# Australian
## Bachelors
### OUTBACK HEROES

MELANIE
MILBURNE

FIONA
LOWE

AMY
ANDREWS

MILLS & BOON

Mills & Boon, an imprint of Harlequin (UK) Limited, Eton House,
18-24 Paradise Road, Richmond, Surrey TW9 1SR

AUSTRALIAN BACHELORS: OUTBACK HEROES
© Harlequin Enterprises II B.V./S.à.r.l. 2011

*Top-Notch Doc, Outback Bride* © Melanie Milburne 2009
*A Wedding in Warragurra* © Fiona Lowe 2008
*The Outback Doctor's Surprise Bride* © Amy Andrews 2008

ISBN: 978 0 263 88997 0

013-1011

Harlequin (UK) policy is to use papers that are natural, renewable
and recyclable products and made from wood grown in sustainable
forests. The logging and manufacturing processes conform to the
legal environmental regulations of the country of origin.

Printed and bound in Spain
by Blackprint CPI, Barcelona

# Top-Notch Doc, Outback Bride

## MELANIE MILBURNE

**Melanie Milburne** says: 'I am married to a surgeon, Steve, and have two gorgeous sons, Paul and Phil. I live in Hobart, Tasmania, where I enjoy an active life as a long-distance runner and a nationally ranked top ten Master's swimmer. I also have a Master's Degree in Education, but my children totally turned me off the idea of teaching! When not running or swimming I write, and when I'm not doing all of the above I'm reading. And if someone could invent a way for me to read during a four-kilometre swim I'd be even happier!'

To my dear friend and confidante
Fiona Abercrombie-Howroyd.
You never fail to amaze me with how you take life
on with both hands, and when someone raises the
bar you don't balk but leap right over it. I am so
proud of you and both of your gorgeous boys.

# CHAPTER ONE

IT WASN'T the worst flight Kellie had ever been on but it certainly came pretty close. The three-hour delay at Brisbane airport had been annoying enough, but when she had finally boarded the twenty-seat regional service area plane she found a man was already sitting in *her* window seat.

'Er…excuse me,' she said, holding her boarding pass up. 'I think you are in the wrong seat. *I* am 10A, you must be 10B.'

The man looked up from the thick black book he was reading. 'Would you like me to move?' he asked in a tone that seemed to suggest he thought it would be totally unreasonable of her to expect him to unfold his long length from the cramped space he was currently jammed into.

Something about the slightly arrogant set to his features made Kellie respond tartly, 'I do, actually, yes. I always have a window seat. I specifically ask for it each time. I feel claustrophobic if I can't see outside.'

Using his boarding pass as a bookmark, the man got to his feet and squeezed out of the two-seat row, his tall figure towering over Kellie as he brushed past her to allow her room to get in.

She felt the warmth of his body and her nostrils began to flare slightly as she tried to place his aftershave. Living with six men had made her a bit of an expert on male colognes, but this time she couldn't decide if the primary citrus scent was lime or lemon based.

She gave him a cool little smile and wriggled past him to sit down, but just as he was about to resume his seat she realised she didn't have enough space under the seat in front for her handbag as well as her hand luggage. 'Um…' she said, swivelling back around to face him. 'Would you mind putting this in the overhead locker for me?'

He *did* mind, Kellie could tell. He didn't say a word but his impossibly dark blue eyes gave a small but still detectable roll of irritation as he took her bag and placed it in the compartment above.

He sat back down beside her and, methodically clipping his belt into place, returned to his book, his left arm resting on *her* armrest.

Kellie inwardly fumed. It happened just about every time she flew and it was *always* a man, although she couldn't help noticing that this one was a great improvement on any of the passengers she'd been seated next to in the past. He even smelt a whole lot better too, she decided as she caught another faint but alluring whiff of lemon-lime as she leaned down to stuff her handbag underneath the seat in front.

While she was down there she noticed he was wearing elastic-sided boots. They weren't dusty or particularly scuffed, which probably meant he was a cattle farmer who had dressed in his best to fly down to the big smoke on business and was now returning home. His long legs were encased in moleskin trousers and the sleeves of his light blue cotton shirt were rolled halfway up his lean but strong-looking and deeply tanned forearms.

Yep, definitely a farmer, Kellie decided, although she couldn't see any sign of him having recently worn a hat.

Didn't all Queensland cattle farmers wear hats? she mused. She noted his dark brown hair wasn't crumpled but neatly styled, so neatly styled, in fact, she could make out the tiny grooves from a recent comb that had passed through the thick wavy strands.

She sat back in her seat and for the sake of common politeness forced herself to give him a friendly smile. 'Thank you for moving. I really appreciate it.'

His dark eyes met hers and assessed her for a moment before he grunted, 'It's fine,' before his head went back to the book he was holding.

*Right, then*, Kellie thought sourly as she searched for both ends of her seat belt. *Don't make polite conversation with me, then. See if I care.*

She gave the left hand belt end a little tug but it wouldn't budge from where it was lodged. 'Er…excuse me,' she said with a frosty look his way. 'You're sitting on my seat belt.'

The man turned to look at her again, his tanned forehead frowning slightly. 'I'm sorry, did you say something?' he asked.

Kellie pointed to the unclipped device in her hand. 'I need the other end of this and, rather than go digging for it myself, I thought it would be polite to ask you to remove it yourself,' she said with a pert tilt of her chin.

Another faint flicker of annoyance came and went in his gaze as he removed the buckle and strap from the back of his seat and handed it to her silently.

'Thank you,' she said, her fingers brushing against his in spite of her effort to avoid doing so. She gave her fingers a quick on-off clench to remove the tingling sensation the brief touch had caused, but still it lingered under the surface of her skin as if he had sent an electric charge right through her body.

That he wasn't similarly affected couldn't have been more

obvious. He simply returned to his book, turning the next page and reading on with unwavering concentration, and even though the flight attendant asked for everyone's attention while she went through the mandatory safety procedure, he remained engrossed in whatever he was reading.

*Typical thinks-he-knows-it-all male*, Kellie thought as she made a point of leaning forward with a totally absorbed expression on her face as the flight attendant rattled off her spiel, even though Kellie knew she herself was probably better qualified if an emergency were to occur given what had happened two years ago on another regional flight.

But, then, after four years in a busy GP practice she felt she had enough experience to handle most emergencies, although she had to admit her confidence would be little on the dented side without her well-equipped doctor's bag at hand. But at least it was safely packed in the baggage hold along with her four cases to tide her over for the six-month locum in the Queensland outback, she reassured herself.

Once the flight attendant had instructed everyone to sit back and enjoy the one-and-a-half-hour flight to Culwulla Creek, Kellie took a couple of deep calming breaths as the plane began to head for the runway, the throb and choking roar of the engines doing nothing to allay her fears. She scrunched her eyes closed and in the absence of an available armrest clasped her hands in her lap.

*You can do this.* She ran through her usual pep talk. You've flown hundreds of times, even across time zones. You know the statistics: you have more chance of being killed on the way to and from the airport than during the actual flight. One little engine failure in the past doesn't mean it's going to happen again. Lightning doesn't strike in the same place twice, right?

The plane rattled and rumbled down the runway, faster and

faster, until finally putting its nose in the air and taking off, the heavy clunk of landing gear returning to its compartment making Kellie's eyes suddenly spring open. 'That was the landing gear, right?' she asked the silent figure beside her. 'Please, tell me that was the landing gear and not something else.'

The bluer-than-blue eyes stared unblinkingly at her for a moment before he answered. 'Yes,' he said, but this time his tone contained more than a hint of sarcasm. 'That was the landing gear. All planes have it, even ones as small as this.'

'I knew *that*,' Kellie said huffily. 'It's just it sounded as if…you know…something wasn't quite right.'

'If everything wasn't quite right, we would have turned back by now,' he pointed out in an I-am-so-bored-with-this-conversation tone as he returned his attention to his book.

Kellie glanced surreptitiously at the book to see if she recognised the title but it wasn't one she was familiar with. It had a boring sort of cover in any case, which probably meant he was a boring sort of person. Although he was a very good-looking boring person, she had to admit as she sneaked another little glance at his profile. He was in his early thirties, thirty-two or -three, she thought, and had a cleanly shaven chiselled jaw and a long straight nose. His lips were well shaped, but she couldn't help thinking they looked as if they rarely made the effort to stretch into a smile.

Her gaze slipped to his hands where he was holding his book. He had long fingers, dusted with dark hair, and his nails were short but clean, which she found a little unusual for a cattle farmer. Didn't they always have dust or cattle feed or farm machinery grease embedded around their cuticles? But perhaps he had been away for a week or two, enjoying the comforts of a city hotel, she thought.

Kellie shifted restlessly in her seat as the plane gained

altitude, wondering how long it would be before the seat-belt sign went off so she could visit the lavatory. She mentally crossed her legs and looked down at her handbag wedged under the seat. She considered retrieving the magazine she had bought to read but just then the flight attendant announced that the captain had turned off the seat-belt sign so it was now safe to move about the cabin.

Kellie unclipped her belt and got to her feet. 'Excuse me,' she said with a sheepish look at the man sitting beside her. 'I have to go to the toilet.'

His gaze collided with hers for another brief moment before he closed the book with exaggerated precision, unclipped his seat belt, unfolded himself from the seat and stood to one side, his expression now blank, although Kellie could again sense his irritation. She could feel it pushing against her, the invisible pressure making her want to shrink away from his presence.

She squeezed past him, sucking in her stomach and her chest in case she touched him inadvertently. 'Thank you,' she said, feeling her face beginning to redden. 'I'll try not to be too long.'

'Take all the time you need,' he said with a touch of dryness.

Kellie set her mouth and moved down the aisle, her back straight with pride, even though her face was feeling hot all over again. *Get a grip*, she told herself sternly. Don't let him intimidate you. No doubt you'll meet thousands…well, hundreds at least…of men just like him in the bush. Besides, wasn't she some sort of expert on men?

Well…apart from that brief and utterly painful and totally embarrassing and ego-crushing episode with Harley Edwards—yes, she was.

When Kellie came back to her seat a few minutes later she felt more than a little relieved to find her co-passenger's seat empty. She scanned the rest of the passenger rows to see if he had changed seats, but he was up at the front of the plane, bending down to talk to someone on the right-hand aisle.

Kellie sat back down and looked out of the window, the shimmering heat haze of the drought-stricken outback making her think a little longingly of the bustling-with-activity beach-side home in Newcastle in NSW she had left behind, not to mention her father and five younger brothers.

But it was well and truly time to move on; they needed to learn to stand on their own twelve feet, Kellie reminded herself. It was what her mother would have wanted her to do, to follow her own path, not to try and take up the achingly empty space her mother's death had left behind six years ago.

The man returned to his seat just as the refreshment trolley made its way up the aisle. He barely glanced at her as he sat back down, but his elbow brushed against hers as he tried to commandeer the armrest.

Kellie gave him a sugar-sweet smile and kept her arm where it was. 'You have one on the other side,' she said.

The space between his dark brows narrowed slightly. 'What?'

She pointed to the armrest on his right. 'You have another armrest over there,' she said.

There was a tight little silence.

'So do you.' He nodded towards the vacant armrest against the window.

'Yes, but I don't see why you get to have the choice of two,' she returned. 'Isn't that rather selfish of you to automatically assume every available armrest is yours?'

'I am not assuming anything,' he said in a clipped tone, and, shifting his gaze from hers, reached for his book in the seat pocket, opened it and added, 'If you want the armrest, have it. It makes no difference to me.'

Kellie watched him out of the corner of her eye as he read the next nine pages of his book. He was a very fast reader and the print was rather small, which impressed her considering how for years she'd had to bribe and threaten and cajole each of her brothers into reading anything besides the back of the cereal packet each morning.

The flight attendant approached and, smiling at Kellie, asked, 'Would you like to purchase a drink or snack from the trolley this afternoon?'

Kellie smiled back as she undid the fold-down table. 'I would love a diet cola with ice and lemon if you have it.'

The flight attendant handed her the plastic cup half-filled with ice and a tiny sliver of lemon before passing over the opened can of soda. 'That will be three dollars,' she said.

Kellie bit her lip. Her bag was stuffed as far under the seat in front as she could get it and, with the tray table down, retrieving it was going to take the sort of flexibility no one but Houdini possessed. 'Er…would you mind holding these for me while I get my purse from my bag?' she asked.

He took the cup and can with a little roll-like flutter of his eyelids but didn't say a word.

Kellie rummaged in her bag for her purse and finally found the right change but in passing it over to the flight attendant somehow knocked the opened can of cola out of the man's hand and straight into his lap.

'What the—' He bit back the rough expletive that had come to his lips and glared at her as he got to his feet, the dark bubbles of liquid soaking through his moleskins like a pool of blood.

'Oops…' Kellie said a little lamely.

'I'll get some paper towels for you, Dr McNaught,' the flight attendant said, and rushed away.

Kellie sat in gob-smacked silence as the name filtered through her brain.

*Dr McNaught?*

She swallowed to get her heart to return to its rightful place in her chest. It couldn't be…could it?

*Dr Matthew McNaught?*

She blinked and looked up at him, wincing slightly as she encountered his diamond-hard dark blue glare. '*You're* Dr Matthew McNaught?' she asked, 'from the two-GP practice in Culwulla Creek?'

'Yes,' he said, his lips pulled tight. 'Let me guess,' he added with a distinct curl of his top lip. 'You're the new locum, right?'

Kellie felt herself sink even further into the limited space available. 'Y-yes,' she squeaked. 'How did you guess?'

# CHAPTER TWO

THE flight attendant came bustling back just then with a thick wad of paper towels and Kellie watched helplessly as Dr McNaught mopped up what he could of the damage.

'I hope it doesn't stain,' Kellie said, trying not to stare too long at his groin. 'I'll pay for dry-cleaning costs of course.'

'That won't be necessary,' he said. 'Besides, there's no dry cleaner in Culwulla Creek. There's not even a laundromat.'

'Oh…' Kellie said, wondering not for the first time what she had flung herself into by agreeing to this post. 'I'm not usually so clumsy. I have a very steady hand normally.'

He gave her a sweeping glance before he resumed his seat. 'You're going to need it out here,' he said. 'The practice serves an area covering several hundred square kilometres. The nearest hospital is in Roma but all the emergency or acute cases have to be flown to Brisbane. It's not going to be a walk in the park, I can tell you.'

'I never for a moment thought it would be,' Kellie said, a little miffed that he obviously thought her a city girl with no practical skills. 'I'm used to hard work.'

'Have you worked in a remote outback area before?' he asked.

Kellie hesitated over her answer. She was thinking her six-week stint in Tamworth in northern New South Wales probably wouldn't qualify. It was a regional area, not exactly the outback. 'Um…not really,' she said. 'But I'm keen to learn the ropes.'

His eyes studied her for a moment. 'What made you decide to take this post?' he asked.

'I liked the sound of working in the bush,' she answered. *And I desperately needed to get away from my family and my absolutely disastrous love life*, she mentally tacked on. 'And six months will just fly by, I imagine.'

'It's not everyone's cup of tea,' he said. 'The hours are long and the cases sometimes difficult to manage, with the issues of distance and limited resources.'

'So who is holding the fort right now?' she asked.

'There's a semi-retired GP, David Cutler, who fills in occasionally,' he said. 'He runs a clinic once a month to keep up his skills but his health isn't good. His wife, Trish, is the practice receptionist and we have one nurse, Rosie Duncan. We could do with more but that's the way it is out here.'

Kellie let a little silence slip past before she asked. 'How long have you been at Culwulla Creek?'

His gaze remained focused on the book in the seat pocket in front of him. 'Six years,' he answered.

'Wow, you must really love it out here,' she said.

He hesitated for a mere sliver of a second before he answered, 'Yes.'

Kellie watched as his expression closed off like a pair of curtains being pulled across a window. She had seen that look before, far too many times, in fact, on the faces of her father and brothers whenever she happened to nudge in under their emotional radar. It was a male thing. They liked to keep some things private and somehow she suspected Dr Matthew McNaught, too, had quite a few no-go areas.

'By the way, I'm Kellie Thorne,' she said offering him her hand.

His hand was cool and firm as it briefly took hers. 'Matthew McNaught, but Matt's fine.'

'Matt, then,' she said, smiling.

He didn't return her smile.

'So…' She rolled her lips together and began again. 'Do you have a family out here with you? A wife and kids perhaps?'

'No.'

Kellie was starting to see why he hadn't been successful thus far in landing himself a life partner. In spite of his good looks he had no personality to speak of. She felt like a tennis-ball throwing machine—she kept sending conversation starters his way but he didn't make any effort to return them.

Not only that, he hadn't once looked at her with anything remotely resembling male interest. Kellie knew she was being stupidly insecure thanks to her disastrous relationship—if you could call it that—with Harley Edwards, but surely Matt McNaught could have at least done a double-take, like the young pilot had on the tarmac before they had boarded the plane.

Kellie had looked in enough mirrors in her time to know none of them were in any danger of breaking any time soon. She had her mother's slim but still femininely curvy figure and her chestnut brown hair was mid-length, with just a hint of a wave running through it. Her toffee-brown eyes had thick sooty lashes, which saved her a fortune in mascara. Her teeth were white and straight thanks to two and a half years of torture wearing braces when she'd been in her teens, and her skin was clear and naturally sun-kissed from spending so much time with her brothers at the beach.

Maybe he was gay, she pondered as she watched him read another chapter of his book. That would account for the zero interest. Anyway, she wasn't out here on the hunt for a love life, far from it. So what if her one and only lover had bludgeoned her self-esteem? She didn't need to find a replacement just to prove he was a two-timing sleazeball jerk with…

OK. That's enough, Kellie chided herself as she wriggled again to get comfortable. Get over it. Harley probably hasn't given you another thought since that morning you arrived to find him in bed with his secretary. Kellie winced at the memory and looked out of the window again, letting out the tiniest of sighs.

This locum position couldn't have come at a better time and the short time was perfect. Living in the outback for a lengthy time was definitely not her thing. She would see the six months out but no longer. She had been a beach chick from birth. She had more bikinis than most women had shoes. Not only that, she was a fully qualified lifesaver, the sound of the ocean like a pulse in her blood. This would be the longest period she had been away from the coast but it would be worth it if it achieved what she hoped it would achieve.

The seat-belt light suddenly came on and the captain announced that there might be some stronger than normal turbulence ahead.

Kellie turned to Matthew with wide eyes. 'Do you think we'll be all right?' she asked.

He looked at her as if she had grown a third eye. 'You *have* flown before, haven't you?' he asked.

'Yes, but not usually in something this small,' she confessed.

He let out a sound, something between derision and incredulity. 'You do realise you will be flying in a Beechcraft twin engine plane at least once if not three or four times a month, don't you? It's called the Royal Flying Doctor Service and out here lives depend on it.'

Kellie gave a gulping swallow as the plane gave a stomach-dropping lurch. 'I know, but someone will have to stay at the practice surely? Tim Montgomery said it in one of the letters he sent,' she said. Biting her lip, she added, 'I was kind of hoping that could be me.'

His eyes gave a little roll. 'I knew this was going to happen,' he muttered.

'What?' she asked, wincing as the plane shifted again.

His blue eyes clashed momentarily with hers. 'This is no doubt Tim and his wife Claire's doing,' he said. 'I asked for someone with plenty of outback experience and instead what do I get?'

'You get me,' Kellie said with a hitch of her chin. 'I've been in practice for four years and I'm EMST trained.'

'And you have a fear of flying.' He settled his shoulders back against the seat. 'Great.'

Kellie gritted her teeth. 'I do *not* have a fear of flying. I've been on heaps of flights. I even went to New Zealand last year.'

She could tell he wasn't impressed. He gave her another rolled-eye look and turned back to his book.

'What are you reading?' she asked, after the turbulence had faded and the seat-belt light had been turned off again. Talking was good. It helped to keep her calm. It helped her not to notice all those suspicious mechanical noises.

'It's a book on astronomy,' he said without looking up from the pages.

'Is it any good?'

Matt let out a frustrated sigh and turned to look at her. 'Yes, it is,' he said. 'Would you like to borrow it?' *Anything to shut you up*, he thought. What was it with this young woman? Didn't she see he was in no mood for idle conversation? And what the hell was she doing, arriving a week earlier than expected?

She shook her head. 'Nope, I don't do heavy stuff any more. The only things I read now are medical journals and magazines and the occasional light novel.'

'I'm doing a degree in astronomy online through Swinburne University,' Matt said, hoping she would take the hint and let him get on with his chapter on globular clusters. 'There's a lot of reading, and I have an exam coming up.'

'You're a very fast reader,' she said. 'Have you done a speed-reading course or something?'

Matt's eyes were starting to feel strained from the repeated rolling. 'No, it's just that I enjoy reading,' he said. 'It fills in the time.'

'So it's pretty quiet out here, huh?' she asked.

Matt looked at her again, *really* looked at her this time. She had a pretty heart-shaped face and her eyes were an unusual caramel brown. He couldn't quite decide how long her hair was as she had it sort of twisted up in a haphazard ponytail-cum-knot at the back of her head, but it was glossy and thick and there was plenty of it, and every now and again he caught of whiff of the honeysuckle fragrance of her shampoo.

She had a nice figure, trim and toned and yet feminine in all the right places. Her mouth was a little on the pouting side, he'd noticed earlier, but when she smiled it reminded him of a ray of bright sunshine breaking through dark clouds.

'No, it's not exactly quiet,' he answered. 'It's different, that's all.'

She gave him another little smile. 'So no nightclubs and five-star restaurants, right?'

Matt felt a familiar tight ache deep inside his chest and looked away. 'No,' he said. 'No nightclubs, no cinemas, no fine dining, no twenty-four-hour trading.' *And no Madeleine*, he added silently.

'What about taxis?' she asked after a short pause. 'Do you have any of those?'

His eyes came back to hers. 'No, but I can give you a lift to Tim and Claire's house. I take it that's where you're staying?'

She nodded. 'It was so kind of them to offer their house and the use of their car while I'm here. They sent me the keys in the mail. Believe me, that would never happen in the city. People don't lend you anything, especially virtual strangers.'

Matt wondered again what had attracted her to the post. He even wondered if Tim and Claire and Trish had colluded to make the job as attractive as possible in order to secure a female GP, a young and single female GP at that—or so he assumed from her ring-free fingers.

'So what do people do out here in their spare time?' she asked. 'Apart from reading, of course.'

'Most of the locals are on the land,' he said. 'They have plenty to do to keep them occupied, especially with this drought going on and on.'

'That's what I thought you were at first,' she said. 'I had you pegged as a cattle farmer.'

'I've actually got a few hectares of my own,' he said, doing his best to ignore the brilliance of her smile. 'I bought them a couple of years back off an elderly farmer who needed to sell in a hurry. I've got some breeding stock I'm trying to keep going until we get some decent rain.'

'Is that where you live?'

'Yes, it's only a few minutes out of town.'

'So do you have horses and stuff?' she asked.

Matt looked longingly at his book. 'Yeah, a couple, but they're pretty wild.'

'I love horses,' she said, snuggling into her seat again. 'I used to ride a bit as a child.'

The captain announced that they were preparing to land and she looked out of the window at the barren landscape. 'So where's the creek?' she asked, and, turning back to him, continued, 'I mean, there has to be a creek somewhere. Culwulla Creek must be named after a creek, right?'

Matt only just managed to control the urge to roll his eyes heavenwards yet again. 'Yes, there is, but it's practically dry. There's been barely a trickle of water for more than three years.'

Her face fell a little. 'Oh…that's a shame.'

'Why is that?' he found himself asking, even though he really didn't want to know.

'I live by the beach,' she said. 'I swim every day, rain or shine.'

Matt felt his chest tighten again. Madeleine had loved swimming. 'That's one hobby you'll have to suspend while you're out here,' he said in a flat, emotionless tone. 'That is, unless it rains.'

'Oh, well, then,' she said with a bright optimistic smile. 'I'd better start doing a rain dance or something. Who knows what might happen?'

Who indeed, Matt thought as the plane descended to land.

Kellie unclipped her seat belt once the plane had landed and reached for her handbag. Matt had risen to retrieve her bulging cabin bag from the overhead locker and silently handed it to her before he took out his own small overnight travel case.

'So how far is it to town?' she asked as they walked across the blistering heat of the tarmac as few minutes later.

'Ten minutes.'

'Tim and Claire's house is a couple of streets away from the practice, isn't it?' she asked as they waited for her luggage to be unloaded.

'Yes.'

She waved away a fly. 'Gosh, it's awfully hot, isn't it?'

'Yes.'

*Right*, Kellie thought, that's it. I'm not even going to try and make conversation. She'd spent the last six years with a house full of monosyllabic males—the last thing she needed was another one in her life.

She looked up to see an older woman in her mid-fifties coming towards them. 'How did the weekend go, Matt?' she asked in a gentle, concerned voice.

Kellie watched as Matt moved his lips into a semblance of a smile but it was gone before it had time to settle long enough to transform his features.

'It was OK,' he said. 'John and Mary-Anne were very welcoming as usual, but you know how it is.'

The older woman grimaced in empathy. 'It's tough on everyone. Birthdays are the worst.'

'Yeah,' he said with another attempt at a smile. 'They are.'

Kellie was intrigued with the little exchange but before she had time to speculate any further, the older woman glanced past Matt's broad shoulder and smiled. 'Well, hello there,' she said. 'Welcome to Culwulla Creek. Are you a tourist or visiting a friend?'

'I'm the new locum filling in for Tim Montgomery,' Kellie said, extending her hand. 'I'm Kellie Thorne.'

'Oh, my goodness, aren't you gorgeous?' the woman gushed as she grasped both of Kellie's hands in her soft motherly ones. 'I had no idea they had someone so young and attractive in mind.'

Kellie felt her face go hot but it had nothing to do with the furnace-like temperature of the October afternoon. She smiled self-consciously as she felt the press of Matt

McNaught's gaze as if he was assessing her physical attributes for the first time.

'I'm Ruth Williams,' the older woman said. 'It's wonderful you could come to fill in for Tim while he and Claire are overseas. So tell me, where are you from?'

'Newcastle, in NSW. I did my medical training and internship there as well,' Kellie answered.

Ruth smiled with genuine warmth. 'What a thrill to have you here. We've never had a female GP before, have we, Matt?'

'No,' Matt said, frowning when he saw the luggage trailer lumbering towards them. In amongst the usual assortment of black and brown and battered bags with a few tattered ribbons attached to various handles to make identification easier, there were four hot pink suitcases, each of which looked as if their fastenings were being stretched to the limit.

Kellie followed the line of his gaze and mentally grimaced. Maybe she had overdone it on the packing thing, she thought. But how was a girl to survive six months in the bush without all the feminine accoutrements?

'I take it these are yours?' Matt asked, as he nodded towards the trailer.

She captured her bottom lip for a second. 'I have a problem travelling lightly. I've been working on it but I guess I'm not quite there, huh?'

He didn't roll his eyes but he came pretty close, Kellie thought but she also thought, she saw his lips twitch slightly, which for some inexplicable reason secretly delighted her.

'It's all right, Dr Thorne,' Ruth piped up. 'Dr McNaught has a four-wheel-drive vehicle so it will all fit in.'

'Er…great,' Kellie said, watching fixatedly as Matt's biceps bulged as he lifted each case off the trailer.

'I'm afraid there are no basic foodstuffs at Tim and Claire's house,' Ruth said with a worried pleat of her brow. 'I would have bought you some milk and bread but we thought you were coming next week so I didn't organise anything, and the corner store will be closed by now.'

'It's all right,' Kellie assured her. 'I had lots of nibbles in the members' lounge while I waited for the flight to be called and I've got some chocolate in one of my bags. My brothers gave it to me. That will tide me over.'

'That was sweet of them,' Ruth said. 'How many brothers do you have?'

'I have five,' Kellie answered, 'all younger than me.'

Ruth's eyes bulged. '*Five?* Oh, dear, your poor mother. How on earth does she cope?'

Kellie concentrated on securing her handbag over her shoulder as she reached for one of the pink suitcases. 'She died six years ago,' she said, stripping her voice of the raw emotion she—in spite of all her efforts—still occasionally felt. 'That's why I took this outback post.' *Or, at least, one of the reasons*, she thought. 'My father and brothers have become a bit too dependent on me,' she said. 'I think they need to learn to take more responsibility for themselves. It's well and truly time to move on, don't you think?'

Matt still wore a blank expression but Ruth touched Kellie on the arm and gave it a gentle comforting squeeze, her warm brown eyes misting slightly. 'Not everyone moves on at the same pace, my dear, but it's wise that you're giving them the opportunity,' she said. 'It's very brave of you to come so far from home. I hope it works out for you and for them.'

'Thank you,' Kellie said, glancing at the tall, silent figure standing nearby, his expression still shuttered. 'I hope so, too.'

## CHAPTER THREE

IT WAS quite a juggling act, getting the whole of Kellie's luggage into the back of Matt's vehicle, even though he had only his carry-on bag with him. But there were other things in the rear of his car—tow ropes, a spare tyre and what looked to be his doctor's bag, as it was very similar to hers, and a big box of mechanical tools, as well as a few pieces of hay scattered about.

Kellie stood to one side as he jostled everything into position and once the hatchback was closed she moved to the passenger side, but before she could open the door he had got there first and opened it for her.

'Thanks,' she said, feeling a little taken aback by his courteous gesture. Over the years she had become so used to her brothers diving into the family people-mover, each vying for the best seat with little regard for her comfort, that his gallantry took her completely by surprise.

'Mrs Williams seems like a lovely lady,' she said as she caught sight of the older woman driving off ahead of them to the road leading to town. 'Did she come out to the airport just to see you? She doesn't appear to have picked anyone up.'

'Ruth Williams comes out to meet every flight,' Matt said as he shifted the gears. 'She's been doing it for years.'

'Why is that?' Kellie asked, turning to look at him.

His gaze never wavered from the road ahead. 'Her teenage daughter disappeared twenty years ago. Ruth has never quite given up hope that one day Tegan will get off one of the thrice-weekly flights, so she meets each one just in case.'

Kellie frowned. 'How terribly sad. Did her daughter run away or was it likely to have been something more sinister?'

His dark blue eyes met hers for a moment before returning to the long straight stretch of road ahead. 'She went missing without trace,' he said. 'As far as I know, the case is still open.'

'Did she go missing from here?' she asked.

'Yes,' he answered. 'She was fourteen, nearly fifteen years old. She caught the bus home from school, she was seen walking along the main street at around four-thirty and then she disappeared. No one has seen or heard from her since. The police lost valuable time thinking it was just another bored country kid running away from home. Tegan had run away a couple of times before. Ruth's now late husband, Tegan's stepfather, apparently wasn't the easiest man to live with. It was understandable that they assumed the girl had hitched a ride out of town. She was a bit of a rebel around these parts, truanting, shoplifting, driving without a licence, that sort of thing.'

'But no one's ever found out what happened to her?' Kellie asked with a frown.

He shook his head. 'There was no sign of a struggle or blood where she was last seen alive and her stepfather had an iron-clad alibi once the police got around to investigating things a little more thoroughly. And, of course, even after two decades there has been no sign of her body.'

Kellie was still frowning. 'So after all these years Ruth doesn't really know if her daughter is alive or dead?' she asked.

'No, but, as I said, she lives in hope.'

'But that's awful!' she said. 'At least when my mum died we had a few months' warning. I miss her terribly but at least I know where she is. I was there when she took her last breath and I was there when the coffin was lowered in the ground.'

Matt felt his gut clench but fought against it. 'What did your mother die of?' he asked.

'Pancreatic cancer,' she said. 'She became jaundiced over-night and started vomiting and within three days we had the diagnosis.'

'How long did she have?'

'Five months,' she said. 'I took time off from my surgical term to nurse her. She died in my arms…'

Matt felt a lump the size of a boulder lodge in his throat. 'At least you were there,' he said, his tone sounding rough around the edges. 'Spouses and relatives don't always get there in time.'

'Yes…' she said, looking down at her hands. 'At least I was there…'

Silence followed for several minutes.

'So where did you go on the weekend?' Kellie asked.

Matt's hands tightened fractionally on the steering-wheel. 'I went to visit some…' He paused briefly over the word. 'Friends in Brisbane. It was their daughter's thirtieth birthday.'

'It was my birthday a week ago,' Kellie said. 'I'm twenty-nine—the big one is next year. I'm kind of dreading it, to tell you the truth. My family wants me to have a big party but I'm not sure I want to go to all that fuss.' She swung her gaze his way again. 'So was your friend's daughter's party a big celebration?'

His eyes were trained on the road ahead but Kellie noticed he was gripping the steering-wheel as if it was a lifeline. 'No,' he said. 'It was very small.'

Another silence ticked away.

'How old are your brothers?' Matt broke it by asking.

'Alistair and Josh are twins,' she said. 'They're four years younger than me at twenty-five. Sebastian, but we always call him Seb, is twenty-three, Nick's twenty and Cain is nineteen.'

'Do they all still live at home?'

'Yes and no,' she said. 'They're a bit like homing pigeons—or maybe more like locusts—swooping in, eating all the food and then moving on again.'

Matt noticed her fond smile and marvelled at the difference between his life and hers. He had grown up as an only child to parents who had eventually divorced when he'd been seven. He had never quite forgiven his mother for leaving his father with a small child to rear. And his father had never quite forgiven him for being a small, dependent, somewhat insecure and shy boy, which had made things even more difficult and strained between them. He couldn't remember the last time he had spoken to either of his parents. They hadn't even met Madeleine.

'What about you?' Kellie asked. 'Do you have brothers or sisters?'

'No.'

'Are both your parents still alive?'

'Yes.'

'Do you ever answer a question with more than one word?' she asked.

The distance between his brows decreased. 'When I think it's appropriate,' he said.

'You're not the easiest person to talk to,' she said. 'I'm used to living in a household of six men where I have to shout to get a word in edgeways, unless they're in one of their non-communicative moods. Talking to you is like getting blood out of a stone.'

Matt felt his shoulders tensing. 'I'm not a chit-chat person. If you don't like it, tough. Find someone else's ear to chew off.'

She sent him a reproachful look. 'The least you could do is make some sort of an effort to make me feel at home here. This is a big thing for me. I'm the one who's put myself out to come here to fill a vacancy, a vacancy, I might add, that isn't generally easy to fill. Outback postings are notoriously diffi-cult to attract doctors to, especially given the timeframe of this one. You should be grateful I've put my hand up so willingly. Not many people would.'

'I am very grateful, Dr Thorne, but I had absolutely nothing to do with your appointment and I have some serious doubts about your suitability.'

'*What?*' she said, with an affronted glare. 'Who are you to decide whether I'm suitable or not?'

'I think you've been sent here for the wrong reasons,' he said.

Kellie frowned at him. 'The wrong reasons? What on earth do you mean? I'm a GP with all the right qualifications and I've worked in a busy practice in Newcastle for four years.'

He was still looking at the road ahead but she noticed his knuckles were now almost white where he was gripping the steering-wheel. 'This is a rough-and-tough area,' he said. 'You're probably used to the sort of facilities that are just not available out here. Sometimes we lose patients not because of their injuries or illnesses but because we can't get them to help in time. We do what we can with what we've got, but it can do in even the most level-headed person at times.'

Kellie totally understood where he was coming from. She had met plenty of paramedics and trauma surgeons during her various terms to know that working at the coal face of tragedy was no picnic. But she had toughened up over the years of her training and with the help of her friends and family had come to a point in her life where she felt compelled to do her bit in spite of the sleepless nights that resulted. She had wanted to be a doctor all her life. She loved taking care of people and what better way to do that than out in the bush where patients were not just patients but friends as well?

'Contrary to what you think, I believe I'll manage just fine,' she said. 'But if you think it's so rough and tough out here, why have you stayed here so long?'

'I would hardly describe six years as a long time,' he said, without glancing her way.

'Are you planning to stay here indefinitely?' she asked.

'It depends.'

'On what?'

He threw her an irritated look. 'Has anyone ever told you you ask too many questions?'

Kellie bristled with anger. 'Well, *sor-ry* for trying to be friendly. Sheesh! You take the quiet, silent type to a whole new level.'

He let out a sigh and sent her a quick, unreadable glance. 'Look, it's been a long, tiring weekend. All I can think about right now is getting home and going to bed.'

'Do you live alone?' she asked.

His eyes flickered upwards, his hands still tight on the steering-wheel. 'Yes.'

Kellie looked out at the dusty, arid landscape; even the red river gums lining the road looked gnarled with thirst. 'I guess this isn't such a great place to meet potential partners,' she mused. Swivelling her head to look at him again, she added, 'I read this article in a women's magazine about men in the bush and how hard it is for them to find a wife. It's not like in the city where there are clubs and pubs and gyms and so on. Out here it's just miles and miles of bush between neighbours and towns.'

'I'm not interested in finding a wife,' he said with an im-placable edge to his tone.

'It seems a pretty bleak existence,' she remarked as the tiny township came into view. 'Don't you want more for your life?'

His dark blue eyes collided with hers. 'If you don't like it here, there's another plane out at five p.m. on Saturday.'

She sent him a determined look. 'I am here for six months, Dr McNaught, so you'd better get used to it. I'm not a quitter and even though you are the most unfriendly colleague I've ever met, I'm not going to be run out of town just because you have a chip on your shoulder about women.'

His brows snapped together irritably. 'I do not have a chip on my shoulder about women.'

Kellie tossed her head and looked out at the small strip of shops that lined both sides of the impossibly wide street. It was certainly nothing like she was used to, even though Newcastle was nowhere near the size of Sydney or Melbourne, or even for that matter Brisbane.

Culwulla Creek had little more than a general store, which was now closed, a small hardware centre, a hamburger café, a service station, a tiny school and a rundown-looking pub that was currently booming with business.

'The clinic is just over there in that small cottage,' Matt said, pointing to the left-hand side of the road just before the pub. 'I'll get Trish to show you around in the next day or so once you've settled in at the Montgomerys' house.'

As they drove past the pub, people were spilling out on the street, stubbies of beer in hand, squinting against the late af-ternoon sunlight.

'G'day, Dr McNaught,' one man wearing an acubra hat and a cast on his right arm called out. 'How was your weekend in the big smoke?'

'Shut up, Bluey,' another man said, elbowing his mate in the ribs.

Matt slowed the car down and leaned forward slightly to look past Kellie in the passenger seat. 'It was fine. How's your arm?'

The man with the hat lifted his can of beer with his other arm and grinned. 'I can still hold my beer so I must be all right.'

Kellie witnessed the first genuine smile crack Matt's face and her heart did a funny little jerk behind her chest wall. His dark blue eyes crinkled up at the corners, his lean jaw relaxed and his usually furrowed brow smoothed out, making his already attractive features heart-stoppingly gorgeous.

'Take it easy, Bluey,' he said, still smiling. 'It was a bad break and you'll need the full six weeks to rest it.'

'I'm resting it,' Bluey assured him, and peered through the passenger window. 'So who's the little lady?'

'This is Dr Thorne,' Matt said, his smile instantly disappearing. 'She's the new locum.'

Kellie lifted her hand in a fingertip wave. 'Hi, there.'

Bluey's light blue eyes twinkled. 'G'day, Dr Thorne. How about joining us for a drink to get to know the locals?'

'I have to get her settled into Tim and Claire's house,' Matt said before Kellie could respond. 'She has a lot of baggage.'

Kellie glowered at him before turning back to smile at Bluey. 'I would love to join you all,' she said. 'What time does the pub close?'

Bluey grinned from ear to ear. 'We'll keep it open just for you, Dr Thorne.'

Matt drove on past the tiny church and cemetery before turning right into a pepper corn-tree-lined street. 'Tim and Claire's house is the cream one,' he said. 'The car will be in the garage.'

Kellie looked at the cottage with interest and trepidation.

It was a three-bedroom weatherboard with a corrugated-tin roof, a large rainwater tank on one side and a shady verandah wrapped around the outside of the house. There was no garden to speak of, but not for want of trying, she observed as she noted the spindly skeletons of what looked to be some yellowed sweet peas clinging listlessly to the mid-height picket fence. There were several pots on the verandah that had suffered much the same fate, and the patchy and parched lawn looked as if it could do with a long soak and a decent trim. There were other similar cottages further along the street, although both of the houses either side of the Montgomerys' appeared to be vacant.

Fixing an I-can-get-through-this-for-six-months expression on her face, Kellie rummaged for the keys she had been sent in the post as Matt began to unload the luggage. She walked up to the front door and searched through the array of keys to find the right one, but with little success. She was down to the last three when she felt Matt come up behind her.

'Here,' he said. 'Let me.'

Kellie felt the brush of his arm against her waist as he took the keys and her heart did another little uncoordinated skip in her chest. She watched as his long, tanned fingers selected the right key and inserted it into the lock, turning it effortlessly before pushing the door open for her.

'You go in and have a look around while I bring in your bags,' he said as he opened the meter box near the door and turned a switch. 'The hot water will take a couple of hours to heat but everything else should be OK. There's an air-conditioning control panel in the lounge, which serves the main living area of the house.'

Kellie looked guiltily towards his car where her bags were

lined up behind the open hatchback. 'I don't expect you to be my slave,' she said. 'I can carry my own bags inside.'

'Then you must be a whole lot stronger than you look because I nearly bulged a disc loading them in there in the first place.'

She put her hands on her hips as if she was admonishing one of her younger brothers. 'I *am* here for half a year, you know,' she said. 'I need lots of stuff, especially out here.'

'I hate to be the one to tell you this but the sort of stuff you need to survive out here can't be packed into four hot pink suitcases, Dr Thorne,' Matt said, stepping back down off the verandah to his car.

'What *is* it with you?' she asked, following him to his car in quick angry strides. 'You seem determined to turn me off this appointment before I've even started.'

Matt carried two of her cases to the verandah as she yapped at his heels like a small terrier. She was exactly what this town didn't need, he thought. No, strike that—she was exactly what *he* didn't need right now. He wasn't ready. He wondered if he ever would be ready and yet...

'Give me that bag,' she demanded. *'Now.'*

Matt mentally rolled his eyes. She looked so fierce standing there with her hands on her slim-as-a-boy's hips, her toffee-brown eyes flashing. For a tiny moment she reminded him of...

He gave himself a hard mental slap and handed her one of the bags. 'I'll bring in the rest,' he said. 'And watch out for snakes as you go in.'

She stopped in mid-stride, her hand falling away from the handle of her bag. 'Snakes?' she asked. 'You mean...' She visibly gulped. 'Inside?'

# CHAPTER FOUR

'SNAKES are attracted to water,' he said as he picked up another one of her bags. 'This has been one of the longest droughts in history. They can slink in under doors in search of a dripping tap. One of the locals had one come in under the door a few blocks from here. They lost their Jack Russell terrier as a result. I just thought I'd warn you. It's better to be safe than sorry.'

Kellie eyed the open front door with wide, uncertain eyes. Snakes were fine in their place, which for her had up until this point been behind a thick sheet of glass at a zoological park. She had never met one in the wild, and had certainly never envisaged meeting one in her living space. She was OK with rats and mice; she was even fine with spiders—but *snakes*?

She suppressed a little shudder and straightened her shoulders as she faced him coming up the verandah steps with a bag in each hand. 'I suppose the next thing you'll be telling me is the house is haunted.'

Something shifted at the back of his eyes. 'No, it's not haunted,' he said, and moved past her to take the bags he was carrying to one of the bedrooms off the passage.

Kellie followed him gingerly down the hallway, her eyes darting sideways for any sign of a black or brown coil lying in wait to strike, but to her immense relief nothing seemed to be amiss. It looked and felt like any other house that had been unoccupied for a while—the air a little hot and stale and the blinds down over the windows, which added to the general sense of abandonment.

The sudden wave of homesickness that assailed her was almost overwhelming. A house was meant to be a home but it couldn't be that without people in it and she—for the next few months—was going to be the only person inside this house.

It was a daunting thought, Kellie realised as she wandered into the kitchen. The layout was modern but very basic, as if Tim and Claire Montgomery had not wanted to waste money on top-notch appliances and joinery.

The rest of the house was similar, tasteful but modestly decorated, the furniture a little dated though comfortable-looking.

Matt came back in with the last of her bags and put them in the largest of the three bedrooms before he came back out to the sitting room where she was trying to undo one of the two windows. 'What's the problem?' he asked.

'I want to air the house but I think this window is stuck,' she said giving it another rattle.

'Here, let me have a go.'

Kellie stepped back as he worked on the latch and pushed the window upwards with his shoulder, the timber frame creaking in protest.

'It needs to be shaved back a bit,' he said, inspecting the inner section of the window. 'I'll send someone around to fix it for you.'

'Thanks, I'd appreciate it.'

He reached into his back pocket and took out his wallet. Flipping it open, he pulled out a business card and handed it to her. 'Here are my home and mobile and the clinic numbers.'

Kellie caught a brief glimpse of a photograph of a young woman just before he closed his wallet. 'Who is that?' she asked.

His expression closed down and his tone was guarded and clipped as he responded, 'Who is who?'

'The woman in your wallet,' she said.

His brows moved together in a frown. 'Do you make it a habit of prying into people's wallets?' he asked.

'I wasn't prying,' she protested. 'You had it open so I looked.'

'Would you like to count how much money I have in there while you're at it, Dr Thorne?' he asked with a sardonic curl of his lip.

Kellie glared up at him. 'If that is your girlfriend in your wallet then I don't know what on earth she sees in you,' she said. 'You're the most obnoxiously unfriendly man I've ever met and let me tell you I've met plenty. I just didn't realise I had to travel quite this far to meet yet another one.'

Blue eyes battled with brown in a crackling-with-tension silence that seemed to go on indefinitely.

Kellie was determined not to look away first. She was used to the stare-downs of her brothers but something about Matthew McNaught's midnight-blue gaze as it wrestled with hers caught her off guard. She found herself blushing and averted her head in case he saw it. 'Thank you for the lift and bringing in my bags,' she said in a curt tone. 'No doubt I'll see you at the clinic some time.'

'Yes, I expect you will.' His tone was equally brusque.

Kellie listened as his footsteps echoed down the hall. She heard the screen door squeak open and close and then the creak of the weathered timber of the verandah as he stepped on it before going down the three steps leading to the pathway to the gate. She heard his car start then the grab of the wheels on the gravel as he backed out of the driveway and the growl of the diesel engine as he drove back the way they had come, turning right, away from town at the corner.

And then all Kellie could hear was the sound of her own breathing. It seemed faster than normal and her heart felt like it was skipping every now and again just to keep up.

She turned from the window and looked at the space where moments before Matt had been standing, frowning at her, those incredibly blue eyes searing and yet shadowed at the same time...

A sudden knock on the front door made her nearly jump out of her skin but when she heard Ruth Williams's friendly voice calling out, her panic quickly subsided. 'Dr Thorne? I managed to get some milk and bread for you. I rang Cheryl Yates who runs the general store and she made up a survival pack for you. You can pay her later.'

Kellie pushed open the screen door. 'That was very thoughtful of you both.'

'Not at all,' Ruth said, handing over the basket of groceries.

'Please come in,' Kellie said. 'I'm still finding my way around but I can rustle us up a cup of tea if you'd like one.'

'I would love one,' Ruth said, puffing slightly. 'I think Cheryl's even put some of those fancy teabags in here somewhere and some chocolate biscuits. You'd better put them in the fridge, though, as this heat would melt stone.'

'Yes, it is rather hot, isn't it?' Kellie answered as she led the way to the kitchen. 'But I'm sure I'll get used to it in a day or two.'

'You know when you first stepped off the plane with Dr McNaught I thought I was seeing a ghost,' Ruth said as she started to help unpack the groceries.

Kellie turned and looked at her. 'A ghost?'

Ruth's smile had a hint of sadness about it. 'Yes. Although

your hair is a different colour, you reminded me a bit of Madeleine,' she said, 'Dr McNaught's fiancée.'

Kellie felt her eyes widen in surprise. No wonder he'd said he wasn't looking for a wife, although she couldn't imagine who would be brave enough to take him on. 'Dr McNaught is engaged?' she asked.

'Was engaged,' Ruth corrected. 'She was killed in an accident two days before their wedding.'

'Oh, dear…' Kellie said, a wave of sympathy washing over her, followed by a rising tide of insight into why Matt was so standoffish and formal. She mentally cringed at his dislike of her prying into the photograph in his wallet.

'He doesn't talk about it much, of course,' Ruth went on. 'But that's the male way, isn't it?'

Kellie nibbled at her lip. 'Yes…yes, it certainly is…'

Ruth handed her a carton of milk. 'It was her birthday on Saturday,' she said. 'That's why he went to Brisbane—to visit her parents.'

'That was nice of him,' Kellie offered, still feeling utterly wretched about her rapid judgement of him.

Ruth gave her another sad smile. 'Yes, he does it every year.'

Kellie put the milk in the fridge and filled the kettle before she sat down opposite the older lady. 'Dr McNaught told me about your daughter,' she said. 'It must be very hard for you…you know, not knowing where Tegan is or what happened to her.'

Ruth let out a little sigh. 'It is hard,' she said. 'The hardest thing after all this time is that no one is actively searching for her any more. I feel that I'll go to my grave without knowing what happened to her.'

'The police keep most missing-person files open, though, don't they?' Kellie said. 'I've seen a few news stories about old cases that have been solved, using DNA to match perpetrators to crimes.'

'That's true,' Ruth said, 'but out here there isn't the manpower to do any more than maintain law and order. Doctors aren't the only people who resist remote country appointments— police are pretty thin on the ground out here, too.'

Kellie met the older woman's brown eyes. 'You don't believe she's dead, do you?' she asked.

Ruth held her gaze for several moments. 'No,' she said. 'I feel it in here.' She placed a hand over her heart. 'She's out there somewhere, I just know it.'

Kellie felt deeply for the poor woman. She had a pretty clear idea of the process of denial—she had witnessed it in her father for the last six years. He still acted as if her mother was going to walk in the door. He even occasionally spoke of her in the present tense, which made the job of getting on with his life so much harder for him and his family, not to mention Aunty Kate.

'Well, I must let you settle in,' Ruth said a few minutes later after they had finished the tea. 'It's an isolated place out here—but it's not an unfriendly one.'

'I'm very glad to hear that,' Kellie said with genuine feeling. 'This is a leap into the unknown for me. I'm right out of my comfort zone but I need the challenge right now.'

'Well, it will certainly be challenging, it always is when the unexpected happens in places as far out as this,' Ruth said as she gathered up her bag. 'But Matthew McNaught is a very capable doctor. He's experienced and caring. I am sure you'll enjoy working with him, especially once you get to know him. This last weekend was a tough one for him. It'll take him a few days to get back to normal.'

'I think we'll get along just fine,' she said to the older

woman with a smile. 'In any case, I've got a week up my sleeve to get a feel for the place. I kind of figured it would be wise not to rush headlong into a close community like this.'

'You might not have any choice, my dear,' Ruth said with a sombre look. 'Things can happen out here in a blink of an eye.'

Soon after Ruth left Kellie decided to walk the short distance to the pub. She had always enjoyed male company and while the pub looked nothing like the family-friendly bistros she was used to, she didn't see any harm in getting to know some of the locals in a relaxed and casual atmosphere.

She was barely in the door before Bluey, the man with the broken arm, came ambling over. 'What would you like to drink, Doc?'

Kellie smiled so as not to offend him. 'It's fine, really. I'll get my own.'

'Nah,' he drawled as he winked at his two mates. 'It's been a long time since I bought a pretty lady a drink. Don't spoil it for me. What'll you have?'

Kellie agreed to have a lemonade, lime and bitters and sat at the table with Bluey and his cronies, who turned out to be two other farmers looking as though they had spent many a long day in the sun.

'So what brings a nice girl like you out to a place like this?' Jeff, the oldest of the three, asked.

'I saw Tim Montgomery's advertisement in the *Australian Medical Journal* and thought it would be a great chance to do my bit for the bush,' she answered. 'A house, a car and a job all rolled into one sounded too good to miss.'

'It sounds too good to be true, right, Jeff?' Bluey said with a gap-toothed grin.

Kellie wasn't sure what he meant and didn't have time to

ask as just then she heard a commotion from behind the counter of the pub.

'Quick, call the doctor!' a female voice shrieked. 'I think I've cut off my finger!'

Kellie leapt to her feet and approached the bar. 'Can I help?' she asked. 'I'm a doctor.'

The face of Bruce, the barman, was ashen as the woman was clutching a blood-soaked teatowel to her right hand. 'It looks pretty bad,' he said. 'Perhaps I'd better call Matt McNaught.'

Kellie stood her ground. 'By the time Dr McNaught gets here I could at least stem the bleeding and assess the damage.'

'Good point, but I'll give him a call in any case. He'll know what to do, you being new in town and all,' Bruce said, and lifted a section of the bar to allow her access to where the woman was sitting visibly shaking as she cradled her hand against her chest.

Kellie introduced herself to the woman, Julie Smithton, who told her she had been using a sharp knife to cut up some lemons when the knife had slipped and cut through the top of her finger.

'Let me have a look at the damage,' Kellie said, gently taking the woman's hand in hers. She carefully unpeeled the teatowel to find a deep laceration across the palmar surface, indicating there was a possibility the flexor tendon could be severed.

'Have I cut it off?' Julie asked in a thread-like voice.

Kellie smiled reassuringly. 'No, Julie, you haven't. The finger's completely intact. But it looks like you might have damaged a tendon. Do you think you can try and bend your finger, like this?' She demonstrated the action of moving her index finger up and down in a wave-like action.

Julie gingerly lifted her hand but even though she was clearly trying to move her finger there was no flexion response. 'I can't do it,' she cried.

'It's all right,' Kellie said gently. 'It's something that can be easily fixed with a bit of microsurgery. You'll be back to normal in no time.'

Julie's eyes flared in fear. 'Microsurgery?'

'Yes,' Kellie said. 'It's done by a plastic surgeon, but it will soon be—'

'But can't Dr McNaught do it?' Julie asked. 'I don't want to travel all the way to Brisbane. I've got three kids.'

'Who's looking after them now?' Kellie asked.

Julie lowered her eyes. 'They're on their own at the house,' she mumbled. 'They're not little kids any more. I guess they might be all right for a day or so.'

'What about their father?' Kellie asked. 'Couldn't he look after them?'

A dark, embittered look came into the young woman's eyes. 'He left us close to three years ago. Got himself a new family now in Charleville, last I heard.'

Kellie looked at the woman's prematurely lined and weather-beaten face and wondered how old she was. She wasn't sure but she didn't think she was that old, but clearly the strain of bringing up three children on her own had taken its toll, not to mention the unforgiving outback climate.

'You'll only be in hospital a few days, five at the most,' Kellie said. Turning to the hovering Bruce, she asked, 'Do you have a first-aid kit here, Bruce? My doctor's bag is back at the cottage. And I'll need the number of the flying doctor service. I left the card Dr McNaught gave me with all the contact numbers on it back at the cottage.'

Once the call had been made Julie asked to be taken to her

house to see her kids and organise things before the flying doctor arrived.

'I'll take you,' Bluey offered as he came to where they were gathered.

'Yeah, right,' Julie said with a look of disdain. 'You're exactly what I need right now, a broken-armed drunk to come to my rescue in a beat-up hulk of a car.'

Bluey looked affronted. 'I'm no drunk, Jules. I've only had two light stubbies. Sure, there's a spot of rust or two in the old Holden, but I can drive it with one arm tied behind my back...' he grinned and added, 'or my front.'

'What's going on?' Matt's voice sounded deep and controlled as he came in, carrying a doctor's bag in one hand.

'Julie has a lacerated flexor tendon and I've organised transport to Brisbane with the flying doctor service,' Kellie informed him. 'I called them and they're only half an hour away on another trip from the station out at Gunnawanda Gully.'

Matt took Kellie aside and, looking down at her seriously asked, 'I notice you have blood on your hands,' he said. 'Do you realise you should be wearing gloves? You could put yourself at risk of infection.'

Kellie felt a little tremor of unease pass through her. 'I didn't have my doctor's bag with me,' she said. 'I simply responded to a call for help and acted accordingly.'

'There's no point putting yourself at risk,' he admonished her. 'Once you had established it wasn't a life-threatening injury you should have taken universal precautions. You should have called me and met me at the clinic where we could have explored the wound, gloved up at the very least.'

'I realise that but—'

'Furthermore, if it turns out Mrs Smithton doesn't have a tendon injury, you would have wasted thousands of dollars of community money, getting an air ambulance out here for nothing.'

Kellie was incensed. She knew a tendon injury when she saw one—her brother Seb had severed his during an ice-hockey match when he'd been sixteen—so she considered herself somewhat of an expert on that particular injury.

'Not only that…' Matt was still dressing her down like a junior colleague. 'You are not officially on duty until next week.'

'I don't see why that should make any—'

Matt ignored her to turn back to the group surrounding Julie. He opened his bag and, putting on some surgical gloves, gently inspected the wound. 'What about if I call Ruth Williams?' he asked Julie. 'She'll be happy to help you out with the boys.'

'I called her a few minutes ago,' Bruce piped up. 'She's gone to the house to get some things together for Julie for the hospital. She said she'll meet you at the airstrip.'

'Good,' Matt said, and stripped off his gloves. 'You'll be OK, Julie. It's a bit of bad luck but it could have been a lot worse.'

'I don't see how,' Julie said with a despondent set to her features. 'I won't be able to work for a couple of weeks and I need the money right now.'

Matt put his hand on her shoulder and gently squeezed. 'The boys will be fine, Julie. Ruth will love being with them, don't worry. I'll keep my eye on things as well, OK?'

Julie gave him a grateful look. 'The new doctor's nice, isn't she?' she said. 'Very pretty too, don't you think?'

Matt concentrated on zipping up his doctor's bag. 'I hadn't really noticed.'

Kellie felt that all too familiar ache of inadequacy as she overheard the exchange. Maybe she should do something about her hair, she thought, tucking a wayward strand behind one ear. A few highlights, maybe even a trim, or even a new style would give her ego a much-needed boost. Not that she'd noticed a hairdresser's anywhere in town. Culwulla Creek was hardly the place to prepare for a Miss Universe line-up, Kellie realised, but a girl—even a girl living in the dry dusty outback—needed a lift now and again, didn't she?

'I think she's just what this town needs,' Julie said. 'Tim and Claire will be delighted to know they chose exactly the right person to fill the position.'

'The flying doctor's just landed,' Bluey announced as he popped his head around the door. 'Do you want me to come with you and hold your hand, Jules?' he asked. 'I've got nothing planned for the next few days.'

Julie gave him another scornful look. 'That'd be the blind leading the blind, wouldn't it?'

Bluey grinned boyishly. 'You break me up, Jules.'

Kellie looked at Matt, who was smiling at the exchange. It wasn't a broad smile by any stretch of the imagination but it was enough to make his dark blue eyes crinkle up at the corners and his normally rigid mouth relax. Kellie couldn't help thinking how sensual it looked without its tightened contours.

He turned and caught her staring at him and his smile instantly faded. 'Is there something wrong, Dr Thorne?' he asked.

Kellie met his gaze. 'No,' she said, suddenly feeling a little embarrassed under his frowning scrutiny.

He held her look for a tense moment. 'Excuse me,' he said. 'I have a patient to see to. I'll let you get back to your socialising.'

Kellie couldn't help thinking there was a hint of criticism in his tone. He made it sound as if she had nothing better to do than sit around and drink cocktails with the locals while he got on with the job of being the only reliable, hard-working doctor in town. 'I'd like to come with you to the airstrip,' she said with a little jut of her chin. 'I need to learn the ropes and now is as good a time as any.'

He looked as if he was about to disagree, but perhaps because of the assembled group nearby he appeared to change his mind. 'All right,' he said, letting out a sigh that sounded like something between irritation and resignation. 'Follow me.'

# CHAPTER FIVE

KELLIE thought the airstrip looked even smaller than when she had arrived there only hours earlier. The arrivals building was no bigger than a suburban garden shed, and the red gravel runway looked too small for a car to brake suddenly, let alone an aircraft.

Before the plane had landed a team of locals had performed the mandatory 'roo shoo' which involved a couple of cars driving up and down the strip to clear away any wildlife such as kangaroos, emus or possums. Kellie could see one or two of the drivers standing chatting to the pilot as she and Matt approached.

Once Julie was settled on board, Brian King, the pilot, Nathan Curtis, the doctor, and Fran Bradley, the nurse, quickly introduced themselves.

'It's great to meet you,' Fran said with a friendly smile. 'I know of a few women out on the land who'll be glad to know you've joined the outback clinic team.'

Kellie swallowed as she looked at the aircraft. 'Er…yes, I'm sure it will be heaps of fun…'

'Dr Thorne isn't too keen on flying,' Matt said with an unreadable expression.

Kellie glowered at him. 'I'm sure I'll get used to it if it's not too rough.' She turned back to the nurse. 'I had a scary trip back from a rotation I did in Tamworth a few years ago. We had to make an emergency landing when one of the engines failed. A few of the passengers were seriously injured. I'm afraid I've been a bit of a coward ever since.'

Brian smiled reassuringly. 'We'll do our best to keep you safe out here,' he said. 'We don't take unnecessary risks. I've only had to make one emergency landing in twenty years of flying in the outback.'

'That's very good to know,' Kellie said, with another nervous glance towards the plane which, in her opinion, looked like it wouldn't look out of place in a child's toybox.

Julie was soon loaded on board and everyone stood back as the engine turned over in preparation for take-off. On the way back to his car Matt stopped to chat to Ruth. 'Are you sure you'll be able to manage Julie's boys?' he asked with a concerned pleat of his brow.

'I'll be fine,' Ruth assured him. 'They'll keep me on my toes, no doubt, but it will be good for me. Take my mind off things.'

'Can I help in any way?' Kellie asked. 'It's not as if I'm not used to handling boys and I don't start at the clinic until next week.'

'If you'd like to, that would be lovely,' Ruth said. 'Julie's house is on Commercial Road, number fifteen, I think it is from memory—no one really bothers with numbers out here. Anyway, it's the house next door to the old community centre.'

'I'll find it,' Kellie said with a confident smile.

Matt opened the car door for Kellie once Ruth had driven off. 'You may have had plenty of experience handling your brothers but I can assure you Julie's boys are something else. They've been running wild for years. I've had each of them for patients with every injury imaginable. How one of them hasn't been killed before now is little short of a miracle.'

Kellie waited until he was behind the wheel before asking, 'How old are they?'

He frowned as if searching his memory. 'Ty is fifteen, Rowan fourteen and Cade is twelve.'

'And how old is Julie?'

'She's not long turned thirty-one, I think.'

Kellie lifted her brows. 'Gosh, she did start young. She was, what, just sixteen when she had the oldest boy.'

'Yes, but out here that's not unusual,' he said. 'I have several patients who are teenage mothers. It's tough on them as they can't really get out of the cycle of poverty without an education to fall back on. They end up having a couple more kids and living on welfare for years on end.'

Kellie couldn't help thinking of how different her life had been in spite of her mother's untimely death. She at least had been able to complete her training even while juggling her father's and brothers' needs. She hadn't really realised until now how lucky she was to have done so. She could so easily have chosen another path, like so many others did in times of grief and trauma.

'Ruth told me about your fiancée,' she said after a lengthy silence. 'I'm sorry…I didn't realise how tough this weekend must have been for you.'

All the air inside the car seemed to be sucked out on the harshly indrawn breath he took. 'It's fine,' he said. 'I'm over it. Life moves on. It has to.'

Kellie glanced at his white-knuckled grip on the steering-wheel and wondered if that was entirely true. He reminded her of her father, stoic and grittily determined to ignore how much life had changed, pretending he was coping when each day another part of him seemed to shrivel up and die.

'What did she do?' she asked, after she'd let another little silence pass. 'Was she a doctor, like you?'

'No,' he said, staring at the road ahead. 'She was a teacher.'

'What grade?'

'First grade.'

'How did you meet?'

He glanced at her as if he found her questions both annoying and intrusive. 'We went to school together.' He looked forward again and paused for a second or two before adding, 'We dated since senior high school.'

*Oh, boy*, Kellie thought. Losing a childhood sweetheart was a tough call. So many memories were intertwined. It was almost impossible to move forward without some sort of survival guilt. Her father was living proof of it. He and her mother had met on the first day of high school and had never had eyes for anyone else but each other.

Kellie, on the other hand, had had plenty of casual male relationships during her adolescence but after her mother had died her only serious relationship had been with Harley Edwards. It worried her that with just under a year until she turned thirty she was way behind her peers in terms of experience. But with the responsibilities of juggling both her studies and her needy family she hadn't had time to socialise in the same way her peers had done.

When Harley had come along, with his easygoing charm, she hadn't given the relationship enough thought before she had committed herself to being his lover. She had known enough about her body and its responses to know she had often been a little short-changed when it had come to their very occasional intimate moments. She had always put it down to overwork and tiredness on her part, but after feeling the fine sandpaper-like touch of Matt McNaught's hands earlier, she wondered if had more to do with not meeting the right person.

She glanced at Matt's hands again and suppressed a tiny shiver. They looked like the sort of hands that would know their way around a woman's body. Long fingered and strong, capable and yet gentle when he needed to be. She had seen that when he had examined Julie's wound earlier.

'Look, if you're really not keen about flying out here, I'm quite happy to do the remote clinics while you hold the fort in town,' Matt said into the silence. 'I hadn't realised you'd had such a frightening experience. An emergency landing would be enough to shake anyone's confidence.'

Kellie felt her heart swell at his gesture of consideration for her feelings. 'Thank you, but I really think I need to conquer my demons,' she said. 'That's part of the reason I came out here. I hate being beaten by something. I knew it would be tough and that there would be flying involved, but patients have to take priority over personal feelings, right?'

He met her gaze briefly. 'Out here patients always take priority,' he said. 'Our feelings don't come into it at all.'

'I guess they don't if you've got them locked away so tightly no one can even get close,' she commented wryly.

His mouth tightened into a flat white line. 'If I choose not to wear my heart on my sleeve, that's surely my business and no one else's,' he said in a curt tone. 'Ruth had no right to tell you all the details of my private life. She was way out of line.'

'She cares for you,' Kellie countered. 'In fact, I think she understands more than most what you're going through.'

He was still looking straight ahead. 'I suppose you mean because we've both lost someone we loved.'

'Yes. She's a mother who has lost her daughter,' she said. 'You're a man who has lost his fiancée. You have a lot of common ground. Grief is a great leveller—sure, we experience it in different ways but it's still grief. Take Julie, for instance. She's lost the father of her children, not from death but because her husband decided he wanted something other than what she could offer. She's left to bring up three boys on her own. In some ways she might have coped better if her husband had died rather than being left to live with the stigma of being rejected for another woman.'

Matt frowned as he thought about what Kellie had said. He had tried over the years to move on from his grief and each year he felt as if he had taken a few more important steps away from it. But then as Madeleine's birthday crept up on him each October he felt the guilt start to gnaw at him, like a tiny pebble inside one of his shoes. It didn't help that Madeleine's parents expected him to be the same broken man he had been six years ago.

For the first time since he had been travelling to Brisbane each year, Matt had felt like a fraud. He had felt almost sickened this time by the way John and Mary Donaldson persisted in maintaining their daughter's bedroom like a shrine to her memory. It was as if Madeleine's parents had never quite accepted their daughter was finally gone. Madeleine's clothes were still hanging in the wardrobe, even her wedding dress and veil this time had reminded Matt of that scene out of Charles Dickens' *Great Expectations* where the jilted Miss Haversham lived in a constant state of wearing her wedding finery, even as it creased and rotted around her aging form.

Madeleine's bed was still made up as if she was coming home to slip in between the neatly pressed sheets, her school trophies and certificates and university degree were on the wall, and her bedside clock was plugged in as if her slim hand would reach out and switch off the alarm the next morning…

Matt gripped the steering-wheel even tighter, fighting against the groundswell of feeling rising inside him. He realised it wasn't grief but frustration that Madeleine's parents were not just holding onto their daughter, but to him as well. 'I'm dealing with it in my own way and in my own time,' he said. 'I don't like talking about it—it brings it all back.'

'I felt the same about my mother's death for ages,' Kellie said. 'I could barely mention her name. But I've come to realise it's much healthier to deal with what you're feeling at the time rather than push it aside. It festers under the surface otherwise, and you can't move on with your life.'

'As a child, no matter what age you are, you more or less expect to outlive your parents,' he said tightly. 'It's not the same thing at all, losing the person you were expecting to marry a couple of days later. There are issues that crop up from time to time, reminders, that sort of thing. It never seems to go away.'

Kellie took a moment to absorb what he'd said to consider if she agreed with it or not. Losing her mother had been devastating. It had been devastating for her father and brothers as well as it had come right out of the blue. One moment their forty-seven-year-old active and energetic mother had been happy and healthy, doing all the things loving mothers did, and the next she had been diagnosed with a terminal illness.

It had felt at the time like the family had suddenly slammed head first into a brick wall. Life was never going to be the same again and each of them had known it. Yes, they'd had a few months to say what had needed to be said so their mother could die in peace, but it hadn't really lessened the grief. If anything, it had prolonged it, as they had watched her waste away before their eyes, each of them watching helplessly until she'd taken her final breath and slipped away.

'I'm not sure I totally agree with you,' she said. 'I miss my mother terribly. There are still days when I reach for my phone to call or text her about something and then I realise she's not here any more. I know for a fact it will get worse if or when I become a mother myself. I have my father, of course, who is absolutely wonderful but no one can ever replace your mother.'

'Yes, well, I've managed without one for the last twenty-six years so I'm not sure I totally agree with you,' he returned.

Kellie looked at the embittered set of what she could see of his features as he continued to focus fixedly on the road ahead. 'You lost your mother when you were a kid?' she asked, frowning.

'She left when I was seven,' he said taking the turn into the street where the Montgomerys' cottage was situated. 'Apart from the occasional birthday card and cheap Christmas present up until I was about ten, I haven't seen or heard from her since.'

'I'm sorry to hear that,' she said, biting her lip as she thought of how hurt he must have felt at such a young age. Her experience with her younger brothers made her very much aware of how incredibly sensitive young boys were. They hid it to protect themselves but it didn't mean they were incapable of deep feelings.

'What about your father?' she asked.

'My father?' His mouth twisted cynically. 'My father still likes to think if it hadn't been for me my mother wouldn't have run off with another man. The burden of looking after a small child, or so he thinks, was the reason she took off for greener pastures. I see him when duty calls, which basically means when he runs short of money, but other than that I keep my distance.'

'That's so sad,' she said with deep sincerity. 'Do you have any siblings?'

'No.'

Soon after that he pulled into the driveway of the cottage but he didn't kill the engine. Kellie knew he had probably regretted revealing as much as he had and was keen to get away before she got even further under his carefully guarded emotional radar.

'Thank you for the lift,' she said, opening the passenger door before he could stride around to do so.

'No trouble,' he said, not even looking her way. 'I'll send someone around tomorrow to fix that window for you. They're probably all a bit stiff. It's the heat at this time of year. It practically melts the paint.'

'Thanks,' she said with a little smile. 'I'd really appreciate it.'

She stood and watched as he drove away in a cloud of dust, the fine red particles his car stirred up making her eyes suddenly start to water.

Kellie spent a restless night in the cottage. The heat, in spite of the air-conditioning, was oppressive and there were noises throughout the night that had her senses constantly on high alert. First she thought she heard footsteps on the roof, but after she heard the distinctive territorial screech of a possum she settled down again.

A few minutes later she heard two cats spitting and yowling just outside her bedroom window. She got out of bed and, pulling aside the curtains, gritted her teeth as she opened the stiff window just enough to lean out and shoo the snarling cats away.

She was just about to close the window when she caught sight of a shadow moving stealthily across the neighbouring vacant property. Her blood stilled in her veins, her heart missed a beat, her throat closing over with fear as she saw the figure disappear into the scrub at the back of the block.

Sleep was almost impossible after that. The old house seemed to be full of squeaks and creaks; even the sound of the refrigerator intermittently regulating its thermostat was enough to have Kellie springing upright in bed each time in wide-eyed terror.

She hadn't realised living alone would be so…so…creepy.

What if someone was inside the house right now? What if they were not aware it was currently occupied and were on their way in? Kellie had heard of intruders reacting violently when confronted by the occupant of a residence they had assumed was vacant.

'I need to get myself a dog,' she said, not even realising she had spoken out loud until she heard the eerie echo of her voice in the stillness of the darkness.

The cats started up again outside her bedroom window and Kellie lay back on her pillow and began counting all the different breeds of dogs she could until through sheer exhaustion she finally drifted off to sleep…

# CHAPTER SIX

THE morning sun was bright but without the sting of the day before so Kellie decided to use the cooler air to get in some exercise. Although the rolling ocean was her usual choice she was no stranger to jogging, and out here where the roads were seemingly endless and with little traffic she felt she could clear her head and prepare herself mentally for the months ahead.

She was well on her way when she realised it might have been a good idea to bring a water bottle with her and maybe even a map of the local area. She had taken a few left and then right turns on side roads to break the monotony of the long straight road but now she wasn't quite sure which way led back to town. The flat dry landscape all looked the same. An occasional gnarled gumtree offered a landmark now and again but as soon as she turned in another direction there was another one just like it.

The sun was beating down with increasing force and her mouth started to feel like she had been sucking on a gym sock for hours. The thought of something wet and cold was almost enough to make her begin to hallucinate. She even thought she could hear the rattle of ice cubes in a glass and the slight tang of a twist of lemon…

She bent down, her hands on her knees as she dragged in

a couple of dry, rasping breaths. Her brand-new running shoes were no longer pristine and white. Instead, they were stained with the ochre-coloured dust of the outback.

She gradually became aware of the sound of a motorbike on her left and she straightened to see a man approaching from behind a fenced property, where a herd of cattle was watching from the limited shade of a cluster of gumtrees, their wide eyes seeming—along with the motorbike rider and the kelpie riding on the back—to be seriously questioning her sanity.

Matt's first words confirmed her impression. 'What the hell are you doing this far out here without water?' he barked.

Kellie hated the ditsy, helpless female role. There was no way she was going to admit she had made a mistake, even if she knew she had indeed made one and a potentially life-threatening one at that. 'It's barely seven in the morning,' she said. 'I've only been running for half an hour or so.'

He frowned at her darkly. 'Then you must be an Olympic champion because you're at least nine kilometres from town. If you turn back now that will be a eighteen-kilometre round trip, which is just asking for muscle meltdown without adequate fluids in this sort of heat.'

Kellie narrowed her gaze to take in the acubra hat on his head. 'Well, now, Dr McNaught,' she said in a pert voice. 'Aren't you a fine one to be preaching health and safety issues with me when you're not wearing a helmet? You could have a fall off that bike of yours and end up concussed or brain injured.'

His jaw clenched slightly as his dark blue eyes tussled with hers. 'I'm on private property and driving at less than forty kilometres per hour.'

Kellie planted her hands on her hips and continued to stare him down. 'You could be driving at ten kilometres an hour and still come off and hit your head against a rock or something,' she pointed out.

He took off his hat and wiped his sweaty brow with the back of his hand. 'Yeah, well, it's too hot to wear one.'

'I'm afraid that excuse won't quite cut it with the cops if they pull you over on the road,' she countered, trying not to stare at the bulge of his biceps as his hands returned to grip the handlebars of the bike.

His eyes nailed hers. 'I don't ride my bike on the road.'

The dog, who up until this point had been perched—somewhat precariously in Kellie's opinion—on the back of the bike jumped off, and with an agility she could only envy wriggled on its belly underneath the fence and came over to nuzzle against her.

She bent down in delight and gave his velvet ears a gentle stroke, crooning to him softly. 'Well, hello, there, gorgeous boy. Have you been helping your daddy on the farm? What a good dog you are, and very clever too. I saw you balancing there like a gymnast on the back of that big bad old bike. Not many of the city dogs I know could do that.'

Matt felt like rolling his eyes but secretly he was a little impressed. Spike wasn't usually so good with strangers. He was a cautious dog, leaning a little towards the anxious if anything, but that was because he had been badly mistreated before Matt had rescued him from the dogs' home in Brisbane.

He watched as the dog melted under her touch, Spike's brown eyes turning to liquid as Kellie tickled him under the chin.

'Here, Spike,' he called, and whistled through his teeth.

Spike pricked his ears and looked at him, but then turned back to Kellie and rolled over in the dust, exposing his belly for a scratch.

'Oh you darling, *darling* boy,' Kellie gushed, scratching and stroking him simultaneously. 'You like that, huh? Yeah, well, I've never met a man yet who didn't like his stomach stroked, or his ego, too, for that matter. But you don't strike me as the overblown-ego type. You're a real sweetie, aren't you?'

Matt could feel his blood surging to places it hadn't surged to in years as he watched Kellie's hand move over his dog's exposed belly. But then the long length of her toned legs in those shorter-than-short running shorts was enough to set anyone's blood boiling, he thought. Her soft, sensual voice was like a whispery caress along the stiffness of his spine, and his deep abdominals switched on with a deep clench-like kick as he thought of how it would feel to have those slim, soft fingers skating over his naked flesh...

Kellie grinned as she straightened, the dog still nudging her hand with its head. 'He's so *cute*,' she said. 'I was just thinking last night how much I'd love to have a dog. Do you know anyone who's got one for sale?'

Matt hastily assembled his features into a stern frown. 'Dogs are not like toys to be picked up and played with at random. It takes commitment and patience to own and train one, especially a working dog. Besides, what would you want with a dog? You're only here for a few months. What will you do with it when you leave?'

She rolled her eyes at him. '*Duh!* I'll take it with me, of course,' she said. 'I love dogs. We've had dogs ever since I was a toddler. Our last one only died a few months ago. That was another reason I took this post. I couldn't bear to leave before Sadie lived her last days. I wanted to be there when she died.'

'And were you?'

Kellie couldn't quite read his expression due to the angle of the morning sun. 'Yes,' she said. 'I was the one who took her to the vet when I realised things were rapidly going downhill. When she was put down the vet left me alone with her and she died cradled in my arms. It was one of the most moving experiences of my life. It reminded me of my mother's death. It made me realise no one should ever die alone, not even the family pet.'

Matt looked at Spike, who was still licking Kellie's fingers as if they were coated in thick chocolate. 'If you want to share the space with Spike on the back, I'm willing to give you a lift back to the homestead and then on to town,' he said gruffly.

She raised her brows at him. *'On the bike?'*

'Only back to the homestead,' he clarified. 'After that you can have the assurance of airbags, stability control and ABS brakes all the way into town.'

'We-ll,' she said, shifting her lips from side to side as she considered his offer.

'I promise to drive extra-slowly,' he added.

'OK, then,' she said, and moved towards the fence with the dog at her side. 'Now, then, Spike, I'm not sure I'm going to do it your way. I think I'll go over the top.'

Matt propped his bike on its stand so he could offer his assistance but she had already snagged her jogging shorts on the top rung of barbed wire by the time he got there.

She looked down at him sheepishly, her perfect small white teeth sinking into her plump bottom lip. 'Oops,' she said, giving her shorts a little tug.

'Here,' he said, moving closer. 'Hold onto my shoulders and I'll unhitch you.'

Kellie put her hands on his shoulders, her belly giving a little quiver of reaction as she felt his hard muscular warmth seeping through the palms of her hands. Her fingers dug in a little further as she felt one of his hands releasing the fabric against her bottom and a shiver ran up like a startled mouse the entire length of her spine. Wow! Those hands of his sure had some magic about them, she thought as she hastily tried to disguise her reaction.

'There,' he said, his voice sounding a little scratchy. 'You're undone.'

'Th-thanks,' she said, locking gazes with him, her hands still on his shoulders.

The sounds of the bush seemed to Kellie to intensify the fact that apart from the dog and the herd of cattle they were not only totally alone but still physically touching.

Her fingers splayed experimentally, relishing the feel of toned male flesh, her belly doing another little flip-kick movement when she saw the dark unshaven stubble on his jaw. She suddenly wanted to run her fingers over the prickle of his skin, to feel it against the softness of hers, on her face, her mouth, her breasts and the silk of her inner thighs.

She looked back into his deep blue gaze and saw the unmistakable flare of male desire burning there. Her chest began to feel as if a moth was fluttering inside the soft cage of her lungs.

His hands went to her waist, the long fingers resting against her for perhaps a second or two longer than necessary before he lifted her from the fence. Kellie felt every angle and plane of his tall lean body on the way down, her breasts brushing against his pectoral muscles, her belly against the hard buckle of his belt, her trembling thighs against the rock-hard length and strength of his.

He set her on the ground and stepped back from her, his expression instantly shutting her out. 'Come on, then, hop on,' he said tonelessly, kicking the bike stand with his foot before straddling the bike.

Kellie had never realised how arrantly masculine such a simple action could be. 'Um…where's Spike going to sit?'

she asked, trying to sound calm and cool and totally unaffected when inside she felt every secret place pulsing with a need she had never felt in such strong, insistent waves before.

'He'll run alongside,' Matt said, and gave the dog a signal with one of his hands. 'It's not far and he'll enjoy the exercise.'

Kellie put one leg over the bike and moved as close to him as she dared, her inner thighs having to stretch to accommodate the muscular width of his. 'R-rightio,' she said a little uncertainly. 'I'm all set.'

He started the bike with a downward thrust of one booted foot. 'Put your arms around my waist,' he instructed. 'The ground's pretty rough in spots.'

'Er…right…' Kellie said, and nestled closer, her arms going around his trim taut middle, while her mind went to places she wasn't sure it should be going.

For instance, she knew if she inched her fingers just a teeny bit closer she could touch his male outline, the unmistakably *hard* male outline of him she had felt on her little sensual slide down his body. Or if she nudged herself even closer against his back, her feminine mound would be able to feel the tautness of his buttocks…

'Everything all right back there?' Matt asked after a journey of about fifty metres.

'Er…yes…fine…just fine…' she answered, wriggling back a bit.

Within a few minutes Kellie could see the homestead in the distance, the colonial design with its wrap-around veranda and large rainwater tanks an iconic image of rural life on the land.

The effects of the longstanding drought, however, were clearly visible. The gardens surrounding both residences looked worn down by thirst and the various trees offering what they could in terms of shade had a thick coat of red dust on their leaves.

Matt brought the bike to a standstill near one of the large sheds a short distance from the homestead and Kellie dismounted even before he had turned off the engine.

'How far behind will Spike be?' she asked.

'He'll probably stop for a quick dip in the home paddock dam,' he said, taking off his hat and brushing back his hair with his hand. 'And speaking of water, let's get you inside and rehydrated.'

Kellie followed him up the four well-worn steps to the front door, the cooler shade of the veranda an instant relief from the now fierce heat of the sun. Inside the house was even cooler, the long hallway with its polished timber floors and the smell of furniture polish and cedar making her feel as if she was stepping back in time to a previous era.

She looked around with interest as he led her to the kitchen. 'Wow, this is such a lovely house, Matt,' she said. 'It must be, what, a hundred and fifty years old?'

'Something like that,' he said, handing her a tall glass of water he had poured from a covered jug in the fridge.

Kellie felt the brush of his fingers as she took the glass and, averting her gaze, took a few sips even though she felt like throwing her head back and downing the contents in one gulping swallow.

'Help yourself to more water and feel free to make yourself tea or coffee,' he said as he headed to the door. 'Everything's there on the bench near the kettle. I'm just going to have a quick shower before we head into town.'

'Thanks,' she said and once he had left the room she quickly refilled her glass and drank deeply.

Kellie heard the sound of water being lapped thirstily

outside. She looked out of the window and was pleased to see Spike had made his way back and after his drink was making himself comfortable in the shade of the rainwater tank.

She wandered from the kitchen to the comfortable-looking sitting room across the hall, the sound of an ancient grandfather clock ticking yet again reminding her of how many generations of farmers had lived here.

Her gaze went to the mantel above the fireplace where there was a photograph of a young woman, the same woman she had caught a glimpse of in Matt's wallet the day before. She picked up the frame and looked into the features of his late fiancée, her long ash-blonde hair, almond-shaped green eyes and wide happy smile marking her as a stunningly beautiful woman.

The floorboards creaked as Matt stepped into the room and Kellie turned around, suddenly feeling like a child who had been caught with their hand in the cookie jar. 'I was just…um…having a look around,' she said, still holding the photograph.

He walked across the room, took the frame from her hands and looked down at it for an infinitesimal moment, before turning and carefully setting it back on the mantel in exactly the same position. Kellie got the impression he thought she had deliberately desecrated his shrine for his fiancée. She could see the tension in his shoulders as he stood with his back to her, still looking at the photograph.

'What was her name?' she found herself asking.

'Madeleine,' he answered after a slight pause.

'She was very beautiful,' Kellie said, not sure what else to say to fill the awkward silence.

'Yes…' He turned around to look at her, his expression showing none of the emotion she could hear in his voice. 'Yes, she was…'

The grandfather clock timed the next silence.

Kellie breathed in the clean scent of Matt, the tantalising combination of citrus-based shampoo and soap and aftershave activating all her senses. His dark brown hair was still wet, although it looked as if he had used his fingers rather than a comb to push it into place. His jaw was cleanly shaven now but it looked as if the razor had nicked him just below his chin on his neck. She could see the pinkish graze and she felt an almost uncontrollable urge to close the small distance between their bodies and salve the tiny wound with the tip of her tongue.

She ran her tongue over her parched lips instead, more than a little shocked at how she was reacting to him. She couldn't remember a time when she had felt so physically aware of a man. Her whole body was on high alert, her skin tingling to feel more of his touch. She could still feel the warm imprint of his hands where they had rested on her waist earlier, the nerve endings still fizzing like thousands of champagne bubbles under her skin.

'Matt, I was— Oh, sorry,' a gruff male voice said from the door. 'I didn't know you had company.'

'It's all right, Bob,' Matt said, turning to face the man. 'This is Kellie Thorne, the new GP filling in for Tim Montgomery. Kellie, this is Bob Gardner, my manager.'

Kellie smiled and took the older man's heavily calloused hand in hers. 'I'm very pleased to meet you, Bob,' she said with a bright and friendly smile.

'Nice to meet you, Dr Thorne,' Bob said. 'My wife Eunice would like to meet you some time. She's away at the moment, visiting our daughter in Cairns, but when she gets back I'm sure she'll invite you over for a meal or something.'

'I'll look forward to it,' Kellie said still smiling.

'What did you want to talk to me about, Bob?' Matt asked.

'That heifer we were worried about has delivered her twin calves without any dramas,' Bob said. 'But I thought we should still get a couple of antibiotic injections from Jim Webber just in case she comes down with milk fever.'

'Good idea,' Matt said. 'I'll drop in on my way home from the clinic, unless you're going to town.'

'I've got to see about that pump part so I can get them then,' Bob said. He turned again to Kellie and smiled. 'I hope you settle in quickly, Dr Thorne, and enjoy your time with us. Lord knows, Matt here could do with the back-up. He works too hard but that's life in the bush, I guess.'

'I'm looking forward to helping out in any way I can,' she said. 'In fact, the sooner the better.'

'Well…be seeing you,' Bob said, and, brushing off his hat, stepped out of the room.

Matt pushed back his partially dry hair with one hand. 'Wouldn't you like a couple more days to look around a bit first?' he asked. 'To settle in and find your way around?'

She shook her head, making her glossy chestnut ponytail swing from side to side. 'No, I've seen enough. I more or less know what I'm in for. I'm itching to get started.'

Matt felt a tiny wry smile lift one corner of his mouth. 'You really like diving into things boots and all, don't you?'

She gave him one of her high-wattage smiles in return. 'No point in living life unless you live it to the full, right?'

Matt had to force himself not to glance back at Madeleine perched on the mantel in her silver frame, but he felt her rainforest-green eyes watching him all the same. He had been promising himself he would put her away…well, not exactly in *that* sense. But he had come to realise recently there would always be a part of him that would think of Madeleine with deep affection. *What? Not love?* That tiny voice of conscience spoke inside his head, louder than it had in years.

Matt had thought he had loved Madeleine. They had been together for so long it was hard to say when the feelings he had assumed were love had started. As a young couple together for such a long time they had sort of gradually drifted into a deeper and deeper relationship. One thing had followed another and before he'd known it they'd been having an engagement party, and then a little while after that they had started planning a wedding…

He gave an inward grimace. Perhaps it was well and truly time to send Madeleine's photograph back to her parents. No doubt they would find a space for it among the unopened wedding presents and uncut wedding cake.

He gave himself a mental shake and reached for his keys. 'Let's get moving,' he said, and led the way out to his car.

# CHAPTER SEVEN

THEY had barely travelled a kilometre or two on the way into town when Matt got a call on his mobile. Because he used his hands-free device to answer while he was driving, Kellie heard every word of the exchange.

'Matt, there's been an incident at Coolaroo Downs,' a female voice said. 'Apparently one of the jackaroos had some sort of altercation with a bull. I'm not sure how serious it is. You know what Joan Dennis is like these days—she panics if someone falls off a fence. It might be just a graze for all we know. The volunteer ambos are on their way but I thought you should see what gives before we call in the flying doctor.'

'Thanks, Trish,' Matt said. 'I'll head back that way now. I have the new GP with me but rather than drop her in to the clinic I think she'd better come with me just in case this is serious. Can you let the clinic patients know I might be half an hour or so late?'

'Sure,' Trish said. 'So...' An element of feminine intrigue entered her voice. 'What's she like?'

Matt tried to ignore the way Kellie's toffee-brown gaze turned towards him. He couldn't see it but he sure as hell could feel it. 'She's...er...with me right now,' he said.

'Yes, I know, that but what is she *like*?' Trish probed. 'Is she good-looking?'

'All right, I guess,' he said, wincing when he felt the laser burn of Kellie's look.

'All right as in what?' Trish kept on at him. 'As in girl-next-door or model material?'

Matt mentally rolled his eyes. 'Somewhere in between,' he answered, chancing a glance Kellie's way and then wishing he hadn't. Didn't he know enough about women to know they all wanted to be considered the most beautiful woman that ever walked the planet? Not that Kellie wasn't beautiful or anything. She was absolutely gorgeous now that he came to think about it. She had a natural elegance about her—in fact, he reckoned she'd look as fabulous in a slinky evening gown with full make-up and exotic perfume and glittering jewellery as she did in a ripped pair of running shorts with her hair limp with perspiration and her cheeks pink from exertion.

Ever since Matt had felt the slim slide of Kellie's body down his that morning out by the fence, he had been having some very disturbing and rather erotic thoughts about her. But he didn't like being manipulated and it seemed to him the whole town was conspiring to hook them up as a couple. When it came time for him to think about another relationship he would do it his way, the old-fashioned way, not because everyone felt sorry for him and had brought in their version of a mail-order bride.

Trish's voice cut through his private thoughts. 'So do you think you might ask her on a date or something?' she asked.

'Trish, I'm on hands-free here and Dr Thorne is hearing every word,' he said, wishing he'd thought to say it earlier, like about three sentences back.

'Oh… Well, then…' Trish quickly recovered and added, 'Hi, there, Dr Thorne. I'm Trish, the receptionist. We've been looking forward to having you join us.'

'I've been looking forward to being here, too,' Kellie said.

'In fact, so much so I'm prepared to get my hands dirty straight away. Dr McNaught has asked me to start a few days early.'

'Well, thank the Lord for that,' Trish said. 'We've been run off our feet while Matt was away on the weekend, and my husband David is supposed to be taking it easier these days. You're just what this place needs—a bit of new blood and young and single and female to boot.'

'Got to go, Trish,' Matt said curtly. 'Keep the phone line as free as you can until we see what gives.'

'Will do,' Trish promised, and promptly hung up.

Matt drove a few more kilometres down the seemingly endless road before he took a right turn into a property marked as Coolaroo Downs, the car rumbling over each of the cattle grids making Kellie rock from side to side in her seat.

He frowned as the cattle yards eventually came into view. 'This looks a little more serious than I thought,' he said. Glancing in the rear-view mirror, he added, 'I hope to God the ambulance isn't too far behind us.'

Kellie felt a tight knot of panic clutch at her insides as Matt parked the car a short distance from the small cluster of people hovering around the body of a young man lying on his back, a dark stain of blood spreading from his abdomen to the dusty ground beneath him.

Matt went round to the rear hatch to retrieve his emergency bag and drug pack. 'Here, take this,' he said, handing Kellie the drug pack, as they were met by Jack Dennis, the property owner.

'It's Brayden Harrison, our junior jackaroo,' Jack said, his face pale beneath his leathery tan. 'Didn't see our stud bull coming straight for him. When he turned, he got gored and thrown into the air. It's bad, Doc. I don't think he's going make it.'

From what Kellie could see, she thought Jack could be right, and sending a quick glance at Matt she could see he thought the same. Brayden was on his back, as white as a sheet and unconscious, hardly breathing. There was a large pool of dark blood still collecting by his side, coming from a wide slash in his abdomen, with a loop of bowel visible through the torn flannelette shirt.

Matt set his emergency pack down beside Brayden, and opened it out to reveal the colour-coded sections for trauma management. 'Jack, has the air ambulance been called?' he asked.

'Yes, Joan called them soon after she called you, but they told her they were on another call to Roma.'

'Have someone go up to the house and tell Joan to ask them to divert here now. There's every chance this is going to be a fatality unless we can pull off a miracle here,' Matt said. Turning to Kellie, he went on, 'He's in shock and unconscious. Put on gloves and goggles and come round to the side and stabilise his neck while I intubate him.'

Kellie held the neck steady, while Matt, now also with gloves and goggles on, gathered the laryngoscope and size 7 endotracheal tube. There was no suction, and the sun was bright, flooding out the light of the laryngoscope.

'Jack, hold this space-blanket over his head to make it darker so I can see down his throat,' Matt instructed with a calm confidence Kellie couldn't help admiring.

Under the cover of the blanket, Matt inserted the endotracheal tube, inflated the cuff and attached the respirator bag. There was no oxygen, only air to ventilate with.

'OK, I'll ventilate while you fit a hard cervical collar, Kellie. They're in the airway section,' Matt instructed.

Kellie retrieved and fitted the collar, then under Matt's instruction took over ventilation with the bag. Matt listened to the chest with his stethoscope, and then percussed the chest.

'There's very little air entry on the right and it's dull to percussion. I'd say he's got a haemothorax. He's also losing a lot of blood from the abdominal wound.'

Taking a pair of scissors, Matt cut away the front of the patient's shirt to reveal a ragged gash in the right upper quadrant of the abdomen, with a loop of bowel protruding and dark blood oozing out. Taking a pack of gauze dressings and a few ampoules of saline, Matt covered the bowel and compressed it back into the abdomen, then covered the whole wound with several large dressing packs and taped them down. He then inserted a 14-gauge cannula into a vein in the arm, and attached it to a litre bag of normal saline.

'Jack, here, squeeze this bag firmly to push the fluid in,' Matt directed, handing over the IV set to the cattle farmer.

One of the station hands came back down from the house to inform them, 'The flying doctor's diverting here. They should be overhead in about ten minutes.'

'Good,' Matt said, and inserted a second IV line into the other arm, and got the station hand to hold up the IV fluid bag.

Matt knew he had two more bags of saline in the kit which would hopefully be enough till help arrived. The flow of blood had now stopped, at least externally.

'OK, all we can do now is hold the fort and support his airway and circulation till we get more gear,' Matt said. 'I'll take over ventilation, Kellie. Can you do his obs?'

'Sure,' Kellie answered, becoming even more impressed at Matt's level-headedness under intense pressure and circumstances that were far from ideal. The dust and heat was bad enough but with the stickiness of blood the bush flies were starting to swarm around. 'Pulse is 120, BP 80 systolic,' she said. 'The first bag's through. I'll put up the next one.'

Seemingly from nowhere, the roar of a plane at low altitude

passed directly overhead, en route to the airstrip on the other side of the homestead.

'Thank God.' Matt breathed a sigh of relief. 'We might just pull this off yet.'

The final bag of saline was almost through when one of the station's four-wheel-drive vehicles arrived with the air ambulance crew in the back, together with a stretcher and several emergency kits. One of the ambulance crew jumped out, carrying two packs of equipment.

'Hi, I'm Marty Davis. We haven't got a doctor—he's in Roma with a placenta praevia. They've got things under control there but we're on our own here. What have you got?'

'Brayden Harrison, one of the jackaroos, has been gored by a bull and is in very bad shape,' Matt informed him. 'He's in haemorhagic shock, he's got a haemothorax and an open abdominal wound. Have you got any plasma expander? We've just exhausted our normal saline and we're still way behind.'

Kellie connected both of the bottles Marty produced to the IV lines while Matt instructed Marty and his partner, Helen, to position the stretcher beside the patient. While Kellie took over ventilation, Matt supervised the transfer onto the trolley and into the back of the four-wheel drive.

'He's still bleeding internally. I want to get him to the plane and put in a right intercostal catheter to re-expand his right lung. Have you got underwater drainage?' Matt asked.

'Yes, we've got a full set of stuff for chest wounds on the aircraft,' Helen said.

'Let's go, then,' Matt said. Exchanging a quick glance with Kellie, he asked, 'Are you OK to fly with me to Brisbane? I'll need you to ventilate him while I manage his IV fluids and abdominal wound.'

'Of course,' she said, although she could feel her stomach already beginning to tighten in apprehension.

Once they reached the aircraft, the two ambulance personnel loaded the patient, while Kellie and Matt set up the intercostal tray.

Kellie helped Matt wash his hands with some sterile water and surgical scrub solution.

'Thanks,' he said, locking gazes with her momentarily before he donned sterile gloves.

She watched as Matt prepped the right side of the chest before performing the necessary procedure that would stem the flow of blood. Some tense minutes later when he unclamped the tube, about 300 ml of blood drained into the bottle, with a small ongoing leak of blood after that.

'Hopefully his chest bleed will stop,' Matt said as he fixed the tube to the skin with a heavy suture and sticky plaster.

'You did an amazing job back there,' Kellie said, meeting his eyes across the now relatively stable patient. 'You stayed so calm and in control.'

Matt gave her a quick movement of his lips that could have almost passed for a smile. 'You were a damned good assistant,' he said. 'It makes a huge difference when everyone knows what to do and when to do it.'

'Thanks,' she said, feeling a blush spreading over her cheeks. 'But I was glad you were the one in charge.'

'I'm sure you would have coped just as well,' he said, checking the patient's condition again. 'Come on, Brayden, hold it together, mate. Not long now.'

Kellie heard the slight note of desperation in Matt's voice. 'Do you know him personally?' she asked softly.

His eyes connected with hers before looking away again to focus on the young man lying between them. 'I met him a few months ago. He came to see me about a plantar wart on his foot.' His frown deepened as he continued, 'He's nineteen years old. He was a little undecided about what to do after he finished school, so rather than waste his parents' money at university doing a course he might never use he came out to the bush for a gap year.' He let out a ragged sigh as his eyes came back to hers. 'He's just a kid…'

Kellie put her hand on his arm. 'He'll make it, Matt,' she said. 'You've done everything possible to get him this far. He *has* to make it.'

Matt looked down at her smooth hand resting against the dark tan of his skin. She had pretty fingers, long and slender with short but neat nails. The skin of her palm was soft and warm, and he found himself wondering what it would feel like to have her massage the aching tension out of his neck.

He pulled his hand away as if by doing so he could tug himself away from where his thoughts were wandering. It had been so long since he had felt a woman's touch. He had locked his physical needs away the day Madeleine had died. For six long lonely years he had ignored the natural and instinctive stirrings of his body, distracting himself with work until there hadn't been time or energy to think about what he was missing.

No one in all that time had made his skin lift and tighten simultaneously at the merest touch. No one's eyes had met his and seen more than he'd wanted them to see. No one's smile had melted or even chipped at the stone of sadness that weighed down his soul.

But Dr Kellie Thorne with her feather-light touch and brown eyes and beautiful smile certainly came close.

Perhaps a little too close.

# CHAPTER EIGHT

ONCE the patient was transferred in Brisbane to the nearest trauma centre, Matt looked up at the flight information board and frowned. 'I hate to be the one to tell you this but it looks like we're going to have to cool our heels here for a while.'

Kellie looked up at the screen. 'Why?'

Brian King, the pilot who had flown the patient down, came over to where they were standing. 'There are electrical storms all over the region,' he explained. 'Most of the regional flights have been grounded overnight.'

'*Overnight?*' Kellie blinked a couple of times. 'But I've got nothing with me. Look at me.'

Both men turned and looked at her.

Kellie felt her face go red when Matt's dark blue gaze lingered the longest. 'I'm covered in blood and dust,' she said, and added mentally, *And I'm wearing a pair of ripped high-cut running shorts and a vest top, and I haven't had a shower and I've never felt so unfeminine and unattractive in my life.* 'Anyway, where would we stay?' she asked.

'There's a hotel close to the airport we use at times like this,' Brian said. 'They do a cheap rate for medical personnel. I'd offer you a bed at my place but we're in the middle of renovations. There's barely room for the wife and kids.' He turned to Matt. 'Will you stay at your…er…fiancée's parents'?'

'No,' Matt said, his expression as blank as a bare wall. 'They've got relatives staying with them this week. I'll be fine at the hotel with Dr Thorne.'

'I reckon the flights will be back to normal in the morning,' Brian said. 'Are you guys right to get a taxi? I've got to go through a couple of checks with the safety crew.'

'Sure,' Matt said. Giving Kellie a follow-me nod, he led the way outside to the taxi rank.

Kellie could feel every person's eyes on her as she stood beside Matt in the queue. An older couple in front had even made a point of stepping away from her, their wrinkled brows frowning in disapproval as they'd taken in her dishevelled appearance.

She felt Matt's broad shoulder brush against her. 'Ignore them,' he said in a low voice.

She looked up at him and asked in an undertone, 'Do I smell?'

His expression contained a hint of wryness. 'I've smelt worse.'

'Thanks,' she said, rolling her eyes. 'That's very reassuring.'

A flicker of a smile lit his gaze. 'Believe me, you'll feel like a million dollars after a shower and something to eat,' he said, as he led her to the next available taxi.

It was a short trip to the hotel, where the receptionist at the front desk smiled apologetically at Matt's request for two rooms. 'I'm terribly sorry, sir, but we only have one room available.'

Matt frowned. 'One room?'

'I'm afraid so,' she answered. 'With so many regional flights being cancelled at short notice, we filled up very quickly.'

'I don't mind sharing a room,' Kellie piped up helpfully.

Matt's frown brought his brows almost together as he looked down at her for a moment.

'It's only for one night,' she said, conscious of the receptionist's speculative look.

'It's a queen-sized suite,' the receptionist chipped in. 'But if you would like a roll-out bed brought in I can organise Housekeeping to have one delivered to your room.'

'Yes,' Matt said. 'That would be very much appreciated.'

'We're not a couple,' Kellie explained.

'Brother and sister?' The receptionist took a wild guess.

'No,' Kellie said with a little laugh. 'I've already got five brothers. The last thing I need is another one.'

The receptionist smiled as she handed Matt a form to sign. 'It's room four hundred and twenty-five,' she said. 'You'll need your swipe card. I hope you enjoy your stay.'

When the doors of the first available lift opened Kellie stared in dismay at her reflection in the mirrored wall at the back. 'Oh, my God!' she wailed. 'Why didn't you tell me I looked like this?'

Matt reached past her to press the button for their floor. 'You don't look that bad,' he said with what he hoped was an indifferent look.

She groaned as she rubbed at the smear of blood over her right cheek with the bottom of her top. 'I look like an extra from a horror movie,' she said. 'The least you could have done is said something. No wonder people were staring.'

'Yes, well, they probably weren't staring at your face,' Matt said dryly, doing his level best not to stare at the strip of tanned and toned abdomen she had exposed by lifting her top to clean her face.

She let the top fall back down. 'What do you mean?'

He put an arm out to hold the lift doors open. 'I think that rip in your shorts is getting bigger,' he said. 'I hope for the sake of your dignity there's a complimentary sewing kit in the room.'

Kellie clutched at her behind and felt the lace of her knickers. 'Oh, no!'

'Don't worry,' he said, leading the way down the hall. 'There's no one about. This is our room right here.'

*Our room.*

Matt felt himself flinch as he said the words. Those words... How many times had he and Madeleine used them over the years? Our first date, our love, our engagement, our future...

He stared at the swipe key in his hand, wondering if he should have tried another hotel. Why hadn't he thought of it earlier? It wasn't as if the whole of Brisbane would have been booked out. There were numerous hotels all over the city and even if some of them were beyond the health department budget, he could have paid for a couple of rooms himself.

'Hurry up!' Kellie said at his side. 'Open the door. I don't want anyone else to see like me this.'

He drew in a breath and opened the door, but before he could reach for the light switch she had rushed past him and headed straight to the bathroom.

While she was in the shower someone from Housekeeping arrived with a roll-out bed, which, once it was set up, shrank the space to give the room an alarmingly intimate feel.

Matt swung away and looked out of the window, trying not to think of Kellie's naked body standing under the shower next door. His whole body felt tense, his blood surging to his groin at the thought of spending the night in the same room as her with less than a metre of space to separate them. He was angry at himself, angry that he was allowing sheer animal attraction to override his common sense.

He closed his eyes and tried to think of Madeleine, but her

features seemed less defined, blurry almost, as if she was slowly but inexorably moving out of focus. He clenched his fists and tried to recall the scent of her perfume but even that, too, had drifted out of his reach.

'I'm all done,' Kellie said as she came out of the bathroom.

Matt slowly turned from the window, his lower belly kicking in reaction at the sight of her in one of the hotel's fluffy white bathrobes, her wet hair loose about her shoulders, the fresh orange-blossom fragrance of the shampoo and shower gel she had used filling his nostrils.

'I've washed out my things and left them to dry over the shower screen,' she said. 'I hope they won't be in your way while you shower.'

'Right…' he said, moving past her. 'Er…do you want to have a look through the room-service menu? It takes them about forty minutes to deliver it. You can order for me.'

'What would you like?' she asked.

Matt wasn't sure he could even admit that to himself without another pang of shame slicing through him. 'Anything,' he said. 'Surprise me.'

Kellie frowned as the bathroom door closed and locked behind him. After a moment or two she let out a little sigh, reached for the room-service menu and started reading.

Matt told himself he wasn't even going to look at the tiny pair of black lace knickers hanging over the glass shower screen, but as he blindly reached for the bath gel they fell off and landed at his feet. He waited a beat or two before bending to pick them up, his fingers almost of their own accord squeezing the moisture out of them.

He hung them back up with careful precision and quickly finished his shower, but somehow the thought of Kellie standing where he was standing just minutes before, the water coursing over and caressing her slim form, unsettled him far more than he wanted to admit.

She was sitting with her legs curled underneath her on the roll-out bed, reading a tourist brochure, when he finally came out of the bathroom. She looked up and smiled at him in that totally engaging way of hers and informed him, 'I've ordered you a steak with kipler potatoes and green vegetables. Is that OK?'

His stomach grumbled in anticipation. 'That's perfect,' he said as he rubbed his wet hair with his towel. 'What are you having?'

'I couldn't decide between the barramundi fillets with mango chilli salsa or the chicken with pesto and pine-nut stuffing or the loin of lamb with rosemary and garlic.'

He tried not to stare at the soft plumpness of her mouth. 'So…what did you decide?' he asked.

She tilted her head at him. 'What do *you* think I chose?'

'The fish,' he said, feeling an involuntary smile pull at the corners of his mouth. 'Definitely the fish.'

Her eyes went wide with surprise. 'How on earth did you guess that?'

He gave his head another quick rub with the towel. 'You're a beach chick,' he said. 'You've probably grown up with fish bones between your teeth.'

She grinned at him. 'I did, too,' she said. 'My brothers and I were taught to fish when we were still in nappies. I think I still hold the record for the most flathead caught in one outing.'

Matt marvelled yet again at how different their family backgrounds were. His father had taken him fishing once but it had been a disaster from start to finish. If the rain hadn't been bad enough, the seasickness Matt had felt on the way home across the bay had made it a day to remember for all the wrong reasons. He could still recall his father's scowling expression, as if Matt had been personally responsible for both the lack of fish and the inclement weather.

'You sound like you had a very happy childhood,' he said as he tossed his towel over the back of a chair.

'I did,' she said with another little smile. 'I hope when I get married and have kids, I'll be able to give them the sort of childhood I had.'

A stretching silence made the room seem ever smaller.

'I'm sorry….' Kellie said, biting her lip. 'I guess that was a bit insensitive of me.'

He gave her an unreadable look. 'No, not at all.'

Another beat or two of silence passed.

'Tell me about her,' Kellie said softly.

'Tell you about who?'

'Madeleine. Your fiancée. What was she like?'

Matt felt his chest start to tighten but after a moment's hesitation he found himself telling her more than he had told anyone. 'She was beautiful, a bit on the shy side but when she got to know you she would come out of her shell a bit more. She was an only child like me so we had a lot in common right from the start. We both found it hard to make friends easily. It took us time to learn to trust people.'

He took in a breath and continued, 'She loved music, not that techno modern stuff but mostly classical. She played the piano and the flute like a pro but she couldn't cook for peanuts.' He gave a ghost of a smile that barely touched his mouth and went on, 'I think it was because her mother and father did everything for her. Being their only child, it was understandable she was treated like a princess.'

'Her parents must miss her dreadfully,' Kellie said into the small silence.

His eyes met hers. 'Yes…' He released a long, rough-around-the-edges sigh. 'She was their life, their entire focus for living. They're like empty shells now.'

Kellie moistened her dry lips. 'It's nice that you keep in contact with them,' she said. 'Not many men in your situation would think to do that.'

He gave a rueful twist of his mouth but it wasn't anywhere near a smile. 'I'm not sure if it helps or hinders them, to tell you the truth,' he confessed. 'If I don't call them regularly I feel guilty, but when I do call it sort of stirs it all up again for them, you know?'

She nodded. 'I do know…'

He ran a hand through his still damp hair and sighed again. 'It's been six years and yet it sometimes feels as if it was yesterday.'

'What happened?' Kellie asked.

He sat on the end of the queen-sized bed, his legs so close that Kellie knew if she uncurled hers from beneath her they would touch his, knee to knee.

She watched the pain of remembering moving like a shadow over his face. It thinned his mouth, it tightened his jaw and it left his dark blue gaze achingly empty as it connected with hers.

'We had an argument the night before,' he said, a frown bringing his brows almost together over his eyes. 'I don't even remember what it was about now, something silly to do with the wedding seating arrangements, I think. She left in a huff and I was my usual pigheaded self, brooding over it for hours without doing anything to sort things out.'

Kellie sat in silence, somehow sensing he was letting his guard down in a way he had never done before. It made her feel an intimate connection with him, unlike anything she had felt with anyone else in the past.

His mouth contorted again as he continued, 'She was

spending the week with her parents so I didn't bother ringing her the next morning. I planned to go round that evening with flowers and an apology but, of course, I was too late. A car ran a red light and ploughed straight into her on her way to school that morning. She died a few minutes later at the scene.'

'I'm so sorry,' Kellie said in a voice whisper soft.

He brought his gaze back to hers, the bleakness of it making her ache for him. 'I often lie awake at night and wonder what she was thinking in those final moments as her life ebbed away,' he said. 'I wonder if she was thinking about me, our wedding and all the plans we'd made.'

Kellie brushed at her eyes. 'It must have been an absolute nightmare for you. I don't know how you coped.'

He gave her a crooked smile but it was grim, not humorous. 'It felt like a nightmare at the time,' he said. 'I kept thinking surely someone's going to tap me on the shoulder and say "April Fool" or something, but each day was the same as the one before. The grief was like a thick fog, I couldn't see through it and no one could get to me through its black heavy shroud. I even thought about…you know…ending it all.'

'What stopped you?'

His gaze meshed with hers. 'See these?' he asked, holding out his hands palms upwards.

Kellie nodded.

He looked down at his outstretched hands. 'These hands have been trained to save lives. I gave up years of my life to train to be a doctor. I had to work harder than most as I didn't have the support of my parents, who were too busy feuding with each other to take much notice of me. I thought it would be selfish of me to end it all when I could put my life to much better use.'

'So you came out to the bush.'

His eyes came back to hers. 'Yes. Out here I can make a difference. My life counts for something, even though it is not the life I had originally planned for myself.'

Kellie leaned forward and took his hands in hers and gently squeezed. 'You are an absolutely *amazing* doctor, Matt,' she said. 'You saved Brayden Harrison's life today.'

'He's not out of the woods yet,' he reminded her, but Kellie couldn't help noticing he didn't pull out of her tender hold.

'Perhaps not,' she said. 'But he's in with a chance, a chance he wouldn't have had if you hadn't been there to do what needed to be done.'

His fingers curled around hers, his slightly rough touch against her smooth one sending her pulse skyrocketing. She ran her tongue over her lips again, mesmerised by the dark intensity of his gaze as it held hers.

The doorbell of the suite sounded, announcing the arrival of their meals, and broke the moment. Matt dropped her hands as if they were hot coals and strode over to the answer the door.

The trolley was wheeled in and Matt gave the young attendant a tip on his way out before coming back to where Kellie was still curled up on the makeshift bed.

'We should eat this before it gets cold,' he said, without meeting her gaze.

Kellie knew he was regretting his earlier outburst of guilt and grief. She had experienced it so many times with her brothers, the way they let their guard down and then pulled away from her as if they were worried she would exploit their brief vulnerability. 'Matt?' she said softly.

He took the lid off one of the plates. 'This is your fish,' he said, and handed it to her with a closed-off expression.

'Don't shut me out,' she said, ignoring the outstretched

plate. 'Come on, Matt, you just let me into your deepest pain and now you're shoving me away.'

He blew out a breath and slapped the plate back down on the trolley. 'Don't eat it, then, see if I give a damn.'

She got to her feet and tugged at his arm. 'Matt, look at me,' she said. 'Stop feeling sorry for yourself. You can't bring her back no matter how much you want to. It wasn't your fault she died. You weren't to blame.'

He brushed off her arm, his eyes blazing as they hit hers. 'What would you know?' he barked at her savagely. 'What the hell would you know about how I feel?'

'I know more than you realise,' she said with quiet dignity. 'I know that you feel somehow responsible for Madeleine's death. I also know you are punishing yourself as if in some way that will make things right, but it won't, Matt. You won't make things right by doing wrong things.'

'What wrong things am I doing?' he asked, still glaring at her heatedly.

She came over to where he was standing, so close he had no where to go but back up against the wall. 'You didn't die in that accident with her, Matt,' she said. 'You're still alive and entitled to live a fulfilling life. You have the right to enjoy what life has to offer, you don't have to be a hermit out there in the bush. You can have a new love, maybe even a happy future, with marriage and babies.'

His lip curled in a sneer. 'Is that why you came out here?' he asked, 'to find a husband and sperm donor?'

Kellie flinched away from his crude bitterness. 'I came out here because I needed a change of scene. My family has become too dependent on me and my love life totally sucks, so all round it seemed like a good solution.'

He moved past her to lift the lid off the other plate. 'I'm

not interested in auditioning for the role of fill-in partner while you sort out your relationship and family issues. When I feel ready to look for another relationship I will do so in my own good time and not a minute before.'

'Only because you're afraid of being hurt again,' she said. 'It's understandable. My father is the same but it doesn't mean either of you don't deserve to live life to its fullest potential. You are, what, thirty-three or -four? You have more than half your life ahead of you. What are you doing, locking yourself away from all that life has to offer?'

He picked up the napkin-wrapped cutlery and sat on the bed with his plate balanced on his lap. 'I'm happy with my life the way it is. I work, I eat and I sleep.'

Kellie gave her eyes a roll of exasperation. 'Yes, but you do it all alone.'

'Only the sleeping part,' he said, sticking his fork into a floret of broccoli and popping it into his mouth.

Her eyes widened. 'You've been celibate for *six* years?'

Matt frowned at her. 'What's wrong with that?' he asked. 'Lots of people choose to be celibate.'

'I know but don't you think it's time you lived a little?'

'I told you, Kellie, I like my life the way it is for the moment,' he said. 'I'm sorry if Trish and the Montgomerys gave you the impression I was a likely candidate for a six-month fling but I prefer to choose my own partners, not have them thrust on me.'

Kellie glared at him. 'You think I would agree to a match-making scheme like that?' she asked. 'Get real, Matt. I like to choose my own partners too, not that I've been particularly good at it or anything, but don't for a moment think I would consider *you* as a potential lover, far from it.'

He pushed his half-eaten meal to one side and got to his

feet. 'I'm going out for some fresh air,' he said, tossing his napkin down on the bed. 'Don't wait up.'

Kellie blew out a frustrated sigh and pushed her half-eaten meal away. OK, so maybe that had been a bit harsh, she thought. The truth was she had more than once considered Matt as a potential lover, but after Harley's brazen two-timing Kellie was damned if she was going to play second fiddle to another woman again: dead or alive.

## CHAPTER NINE

WHEN Matt came back to the suite at close to two a.m. Kellie was sound asleep, her small body curled up like a child's, one of her hands underneath her cheek, the other hanging down over the side of the bed.

He stood looking at her in the lamplight, feeling guilty for drinking in the sight of her while she was totally unaware of his presence. It seemed voyeuristic, exploitative even, but he couldn't seem to pull his gaze away.

She had obviously dispensed with the bathrobe for it was now hanging off the edge of the bed near her feet. Somehow the thought of her naked beneath that thin cotton sheet stirred his senses more than he would have thought possible. She had such a neat body, lean and athletic but unmistakably feminine.

He went rigid when she suddenly rolled over with a little murmur, the sheet slipping to reveal the creamy curve of one small but perfect breast. He knew he shouldn't be staring—he was a doctor, for pity's sake! He'd seen more breasts than he could count, and yet the sight of that creamy globe with its dusky brown nipple took his breath away.

Her soft mouth opened slightly on a sigh and she nestled back down into the pillow, but just when Matt thought it was safe to draw in a breath she suddenly opened her eyes. She sat bolt upright, her mad scramble for the sheet to cover herself affording him an even better view of her body than she had probably intended.

'What the hell do you think you're doing?' she railed at him. 'You scared me half to death!'

'Sorry,' he mumbled gruffly. 'I didn't mean to wake you. I was just…'

'You were just what?' She glared at him. 'Having a little peek while you thought no one was looking?'

He raked a hand that wasn't quite steady through his hair. 'It wasn't like that at all,' he lied, a tide of colour heating the back of his neck. 'I was trying to get to my bed without disturbing you in the process.'

'How long have you been standing there?'

His eyes shifted away from her accusing narrowed ones. 'Not long.'

'How long?'

'Can we, please, drop this?' he asked. 'Look, I have no designs on you so you can rest easy.'

She hugged her knees under the sheet, her expression looking a little downbeat. 'So…what you're saying is you don't find me in the least bit attractive?'

Matt frowned at the edge of insecurity in her tone. 'Of course I find you attractive,' he said. 'You're very attractive— gorgeous, in fact. Why on earth would you think otherwise?'

She gave her bottom lip a bit of a nibble before she answered. 'I don't know… I guess I'm not all that confident on the dating scene. I think I spent too much time sweating over making dinner for my father and my brothers instead of getting hot and sweaty in a nightclub with the rest of my friends. I keep thinking there must be something wrong with me. My ex certainly made it clear I wasn't enough to hold his interest.'

'Yeah, well, if you ask me, your ex was a jerk,' Matt said, pulling down the covers on the queen-sized bed in case he was tempted to cross the floor and pull her into his arms and show her how achingly beautiful she was.

A little silence passed.

'If the tables had been turned, would you have expected Madeleine to put her life on hold indefinitely?' Kellie asked.

'Look, Kellie,' he said injecting his tone with impatience at her persistence over his lack of a love life. 'I'm not putting my life on hold. But even if I was, it's not the same thing. It's so much harder for women.'

'How?' Kellie asked. 'Grief is grief. I don't think either gender has an exclusive take on it.'

'The issue of fertility puts a very definite take on it,' he pointed out. 'As a man, if I chose to I can have children at almost any age. Of course, in my twenties, thirties or forties would be ideal, but for women that isn't the case. They have limited time in which to select a suitable partner to father their child or children.'

'Did you and Madeleine plan to have children?'

Matt turned from the bed to look at her. 'It was something we discussed once or twice.' He looked away again, not comfortable adding how often he had shied away from the topic. Madeleine had been a few more steps ahead of him, now that he thought about it. It had been her idea to get engaged, her idea to bring the wedding forward and very definitely her idea to begin a family straight afterwards. It wasn't that Madeleine wouldn't have made a great mother, it was just he had never really seen himself settling down into suburbia in quite the way she had planned. It was a disturbing realisation that two people who had claimed to be in love had not really been in tune with each other's wants and desires. Was that why he was still punishing himself? he wondered. It wasn't that he had loved Madeleine too much—it was more that he hadn't loved her enough…

Kellie lay back on her pillow with her hands propped behind her head. 'My mother would have loved to be a grandmother,' she said on the end of little sigh. 'She told me that being a mother was great but it was so exhausting she couldn't wait to be a granny so she could hand back the little ones at the end of the day. I feel sad she won't be around for my babies, to love and indulge them as a doting granny should. My dad will do his best but it won't be the same, will it?'

Matt sat on the edge of his bed. 'I'm sure he will do what he can to be a good grandfather,' he said, rather unhelpfully.

She turned her head to look at him, a soft smile curving her mouth. 'I'm hoping my time away in the bush will bring about a romance.'

He automatically tensed. 'So I was right about Tim and Claire?' he said, clenching his jaw. 'I knew it. I just knew they wouldn't be able to help themselves.'

She gave him a blank look. 'What have Tim and Claire got to do with my father and my aunt?'

It was Matt's turn to deliver the blank stare. 'Your father and your aunt?'

'Yes,' Kellie said. 'My aunt has been in love with my father for the last five years, ever since she watched him nurse my mother through her illness. Aunty Kate's husband left her for another woman years ago, and for as long as I can remember she has always been there for all of us, working tirelessly in the background, dropping in meals or doing loads of washing and ironing without being asked. My father has more or less been oblivious to it because I've been there to pick up where she left off. I thought it would be best if I moved out so she could show Dad how much she does for us and for him. He's a bit on the slow side, if you know what I mean.'

'He's probably not quite ready to move on,' he said pragmatically. 'You can't force him.'

'I know, but Aunty Kate loves him,' she said. 'She's loved him for years. I've known it, my brothers have known it even though they are about as emotionally deficient as boys can be, but my father seems completely ignorant of it.'

'Then perhaps it was a good move of yours to come out to the bush,' he said. 'You sound to me like the glue that holds your family together.'

'I'd never thought of it quite like that. That's great way to put it.' Her smile faded a little as she asked, 'But what if they fall apart while I'm gone?'

'I'm sure they won't,' Matt said. 'They've probably got into a pattern of learned helplessness. They'll soon snap out of it.'

'Yes, well, that's the plan,' she said with another little smile.

Matt could see that Kellie was a warm-hearted person who had a mission in life to spread love and goodwill to others. He also knew from what she had briefly intimated that her love life was lacking something, but it didn't mean he was the person to step up to the plate to take the next ball, certainly not with the whole of Culwulla Creek on the sidelines, cheering him on.

Anyway, life was *so* damned capricious.

Doctors knew that more than most. They diagnosed terminal illnesses on a weekly, sometimes even daily basis. He had done it himself. So many faces drifted past him, shocked faces, devastated faces, faces that communicated their frustration in their but-I've-not-done-all-I've-set-out-to-do expressions of despair.

They were all the same, just like him: cheated of what life had promised but had failed to deliver.

Was it his fault?

No, and the rational part of him knew Madeleine's death wasn't really his fault. It was the driver running the red light, it was the rush hour, it was a hundred other things that had been going on in the universe at that particular moment, but yet still he felt somehow responsible. What if she had been thinking about *him* at that moment and not seen the car on her right? What if she had been thinking about the seemingly endless list of jobs to do before their wedding? Or, like him, having last-minute doubts? It had been a stressful time, especially as Madeleine hadn't wanted to take any time off school and therefore everything had had to be packed into those last couple of days before the term finished. What if *he* had done more of those little jobs for her so she hadn't been so rushed off her feet?

The what-ifs had been what had kept him awake most nights in those early days and tortured far too many of his days as well. Work out here in the bush was his only panacea and so far it had done a reasonable job...well, it had until Kellie had come to town with her big smile and adorable dimples.

'We'd better get some sleep,' he said, feigning a yawn. 'The first flight is at eight. I organised it when I went out earlier. We were lucky as there were only two seats left.'

'I hope I get the window one,' she said, turning on her side and propping herself on her elbow.

Matt decided it would be wise to turn out the lamp as soon as he could so he didn't have to keep staring into those beautiful brown eyes. The soft light in the room made her gaze melting and soft, so soft he could feel himself drowning in it every time she looked at him. He muttered something about using the bathroom and came out a few minutes later dressed in the other bathrobe provided by the hotel. She was still lying facing him, her eyes widening slightly when he got between the covers without taking off the bathrobe.

'You're going to cook, wearing that to bed,' she informed him knowledgably. 'I had to toss mine off hours ago.'

*I wish you hadn't reminded me of that*, Matt thought as he turned off the lamp and flopped down on the pillow. The thought of her satin skin covered only by the thin threads of a cotton sheet was almost too much for his mind to cope with.

There was barely a beat of silence before her voice split the silence.

'Matt?'

He affected a bored, I'm-almost-asleep tone. 'Hmm?'

'Do you think you could leave the lamp on?' she asked in a beseeching whisper.

Even though his eyes were closed Matt still rolled them behind his eyelids. 'What on earth for? Do you want to read or something? It's close to three in the morning.'

'No but it's so dark in here…'

He thumped the pillow to reshape it. 'It's supposed to be dark,' he said dryly. 'It's the middle of the night.'

'Yes, but I like to be able to see my way to the bathroom,' she said. 'I don't want to break a leg or something, stumbling in the dark.'

'Do you need the bathroom?'

'Not right now, but I might later.'

Matt removed his bathrobe under the cloak of darkness and placed it over the nearest chair before switching on the bedside lamp, turning the dimmer switch as low as it could go. 'There, it's on now so close your eyes and go to sleep.'

There was another beat or two of silence.

'Matt?'

He inwardly groaned. 'Yes?'

'Have you ever wondered what it would be like to be totally blind?' she asked.

He counted to five. 'Not lately, no.'

He heard the rustle of the bedclothes as she shifted her position. 'I do, a lot,' she said. 'I had a young female patient who was blind from retinoblastoma. She had lost both eyes by the time she was two years old. She told me what it was like, how she has to read people not by their faces or body language but by using other senses. She has to memorise every place she visits. No one can move a single piece of furniture at her house otherwise she'll bump into it. I think about it a lot—you know how you would have to adjust in so many little ways.'

'Do we have to talk about this now?' he asked, smothering a weary yawn, not a feigned one this time.

'No, it's just ever since I met her I feel like I have to have light around me,' she said. 'It reminds me of what so many people, me included, take for granted.'

'You do realise you are contributing unnecessarily to global warming?' he asked.

Kellie turned to look at him. He had dispensed with the bathrobe and was now lying on his back with his eyes closed, his arms propped behind his head, his biceps bulging, and his stomach flat and naked to his waist where the thin cotton sheet was resting. His chest was as tanned as the rest of his body, not entirely hairless but not overly so. The trail of black curly hair burrowed below the sheet to where it loosely covered his groin.

Kellie knew she shouldn't be staring but it had been a very long time since she had seen a man in such fabulous physical condition. Her pulse fluttered like a trapped moth beneath her skin.

She was less than a metre away from him. She could reach

out with one of her hands and slide it down his ridged abdomen; her fingers could splay over his maleness, stirring it to fervent life with the merest brush of her fingertips.

'It'd be tough, though, don't you think?' she asked, forcing her mind away from the temptation of his body. 'Being blind, I mean.'

Matt opened his eyes and turned to look at her and then wished he hadn't. The shadow of her cleavage was right in his line of vision and the delicious curves of her breasts were outlined by the sheet tucked against her. Even if he closed his eyes again he knew it would be impossible to erase that vision from his mind.

Possibly for ever.

'Aren't you exhausted?' he said. 'You've had a tough day, by anyone's standards.'

She wriggled under the bedclothes again and let out a tiny sigh. 'I guess I am a *bit* tired…'

*Thank God*, Matt thought as he watched her eyelids start to droop. He watched as she drifted off, her mouth relaxing into a soft plump curve, her slim form covered by the sheet making him wish he could run his hand over her, exploring every dip and curve of her body.

He clenched his hands into fists, scrunching his eyes shut, but the gentle sound of her breathing kept him awake for most of the night.

Bright morning sunlight pierced Kellie's eyelids and she sat bolt upright and rubbed at her eyes. 'Hey,' she said, glancing at her watch. 'Aren't we supposed to have left by now?'

Matt dragged his head off the pillow and looked at the bedside clock through slitted eyes. He muttered a stiff curse and threw off the bedclothes without thinking.

He suddenly saw Kellie's eyes go wide and then the delicate rise of colour rush up over her face. He reached for the bathrobe he'd discarded the night before and, tying it with more haste than security, lunged for the phone.

Kellie overheard every word of the exchange, realising as the heated conversation went on they would have to hurry or they would miss the only flight to Culwulla Creek that day, which would mean a long road trip in a hire car from Brisbane.

Using the sheet as a cover, she scuttled into the bathroom and tried not to think about what she had seen in that brief lapse when he had leapt from the bed, although she knew it was going to be very hard to erase it from her mind.

Matt was built like a bodybuilder, not the over-the-top anabolic steroids type but the type that sent female pulses soaring. Pumped muscles, leanness where leanness looked best, like on the flat planes of a stomach that looked as if it had been carved from a slab of marble.

When she came out dressed in her rinsed-out shorts and top and running shoes he was dressed and ready to go. 'We have to hurry,' he said, scooping up his doctor's bag. 'They're holding the flight for us but only because we're medical personnel.'

The attendant smiled at Matt as he led the way up the gangway. 'Well done, Dr McNaught,' she said, 'and with three minutes to spare.'

Matt gave her a brief smile in return and, nodding in apology to the already seated and belted passengers, indicated for Kellie to precede him. 'You can have the window seat,' he said with a deadpan expression. 'And the armrest too, if you want it.'

Kellie grinned up at him as she wriggled into the seat. 'Is that a sense of humour I see peeking out from behind that gruff exterior of yours?' she asked.

His expression remained bland but she saw his lips twitch slightly as he took his seat and began rummaging for his end of the seat belt.

'Is this what you're looking for?' she asked, holding up the clip-in end of the belt, her eyes twinkling mischievously.

Matt took it from her slim warm fingers, his body tingling all over at that merest of touches. She was smiling at him in that impish way of hers, the mixture of tomboy and sexy siren that befuddled his brain and other parts of his anatomy. He could feel the way his groin was already tightening, the ache building even more when she ran her tongue over the pink sheen of her lips in that slightly nervous, uncertain manner of hers. He thought of that soft mouth exploring him, the tip of her tongue tasting the essence of him, licking from him the life force that was banked up inside him to the point of bursting. All night he had thought of her hands skating over him, discovering his contours, feeling the length and deep throbbing pulse of him in the slim sheath of her body, the feminine heart of her convulsing around him as he drove himself to paradise...

Kellie peered at him curiously. 'Are you all right, Matt?' she asked.

Matt gave himself a mental shake and resettled in his seat, wincing as he had to accommodate a little more of himself than normal. 'I'm fine,' he muttered. 'These seats are so damned uncomfortable. There's not enough leg room.'

'That's because you're so tall,' she said, pushing his elbow off the armrest and smiling at him playfully.

Matt reached for the in-flight magazine in the seat pocket, even though he'd read it a thousand times before. Those long legs of hers were still in his line of vision. He couldn't help imagining them looped around his, her mouth on his, her tongue mating with his as they strove for mutual fulfilment.

He felt her shoulder lean into him. 'Interesting article?' she asked.

He schooled his features into impassivity as he looked at her. 'Absolutely riveting,' he said, and turned back to the piece on emu-oil investment.

# CHAPTER TEN

RUTH WILLIAMS was at the airstrip when they alighted from the plane. 'I organised one of Jack Dennis's boys to take your car to the clinic,' she said to Matt. 'I didn't want to leave it out here overnight, especially with your medical equipment on board. I can give you a lift back into town.'

'Thanks, Ruth,' Matt said. 'That was thoughtful of you.'

Ruth turned to Kellie. 'You must be exhausted. What a drama to face on your first official day with us.'

'Yes, it was,' Kellie said, looking down at herself ruefully. 'That's the longest run I've ever been on. Next time I'm going to take an overnight backpack just in case.'

Ruth gave her a rueful look. 'I did warn you things can happen out here in the blink of an eye.'

'Yes, well, I'm a believer now,' Kellie said as they made their way to Ruth's car.

The clinic was fully booked so Ruth dropped off Matt before taking Kellie to the Montgomerys' cottage so she could get changed and drive herself back to town.

By the time Kellie made it back to the clinic the waiting room was full. Every available chair was taken and three male patients were standing. A small child was howling piteously in one corner, his harried mother doing what she could to placate him while nursing an infant at her breast.

Trish gave Kellie a relieved smile as she ended the call she was on. 'Welcome to Mayhem Medical Clinic,' she said. 'I know you're not going to believe this, but it's not always as busy as this.'

Kellie straightened her shoulders. 'I'm ready for a challenge,' she said. 'That's why I'm here.'

'Good,' Trish said, handing her the file on top of the stack on the reception counter. 'Angela Baker is your first patient. You won't get much more challenging than that.'

Kellie suppressed a frown, hoping the patient hadn't overheard Trish's comments. She hadn't appeared to, although perhaps it was because her son was now having a full-on tantrum in the middle of the waiting-room floor.

'Angela?'

The young flustered woman got to her feet, almost dropping the baby in the process.

'Here,' Kellie said as she reached for the baby and the nappy bag the young mother was carrying. 'Let me help you.'

'Thanks,' Angela mumbled as she reached for one of her toddler's flailing arms. 'Come on, Charlie. It's time to see the doctor.'

The little boy opened his mouth even wider, his reddened eyes streaming with tears. Kellie felt sorry for both the toddler and his poor mother, who looked like she was close to tears herself. She looked far too thin for someone who had not long had a baby. Her cheeks were sunken and her hair looked like it hadn't seen a brush in a couple of days at least.

It took a bit of cajoling but eventually Charlie shuffled in with his mother and sat down on the floor to play with the small basket of toys in Tim Montgomery's room.

Kellie was glad she had come to the post with experience as she hadn't had time to check the facilities out first. The room was fairly well equipped and organised in such a way that she didn't think she would have too much trouble finding what she needed.

The baby became restless as it was still hungry so Kellie handed her back to Angela so she could run her eyes over the file to familiarise herself with the young woman's history. There wasn't a great deal of information, apart from the two pregnancies which had both progressed more or less normally. Tim's writing was a little difficult to read in places but she could see that Angela was a nineteen-year-old girl. She wasn't married but lived with the father of her children on the edge of town.

'Right.' Kellie smiled as she looked up from the notes. 'What can I do for you, Angela?'

'I think there's something wrong with Charlie,' Angela said, not quite meeting Kellie's gaze. 'He's been crying a lot and keeps trying to hit the baby.'

'Lucy is, what…?' Kellie glanced at the notes again. 'Just ten weeks old and Charlie is nineteen months old. It's perfectly normal for him to be a little put out by the presence of a new baby. He's had you to himself for all that time. He's only a baby himself so it will take him a little while to adjust, but I'll run a few standard tests to reassure you.'

Charlie was surprisingly obliging when Kellie approached him. She crouched down to his level, brushed back his dark brown hair from his face and told him she was going to see how much he had grown over the past few months.

Once she had finished her examination she handed him one of the more colourful toys and he played contentedly while she turned her attention to Angela and the baby.

Lucy was as cute as a button. Kellie felt every maternal urge pulling cathedral-like bells on her biological clock as she examined the tiny wriggling infant.

Lucy, like her brother, had big brown eyes and beautiful skin. Her weight and length were normal and she even gave Kellie a gummy smile, which sent the clanging bells inside Kellie's head into overdrive.

Once the baby was settled back in Angela's arms Kellie asked a few questions about the young woman's health and diet, suggesting she might need to eat a bit more because she was breastfeeding. 'I imagine it's a difficult time, juggling the needs of two small children, but you need to take care of yourself. I'd like to run a few tests just to make sure your haemoglobin is fine and your thyroid function is normal.' She waited a beat before adding, 'I notice you have a slight tremor in your hands. How long have you had that?'

Angela's eyes moved away from hers. 'I don't know… A little while, I guess…' She brought her head back up after a moment and said somewhat defensively, 'I don't drink. As soon as I knew I was pregnant I stopped.'

'That's good, Angela,' Kellie said with an encouraging smile. 'That was a very sensible thing to do. Alcohol crosses the placenta and it also passes through breast milk so it's best to avoid it.'

'It's hard…you know?' Angela said, looking down at the baby. 'There's no one to help me. Shane doesn't see it as his thing. He thinks it's women's work to look after the kids. I never get a break.'

'Would you be interested in being part of a mothers' group if I set one up?' she asked.

Angela gave a one-shoulder shrug. 'I guess.'

Kellie smiled. 'I'll make some enquiries and let you know.

You'll need to come back and see me if the blood tests show up anything abnormal.'

Once she had drawn up the blood for testing she helped Angela back out to Reception with the children before reaching for the next patient file.

The rest of the morning whizzed by as patient after patient came in and out. Kellie saw Matt only twice, once when she was out at Reception, quizzing Trish on facilities available for an elderly patient, and then again when she went in search of the toilet. He had been coming out of his consulting room and briefly asked how she was settling in.

'Fine,' she said. 'I have a couple of patients I wouldn't mind talking over with you when you've got a minute.'

'Trish usually leaves a thirty-minute gap for lunch so we can go over them then,' he said. 'The kitchen's out the back. I'm not sure if Trish has had time to show you around. It's been a full-on morning due to yesterday's cancellations.'

The thirty-minute gap became a ten-minute one because Kellie was held up with another young single mother who was finding it difficult to cope with her three young children. Kellie spent most of the consultation handing over tissues as Gracie Young told her of her woes, but it made her all the more determined to try and sort out something for these unfortunate girls.

'I'm sorry I'm late,' Kellie said as she came into the clinic kitchen after seeing Gracie out.

Matt looked up from the paper he was reading. 'That's fine. Trish told me you've seen some of our more difficult patients.'

Kellie frowned as she flicked on the still warm kettle. 'Where is Trish now?' she asked.

'I think she said something about going to the general store for something,' he answered. 'Why?'

She leaned her hips back against the counter and faced him. 'She made a comment about a patient that I thought was a little inappropriate,' she said. 'The waiting room was full and anyone could have heard. The patient hinted that she had heard it as apparently it's quite a common occurrence.'

'Which patient was it?'

'Angela Baker.'

'Do you want me to have a word with Trish about it?' he asked.

She let out a sigh as the kettle clicked off. 'I probably need to talk to her myself.'

'Angela is a hard case, Kellie,' he said. 'Gracie Young is even worse. They both have pretty sad backgrounds, lots of violence and drinking while they were growing up.

'She told me she's stopped drinking.'

His expression took on a cynical edge. 'And you believed her?'

Kellie stood up straighter. 'Yes, I did, as a matter of fact,' she said. 'She loves those kids. She's doing the best she can. It's not easy for her, you know.'

'You won't be able to fix anything in the short time you're here,' he said, lifting his cup to drain its contents.

'As far as I can see, no one is doing anything to turn things around.' She threw back.

Matt stood up and pushed in his chair. 'Listen, Kellie,' he said. 'You're not a social worker or a psychologist or indeed a drug and alcohol counsellor. You're a GP. Your job is to diagnose and treat illness. You'll end up doing more harm than good.'

'I want to start a support group for the young mothers,' she said with a defiant jut of her chin. 'Once or twice a week for just a couple of hours for them to have a cup of tea or coffee together and chat, sort of like a playgroup. I can do some workshops on parenting or cooking classes even. Anything will be better than nothing.'

'I don't want to rain on your campaign to save the world but you really would be wasting your time,' he said. 'Before you're in the air on your way home they will go back to what they're familiar with.'

'How can you be so cynical?' she asked. 'You've lived out here for this long—surely you realise the issues they face?'

'Of course I do, and I do what I can when I can,' he said as he went to the sink to rinse his cup. 'It's heartbreaking to see the destruction of so many young lives.'

'Is there a community centre I could use?'

Matt turned to look at her. 'You really are serious about this, aren't you?'

Her brown eyes glinted with determination. 'Yes.'

He shoved his hands in his pockets, to stop himself from reaching to brush back a wayward strand of her hair off her face. She looked strong and determined but that chestnut strand lying across her left eyebrow gave her a look of endearing vulnerability. Even the pillowed softness of her mouth made him want to bend his head to press his lips against hers. 'All right, I'll see what I can do,' he said, but somehow his voice came out a little croaky.

She smiled and before he could do anything to stop it— even if he had wanted to—she reached up on tiptoe and pressed a little soft-as-a-summer-breeze kiss to his cheek. 'Thank you, Matt.'

His eyes locked on hers, the silence stretching and stretching until Matt thought the room would burst. He knew he should say something but he couldn't get his mind into gear.

He was standing too close to her. Her perfume had bewitched him. He could feel the drugging of his senses as each pulsing second passed.

'I hope I'm not interrupting anything,' Trish said in a sing-song tone as she came in carrying a packet of tea bags.

'No, not at all,' Matt said brusquely, stepping away from Kellie. 'We were just discussing Angie Baker.'

Trish's gaze flicked to Kellie's before returning to Matt's. 'Oh?'

'I know you've had some run-ins with Angie in the past, but I would prefer it if you'd refrain from making your opinions of her public,' he said. 'That's not how this practice is run.'

Trish's mouth tightened for a moment before she released it on a sigh. 'I'm sorry,' she said. 'You're right, of course. I just get *so* frustrated. David and I spent years trying to have a child and it never happened. She just seems to fall pregnant just looking at a man.'

Matt gave her shoulder a little pat. 'Don't be too hard on yourself, Trish. You're doing a great job. Thanks for rescheduling all those patients yesterday. I owe you.'

'Then promise you'll come to this year's bachelors' and spinsters' ball,' Trish said. 'You never been to one before and it's about time you did.'

'I'll think about it,' he said.

'Will you come too, Kellie?' Trish asked with a broad smile. 'You'd have a great time, I'm sure. People come in from miles around.'

'It sounds like fun,' Kellie said. 'When is it?'

'It's next month,' Trish said, 'I'll give you an invitation with all the details on. You'll have a great time and, you never know, you might even meet the love of your life. Believe me, it's happened before. We've had four marriages in four years so you never know whose turn it will be next.'

Kellie carefully avoided looking at Matt in case he saw the blush she could feel creeping along her cheeks. 'I can't see that happening,' she said. 'Besides, I'm not intending to stay out here any longer than six months.'

Trish's hazel eyes began to twinkle as she bustled out to answer the phone. 'You'll have to change her mind, Matt,' she said over her shoulder. 'I'm sure if you put your mind to it, you could do it.'

There was a flicker of irritation in Matt's gaze as it met Kellie's. 'Don't take any notice of her,' he said. 'She, along with just about everybody else in town thinks it's time I found myself a wife. I'm sorry if you were embarrassed by her—she means well in spite of her rather obvious and clumsy attempt to matchmake.'

'It's all right,' Kellie said. 'I understand. I have heaps of friends and colleagues who do the same thing to me. I've been on so many blind dates over the past few years I reckon I could almost qualify for a guide dog.'

The smile that pulled at his mouth made Kellie's heart skip in her chest. It made his dark blue eyes soften and the tight set to his jaw disappear completely.

He held her gaze for a moment or two before turning away, his smile gradually fading. 'I have patients to see,' he said in a gruff tone.

Kellie drew in a breath and let it out in a long unsteady exhalation as the door clicked shut on his exit. *You're in deep trouble, my girl*, she thought as she tipped her undrunk tea down the sink.

## CHAPTER ELEVEN

AFTER she had finished at the clinic Kellie called in at the general store to pay for the things Ruth had bought on her behalf.

Cheryl Yates introduced herself and showed her around the store. 'Of course, it's not up to your city standards, but if you want anything special I can order it in,' she said. 'We're not flash but we're friendly.'

'Thanks, Cheryl.'

Cheryl narrowed her gaze as she looked in the mirror positioned above the cash register. 'Would you excuse me for a moment, Dr Thorne?'

'Sure,' Kellie said, and watched as Cheryl sternly approached a youth of about fifteen who was lingering near the back of the store.

'OK, Ty Smithton,' Cheryl's broad twang bounced off the walls. 'What have you got in your pockets this time?'

'Nuffin', Mrs Yates. I got nuffin.'

'You want me to call the cops or do you want to deal directly with me?' she asked, placing her hands on her hips in a don't-mess-with-me manner.

Kellie couldn't help feeling a carload of burly cops might be preferable to facing the ire of the large-framed woman. The youth scowled and emptied his pockets just as someone came into the store.

'What's going on, Cheryl?' Matt asked.

'Ty here decided he wanted to borrow a few items but he's since changed his mind,' Cheryl said as she escorted the boy to the front door. 'Haven't you, Ty?'

Ty's expression was all brooding surly teenager but Kellie could see beyond it to the lost little boy inside. He reminded her of her brother Nick who had often wound up in trouble in an effort to draw attention to himself.

'How's it going with Mrs Williams looking after you guys?' Matt asked Ty.

'All right, I s'pose,' the boy mumbled.

He gave Ty's shoulder a quick squeeze. 'Go easy on her, mate,' he said. 'She's not as young as your mum, you know.'

'I know…'

Kellie stepped forward. 'Hi, Ty, I'm Kellie Thorne, the new doctor in town. I was thinking about coming to visit Ruth at your place. I can give you a lift if you like then you can show me the way.'

'All right,' Ty said in a grudging tone. 'But it's not far. I can easily walk.'

'Then why don't we do that?' she suggested. 'I need the exercise. I've been cooped up inside all day. A walk in the fresh air is just what I need, and I have no idea where your house is. Ruth did tell me but I've completely forgotten.'

The boy gave an indifferent shrug, which Kellie took to be an affirmative. She turned to Cheryl and snatched up three chocolate bars from the counter. 'I'll take these as well,' she said with a little smile as she handed over some money.

Cheryl turned to Matt once Kellie had left the store with the boy at her side. 'Pretty little thing, isn't she?' she commented.

'Stop it, Cheryl,' he growled. 'You're starting to sound like Trish. I'm sure Tim and Claire have colluded with her about appointing Dr Thorne. In fact, I think the whole town's been in on it. Everywhere I go people give me a knowing look.'

'But she *is* very pretty,' she said. 'And it's well and truly time you moved on. You're young, Matt. Too young to be denying yourself a bit of fun. Why don't you ask her out to your place for a meal?'

Matt schooled his features into a blank mask. 'I'm not interested.'

Cheryl chuckled as she handed him the groceries she had got ready for him earlier. 'You can't fool me, Matt, any more than Ty Smithton or his wayward brothers can. You're interested all right, it's just your head hasn't caught up with your body and your heart.'

Matt frowned as he made his way back to his car. He didn't want to be interested but he just couldn't help it. Kellie was like a magnet he couldn't resist. He felt himself being drawn towards her in spite of his efforts to keep his distance. She exuded life and hope and joy. He had never met someone with such an exuberant boots-and-all mentality before. She went at everything like a bull at a gate, which made him realise how much he had shut himself away over the years. He was lonely, there was no point denying it. He craved the easy companionship of a secure relationship, having been denied it during his formative years.

Madeleine had been so stable, so dependable and reliable. *But totally predictable*, a little voice piped up, seemingly from nowhere.

He got behind the wheel and gripped it with both hands until his knuckles turned white.

He *liked* predictable, at least in his private life. He liked knowing what was going to happen next.

Matt couldn't imagine Kellie being predictable, or at least not from what he had seen from her so far. She was impulsive, for one thing. Her scheme to bring the single mothers together was well meaning but fraught with disaster. She was new to the community. She had no idea of how things worked out here. She would no doubt go in with all her social-conscience guns blazing and end up with some of her bullets ricocheting back to hurt her.

He gunned the engine and put the car into gear. It wasn't his problem if she got hurt. What did he care? He had only met her a couple of days ago. She was a city chick who was here for six months and six months only.

But somehow as he drove towards his property he couldn't quite rid himself of the image of Kellie walking alongside the spotty-faced, scowling Ty Smithton. She had taken the time to stop and speak in a respectful way to a troubled young boy who was hell bent on ruining his life. She hadn't turned up her nose or shrunk away in fear. She had faced the young boy as an equal and asked him to help her.

The least Matt could do was support her during the time she was here, which reminded him he had promised to organise for someone to fix that sticking window.

No reason why it couldn't be him.

Kellie couldn't believe the chaos at the Smithtons' house. Ruth had clearly made some headway but there was still a lot to be done. There was a roomful of clothes that had been washed and dried but not sorted. Kellie had never seen such a mould-ridden bathroom and the boys' rooms were like war zones.

Ruth was clearly finding it harder than she had expected and communicated that once the boys had retreated to their rooms. 'I can't believe how messy they are,' she said as she wiped the benchtops yet again. 'I no sooner clean up after them and they're at it again. *And eat!* I can't believe what they can put away.'

'They're boys and they're fully loaded with testosterone,' Kellie said, 'It's entirely normal for them to eat like gannets, believe me.'

Ruth gave a sigh. 'Tegan was the opposite. She hardly ate a thing, especially after I married Dirk. I often wonder if things would have been different…you know, if I hadn't gone ahead with the marriage. Tegan missed her father—he died when she was eight. I was lonely and then Dirk came along and we got along quite well. I hadn't worked since before Tegan was born so I think I might have been looking for security more than anything. It was a disaster from the word go.'

'Stepparenting is a difficult task for most people,' Kellie offered.

'Yes,' Ruth said, sighing again. 'Dirk wasn't the most patient of men and he had rather strict ideas on what girls should and shouldn't do. There have been rumours over the years that he had something to do with her disappearance but I wouldn't have thought him capable of something like that. But even now I lie awake at night and wonder if I missed something somewhere.'

'I really don't know how you've remained so strong,' Kellie said.

'The first few years were the worst,' Ruth said. 'Dirk passed away eighteen months after Tegan disappeared. He had a massive heart attack. I had to keep myself together in case Tegan came back. I kept thinking what if she had run away and then came back only to find her mother had given up on life? I could so easily have ended it all. I wanted to end the torture of not knowing but I think I'm finally coming to terms with the fact that I might never know the truth.'

'I think it's amazing how you help people in spite of your own suffering,' Kellie said. 'Look at what you've done for Julie and the boys for instance.'

'I spoke to Julie this afternoon and her hand is recovering well,' Ruth said. 'She is being released the day after tomorrow.'

After she had helped Ruth bring some sort of order to the house and spent a few minutes helping the youngest boy, Cade, with his homework, Kellie asked if the three boys were interested in doing some yard work for her.

Ty, the oldest at fifteen, grunted something unintelligible but fourteen-year-old Rowan and twelve-year-old Cade showed a bit of interest, although it was somewhat guarded.

'I thought it might be nice for when Dr and Mrs Montgomery come back if the garden was spruced up a bit.' Kellie explained her plan. 'I know the drought makes things difficult, but if we start now there are still things that can be done to make the place look neat and tidy by the time they return.'

'Are you going to pay us, Dr Thorne?' Cade asked with a wary expression.

'Of course!' Kellie said. 'There's no such thing as a free lunch, right?'

She told them how much she was prepared to pay them and arranged to meet them at the Montgomerys' house on Saturday morning.

Driving into the Montgomerys' driveway a few minutes later, she caught sight of a slinking shape near the rainwater tank at the side of the house. At first she thought it might have been a fox or even a dingo, but when it moved away into the shadows of the night she could see its tail was long and thin not bushy and the colour not golden but more like a patch-work of brown and black and white.

She turned on the back light once she got inside and looked out over the yard but there was no sign of any movement.

A few minutes later her mobile phone rang just as she had taken her last mouthful of her daily allowance of chocolate. 'Hello?' she answered from a full mouth.

'Kellie, it's Matt…' He paused for moment. 'Have I caught you having dinner?'

'No, I had a snatch-and-grab meal with Ruth and the boys. That was my chocolate hit for the day. What can I do for you?'

There was a little silence.

She heard him draw in a deep breath before he spoke. 'I promised to fix that window for you. When would be a convenient time?'

'I thought you were going to get someone else to fix it. I didn't realise you were going to do it yourself.'

'I had to do the same to one of the windows at my place a while back,' he said. 'It's no trouble really.'

'What about tomorrow after work?' she suggested. 'That way I can cook you dinner in payment.'

'I don't expect to be paid,' he said quickly.

'Nevertheless, I insist on cooking you a meal. Besides, you'll be doing me a favour by keeping me company for a few hours. I'm not used to being on my own in such a quiet house. It's sort of creeping me out.'

'Perhaps a dog might be a good idea after all,' he said. 'I've heard there's one hanging about the school, looking for scraps.'

'I think it was here when I got home a while ago. I saw it slink around the back of the tank.'

'You could leave out some food for it and see if it's friendly,' he said. 'But don't approach it unless you're sure. It might take a nip at you.'

'I'll be careful,' she promised.

There was another silence.

'Well…' he said. 'I'd better let you get some sleep. It's been a rough couple of days for you. You must be totally wiped out.'

'I'm pretty used to hard work.'

'You'll certainly get plenty of it out here. You'll have to run the clinic singlehandedly tomorrow as I'm flying out to do the clinic at Warradunga Crossing.'

'You don't need me to come with you?' she asked.

'Although the appointment book isn't full, I thought you'd be better to stay in town in case there's anything urgent,' he said. 'The clinic at the Crossing isn't a big one.'

'And I don't suppose the plane is either, right?'

Matt felt a smile tug at his mouth. 'Not as big as the ones you're used to but it does the job.'

'So what time will you get back?'

'About five,' he said. 'I'll go home, have a shower and get back to your place at about seven, unless you want me to come later?'

'No, that will be fine.'

'Good. I'll look forward to it.'

*Not as much as I will*, Kellie thought as she placed her phone back on the kitchen bench.

Her skin lifted in a faint shiver of anticipation. She knew the old adage about the way to a man's heart being through his stomach might not apply to someone like Matt McNaught, but she was going to have a damn good try.

# CHAPTER TWELVE

KELLIE was putting the last-minute touches to her make-up when she heard the sound of Matt knocking on the front door. She put the pot of lipgloss down and quickly slipped on her high heels and click-clacked her way down the hall.

She opened the door wide and smiled. 'Hi.'

Matt felt as if he had been zapped with a stun gun. He stood there for several seconds, trying to keep his jaw from dropping at the vision of loveliness in front of him. She was wearing a red-and-white sundress with shoestring straps, nipped in at the waist with a shiny patent-leather belt, emphasising her trim body. Her hair was loose about her shoulders; she had done something to enhance the slight wave in it, the cascade of bouncy curls framing her heart-shaped face giving her a casual but elegant look. She smelt of summer, the delicate notes of honeysuckle—or was it orange blossom?—danced around his nostrils like invisible sprites.

'Um…won't you come in?' she asked.

'Er…right,' he said, stepping over the threshold and thrusting a bottle of wine at her. 'I don't know if you like red or white but this is from the Roma vineyard. I thought you might like to try it. It's the oldest vineyard in Queensland. It began in 1863.'

'I've heard of it,' she said, and closed the door. 'I'll open the wine while you play handyman with the window. I got the bedroom one open the other night but it's still a little stiff.'

*Yeah, well, it's not the only thing feeling that way*, Matt thought as she brushed past him. He was glad he was holding his toolkit so he could hide his physical reaction to her.

He went through the house and checked each window, listening to her singing along to the CD player. She had a nice voice, light and pure and enthusiastic as she was about seemingly everything.

*I wonder what she's like in bed.*

The thought was like an intruder inside his head. He tried to evict it but it wouldn't leave. It made it even worse when the last window he had to check was in her bedroom. The intoxicating fragrance of her permeated everything. Even the lightweight curtains smelt of her as he pulled them aside to work the latch.

'How's it going?' she asked from just behind him.

Matt hadn't heard her approach and nicked his finger on the blade of the chisel. 'Er…fine,' he said. 'I'm just about done.'

Kellie frowned when he turned around and began to wind his finger around his handkerchief. 'Have you cut yourself?' she asked.

'It's just a scratch.'

'Let me see.'

'It's nothing,' he said. 'I told you, it's just a little scratch. It will stop bleeding in a second.'

Kellie gave him a reproving look as she reached for his hand. 'You don't need to go all macho on me, Matt,' she said. 'If I can handle what Julie Smithton did to her finger, I think I'll cope with what you've done with yours.'

She unpeeled the handkerchief and inspected the flesh wound. 'Mmm,' she said. 'It looks like it needs some pressure for a bit longer. I'll cleanse it for you and put on a sticky plaster.'

'There's really no need…'

Her eyes met his. 'Why are you being so stubborn about such a little thing?' she asked. 'When was the last time you allowed someone to help *you* for a change?'

He held her gaze for a moment or two. 'All right,' he said, blowing out of sigh of resignation. 'Do what you need to do. I won't put up a struggle.'

Kellie led him by the hand to the bathroom and making him sit on a small stool, attended to his finger with meticulous care. She was acutely aware of his long legs, she had to step around them a couple of times to reach the first-aid cupboard. She was also intensely aware of his hand in hers as she cleansed and dressed the wound. She imagined how it would feel to have those strong, long-fingered hands on her body, touching her face, tilting her head to claim her mouth with his own…

Matt met her brown gaze on a level. She was wearing mascara, which made her long eyelashes even more lustrous. His eyes went to her mouth. This close he could see the tiny sparkles in her lipgloss, making her lips all the more tempting to taste. He watched as the point of her tongue sneaked out to paste a film of moisture on top of the gloss and his insides gave a sudden kick of reaction. It would be so easy to lean forward and—

'There,' she said briskly, scrunching up the wrapping of the sticky plaster. 'I'm all done.'

Matt got to his feet. 'Thank you, but it was totally unnecessary to go to all that fuss over nothing.'

'It wasn't nothing and, besides, I didn't want you to bleed all over the place. Imagine if Tim and Claire come back to find bloodstains all over their bedroom carpet?'

'Good point.'

She turned from the basin, where she had been washing her hands. 'Ready for dinner now?'

'Sure.'

Kellie led the way to the kitchen where she had an Italian chicken dish simmering. She poured two glasses of wine and handed him one. 'Thanks for fixing the windows. I really appreciate it. I'm hopeless at household maintenance. I guess it comes from living with six men. They did that sort of stuff while Mum and I got on with the cooking and housework.'

He took the glass with a brief brush of his fingers against hers. 'Did you resent having to do that?'

She cradled her glass in her hands. 'Not at first. I took over the cooking when Mum got sick. It was hard once she'd gone to stop doing it. Dad and the boys were devastated. The last thing they needed was a huge shopping list and a week's menu thrust in their hands.'

Matt thought about how caring she was, how she had put her needs aside for the sake of her father and younger brothers. 'All the same, it must have been hard, not having a life of your own,' he said. 'What about boyfriends and so on? How did you juggle your professional and social life with your family taking up so much of your time?'

Her smooth brow furrowed slightly. 'It wasn't easy. I'm nearly thirty years old and I've only had one lover. I guess you think that's pretty pathetic, huh?'

He felt his mouth tip upwards in a rueful smile. 'I'm hardly one to criticise. I haven't exactly been out there sowing my wild oats.'

She smiled back at him but he noticed her cheeks were a little pink. 'I guess I should check on dinner…'

Matt watched as she deftly sorted out plates and garnishes and steamed vegetables as if it was second nature to her. He couldn't help wondering what she would think of his microwaved single-serve meals or his two-recipe repertoire of macaroni cheese or savory mince on toast. 'You obviously enjoy cooking,' he said into the silence.

'I love it,' she said handing him a plate loaded with food.

'Was your mother a good cook?' he asked once they were both seated at the small pine table.

'She was fabulous,' she said, passing him the pepper grinder. 'I stood on a step-stool by her side for as long as I can remember. I think she would have loved to have been a chef but she didn't get the opportunity. She got pregnant with me while she was at college so that put an end to that.'

'Was she bitter about it?'

She met his gaze across the table. 'No, of course not. She loved being a mother.'

He looked into the contents of his glass. 'My mother was the opposite. She also fell pregnant by mistake but it was made very clear to my father and me that it had ruined her life.'

Kellie felt her heart contract. 'Did she tell you that?'

He forked up some of the casserole. 'I seem to remember it was a recurrent theme before she finally left.'

'You must have been so hurt.'

He gave an indifferent shrug. 'I don't dwell on it much. It happened and I can't change it. My father, on the other hand, lets it eat away at him even now. He hasn't moved on. He talks about nothing else whenever I call him, which isn't often. He can't seem to accept that she's not coming back.'

'And you don't think you're a little bit like him in that regard?'

He frowned as he met the challenge of her gaze. 'What are you saying?'

She put down her fork and picked up her wineglass. 'If you can't see it, I'm not going to hit you over the head with it.'

His frown deepened. 'I suppose by that you mean Madeleine.'

'You're still carrying a photo of her in your wallet,' Kellie said. 'You have a shrine built to her in your home. You visit her parents every year on her birthday. If that doesn't demonstrate how stuck you are then what will?'

'I can hardly wipe her from my memory as if she never was a part of my life,' he bit out.

'No, of course not, but I'm sure she wouldn't have wanted you to live the way you are doing,' Kellie argued.

'You know nothing of how I live my life.' *Or how I'm about to change it*, he added silently.

She gave him a wry look. 'Going on what I've seen so far, I think I've got a pretty clear idea.'

He put down his knife and fork, his top lip lifting mockingly. 'So you think you can do something about my sad and sorry situation, do you, Dr Thorne?'

Kellie kept her eyes trained on his. 'I don't see anything wrong in you getting out a bit more, having some fun, dating now and again. What harm would it do?'

He leaned back in his chair, still with his mouth tilted. 'So is this what this is all about?' He waved his hand over the meal between them. 'Is this yet another one of your do-good missions to achieve while you're here?'

Kellie frowned at the veiled insult he had thrown at her. 'I know you think I'm wasting my time with Angie and Gracie but it's not just the young mums around here that need help. Julie's boys do, too. They're bored and restless, that's why they're in trouble all the time. They have low self-esteem and the only way they can get attention is to do something bad. I've arranged for them to do something good for a change. They're coming to help me here on Saturday to clean up the yard a bit. Who knows? It might inspire them to do the same at their house or others in the area.'

Matt looked at the bright sparks of enthusiasm in her eyes and wondered when the last time had been that he had been passionate about anything, *truly* passionate. For most of his life he had taken a back seat when it had come to eagerness. Every time he had been excited about something he had been let down. He remembered one time, not long after his mother had left, he'd thought he'd seen her coming up the front path. He had dashed downstairs, his heart beating like a bass drum in his chest, only to throw open the door to see it was a complete stranger, selling raffle tickets for a charity. The disappointment had been totally devastating. He hadn't realised until then how much he had hoped his life would go back to what it had been. But it was never going to go back and it was up to him now to move forward.

'You think I'm wasting my time, don't you?' she asked.

Matt picked up his wineglass and twirled the contents. 'I think you mean well but you're likely to get swamped with the endless needs of people you can't help in any significant way.'

'I don't care about the destination as much as the journey,' she said. 'I know I haven't got long here but just the fact that someone is taking the time and making the effort to make a difference in someone's life is surely a worthwhile enterprise.'

He put his glass down and met her brown eyes. 'Even if you get hurt in the process?'

'I'd rather get hurt trying. At least it proves I care, and it could make a difference, maybe in just one life but it's still worth it.'

A warm feeling spread like heated honey through Matt's chest as he held her gaze. 'Do you make it a habit to nurture absolutely everyone who crosses your path?' he asked.

She gave him a self-conscious smile. 'It's my mother

complex. It's showing, isn't it? I just can't seem to help it. I pick up every lame duck or stray. I've been doing it since I was a little kid.'

'Speaking of strays, I thought I saw that dog you were talking about on my way to the front door,' Matt said. 'It was sniffing around the tank stand. I forgot to tell you earlier.' *Only because I was completely taken aback by your amazingly sexy appearance*, he tacked on mentally.

'I left some food and water out at the bottom of the back veranda,' she said. 'I hope it hangs around now. That way I can gradually teach it to trust me.'

'My dog Spike was from the dogs' home,' he said. 'He had been treated cruelly by some idiot who thought a working dog should be confined to a small back yard in the city. The guy had him tied up day in, day out and whenever Spike made a sound he would get whipped with whatever was handy.'

'Oh that's terrible,' Kellie gasped. 'How can people be so cruel?'

He gave her a grim look. 'I don't know, but animal cruelty is one thing that truly sickens me.'

'Me, too,' she said with fervour. 'And children. I hate the thought of little kids being hurt. There are so many people who are desperate to have kids and yet others treat their children like punching bags. Why have kids if you can't be patient and loving towards them?'

'Do you want kids?' Matt asked, surprising himself at asking such a candid question.

He watched as her eyes moved away from his, her index finger absently running round the rim of her glass. 'I think there are a few women out there who genuinely don't want to have children,' she said. 'But while I have yet to meet someone who has regretted having a child, I have met plenty who have regretted they didn't.' She brought her eyes back to his. 'You were right about the fertility-issue thing we talked about the other day. It seems harder than ever to find a man who wants to settle down and have kids. If you date a man the same age as you they don't want kids until it's too late for you. If you date someone older they often have kids from a previous relationship so you end up trying to convince him to have another child when he hardly has enough to pay for the ones he has.'

'It sounds like you've thought about this at length.'

She gave him another self-conscious smile. 'I'm on the fast train to thirty,' she said. 'I try not to panic that I might not meet someone in time, but it's hard not to think about it.'

'Is that why you came out here—in the hope of meeting someone?'

Kellie chewed at her lip before answering. 'Not really, I just felt I needed a change. My ex-boyfriend was two-timing me, and like most women in that situation I was the very last to find out. I didn't think Newcastle was big enough for me to lick my wounds in private so I took the first job I saw advertised.'

'So it could just as easily have been Outer Mongolia or Culwulla Creek,' he said with a hint of a wry smile.

She smiled back at him. 'Yes, I suppose so. But just as well it was here as it would have cost me a fortune in excess baggage.'

'Were you in love with your boyfriend?' he asked.

Kellie found his blue gaze suddenly intense and had to lower hers a fraction. 'I'm not sure if I know what it feels like to be in love,' she confessed as she gathered up their plates, 'or at least not personally. I know my mother and father loved each other from the moment they met, but I didn't love Harley that way. I liked his company and we had interests in common but…'

'But?' he prompted as he followed her to the sink with their used glasses.

She brought her eyes back to his. 'But I think something important was missing. I think I realised it from the word go but I was so keen to find someone I ignored it. And then when I found about how he was seeing someone else…well, that was just the boost my ego needed. He even told me it was my fault for not being attractive enough to hold his interest.'

'Yes, well, like I said the other day, Kellie, he was a king-sized jerk,' Matt said, looking down at her mouth. He knew it was a mistake to do so but he couldn't resist the temptation. Her lips were so damned kissable, so soft and supple. A few strands of her chestnut hair had moved forward over her left eyebrow and without even realising he was doing it his hand came out and gently tucked them behind the shell-like curve of her ear.

He watched as she gave a tiny shiver. He felt her tremble against his fingers as they trailed down from her ear over the smooth curve of her jaw to her chin, her brown eyes darkening to the colour of melted chocolate as she looked up at him with uncertainty and vulnerability in her gaze.

Matt could feel his heartbeat, like an out-of-control timepiece in his chest, speeding up, slowing down, skipping a beat here and there and then speeding up again. His breathing became shallow and uneven and his skin prickled all over with the need to feel more of her.

With two of his fingers still beneath her chin, he lifted her face as he lowered his until his mouth touched down on hers, the soft pillow of her lips sending a jolt of reaction coursing through him like a zap of lightning. She tasted of wine and feminine want, her tongue meeting the first explorative stroke of his with electrifying heat.

The kiss took on a life of its own. He had no hope of controlling his response to her mouth under the pressure of his. It was like an uncontrollable bush fire. It had started with a flicker but was now racing away, consuming everything in its path. He felt himself being swept away on a tide of such intense longing he thought he was going to make a complete and utter fool of himself. His body was already fit to explode, the quickening of his blood engorging him to bursting point. Surely she could feel it against her? There was no way of disguising his reaction, she only had to reach down between their tightly locked bodies and examine it for herself. The thought of her doing so made him kiss her with increasing ardour.

He wanted her.

He drove his tongue even deeper into the moist cave of her mouth and groaned.

God forgive him for being human but he *wanted* her…

# CHAPTER THIRTEEN

KELLIE had never been kissed so thoroughly in her life. She had never felt such fervour in a man's lips and tongue, or such incredible need and purpose. His mouth was like a hot brand on hers, searing hers, making her weak with longing. Her body felt the hard probe of his erection, the hot surge of his body making her feel feminine and dizzyingly alive in a way she had never felt before.

His mouth was still locked on hers as his hands moved to her hips, pulling her even tighter against the intimate connection of their bodies. She felt his fingers dig into the curve of her bottom, intensifying their contact to the point where her feminine core pulsed with ripples of desire to feel him fill her, to claim her as his. She rubbed against him enticingly, wanting him, needing him to satisfy the need he and he alone had awakened.

As if someone had flicked a switch in his head he suddenly put her from him, his expression stripped of all emotion as he moved away from her to pace the kitchen.

'M-Matt?'

He shoved a hand through his hair, making it even more disordered than her hands had done moments previously. 'That should never have happened,' he said in a gruff tone, his eyes avoiding hers. 'I'm sorry. I don't want to give you the wrong impression.'

Kellie swallowed to give herself a moment to gather her scattered senses into some semblance of order. 'Are you saying you didn't want to kiss me?' she asked.

He turned around to look at her. 'I'm not going to waste my time denying I didn't want to kiss you but…' He sent his hand through his hair again. 'But I'm not interested in taking this any further.'

Kellie pressed her lips together, trying to quell the ache of disappointment deep inside her being. 'Madeleine's not coming back, Matt,' she said, before she could stop herself. 'She's not coming back, and denying yourself a full life isn't going to bring her back.'

She heard him suck in a harsh breath as he swung away from her. 'Do you think I don't know she's not coming back?' he barked at her. 'I was the one who identified her at the bloody morgue. Don't tell me what I already know.'

Kellie stepped forward to grasp one of his arms. 'But have you accepted it, Matt?' she asked. 'You want to move on, I know you do, but you just won't let yourself.'

He brushed off her hand as if it were a mosquito. 'Stop analysing me, Kellie. Can't you tell rejection when you hear it? I am not interested. Got that? *Not in-ter-ested.*' He drew out the syllables for emphasis.

Kellie felt tears sting her eyes. 'I don't believe you. You just kissed me as if your life depended on it. Your whole body was shaking with desire. Don't insult me by denying it.'

His eyes blazed at her. 'It was a mistake, damn you! You look at me with those big brown eyes of yours and I swear to God any man married, celibate or dead from the waist up would want to kiss you.'

'But you're not married or dead from the waist up. I know that for a fact.'

He frowned at her. 'Stop this, stop it now. I am not going to be drawn into an affair with you just to stroke your ego after being ditched by your two-timing boyfriend.'

Kellie glared at him in affront. 'Is that what you think this is about?'

He sent her a cynical glance. 'You've been hurt and you went bush. It's totally understandable you'd latch onto the first available man to salve your pride.'

She injected her tone with venom. 'And you think I've selected *you* as the first step in my relationship rehab?'

Matt held her fiery gaze for several seconds. 'I think you're very vulnerable just now,' he said, his tone now calm and controlled. 'You're new in town, you've got baggage that needs to be dealt with and I don't want to hurt you any more than you've been hurt. You're a nice person, Kellie. I can see that from how you've responded to the needs of the patients you've come into contact with so far. You're a really lovely young woman who deserves much more than I can offer right now.'

She screwed her mouth up, not quite a pout but somewhere close. 'I wish you hadn't kissed me,' she said. 'No one's ever kissed me like that before.'

Matt couldn't stop himself from tipping up her chin until her eyes met his. 'You know something, Kellie? No one's ever kissed me quite like that either.'

'Didn't Madeleine kiss you like that?' she asked softly, her smooth brow wrinkled in a little frown.

Matt should have known the question was coming but for some reason he didn't have a ready answer. The truth was Madeleine had always been a few steps behind him when it had come to their physical relationship. He had put it down to her sheltered upbringing. She had not been comfortable with outward affection, and sleeping together had been a huge step for her, one she had baulked at several times. If he was entirely truthful he would have to admit he'd always had some reservations about their sexual compatibility, but he had thought the security of marriage would sort them out. Madeleine had grown up in a conservative home. Sex outside of marriage was frowned upon so it was no wonder she had always been a little restrained with him.

'Did she?' Kellie asked.

'Did she what?' Matt asked, trying not to stare at the cushioned bow of her mouth.

'Did Madeleine kiss you like I kissed you?'

He stood there looking down at her for endless seconds. 'No,' he said at last. 'No, she didn't.'

'Did she sleep with you?'

Matt felt as if he was betraying Madeleine's memory by revealing the intimate details of their relationship but still he answered, 'We took things slowly but yes, we did eventually sleep together.'

Kellie turned away to clear the rest of the table. 'I wish I hadn't slept with Harley,' she said, clattering the side plates as she stacked them haphazardly. 'Looking back now, I can see I was being used. I wasn't the one he wanted, I was the fill-in—his little bit on the side.' She gave a shudder of revulsion as she stomped back to the kitchen. 'I am *such* an idiot when it comes to men. You'd think after living with six of them I'd be an expert by now but, no, I have to make a complete fool of myself all over again.'

'You haven't made a fool of yourself,' Matt said gently.

She turned from the sink where she had dumped the rest of the plates and looked up at him. 'Are you sure?'

He gave her a crooked smile. 'We kissed. So what?' His tone was deliberately offhand. 'Lots of people do it. It doesn't have to mean anything.'

She lifted up her hand and with the point of her index finger lightly traced the shape of his bottom lip. 'You have a very nice mouth, Dr McNaught, especially when you smile,' she said, her voice coming out in a slightly breathless whisper.

Matt could feel his bottom lip buzzing with sensation all over again. His insides were coiling with need just looking at that pretty uptilted, heart-shaped face. Her lips were still swollen from his kiss, plump and pink and slightly parted, leaving just enough room for him to slide his tongue in and...

Kellie jerked backwards. 'Did you hear that?' she asked in a hushed voice, her eyes suddenly wide with apprehension.

He looked at her blankly. 'Hear what?'

'That noise outside.'

'What noise?'

'I think there's someone outside,' she said, still whispering. 'I thought I heard someone step on the veranda.'

Matt strained to listen but the only thing he could hear was the sound of one of the oleander trees brushing up against the house in the slight breeze. 'I'll have a look around but I'm sure it's just the wind,' he said.

Kellie waited as Matt did a circuit of the house, taking the torch from the cupboard beneath the sink with him. He came back a few minutes later and reassured her that everything was as it should be.

'But I think your stray has eaten the food you put out,' he said. 'That might have been what you heard.'

'I hope you're right,' she said, hugging her arms around herself.

'Are you going to be OK here on your own?' Matt asked.

Kellie pasted a brave smile on her face. 'Of course I'll be OK. I'm still getting used to the house and living on my own for the first time ever. I'll be fine in a couple of days.'

He picked up his keys. 'Call me if you're worried during the night. I'll come straight over.'

'Thanks, but I'm sure I'll be fine,' she said still rubbing her upper arms as if to ward off a chill. 'I'm not normally such a coward. It's just this house has an odd feel to it. I can't put my finger on it. I just feel uncomfortable.'

'Living in someone else's house is a bit weird,' he said. 'You're surrounded by the Montgomerys' belongings instead of your own.'

'I guess you're right...'

'Is it what I said about snakes that spooked you?' he asked. 'You haven't seen one, have you?'

'No, but that's one of the reasons I want to tidy up the yard a bit,' she said. 'That long straggly grass down the back has to go for a start.'

'It's just normal house, Kellie,' he said. 'A bit neglected, I know but the Montgomerys aren't the house-renovating types. Tim's no handyman and Claire has a chronic problem with her back, which limits what she can do. That's why the garden is the way it is, irrespective of the drought.'

'Who lived here before Tim and Claire?'

'I'm not sure. You'd have to ask someone like Ruth who has lived in the town for most of her life. I do know it was vacant for a long time before the Montgomerys took the post. They bought it for a song, but to tell you the truth I think they'll probably move on once they get back from overseas. Tim hasn't said anything to me but I know Claire is probably going to end up wheelchair-bound so living out here long term is going to be out of the question.'

'So you don't think they'll mind if I clean it up a bit?' she asked. 'It will help them get a better price for it if they want to sell it.'

He smiled one of his fleeting smiles. 'I think it's a nice gesture and they'll appreciate it very much.'

She gave him a bright smile in return. 'And it will kill two…no, *three* birds with one stone. The Smithton boys will gain valuable experience, don't you think?'

'That's if they turn up,' he said with a cynical look.

Her face fell. 'You think they won't show?'

'Ty won't, that's for sure,' he said. 'He's a crime statistic waiting to happen, and Rowan's not much better. As for Cade…well, what sort of role models has he had? He's a nice enough kid but with his brothers in and out of trouble all the time, what hope has he got?'

'I'm not in the habit of giving up on people,' she said. 'I think they will turn up. In fact, I think even Ty will.'

His expression demonstrated he didn't share her view but he softened it saying, 'Thank you for dinner. It's been quite a while since I had a gourmet meal. It was delicious.'

She smiled up at him. 'Thanks for fixing the windows.'

'It was a pleasure.'

Kellie stood there, looking up at him for a beat or two. 'I guess I'll see you at the clinic tomorrow,' she finally said.

His eyes dropped to her mouth for a moment. 'Yes…I expect you will.'

''Night, then…'

His eyes held hers for a little longer than necessary. 'Goodnight, Kellie.'

Kellie watched as he strode down the steps to his car. He didn't look back at her but got into his car and backed out as if he couldn't wait to get away. She watched the red eyes of his taillights disappear into the distance before she let out her breath in one long jagged stream.

'You're only here six months.' She gave herself a little pep talk as she closed and locked the door. 'You don't need the complication of falling in love, understand? So it was a fabulous kiss. So what? There are probably thousands...no, *millions*...of guys who could kiss like that or even better. Matt McNaught is off limits. He's not interested. He told you in no uncertain terms. Do *not* go there.'

For the next few days Kellie concentrated on sorting out the arrangements for using the community centre in between seeing patients. She barely caught a glimpse of Matt—he seemed equally snowed under with a seemingly endless list of patients, including a run of home visits which, due to the distances involved, ate up a lot of time. But even so she couldn't help feeling he was deliberately avoiding having one-on-one time with her, although she knew he had been per-sonally responsible for most of the out-of-hours handyman work done at the community centre. She had seen the paint tins in the back of his car on her way into the clinic and was keen to see him in person to thank him for his support.

'How are your plans going for the mothers' group?' Trish asked as the week drew to a close.

'Their first meeting is next week,' Kellie announced proudly. 'I've organised the delivery of some toys for the little ones to play with while the mothers chat and get to know one another.'

'Gosh, you have been busy,' Trish said. 'Julie Smithton told me you've got her boys coming to help you tomorrow at the Montgomerys' house. She thinks you must have some sort of magic touch when it comes to the male of the species. She can't get them to lift a finger at home.'

Kellie smiled as she picked up the next patient's file. 'I have less than six months to work a miracle. No point wasting time, right?'

'Oh, I almost forgot,' Trish said, reaching over for some blood results and handing them to Kellie. 'These came in this morning. It's Angie Baker's thyroid results.'

Kellie looked at the printout, the raised T4, low TSH and high antithyroid peroxidase antibody levels clearly indicating Graves's disease.

'I'll call her and let her know,' Kellie said. 'She'll have to make a decision about treatment. She won't be able to take medication or radioactive iodine while she's breastfeeding. But surgery when she's got two little ones to look after and not much support would be daunting for her.'

Angie came in later that afternoon looking even more exhausted than previously. Charlie was acting up as usual but as soon as Kellie handed him a bright toy that squeaked when it was squeezed he played quite happily albeit rather noisily, as she discussed Angie's treatment options with her.

'But won't it just go back to normal all by itself?' Angie asked, her dark brown eyes worried.

'That occasionally happens, but usually it just stays over-active, and causes a lot of problems as a result,' Kellie explained. 'It's quite dangerous in the long term to leave hyperthyroidism untreated. It will cause weight loss, heart problems, eye problems, weakness, and make you feel hot, anxious and irritable. We can use blocking medication—sometimes the over-activity goes away after a year or so of treatment, but we'll have to watch your levels with blood tests, and make sure you don't get any eye problems while you're on the tablets, and you'll have to stop breastfeeding.

The other alternatives are radioactive iodine, not a great idea at your age, or surgery to remove the thyroid.'

'I don't want no one slicing my neck open,' Angie said after Kellie had given a brief description of a thyroidectomy.

'I know it sounds very unpleasant,' Kellie said, 'but the scar is barely noticeable after a few months. Most surgeons try and follow the natural crease in the neck.'

'I'll think about it,' Angie said as the baby began to become restless.

Kellie helped her out of the consulting room with Charlie, who had decided he wanted to keep the toy. He clutched it tightly to his little chest and pouted as his mother told him to hand it back.

'Let him keep it,' Kellie said. 'I've ordered some more from Brisbane in any case for the mothers' group and the surgery.'

'It's very kind of you,' Angie said, tucking the baby closer. 'I mean giving that to Charlie as well as what you're doing at the community centre. We've never had anything like that here before.'

'So you think you'll come along with the kids?'

Angie gave her a shy smile. 'Got nothing better to do, have I?'

Kellie smiled back. 'I think it will be a lot of fun. As time goes on we can set up a sort of roster to take turns minding the children while the others have a coffee. It will mean you can each have a little break.'

'Yeah, well, I could really do with one of those,' Angie said wryly, reaching for Charlie, who had slipped out of her grasp and was rapidly heading for the door.

Matt was just coming in and captured the runaway toddler by lifting him up in his arms. 'Hi, there, Charlie,' he said, smiling at the little boy. 'What have you got there?'

Charlie squeezed the toy so it squeaked, his big brown eyes luminous with possessive pride.

'Dr Thorne gave it to him,' Angie said, shyly lowering her gaze.

Matt gave the little boy's back a stroke. 'Hey, you've really grown since I saw you last, little man. How is your baby sister doing?'

Charlie buried his head in Matt's shoulder, the toy still grasped tightly in his hand.

'He loves her to death,' Angie said with a show of dry humour that made Matt smile.

'It's normal, Angie,' he reassured her. 'He's just feeling a little put out that someone else needs you as much if not more than him. How is Shane?'

Angie's gaze dropped even lower. 'I dunno. I haven't seen him since the baby was born. He's gone bush. He started drinking again.'

Kellie felt as if she had been slapped. She'd had no idea Angie's circumstances were so dreadful. She couldn't imagine what it must be like having two tiny infants to look after with absolutely no support from their father. She also felt totally incompetent that she hadn't discovered this information for herself. Why hadn't Angie told her? It made her feel as if she had been remiss in some way, too intent on sorting out Angie's social network without considering the all-important domestic scene.

'Are you still living out at the flats?' Matt was asking.

Angie nodded dejectedly as she patted the fretting baby's back. 'It's not what I want for the kids but what else can I do?' she asked. 'Shane promised he'd look after us but he wants his freedom and to tell you the truth I can hardly blame him. I wouldn't mind a bit of freedom myself.'

Matt glanced at Kellie, who was looking rather pale. He turned back to Angie. 'I'll speak to Ruth Williams about coming round to give you a hand,' he said. 'Julie is back now from her trip to Brisbane so she won't need Ruth's help any more.'

Angie cuddled her children closer. 'I can manage on my own. I don't want no one telling me how to bring up my kids. Anyway, what would she know? Her only kid ran away at fourteen. Some great mother she must have been.'

'Angie,' Matt said in a deep calm voice, 'take the children home and I'll send Ruth round to help you. You can't go on like this, juggling two little ones with little or no support. Ruth loves to help, it's her life. It gives her a purpose. She's on a high after looking after the Smithton boys for a few days. She'll be thrilled to be of use to you, it's just the thing she needs to take her mind off things.'

'We all reckon her Tegan is dead, Dr McNaught,' Angie said. 'The sooner she realises it the better.'

'That is an issue for the police,' Matt said, bending down to pick up Charlie's toy, which he had just dropped, and handing it back to him. 'Anything else is speculation.'

As Angie left the clinic, Kellie whooshed out a sigh heavy enough to lift the strands of her hair that had worked loose from her ponytail.

'Tough day?' Matt asked, watching as she tucked her hair behind her ear.

'You could say that,' she said with another weary sigh. 'I had no idea Angie's partner wasn't on the scene. She never said a word.'

'Don't take it personally, Kellie. A lot of the locals need time to build up trust, especially with authority figures like doctors. She would have told you eventually. For all her problems she still has a sense of pride.'

'She's got Graves's disease,' Kellie said, handing him the blood results from Angie's file.

He read through the pathology for a moment before handing it back. 'Good work,' he said. 'That could easily have been overlooked, especially given her drinking history.'

'Matt, thanks for what you've been doing at the community centre,' she said. 'The paint job looks great.'

He gave an offhand shrug. 'I had nothing better to do.'

There was a short silence.

'Well…' Kellie said with forced brightness. 'I'd better get going. It's been a long week.'

Matt thought of the weekend stretching ahead of him, the long lonely hours of catching up with paperwork and farm accounts with only the dust and flies to keep him company.

Ever since they'd had dinner together the other night he had felt increasingly lonely. Kissing Kellie had been a stupid mistake for it had awakened feelings and urges in him that were now torturing him day and night. Even looking at her now, with her hair all awry, her eyes shadowed with tiredness, he wanted to haul her into his arms and feel that soft mouth move with passion beneath his. He wanted to feel the duck and dart of her tongue playing with his, teasing him, tantalising him. He had been a fool to tell her he wasn't interested. Of course he was interested. It was just that he wanted to take things slowly, to get to know her, to spend time with her away from the prying eyes of the small bush community.

He brushed an imaginary fly away from his face and stepped past her before he gave into the temptation to pull her in to his arms. 'See you on Monday,' he said curtly.

# CHAPTER FOURTEEN

KELLIE looked at the empty bowl on the back step of the veranda the next morning and smiled. Her smile grew even wider when she answered the knock at the front door to find all three Smithton boys standing there.

Ty was leaning indolently against the veranda rail, his demeanour that of a typical bored teenager who looked as if he had only come under duress.

'Hi, guys,' Kellie said cheerily. 'Thanks for coming so early. It's going to be a hot day so it's best if we get cracking.'

The first hurdle she came to was not the lack of co-operation from one-third of her work team but the fact that the ancient-looking lawnmower in the garden shed refused to start.

Ty, who up until this point had been doing nothing more than kicking at the ground with his foot in a surly silence, stepped forward. 'Here, let me have a look. I know a bit about engines.'

Kellie stood back as he set to work tinkering with the old engine. He checked the oil and fuel before he undid the carburetor, cleaning it with a cloth before putting it back together. The engine coughed and choked a couple of times before starting with a splutter.

Kellie grinned at him. 'Wow! That was amazing.'

He gave her an anyone-with-half-a-brain-could-do-it shrug and began to push the mower through the straggly grass.

Kellie inwardly sighed with satisfaction before she turned to the other two boys. 'Stay out of his way, Rowan and Cade, in case anything flies up,' she cautioned. 'There's no catcher on the mower and I don't want any of us to lose an eye or something.'

'What can I do?' Cade asked eagerly.

Kellie smiled as she handed him a rake with two of its teeth missing. 'How about you rake up what you can where Ty's mowed while Rowan and I empty all the dead pots and pull that dead vine off the fence. We'll put all the rubbish in one heap and I'll organise for someone to get rid of it later.'

A couple of hours later there was a pile of rubbish almost as high as Cade. The yard looked a lot neater and although there was still work to be done Kellie didn't want to exhaust the boys to the point where they wouldn't want to come and help again. She brought out ice-cold drinks and some chocolate-chip cookies she'd made the night before, and they sat on the shady side of the veranda out of the heat of the sun.

Rowan and Cade did most of the talking in response to any of the open-ended questions Kellie asked in an effort to build her rapport with them, but Ty remained mostly silent until something caught his eye near the shed.

'Hey, there's that dog that's been hanging around school,' he said, and leapt up to get a pebble to throw at it.

'*No!*' Kellie grabbed him by the arm to stop him. 'Please, don't scare him away. I'm trying to tame him.'

Ty scowled and shrugged off her hand. 'You're wasting your time,' he said, aiming the pebble at a can on the top of the rubbish heap and hitting it with a sharp ping. 'You'll never tame that one. He's totally wild.'

'I think he's frightened, not wild,' Kellie said, watching as the dog peered at them from behind the shed. 'Look at him, he's neglected and filthy.'

'That's because he's been digging,' Rowan said. 'When I was clearing the vine off the fence behind the shed, I saw where he was digging up a bone.'

'A bone?' Kellie asked, as a faint shiver ran up her spine to disturb the hairs at the back of her neck. 'What sort of bone?'

He gave a disinterested shrug. 'I dunno…a bone sort of bone.'

'But I haven't given him any bones,' she said, frowning. 'I've only left out fresh meat and water.'

The three boys exchanged glances.

Ty was the first off the veranda with Rowan close behind. Kellie got there at the same time as Cade and she looked down at the patch of earth where a whitened bone was sticking out of the ground.

Ty bent down but she blocked him with her outstretched arm. 'No,' she said, suppressing a shudder. 'Don't touch it.'

He looked at her as if she was losing her senses. 'What's wrong?' he asked. 'It's just a bone, for God's sake.'

There was a sound from the driveway and a familiar deep voice called out. 'Anyone home?'

Kellie felt such a giant wave of relief flood her she wanted to throw herself into Matt's arms as he came around to where they were standing. The three boys standing there, watching, was the only thing that stopped her, but only just.

'I brought the ute around to take the rubbish away for you,' Matt said. 'Hi, guys,' he addressed the boys. Suddenly noticing the tense atmosphere, he asked, 'What's going on?'

'Rowan found a bone,' Cade piped up. 'Do you think it's human?'

Matt's eyes flicked to Kellie's wide ones. 'Hard to tell,' he said, looking at the specimen for a moment. 'We'd better call the police, though, to make sure.'

'The cops?' Ty and Rowan spoke in unison.

Matt crouched down and examined the bone a little more closely, but refrained from touching it. He knew exactly what sort of bone it was and so did Kellie if the look on her face was anything to go by. But he didn't want the Smithton boys running all over town with the news of a human bone found in the Montgomerys' back yard.

He straightened from the ground and faced the boys. 'It could be someone's Sunday roast, of course, but it's always best to make sure.'

'I've got things to do,' Ty announced cagily.

'Me, too,' Rowan was quick to add.

Cade's eyes were bug-like. 'Do you think there's a dead body buried in Dr Thorne's back yard?' he asked.

Kellie gave a visible shudder.

'Go home, boys,' Matt said firmly. 'Dr Thorne and I will hang around for the police.'

Ty folded his arms in an indomitable pose. 'We're not going until we're paid,' he said.

Kellie brushed the sticky hair out of her eyes. 'I'm so sorry, I almost forgot. I won't be a minute.'

Matt's eyes followed her as she dashed inside the house, returning a short time later and handing each of the boys some notes. They thanked her and left, jostling and nudging each other as they went up the street.

'Are you OK?' Matt asked Kellie once he had called the local sergeant.

She was standing hugging herself as if an arctic breeze was blowing holes into her chest, even though it was close to thirty-eight degrees in the shade. 'I knew there was something about this house,' she said. 'Properties have personalities and this one was giving off spooky signals right from the word go.'

He didn't answer but stood looking down at the bone.

She gave him a worried look. 'Do you think it might be Ruth's daughter?'

Matt had tried not to jump to any conclusions but he would be lying if he didn't admit to thinking the very same thing. But before the forensic team arrived, which, according to Greg Blake, the local sergeant could take several hours, it was probably best for all concerned to keep things low key. He hated the thought of Ruth being confronted with the possibility that her daughter's body was lying behind the Montgomerys' shed. It was every parent's nightmare to have a child go missing but somehow the body-in-the-back-yard scenario made it even more harrowing and gruesome.

He blew out a sigh and turned away from the grisly object. 'This is not turning out to be great start for you in the bush,' he commented wryly.

She gave him a weak smile. 'I admit it's not quite what I was expecting…' she glanced back at the bone '…especially this.'

His gaze swept over the yard. 'You and the boys did a good job,' he said. 'I'm impressed.'

'Ty was a miracle worker on the mower,' she told him. 'He'd make a great mechanic. He seems to have a natural flair for that sort of thing.'

'You did both him and Julie a favour, getting him out of the house for a legitimate purpose,' he said. 'He usually only goes out to make mischief. I don't think he's been to school for the past month. He was suspended for a week for some misdemeanour and hasn't gone back. Julie's been tearing her hair out over him.'

'He's a nice enough kid,' Kellie said. 'He's just hurting deep inside.'

Matt looked at her. 'You know what your trouble is, Kellie Thorne?' he asked. 'You want to mother everyone. Ty has his own mother, he doesn't need another one.'

'Maybe not, but he definitely needs a friend,' she countered. 'He reminds me of the dog I'm trying to befriend. He comes close and then backs off in case he gets hurt again. Ty is grieving the loss of his dad. The younger ones are too, but Ty has just stepped up on the bridge to manhood. He's fifteen and full of raging hormones. He's suddenly been thrust into being the man of the house but he's not quite ready for it. He's feeling the pressure and he's acting up because deep inside he's just a little boy who's missing his dad.'

Matt had to look away in case she saw how much her insights affected him. He was familiar with the feelings of emotional abandonment, not just from his mother but his father as well. He suddenly realised he had been lonely for most of his life. Madeleine had eased it in the only way she had known how, but it hadn't really been enough.

Kellie had loved and lost and was still in there, defending any cause she could get her hands on. He couldn't help admiring her for it. She was a brave young woman who wasn't the least bit daunted by what life threw up at her.

He knew if he wasn't careful he would be in very great danger of falling for her. Maybe he was well on his way. It certainly felt like it, even though he had been fighting it almost from the start. She was like a battery recharger that had somehow plugged into his body, making it come to life again after being shut down for years. He could feel energy flowing through him, lighting up the shadows of his soul, making him feel as if he could live again, and fully at that.

It seemed like an hour but it was only a few minutes before Sergeant Greg Blake arrived with a constable called Tracey Chugg.

'The local coroner's been contacted and the forensic pathologist is on his way,' Greg said. 'Fortunately they were working on a case in Roma. They're flying in shortly.'

Kellie stood back and watched as the scene was protected from further contamination. The area was taped off with crime-scene tape and once the forensic team arrived she was kept busy providing cool drinks as the temperature had soared. The humidity in the air was almost unbearable and when she looked up she could see the clustering of dark, brooding clouds that heralded a storm.

Matt came to stand beside her and looked up at the bruised-looking sky. 'We might get some rain out of this,' he said. 'It certainly feels like it.'

There was a sound of rushed footsteps behind them and as Kellie turned she saw Ruth coming towards them, her face twisted in anguish. 'Is it my baby?' she sobbed brokenly. 'Don't tell me it's Tegan.'

Matt enfolded her in a comforting hug, stroking her while looking over her head to Kellie's empathetic gaze. 'Nothing is certain, Ruth,' he said gently. 'It will take a while to find out how old it is or if the bone is male or female.'

Ruth pulled out of his embrace and scrubbed at her face with her hands. 'For all these years I've felt she was still *alive*. I've know it in *here*.' She thumped at her chest where her heart was. 'I don't want her to be dead. Oh, dear God I don't want her to be dead and buried like a bit of rubbish in someone's back yard…'

Kellie put her hand on the older woman's shaking shoulder. 'The police are doing everything they can to establish who this is,' she said. 'They'll let you know as soon as they find out anything.'

Kellie watched as Matt led Ruth away, his strong arms encircling the older woman's shoulders as he spoke to her in soothing tones. Trish arrived and, after exchanging a few words with Matt, took Ruth to her house out of the way of the police and forensic services team.

Tracey, the constable, came to stand beside Kellie. 'I hear you're new in town,' she said. 'Nice way to start a locum, finding a body in your back yard.'

'Is that what this is?' Kellie asked, sneaking a look around the taped-off area. 'It's not just a humerus in there?'

Tracey nodded grimly. 'Whoever put that body there did so in hurry—it's barely two feet under.'

'Is it male or female?' Kellie asked.

'Can't tell yet,' Tracey said. 'We'll have to send the remains to a forensic anthropologist. He or she will be able to establish what age, race and gender the deceased is. Depending on the state of the remains they can sometimes even establish the cause of death.'

Kellie rubbed at her upper arms in spite of the searing temperature. 'I don't think I can stay here another night,' she said. 'I'm not normally such a wimp but this goes way beyond my comfort zone.'

'You won't have to,' Tracey said. 'The local guys will secure and guard the site until everything is assessed. Is there anyone you can spend a couple of nights with until things are formally cleared up here?'

'She can stay with me,' Matt said as he came up behind them after seeing Ruth off with Trish. 'I have a spare room— a couple of rooms, actually.'

Kellie swung around to face him. 'You don't have to do that,' she said, feeling her colour start to rise in her cheeks.

'It's fine,' he said. 'I have plenty of room.'

'But what about the dog?'

'What dog?' Tracey asked, looking confused.

Kellie turned to the constable. 'I've been trying to tame a stray dog,' she explained. 'I've been leaving food out each night but so far he isn't coming close enough for me to approach him.'

'Is that the one that has been lurking around the school lately?' Tracey asked.

'I think so,' Kellie said. 'It looks very thin and scared.'

'We can get rid of it for you if you'd like,' the constable offered matter-of-factly.

Kellie stared at her. 'You mean…get rid of it as in *shoot* it?'

Tracey gave an indifferent shrug. 'If it's causing you any bother then we can do something about it. There's no dog catcher out here, Dr Thorne. If the dog is being a menace, we have the means to remove it.'

Kellie pulled herself up to her full height, which still left her an inch or two short of the formidable constable. 'No, thank you,' she said crisply. 'The dog isn't being a nuisance to me. I don't want it destroyed or removed from this property.'

'The dog isn't a problem, Tracey,' Matt said to the police officer. 'Now that it's being regularly fed by Dr Thorne, I don't think it will be causing any problems at the school. We'll make sure it's fed each day until you guys think it's OK for Kellie to move back into the house.'

Greg Blake joined them at that moment. He asked Kellie a few questions before turning to Matt. 'The Montgomerys have only been away, what, three weeks?'

'Closer to four,' Matt answered. 'Dr Thorne's been in the house about ten days.'

Greg Blake closed his notebook. 'We'll be in touch as soon as we know anything. I'd better go and chat to Ruth. This will hit her hard.'

'You think it's Tegan Williams buried there?' Matt asked, frowning heavily.

'We won't know until the forensic anthropologist dates the remains,' Greg said. 'But I would say that whoever it is buried there has been there for quite some time, at least ten or fifteen years, maybe even more.'

# CHAPTER FIFTEEN

'POOR Ruth,' Kellie said later that evening once she was settled in at Matt's house. 'I can't imagine what she must be going through right now.'

Matt handed her a glass of white wine and a bowl of crisps before sitting on the sofa opposite. 'I spoke to Trish earlier,' he said. 'She finally managed to persuade Ruth to take a couple of the sedatives I prescribed and she's now sleeping.'

Kellie suppressed another shudder at the thought of the forensic team digging up the rest of the body. She knew it would be a painstaking task as vital clues could be lost if anything was handled incautiously.

'It might not be her,' Matt said into the silence. 'It might be someone else entirely.'

Kellie ran the tip of her tongue over the dryness of her lips. 'Have there been any other missing persons reported from around here over the last ten or twenty years?'

'Thousands of people go missing every year from all over the country,' he answered. 'It's one of the most frustrating tasks for police trying to track a person's last movements. And then, of course, there are some people don't who just don't want to be found. I read about a guy who ran away from home when he was a teenager. He made no contact whatsoever. His parents subsequently died, never knowing what had happened to their son. By sheer chance his younger sister tracked him down thirty years later living in another country. It turned out he'd had a furious row with his parents over a curfew and took off. He was too proud to come home and apologise.'

*'Too proud?'* Kellie gaped at him. 'But that's dreadful! Can you imagine what his family went through for all those years? How could he have been so selfish?'

Matt lifted one shoulder in a shrug. 'You know what kids are like at that age,' he said. 'They tend to see things in black and white.'

'Yes, I guess so,' she said. 'I can remember plenty of slammed doors and shouts of "I'm never coming back" at my house too. But fortunately everyone came back…' She snagged her bottom lip momentarily. 'Except my mother, of course….'

Matt saw the flicker of grief pass over her features and, putting down his glass, got up and joined her on the other sofa. He put his arm around her shoulders and gently squeezed. 'You did a great job with those boys today,' he said. 'It was a shame the day had to end the way it did, but you showed an interest in them few others have done. Ty, for instance. I had no idea he was interested in all things mechanical and I've lived here for six years. You've been here ten days or so and you've already got everyone eating out of your hand.'

She turned her head to look into his eyes, her toffee-brown gaze luminous. 'Not quite everyone,' she said softly.

Matt looked at the tiny dusting of salt on her lips from the crisps she had nibbled on and felt his groin instantly surge with blood. He wanted to taste every salty inch of her, he wanted to feel her softness against his hardness, to explore the curves of her body that he knew instinctively would align perfectly with his. The desire to do so was like a hot river of need racing beneath his skin; he could feel it pumping him to erectness, the ache for fulfilment so overwhelming he knew it would take all his self-control and more to stop himself from sealing her mouth with his.

'You've got salt on your lips,' he said, his voice coming out far too husky.

'Have I?' Her tongue basted her lips. 'All gone?'

His gaze locked on her mouth. 'Er…not quite.'

She did another circuit of her lips with the point of her tongue. 'What about now?'

'There's a tiny bit there,' he said pointing to the lower curve of her bottom lip.

Her tongue came out before he could move away and brushed against his fingertip. It was the most erotic thing he had ever experienced. It sent lightning bolts of electricity to every part of his body. His skin burned with the heat of her touch, and before he had any hope of restraining himself he brought his mouth crashing down on hers.

It was a kiss of pent-up passion, long-denied needs and mutual longing. He could feel her frustration mingling with his in a combustible impact that left no part of him unaffected. His body was out of control, riding a wave of desire so fast and furious he had no hope of keeping his head. He wanted more of her; he wanted to bury himself in her softness, to drive himself to oblivion.

Kellie gasped in delight as his tongue drove through the soft shield of her lips and found hers, tangling with it, taming it in a duel-like dance that signified his ultimate intent. She could feel the hard swell of his erection as he pressed her back down on the sofa, his body a blessed weight on the floating neediness of hers. His thighs bracketed hers, but as his kiss intensified he deftly nudged them apart, settling between them with the full force of his masculinity.

Her body ached and pulsed with need. She arched her back with a wantonness that was totally unfamiliar to her. She had never experienced such an avalanche of emotion before. The twin fires of love and lust burned in the cauldron of her body, each vying for supremacy.

*Love?* Kellie felt herself take a momentary mental back step. Was that what was happening to her? It felt so right being in his arms like this, with his body responding to hers with such urgency and purpose, as if he had waited all this time for her to come along.

When his hands scooped beneath her top and bra and found her breasts, Kellie's whole body shivered in reaction. His palms flattened her, shaped her and moulded her before he bent his head and anointed her with the hot moist cave of his mouth. Her nipples were so tight each stroke of his tongue was exquisite torture, making her squirm beneath him for more of his masterful touch. How on earth had she lived this long without this passionate madness? she wondered as his teeth scraped erotically against her sensitive flesh.

Her body was suddenly a stranger to her; she barely recognised the responses she could feel raging through her. Each nerve had come to fizzing life, dancing and leaping beneath her skin. It seemed like each and every part of her was becoming more and more impatient for his touch.

Her stomach almost caved in with need when he pulled on her bottom lip with his teeth, the sexy movement of his lips and tongue sending her spinning out of control. The stubble on his jaw scraped at the softer skin of her face as he angled his head to deepen the kiss even further, sending her pulse right off the scale.

She tugged his shirt out of his trousers and explored his naked chest with her hands, relishing the feel of hard muscles and the light dusting of hair. She let her fingers move lower, following the trail of hair that went below his waistband, her fingers fumbling with the fastening for a moment before she finally freed him into the soft, worshipful caress of her hands.

He was so very aroused she could smell it on his skin, the musk and salt and urgency a potent combination, sending her senses into overdrive. She had seen a lot of male bodies but none had ever taken her breath away quite like his. Everything about him was perfect; each contour of his body was toned and leanly muscled. The satin strength and the thickness of him that indicated how much she had affected him made her feel utterly feminine and complete in a way she had never felt before.

She wriggled down so she could taste him, the act one she had never felt comfortable with before, but somehow this time it felt so natural, so in tune with what she felt for him she didn't hesitate for a moment. She felt him jerk against her in response, his harshly indrawn breath a clue to how close he was to losing control, but she continued to use her lips and tongue.

Matt suddenly pulled away from her, avoiding her eyes, avoiding further contact and most especially avoiding the mantelpiece where the green watchful gaze of his dead fiancée seemed to be trained on him accusingly. 'I'm sorry,' he said, zipping himself back into place. 'That wasn't meant to happen. In fact, I can't believe it just did.'

Kellie looked at him in bewilderment, her senses knocked off course by his abrupt rejection. She couldn't speak for the emotion clogging her throat. She had thought he had been with her all the way. Was she so naïve and inexperienced that she had totally misread him? Shame flooded her. She felt so exposed and vulnerable she could barely look at him without flinching.

He turned to face her, his expression criss-crossed with a frown. 'It shouldn't have happened, Kellie. You know it shouldn't. We're colleagues who have to work together for six months. It doesn't mean we have to sleep together. It's not written into the contract.'

'But…but you kissed me…' Kellie moistened her still sensitive mouth and continued in the same confused tone, 'I thought you were…you know…developing feelings for me…' She bit her bottom lip until she could feel it swelling around her teeth. 'I've never felt like this before…with anyone… It feels so right. I thought you were starting to feel the same way… Your kiss seemed to indicate…'

He scraped a hand through his hair as he stepped away. 'You can't possibly fall in love with me,' he said, hardly game to believe it was possible. She was an impulsive young woman, caught up in the heat of the moment, no doubt feeling guilty she had become so intimate with him in so short a time. In a few days she would see this episode in a new light. It was up to him to give her an out. It was the gentlemanly thing to do. She had been cruelly hurt before. She needed more time to get to know him before anything between them was established.

'It's her, isn't it?' she asked into the tight silence.

He clenched his shadowed jaw. 'Don't do this, Kellie,' he bit out. 'Don't make this any harder than it is.'

She got to her feet and, moving across to the mantelpiece, turned the photograph of Madeleine around. 'There,' she said stridently. 'Are you available now?'

He glared at her in anger, his hands going to fists by his sides. 'This is not about her, damn you.'

She came up to him and jabbed him in the chest with the point of her index finger. 'You are *alive*, Matt, she is dead.

D-E-A-D. You can't change that. The only thing you can change is how you live your life now.'

He pushed her hand away. 'I don't want this. I don't need the complication of this right now. And if you were honest with yourself, neither do you.'

'Yes, you *do* want this!' she cried. 'You would never have reacted the way you did unless—'

'So where were you on the day they taught male sexual response at medical school?' he said cuttingly. 'Anyone could have achieved the same result you just did. It has nothing to do with feelings and emotions, it's totally physical.'

Kellie swung away, her pride so tattered and torn she felt sick to her stomach. 'I'm s-sorry,' she said, hoping he wouldn't hear the catch in her voice. 'I obviously completely misread the situation. Put it down to my appalling lack of experience…or something…'

A little silence pulsed in the air for a moment.

'Forget about it,' he said gently. 'We were both caught out by today's drama. Emotions can often get out of hand in tense situations.'

She moved towards the sitting-room door, her back turned towards him. 'I think I'll give dinner a miss if you don't mind,' she said. 'I'm very tired. I'm often irrational when I'm overtired.'

'It wasn't your fault, Kellie,' he said. 'If anyone is to blame, it's me. I started it with that kiss. I'm sorry. I stepped way over the line. It's no wonder you jumped to the conclusions you did. Any woman would have done so.'

She turned back to look at him briefly. 'You have to let her go, Matt,' she said softly. 'Some day, some time you have to finally let her go.'

Matt watched her leave the room, his body still on fire, his heart torn between wanting to go after her and claim her as his own and the other part of him wanting to go over to the mantelpiece and turn Madeleine's photograph back to face the room and his conscience.

In the end he drained the contents of his wineglass and left Madeleine facing the wall—he kind of felt she had seen enough for one day.

Kellie was up early next morning in an effort to avoid running into Matt, but she needn't have bothered as he was nowhere in sight. On her way into town she drove past the Montgomerys' house but it was still cordoned off so she carried on to the clinic instead.

'How is Ruth?' she asked Trish, who was already sitting at the reception desk.

'Matt's spending some time with her now,' Trish said. 'She's terribly upset, as you can imagine.'

'Have the police established anything yet?' Kellie asked.

'Not yet. The forensic team is still at the site.'

'Yes, I saw them as I drove past,' Kellie said, trying not to shiver in reaction. 'I used to have such a normal, boring life.'

'You'd better give your family a call to let them know what's going on,' Trish suggested, handing her the newspaper. 'They might find it a little disturbing to hear about it in the press.'

'I called my father late last night,' Kellie said relieved she had done so now that she had seen the headlines. 'He wants me to come straight home.'

'You're not going to, are you?' Trish looked worried.

She blew out a sigh and put the newspaper down. 'No. I made a commitment and I'm determined to see it through.' *Even if I have made the biggest fool out of myself*, Kellie thought.

'So…' Trish gave her a penetrating glance. 'How are you getting on with Matt? I heard you spent the night at his place last night.'

Kellie shifted her gaze to look at the list of patients. 'We're getting on just fine. He's very professional at all times.'

'He's certainly been very supportive of you with the mothers' group project,' Trish observed. 'He's been working the most ungodly hours to see that everything you want gets done.'

'I know what you're thinking, Trish, but it's not going to happen,' Kellie said. 'He's a nice guy and all that but he's in love with a dead woman. I can't compete with that. I don't want to even try.'

'I think you're in with a very good chance. You're the first woman he's shown any interest in whatsoever. I see the way he looks at you. He's never looked at anyone like that before.'

'I think it would be better if everyone left him alone,' Kellie grumbled. 'Besides, who said I was interested in him?'

Trish gave her a knowing look. 'Come on, Kellie, you have one of the most expressive faces this town has ever seen,' she said. 'I know you got off to a rocky start with him but it's obvious as those cute little freckles on the bridge of your nose that you're falling in love with him. In fact, I'd hazard a guess you already *are* a little bit in love with him. I can see it in your eyes. You practically melt whenever his name is mentioned.'

'That's ridiculous.' Kellie attempted to deny it but she knew her colour was probably giving her away. 'What sort of crazy person would fall in love with someone after just a few days? That stuff only happens in movies and paperback novels. Anyway, I didn't come out here to find myself a husband, and if I had Matt McNaught is definitely not husband material. He's married to his memories.'

'People do sometimes fall in love within days, if not

minutes,' Trish countered. 'I fell in love with my husband the moment I met him, I just had to wait for a couple of dates for him to catch up. And as for Matt and his memories, I don't think it will take him too long to realise what's landed right under his nose. In any case, I can't remember the last time he mentioned his late fiancée. I get the feeling he's well and truly ready to move on. The whole town thinks so, too. Nothing would please everyone more than seeing him settle down with someone like you. You've brought life and vigour to this dry old town.'

The first patient arrived, which put an end to the exchange, for which Kellie was rather thankful. She hadn't realised her feelings were so obvious but, then, just thinking about what had happened between her and Matt last night was enough to make her whole body light up with the glow of guilt and shame.

She still couldn't quite believe she had been so bold and brazen. She mentally cringed in embarrassment. She had practically seduced him. No, she *had* seduced him! There was no point pretending otherwise. She had responded to him in such a manner uncharacteristic of her upbringing, out of line with her beliefs and moral standards.

What on earth had she been thinking? Sex didn't equal love. He had told her so himself. He had at least had the decency and sense to call a halt before things had got even further out of hand.

She of all people knew the dangers of casual sex. She had seen enough patients with sexually transmitted diseases to know how risky it was, and yet if he hadn't pulled back she would have been his for the asking. He had gallantly taken some of the blame for kissing her, but where had her self-control been when she'd needed it? Being someone's sex buddy was definitely not in her scheme of things. She wanted marriage and babies and the whole shebang—the white wedding and the honeymoon in paradise. She had dreamed of it since she was a little girl. She had tottered around the house in her mother's high heels, her entire body consumed by the slightly yellowed wedding veil, conjuring up her very own Mr Right. He wasn't supposed to come with baggage. He was supposed to love her and only her. How could she settle for anything less?

Kellie picked up the first patient's file and plastered a smile on her face. 'Mrs Overton?'

Pat Overton was a frail woman in her sixties who had been battling breast cancer for the last five years. Kellie knew from the notes that things did not look promising. Despite a mastectomy with axillary clearance and adjuvant tamoxifen, the cancer had metastasised to the lungs, pleura and thoracic spine. She had refused to go to Brisbane for radiotherapy to the bony involvement—she didn't want to be away from the country-side for even one day and she had already been changed to arimidex, but with no obvious improvement. She had also refused chemotherapy.

Kellie's examination showed a large left pleural effusion and crepitations over most of both lungs. The thoracic spine and some of the ribs were very tender.

It was a levelling moment, to be sitting so close to someone who was so close to death and who obviously knew it. Kellie could see the sad resignation in the older woman's grey-blue eyes and her heart ached for what her family would be going through right now and in the few short weeks ahead.

'I'm so tired of fighting,' Pat said breathlessly. 'I've come to the end of my rope. I've managed on the painkillers Dr Montgomery gave me before he left but I think it's time for something stronger. I was going to see Dr McNaught but I thought it might be nice to meet you. I'd heard you were quite lovely and I can see now it's true.'

'That's very sweet of you but I—'

'He's a good man, Dr Thorne.'

'Yes, I know, he's—'

'He'll make someone a wonderful husband one day.' Pat had cut her off again.

'I'm sure he will. However—'

Pat grasped her by the hand. 'My husband will do the same, I know it. We've been together a long time but that doesn't mean he can't find happiness and companionship with someone else after I've gone. I've tried to tell him but he won't listen. Men can be so stubborn, don't you think?'

Kellie swallowed the lump of emotion in her throat. 'Yes,' she said, 'exasperatingly so.'

Pat smiled and sat back with a sigh. 'Now, give me something to knock the back teeth out of this pain and I'll leave you to get on with your young life. I've had mine and it's been a good one. I've brought up two sons and two daughters and I've had the privilege of being a grandmother six times. I wish I could stay around for the rest but that's not God's plan.'

'I can escalate the pain relief a lot,' Kellie said, discreetly clearing her throat as she reached for the prescription pad. 'I'm going to start you on a medium dose of long-acting morphine. That will ease the breathlessness a little too. We'll up the dose until you feel comfortable.'

'Thank you, Dr Thorne,' Pat said. Reaching out, she touched Kellie softly on the arm, her pain-filled eyes meeting hers. 'Thank you for caring so much.'

Kellie blinked back tears. 'I can't help it, Mrs Overton,' she said.

The older woman smiled. 'Yes, I can see that. It's what everyone loves about you. Even Matt McNaught.'

# CHAPTER SIXTEEN

MATT was in the staff kitchen when Kellie came in, blowing her nose. He looked up from the newspaper and frowned. 'Are you all right?'

She nodded and stuffed the tissue into her bra. 'I've just spent over an hour with Pat Overton.'

'Oh.' His one-word response summed it up completely.

Kellie plucked another tissue out of the box on the counter and buried her reddened nose into it. 'She's so brave and so selfless, it really got to me.'

'She has been very brave about it all,' he agreed. 'Tim and I have often spoken about her courage. She's put up an incredible fight.'

'Why does it happen to such nice people?' she asked looking up at him through tear-washed eyes. 'Why do such lovely people get struck down when there are horrible murderers and rapists on the loose?'

Matt let out a sigh and came over to where she was standing, snivelling into another scrunched-up tissue. He had told himself after last night he wasn't going to touch her again. He had practically drawn an invisible line around her body as a no-go area. But somehow she had this weird effect on him—it was like he was a tiny iron filing and she was a super-sized magnet.

'It happens because life is sometimes totally unfair,' he said, breathing in the sweet scent of her as she nestled against him. 'I don't have any answers, Kellie. I'm the one still asking the unanswerable questions.'

'Pat is worried about her husband,' she said stepping out of his embrace. 'She wants him to move on after she's gone. I wish my mother had said that to my father. I think it would have made it easier for him.'

Matt shoved his hands in his trouser pockets to keep them away from where they really wanted to go. 'It's a personal thing,' he said. 'No one can put a time limit on it. Joe Overton will have to work through it for himself. He and Pat have been together a long time. They've raised a family together and watched their farm go through all the highs and lows of droughts and floods and good years. He will miss her dreadfully when she goes, but at least he's had some warning.'

She pulled out another tissue and wiped at her eyes. 'Do you think that makes it easier?' she asked.

His chest deflated on a sigh. 'I don't know. What do you think? You've been in practice long enough to have seen just about everything there is to be seen. Do you think it makes a difference?'

'I'm not sure…' She chewed at her bottom lip in that little-girl-lost sort of way that did twisting and turning things to his insides every single time. 'I think it varies from person to person. Some people cope really well with the sudden death of a relative, others have trouble coping with watching a loved one go through the process of a drawn-out terminal illness.'

'If Pat Overton is a little too close personally, I'll take over her care for you,' he offered.

She looked up at him, her eyes still red and glistening with tears. 'No. I want to look after her. I want to do whatever I can for her and her family.'

A silence began to shrink the size of the room.

'About last night...' he began awkwardly.

'No,' she said, squeezing her eyes shut and holding up a hand to stall him. '*Please*, don't make me suffer any more embarrassment than I already have. I can't believe I was so...so...out of control. I've never done that...you know... I mean, I've read about it in all those modern women's magazines but I've never actually...well...you know...taken it to that point...'

'Don't worry about it,' he said. 'I told you it wasn't entirely your fault. I could easily have stopped things before they got to that point...' He twisted his mouth ruefully. 'Well, maybe not easily, but I should have all the same.'

Her gaze dropped away from his. 'I'm sorry,' she said. 'I can't imagine what you must be thinking of me. I'm normally the biggest prude out. For years I've been plugging up my ears when my brothers start talking about their sex lives. I just don't want to know what they get up to or who with.'

'It's another one of those personal things,' he said. 'What feels right for one person isn't right for another.'

'I hope I haven't compromised our working relationship,' she said, starting to gnaw at her lip again.

'It's fine, Kellie, really,' he said. 'It was an unusual day. It's not every day you find a skeleton in your back yard. It's no wonder we were both a little out of kilter.' He took a breath and mentally rehearsed what he had really wanted to say but just as he opened his mouth Trish came in.

'Oh, sorry,' she said, with one of her knowing smiles. 'I was just wondering if I could get you two a cup of tea or something?'

Matt silently ground his teeth behind his polite smile. 'No, thank you, Trish,' he said. 'I have a house call to make out at the Fairworth property. I should have left ten minutes ago.'

'How is Ruth managing?' Trish asked.

'She's trying to be strong but it's knocking her around,' he said. 'It will be a huge blow to her if it turns out to be Tegan. She has kept herself going for so long on the hope that her daughter is still alive. I'm really worried about how she will deal with it if the worst comes to pass.'

'I can't imagine the hell Ruth is going through,' Kellie said once Trish had bustled out to answer the phone. 'It must be so hard to keep on hoping when there is really no hope.'

Matt picked up a card and handed it to her. 'I thought you might like to see this,' he said. 'It's from Brayden Harrison. He's out of the induced coma and doing really well. He particularly wanted to thank you after he heard you had been on a run and got waylaid by his injuries.'

Kellie read the card and felt her eyes water again. 'Wow,' she said, tucking the card back into the envelope. 'It makes me glad I chose to be a doctor instead of an orthodontist.'

He gave her a wry smile. 'An orthodontist?'

She nodded. 'It was the braces I had when I was a teenager. I toyed with the idea for a while but then I realised I had another calling.'

'You're a damned good doctor, Kellie,' he said. 'I'm not sure Brayden would be alive today if you hadn't been there with me that day.'

Another silence brought the walls closer together.

'I have to get back to work,' she said, turning away. 'Gracie Young's middle child has an ear infection. I think I can hear her crying in the waiting room. I've squeezed her in between Mr Tate and Mrs Peters.'

'Kellie, wait,' Matt said, hoping Jean Fairworth and her migraine would forgive him another minute or two.

Kellie turned back to look at him. 'Yes?'

His throat moved up and down in a tight swallow. 'I just wanted to say if you want to leave, that would be fine with me. It's not been a pleasant experience so far and I thought if you wanted to pack it in before the six months is up, I wouldn't make a fuss about it. It might take some time but we can find someone else.'

She frowned at him. 'You *want* me to leave? Is that what you're saying?'

Matt felt like kicking himself. What was wrong with him? Why had he said that? Of course he didn't want her to leave. She was an asset to the place. No, she was much more than that. She was the most beautiful, adorable, dimple-cheeked woman he'd ever met and he wanted to spend the rest of his days telling her how much she had come to mean to him. He scraped a hand through his hair and tried again. 'No, that's not what I'm saying, not really.'

'Then what are you saying, Matt?' she asked with a look that would have sent a raging bull ten paces backwards.

He cleared his throat. 'Look, I'm just trying to make things easier for everyone.'

Her brown eyes flashed with sparks of resentment. 'For yourself, you mean. What's worrying you, Matt? That word might somehow get out in town that you allowed yourself to be human for change? That you have needs and desires and urges, just like everyone else?'

He frowned back at her, annoyed with how he had bungled things and equally annoyed at her for not giving him a chance to explain himself. 'You were appointed to this position as a fellow GP, not as a solution to my lack of a love life,' he clipped out. 'I suggest you get on with the tasks assigned you as part of your contract and leave me to deal with my own issues in my own time.'

Kellie's mouth tightened so much her jaw ached. 'You're never going to deal with any of those issues, Matt, because you're an emotional coward. You've never forgiven your mother for leaving you and your father, just like you've never forgiven Madeleine for dying. That's your problem, you know. You're angry at her for getting killed but you can't admit it so you wear your hairshirt way out here in the sticks, making everyone feel sorry for you. It's pathetic, that's what it is—totally pathetic.'

He glared at her in fury. 'I think you might have said quite enough, Dr Thorne,' he bit out. 'I also think you might want to have a rethink about returning to the city where you and your psychology belong. There's no place for it here.'

Kellie pulled back her shoulders as he stalked past, her chest heaving with anger as he left the room with the victory of the last word ringing in her ears.


The police were just leaving the Montgomerys' house when Kellie called in after work. She was assured that everything was fine for her to resume living in the house; they had finally removed the remains and were now waiting for confirmation of the identity of the deceased.

Kellie left some food out in case the stray dog was about before making her way around to Ruth Williams's house. Trish had informed her earlier that afternoon that Ruth had insisted on returning home to wait for the police to contact her.

When Ruth answered the door to Kellie's knock it was clear the waiting was taking its toll. Her face was sunken with anguish, the conflicting lines of grief and hope like a complicated map written on her forehead.

'Oh, Kellie, my dear,' she said, sinking into Kellie's embrace. 'How did you know I needed some company right now?'

'Have you heard anything?' Kellie asked once they were seated in the sitting room.

Ruth shook her head. 'Sergeant Blake said he would call me as soon as he finds out who it is.' She glanced at the phone by her right side and added wearily, 'I hope it won't be too much longer now…'

Kellie's gaze went to a sideboard, where an array of photographs was displayed. 'Is that Tegan?' she asked.

Ruth nodded sadly. 'Yes, that's my girl.'

'She was very beautiful,' Kellie said, and then wondered if she should have used the past tense.

'Yes,' Ruth said with a sad smile. 'She used to love posing for the camera. She loved being the centre of attention, she craved it. I guess that's why she and Dirk clashed so much. She wasn't used to sharing me with anyone after her father died.'

'Is this Dirk?' Kellie asked, picking up a photograph of a sandy-haired man with an open easy smile.

Ruth let out a sigh. 'No, that's my first husband, Tegan's father Alan. Dirk never used to like me having Alan's photo there, but when he passed away I put Alan back.'

Kellie's eyes scanned the rest of the display. 'Do you have any photos of your second husband?'

'Not now,' Ruth answered. 'I sent them to his parents after he died. I didn't really want them any more, to tell you the truth. Alan was my first love. Tegan was right, she told me often enough before she…left. I should never have tried to replace him.'

Kellie swallowed as the older woman's gaze centred on hers. She felt Ruth could see every emotion she was feeling as if they were individually etched on her skin—her escalating feelings for Matt, how she loved him and wanted him to take that step away from the past towards her open arms.

'You will have to be patient, Kellie,' Ruth said with a tender look. 'From the little he's told me, I know Matt's whole life and future was built around Madeleine. She represented the security he had been lacking all his life. Her shock death was like suddenly turning a corner and slamming into an invisible brick wall. He was planning his wedding one day, the next he was organising her funeral. He didn't see it coming, no one does. But he will heal in time—I can already see signs of it. Maybe he feels he can't quite let go just yet because in doing so he will have to finally accept he has lost her for ever. That's the hardest part, realising the one you love isn't coming back.'

Kellie pressed her lips together as the tears started to flow. 'I just want him to make some room in his heart for me,' she said. 'Is that asking too much? I've waited all my adult life to meet someone who makes me feel like this, only to find his emotions are tied up elsewhere. How can I ever be the one he wants when the one he really wants is dead?'

Ruth reached for her hands and held them in the soft warmth of hers. 'Listen to me, Kellie,' she commanded gently. 'You're a beautiful, caring person. Anyone can see that. I saw it the moment you stepped off that plane. I think Matt *is* starting to see what he's missing out on. He's isolated himself out here like a wounded lonely wolf to brood and lick his wounds in private. For six long years he's punished himself for not being able to keep Madeleine safe from the vicissitudes of life.

'But the fact is it's not possible to keep *anyone* we love safe. We have to accept that and live the life we've been given. I've come to realise over the years that life isn't a dress rehearsal—it's actually a one-act play.' Ruth sat back, sighing deeply as she continued, 'I miss my daughter, every day I ache for the years I've lost with her, but I have to press on. Whatever the outcome of the forensic investigation, I have come to realise there are other people in this community who need me. I draw strength from that. It's what keeps me going, it's what has always kept me going.'

Kellie brushed at her eyes with the back of her hand. 'You remind me of my mother,' she said. 'I think if one of my brothers or I had gone missing, she would have been the same as you, waiting indefinitely. She would never have given up hope, not until the evidence was before her to convince her otherwise.'

'There are so many different types of grief, Kellie,' Ruth said. 'Look at Trish and David Cutler, for example. All they ever wanted to do was get married and have babies, but it wasn't to be. The irony is that nowadays they may well have achieved it with a couple of IVF attempts, but that wasn't available then. They were told to go away and forget about it or apply for adoption, but by the time they got around to doing it they were considered too old so they missed out. Life is full of disappointments, though, isn't it? No doubt you've been a doctor long enough now to realise how unfair it all is.'

'Yes, it certainly is,' Kellie agreed, thinking of the lovely and incredibly courageous Pat Overton.

There was a knock at the door and Kellie offered to answer it. 'Thank you, dear,' Ruth said. 'I've been up and down all day. It's probably Julie—she said she'd call around about now.'

Kellie came back into the sitting room with Greg and Tracey. 'It's the police,' she said, unconsciously holding her breath. 'They have some news for you.'

# CHAPTER SEVENTEEN

'HAVE you heard the news?' Cheryl asked Matt when he came to the general store to pick up a special item he had ordered.

'No,' he said, trying to gauge her expression. 'Is it about Tegan Williams?'

'Apparently it's not her,' Cheryl said. 'It wasn't her body buried at the Montgomerys' house. The police have now identified it's a man.'

'Who was he?' Matt asked, frowning.

'Apparently he was an international tourist on a working holiday who came through twenty-five years or so ago,' Cheryl reported. 'The Montgomerys' house used to be a bit of a backpackers' cottage back then. It was a pretty ad hoc arrangement, I seem to recall. I don't think anyone paid much for staying there as it was pretty rundown. Anyway, he was travelling with three friends from Europe, picking up work when and where they could. They didn't stay in town long, a couple of days at the most.'

'So how did he come to be buried in the back yard?' Matt asked.

'Well, it seems after a solid night of heavy drinking, the guys all bunked down to sleep, but during the night one of them vomited and choked to death. When the other two found him dead the next morning they panicked. They felt responsible because they had been the ones to encourage him to drink shot after shot of vodka. They didn't speak much English and were worried they would be charged with manslaughter or something.'

'So they just *buried* him behind the shed and left town?' Matt asked with an incredulous expression.

'Yep,' Cheryl said. 'The federal police finally tracked the two guys down on the basis of the dead man's dental records. There's an international database on missing persons so they were able to find his travelling companions. They told the police everything. Imagine living with that on your conscience for all these years? Hard on the dead guy's family after all this time, but at least now they've got closure. His remains will be sent back for a proper burial. The authorities are seeing to it as we speak.'

'I'd better go and see Ruth,' Matt said, running a hand through his hair. 'She's been to hell and back and she still has no answers.'

'Kellie was with her earlier,' Cheryl said. 'I heard our pretty young doctor spent the night with you. Counting the one in Brisbane, that's two nights you've spent with her so far. So what's going on with you two?'

Matt's brows moved together. 'What do you mean?'

Cheryl's eyes glinted. 'Come on, Matt, what are you waiting for? She's everything a man could want. You'd be a fool to let her slip through your fingers. If you don't snap her up someone else will, and then what will you do? Spend the rest of your life out here sulking about yet another one that got away?'

He picked up his items from the counter, his mouth pulled tight. 'Put it on the tab, Cheryl,' he bit out as he strode out of the store.

\* \* \*

Kellie didn't see much of Matt over the next few days. Apparently there had been a mechanical problem with the plane on one of the outback clinic runs, which had meant he and the pilot had had to stay at one of the grazing properties until it was fixed.

Matt had called her one evening but his conversation had seemed rather stilted so she'd decided to make up an excuse about having to wash her hair. The fact that he hadn't even questioned her rather hackneyed excuse had seemed to suggest he'd been relieved she'd brought an end to an already uncomfortable conversation.

The clinic in town took up as much time as Kellie had available and with her extra commitments at the community centre she was glad she didn't have too much time on her hands to think about Matt.

Kellie was more than delighted at how well the young mothers were getting on. She had conducted several cooking classes with Ruth's help and the girls themselves had come up with the brilliant suggestion of planning a charity dinner prepared by them to raise funds for Christmas presents for the underprivileged kids in town.

A few evenings later, once Matt had got safely back from the regional clinic, his manager Bob Gardner and his wife Eunice invited her out for a meal at their cottage.

Kellie accepted the invitation with enthusiasm, as even though her days at the clinic and the community centre were long, the nights at the Montgomerys' were even longer. Although she had to admit her enthusiasm underwent a quick change once Eunice informed her Matt would be joining them for dinner.

It seemed from the moment Kellie was welcomed effusively in the door by Bob and Eunice, Matt not only evaded addressing a word to her but seemed to be avoiding even looking at her.

Bob was called away to the phone at one point and Eunice bustled out, mumbling something about seeing to the apple crumble in the oven, which left Kellie alone with Matt at the dining table.

The silence was almost palpable.

'Ruth seems to have recovered well,' he finally said, still looking at the contents of his wineglass.

'Yes,' Kellie responded. 'She's been a great help to me with the mothers' group.' She briefly filled him in on the charity dinner the girls had planned, and for her trouble got a mono-syllabic reply.

Another silence passed.

Matt cleared his throat and met her gaze across the table. 'Kellie…I was wondering if we could get together some time to—'

Eunice came in at that point with a fresh jug of iced water. 'Did Dr Thorne tell you about the young mothers' charity dinner?' she asked.

Matt forced himself to smile. 'Yes, it sounds like a great idea.'

Eunice put the jiggling-with-ice jug on the table next to Matt. 'I think it's wonderful what Dr Thorne has done in the short time she's been here, don't you?'

'Yes,' Matt said. Picking up the jug, he concentrated on re-filling everyone's glass.

'Have you thought about staying a little bit longer, Dr Thorne?' Eunice asked. 'Six months isn't very long and David Cutler really needs to hang up his stethoscope. You staying on to help Matt would be the perfect solution all round.'

'Um…I hadn't really thought about staying much longer

than the allotted time,' Kellie said, carefully avoiding Matt's eyes. 'I've put in an application for a posting at Byron Bay. I could have gone back to my old job in Newcastle but my family need more time to get used to being on their own.'

'Oh, well, it's early days yet,' Eunice said, and made her way back out to the kitchen.

Matt looked at Kellie. 'Is it true?' he asked. 'Are you applying for a placement at Byron Bay once your time here is up?'

Kellie picked up her water glass and examined the ice cubes rather than meet his eyes. 'I have a few options I'm exploring at present,' she said. 'I don't recall making any promises about staying longer than the six months.'

Matt swallowed. 'No…I guess you didn't.' He waited before adding, 'I have some business to see to in Brisbane. I'll be away for a couple of weeks at the most. Will you be all right on your own? David Cutler said he'd do what he can to help.'

'Of course,' she said. 'I'll be fine.'

'Good…' he said, looking away again. 'That's good.'

'Matt, you seem a little on edge,' she said, after another beat or two of painful silence. 'I know things have been pretty strained between us since…well, since that night we…I mean I…you know, overstepped the mark, but it seems to be getting worse. Have I done something wrong? I mean, apart from that…that other thing…'

He pushed away his wineglass and met her gaze once more. 'No,' he said, twisting his mouth so that it almost smiled. 'It's not you. It's me.'

Kellie stopped breathing as she looked into those midnight-blue eyes. Her heart gave an irregular thump and her stomach felt hollow in spite of the generous helping of roast beef with all the trimmings she had not long ago consumed.

182   TOP-NOTCH DOC, OUTBACK BRIDE

'I have something I need to do,' he went on. 'I should have done it well before now, but I guess I just wasn't quite ready.'

*What?* Kellie was about to ask when Eunice suddenly came in with a tray loaded with a dish of steaming apple crumble and custard, setting it down before them with a cheerful smile as Bob followed with the jug of cream.

'This is Matt's favourite dessert, isn't it, Matt?' Eunice said, dishing him out a huge helping.

'Not too much cream for me, thanks, Bob,' Matt said as his manager began to tilt the jug over his plate.

'What about you, Dr Thorne?' Bob asked, with the jug poised. 'Are you worried about your heart, like Matt, or do you like to indulge now and again?'

Kellie gave a strained smile. 'I guess a little bit of what you fancy is OK now and again, right?'

Two and a half weeks later Kellie sat on the back steps of the veranda and watched as the dog she had called Sylvie came up to take a treat out of her hand. 'There you go, sweetie,' she said encouragingly. 'That wasn't so hard now, was it?'

It was one of the most satisfying experiences Kellie had had in the time she had spent so far in Culwulla Creek, that and seeing the young mothers' group go from strength to strength.

Julie's boys had even settled down a bit. Ty had decided to go back to school so he could finish his leaver's certificate in order to become a mechanic which had pleased his mother no end.

Ruth had pulled herself back into the swing of things and for the last few days had been madly helping Trish prepare one of the pastoral property's biggest barns for the bachelors' and spinsters' ball, which was being held that evening.

Kellie was in two minds about whether to go or not. She

didn't fancy dancing and flirting playfully with the locals when the only man she wanted to be there wasn't planning to attend. She had heard via Trish that Matt's father had suddenly become ill, and instead of returning to Culwulla Creek as planned Matt had had to travel down to Sydney. Trish didn't seem to have any idea of when he was planning on getting back.

Kellie was all dressed up and ready to go to the ball when she heard the sound of a car pull up outside. She pushed the curtain aside and felt her stomach drop like an out-of-control lift when she saw Matt's tall figure unfold from his car.

She gave her wrists and neck another quick spray of perfume. Drawing in a shaky breath, she made her way to the front door, each step she took making her stomach perform another star jump.

He was stroking Sylvie under the chin when Kellie opened the door. He straightened and gave her a smile. 'Hi.'

'Hi.'

He shifted his weight from one foot to the other. 'You look nice,' he said. 'Great, in fact. You look great. Fabulous…' He cleared his throat. 'Really great.'

'Thank you.'

There was a little silence.

'I see you've tamed the dog,' he said, shifting his weight again.

'Yes, I've called her Sylvie.'

He cleared his throat once more. 'Er…that's a nice name.'

'Yes, it means from the forest,' Kellie said. 'I kind of thought it was appropriate. She sort of came from the bush, which is almost the same thing as a forest, right?'

He nodded and smiled. 'Er…right.'

'So…' She rolled her lips together. 'Are you going to the ball? I'm just about to leave so…' She left the sentence hanging.

'Are you sure you still qualify?' he asked.

She gave him a quizzical look. 'Qualify? What do you mean by qualify?'

He gave a little shrug and reached down again to stroke Sylvie, who was practically sitting on his left foot by now, gazing up at him adoringly. 'It's a bachelors' and spinsters' ball,' he said. 'Only single, unattached people are supposed to go.'

Kellie felt her heart join in with her stomach's complicated gymnastics routine. 'Um…last time I looked I was still single and unattached,' she said, trying to read his exasperatingly inscrutable expression.

His dark blue eyes locked on hers. 'Listen, Kellie, there's no point in me beating about the bush…' He suddenly smiled and corrected himself. 'Or the forest, as the case may be. The thing is I love you.'

She blinked at him. 'You…you do?'

'I do.'

'Wow…' she breathed.

His smile widened. 'Is that all you can say?'

'Oh, wow…' She looked up at him dreamily.

'I want you to marry me,' he said. 'I want you to be my wife.'

'But what about—'

He pressed the pad of his finger against her lips to stop her saying the name out loud. 'She's gone, Kellie. You were right, it was well and truly time to let her go. The thing is, I had done so ages ago but I hadn't really realised it until you came along. That's one of the reasons I went to Brisbane. I took her ashes and her photograph back to her parents and told them I was moving on with my life. I told them I was coming back here to ask you to be my wife. Will you do me the honour of being my partner in life, no matter where it leads us or whatever it throws at us?'

'Oh, wow… Oh, wow…'

Matt grinned at her. 'Is that a "yes" or a "maybe" or an "I'm still thinking about it"?'

Kellie could barely speak for joy. 'You really mean it? You *really* love me?'

He looked down at her tenderly. 'I've been trying to tell you for the last three weeks but every time I worked up the courage, someone would interrupt us,' he said.

'But I thought you were still in love with Madeleine?'

He gave a sigh and held her close. 'After Madeleine was killed, I grieved and heavily. I didn't see the point in having a life when she had been robbed of hers. But the truth is, she wasn't the love of my life. I think that's why I stayed away from another relationship for so long for then I would have to face up to the realisation I hadn't loved her the way she deserved to be loved.'

'Oh, Matt…'

He smiled down at her. 'I guess that's why you got under my skin from day one,' he said. 'You came bouncing into town with your propensity to mother and organise everyone, and I realised how I had never felt that sort of attraction before. It was like being hit right between the eyes.'

'Oh, Matt,' Kellie said again, hugging him tightly. 'I thought you didn't even notice me that first day on the plane.'

He lowered his chin to the top of her head, pulling her closer. 'I would have noticed you from the first second, but the truth was I was struggling with the aftermath of that trip to Brisbane for Madeleine's birthday. I had gone there intending to tell her parents I was ready to reclaim my life, but when I got there, I just couldn't seem to do it. They were so glad to see me, so pathetically grateful, that I felt a heel the whole time I was there.

'You were right when you said that deep down I was angry at Madeleine for dying. It shocked me to hear it but later when I thought about it I realised it was true. Anger is grief's second cousin, depression is its first. I was getting a little too close to both of them until you came along.'

Kellie looked up at him devotedly. 'I think I fell in love with you within the first day or two of meeting you. I didn't want to but I just couldn't help it. But I was so worried you would never be able to move on enough to love me back.'

He tucked a strand of her hair behind her ear with a touch so gentle she felt tears come to her eyes. 'I can't promise you in the months and years to come I won't sometimes think of Madeleine,' he said. 'I know it's not quite the same thing, but it's like asking you to never think of your mother. It's just not possible to forget the people who have touched you in some way during the course of your life. But I can promise you I will love you with my whole heart for the rest of our days. I don't care where we live, be it bush or beach, as long as you're with me I'll be the happiest man on earth.'

Kellie wrapped her arms around him, her smile as wide as it was radiant. 'I didn't really apply for that job at Byron Bay,' she confessed sheepishly. 'So, if it's all right, can I stay here with you?'

Matt grinned as he swept her up in his arms. 'You can stay with me as long as you like, starting from now,' he said, and carried her inside.

# A Wedding
# in Warragurra

## FIONA LOWE

Always an avid reader, **Fiona Lowe** decided to combine her love of romance with her interest in all things medical, so writing Medical Romance™ was an obvious choice! She lives in a seaside town in southern Australia, where she juggles writing, reading, working and raising two gorgeous sons, with the support of her own real-life hero! You can visit Fiona's website at www.fionalowe.com

To my cousin, Annie, for her wholehearted enthusiasm, unwavering support, and shelf-arranging skills. A woman going places in her own life.

# CHAPTER ONE

'BUT it isn't pink.'

Kate Lawson heard the disappointment in the young girl's voice as she browsed in the limited clothing section of Warragurra's answer to Teen Gear. She glanced up and just caught the woebegone expression that matched the voice before a set of very broad shoulders partially blocked her view.

'Not everything in life is pink or purple, Sasha.' The deep, melodious voice carried a smile.

Kate grinned, wishing she could see the man's face. Did he have a clue what he was up against? Shopping with tweens was a minefield. She knew only too well. She had a niece much the same age and a Girl Guide troop that kept her on her toes.

Sasha tossed her head and stuck a hand on her hip. 'I do know that, Dad.'

'So, perhaps it's time to branch out and explore green and blue now that you're twelve.' Patience threaded through the words. He picked up a cute striped vest top. 'What about this?'

Kate watched, fascinated and completely forgetting she was supposed to be finding a gift for her niece. That she was supposed to be ironing her nurse's uniform and polishing her shoes for her first day back at work. Not to mention the million other things that needed doing in preparation for her return to the real world of Warragurra. She'd been gone six months, but she couldn't hide for ever.

Sasha wrinkled her nose at the top that lay across her father's arm.

Long masculine fingers trailed across the fabric. 'It's green but it has a fine pink stripe.' He paused for a beat. 'It matches your beautiful eyes. They're green, just like Mum's.'

His words wove magic. Sasha's expression transformed from sceptical to delighted. 'I'll try it on. And these shorts, too.' Sasha took the hanger from her father's hand, grabbed the matching shorts and marched toward the change room.

Laughter bubbled up inside Kate at the exchange between father and daughter. He was good! Wily, but good. Sasha had no idea she'd just been outplayed. Usually dads lost the fashion battles, which was why mothers took on that role.

He turned toward the change rooms and caught her gaze, giving her a conspiratorial grin. 'Let's hope that saves me from a trip to Dubbo.'

Kate forgot to breathe.

Azure eyes flecked with myriad shades of blue sparkled at her, along with a slightly crooked smile. A smile that belonged to a pirate. A smile formed by a mouth that promised all things deliciously wicked.

Where on earth had *that* thought come from?

She gave herself a mental shake. She wasn't shopping for a man. She wasn't even window-shopping. Shane had cured her of every romantic notion she'd ever held.

Besides, this man was a husband and a father. He had a wife with beautiful eyes. Perhaps that's why the errant thought had played across her mind. He was an unavailable man and her radar had relaxed.

She returned his smile. 'I think your days are numbered and it won't be Dubbo she'll be demanding, but the shopping delights of Sydney.'

'You're probably right.' His grin faded, chased away by a shadow that flickered across his face as he shoved his large hands into the pockets of his chinos.

'Dad, what do you think?' Sasha reappeared and did a twirl in her matching outfit, her eyes anxiously seeking his approval.

'You look gorgeous, sweetheart.'

Sasha rolled her eyes. 'You *always* say that, Dad, even when I'm splattered in mud after soccer.'

'Well, you do.' The love in his voice radiated around the shop.

Kate tried to ignore the slug of loss that turned over inside her like a lead weight. What would it be like to be loved like that?

'Um, excuse me, but do you think this colour suits me?' Sasha directed her question to Kate.

Kate took in the tanned, healthy glow of the child, her shiny chestnut hair and large, green eyes. 'Your dad's right. That green does suit you.' A streak of mischief shot through her. 'And you know what would look really great with it? One of those new belts and a matching bracelet and necklace. They've got a rack of accessories to match each outfit.' She pointed toward the display.

Sasha's eyes widened as she caught sight of the trinkets. 'Ooh, and bags, too.'

The pirate groaned and shook his dark head, his thick curls shaking in resignation. 'Thanks for that.'

His sarcasm wasn't lost on Kate and she laughed. 'My pleasure. I'm happy to help. Have fun.' She picked up the same vest top for her niece and walked toward the checkout, a sense of lightness dancing through her. It had been a long time since she'd felt so carefree in Warragurra.

For the first time she realised she was ready to go back to work. At work she'd be surrounded by the security of familiar faces and colleagues who understood. Armed with support like that, of course she could cope with the town.

A shimmer of anxiety skated along her veins, which she promptly squashed. After all, how bad could coming back to Warragurra really be?

'I need to talk to you.' Jen, the office manager of the Warragurra Flying Doctors' Base, called to Baden as he walked briskly past her desk.

'Sorry, Jen. Can't do it now, I'm late. Sasha had an excursion and somewhere between home and school the permission slip vanished. I've just debased myself totally, begging the vice-principal to bend the rules and allow her to go,' Baden Tremont called over his shoulder as he quickly checked the contents of his medical bag.

'I'm sure you charmed her with that smile of yours but I need to talk to you about—'

Baden briskly snapped the clasps of his large black bag closed. 'Email me.' He strode toward the door, knowing he was cutting his departure way too fine.

Jen jogged behind him, trying to keep up. 'I already did but it bounced back as undeliverable and I've had to change—'

'Did you tell Emily? She can fill me in on the plane.' His hand connected with the doorhandle.

'Yes, but…' Jen's words disappeared, captured by the hot wind and drowned out by the engine noise that surged inside when Baden opened the door.

Hell, he really was late. The early morning flight from Broken Hill was touching down. The smell of burning rubber seared his nostrils as he stepped out onto the already steaming tarmac.

Jen continued talking despite the noise. 'Emily…Kate… flight…'

He only caught a few fragments of the words over the din but he had no time to stop. 'Is Emily late?'

Jen shook her head and threw her hands up in frustration.

He gave her a grin, one that usually got him out of trouble, waved and mouthed, 'Tell me at three.'

His last glance was Jen muttering as she stomped back inside.

He hated being late. But the balancing act of full-time doctor and full-time single father meant he was frequently late both professionally and personally. Five months ago when he'd moved to Warragurra from Adelaide, he'd thought the move to the country would give him more time. He'd got that wrong. Remote areas were medically under-resourced.

He took the plane's steps two at a time as a familiar thrill zipped through him. Life might not be how he'd imagined it four years ago but being part of the Flying Doctors' team went a long way toward providing him with professional satisfaction. He'd accepted that was how things had to be. His life offered professional satisfaction. He didn't expect anything more.

The plane door closed behind him and he signalled to Glen Jacobs, the pilot, that he'd checked the lock. 'Morning, Emily.' He caught sight of his flight nurse's legs as she leaned into a storage compartment.

Funny, he'd only ever seen Emily wear long trousers. Somehow he hadn't imagined her legs to be quite so shapely. Or as long. Come to think of it, he'd never imagined anything about Emily. She barely made it to five feet four and her uniform always seemed to hang off her, giving her a shapeless look. The only thing he regularly noticed was how her hair changed colour every third week.

He and Emily had been a team since he'd arrived in

Warragurra. Steady and reliable, she had a no-nonsense approach and got the job done. Home was often chaotic and sadness crept around the edges but Emily made work easy. She was like one of the boys. Happy to talk cricket, tennis and car engines, she was often found at the pub on a Friday night beating anyone brave enough to take her on at the pool table.

He heard her muffled greeting and kept talking, his back to her as he stowed his bag. 'What's Jen in a flap about? I thought she was telling me you were late.'

'I think perhaps she was telling you I was Kate.'

He turned abruptly at the rich and throaty yet vaguely familiar voice.

A tall, willowy woman met his gaze. A startled look crossed her face, racing down to bee-stung lips, which compressed slightly before relaxing into a hint of a smile. Large brown eyes, their gaze serious, blinked against a flash of surprise. 'H-hello.'

He guessed he looked equally astonished. Unexpected warmth spread through him at seeing her again. A type of warmth he hadn't experienced in a long time. 'Hello.' He extended his hand. 'I'm Baden Tremont and you cost me an extra forty-five dollars yesterday.'

This time she smiled a full, wide smile and the serious edge in her eyes softened, changing her look completely. 'A girl lives to accessorise, Doctor, didn't you know that?'

He laughed. 'I'm learning fast.'

She stepped forward with natural grace, taking his hand with a firm grip. 'I'm Kate. Nurse Practitioner.'

Her smooth skin glided softly against his palm and his mind emptied. A tingle of sensation shot through him, stirring his blood for the first time since Annie's death.

Shocking him to his toes.

He abruptly dropped her hand. He covered his rudeness by

indicating they should both sit down. 'Pleased to meet you, Kate.' Had she mentioned a surname? He forced a smile. 'Call me Baden. We should buckle up. Sorry to have kept you waiting. Is Emily sick?'

Kate slid into her seat, crossing her long legs. Baden's gaze followed the movement as if hypnotised.

*Stop gawking.* He dragged his gaze away and focussed intently on the buckles of the safety harness wondering what the hell was wrong with him.

'I don't think so. She looked her usual hale and hearty self this morning when she flew out to Barcoo Station with Linton.'

Confusion snagged him. 'Linton Gregory? The doctor in charge of A and E at the base hospital?'

She nodded. 'That's right. A couple of times a year he spends two weeks with us. Emily always accompanies him as she has so much experience. It's a good link between the two organisa-tions. Bridge building never goes astray.' Slender fingers expertly snapped the buckles of the harness in place. She tilted her head. 'You're frowning at me—is something wrong?'

He started at the direct question. 'Um, sorry. It's just this has a surreal feeling of being my first day at a new school where everyone else knows each other and how things work. The only problem is that I'm not the new person, you are.'

She laughed. 'I'm not actually new. I've worked for the Flying Doctors for four years. I saw your name on the email that Jen sent out on Friday outlining the changes, so I assumed you were expecting me. Besides, didn't Emily tell you?'

*Your email bounced back as undeliverable.* Jen had tried to tell him but what about Emily? He racked his brains. 'Come to think of it, on Friday night she did thump me on the back after beating me at pool and said, "Doc, you're a good bloke to work with."'

Kate's mouth broadened into a knowing smile. 'That's Emily's code for saying goodbye.'

A thread of unease vibrated deep inside him. Goodbye? *No.* He wanted to keep working with Emily. Emily was safe and uncomplicated. She didn't stir up sensations he'd forgotten existed. Surely Emily was just spending a couple of weeks with Linton as part of the bridge-building exercise.

Of course, that was it. Just a temporary change.

Once he'd embraced the exhilaration of change. He used to actively seek it out, loving to juggle up the mix. But when Annie had got sick, uncertainty had marched into their life, changing it for ever. Now he craved stability for himself and Sasha. Especially for Sasha.

Of course he could cope for a fortnight working with a tall and slender colleague even if her standard-issue blue blouse seemed to hug her in all the right places. She was a nurse, just like Emily. He swallowed a sigh as he caught sight of her toned calves. He didn't suppose it was PC to suggest she wear trousers rather than shorts.

The engines burst into life, their noise immediately killing the conversation. Baden lifted his green headphones over his ears and adjusted the black mouthpiece so he could hear any last-minute instructions from Glen.

He loved take-off. Loved the roar of the engines, the thrust of power, the torque and the pressure against his chest as acceleration increased and the plane tilted for its fast climb. It gave him an endorphin rush every single time. He forgot his unease and relaxed into the power surge.

The red earth of the outback opened out underneath them, endless red sand bound together by green-grey spinifex. A ute far below sent up a plume of dust into the cloudless blue sky as it travelled along a straight road. Kangaroos bounded with purpose in the cool of the morning. In an hour or so they'd be sheltering in the shade of the gnarled gum trees that clearly marked the winding path of the muddy Darling River, once the transportation lifeline of outback New South Wales.

It took a lot of imagination to picture the 'river jam' of a century ago. One hundred paddle steamers had plied the river, their barges groaning with bales of wool as they'd connected the outback stations with the southern cities. In today's drought, the river was a trickle of its former glory.

He glanced across at Kate. Her eyes sparkled and her face glowed as she peered out the window, her fingers spread against the Perspex. She didn't look like an experienced flight nurse. She looked like a child on her first flight.

She turned away from the window and caught him staring at her. She gave an embarrassed shrug and spoke into her mouthpiece. 'I love the view.'

'It's pretty spectacular if you're not into green, rolling hills.'

She nodded. 'I've been in Europe and although I adored the greenness, I've just realised how much I missed this view. There's a certain rugged beauty about scrubby vegetation and red sand.'

Surprise snagged him. It was like putting together a difficult jigsaw puzzle. Right up to this point he'd thought she was a transfer from another base. 'You've seen this view before?'

'Oh, yes, lots of times.' She picked up a procedures folder as if she was going to read rather than talk.

He tried to ignore the irrational feeling of being overlooked. 'But not recently?'

She shook her head, her chestnut bob caressing her cheeks, highlighting the fine line of her jaw. She seemed to hesitate before speaking. 'I've been away for six months. Today is my first day back.'

Suddenly things started to line up in his brain. He vaguely remembered seeing the name Kate Kennedy on orientation documents when he'd first started. It had caught his attention because the Kennedy name meant money in Warragurra. The family construction company built or renovated just about every substantial public building in the town and had contracts on many of the cattle stations.

That's why she hadn't mentioned her last name when she'd introduced herself—typical Warragurra style. His brief experience with the three prominent families in town had been the same. They all assumed you knew them by the nature of their community standing. 'We must have just missed each other. I started in September last year. So you must be Kate Kennedy?'

Her jaw stiffened slightly, the tremor running down her neck and along her arm. 'My surname is Lawson.' The words snapped out, matching the flash of fire in her eyes. Her body language brooked no argument. It clearly said, Get it right and don't ask why.

He recognised her posture. He'd used it often enough himself to deflect questions. But it was a strong response over a name. Perhaps Lawson was her professional name? A lot of his female colleagues retained their maiden names for work.

He let it slide, wanting to establish some working esprit de corps. 'You must have left just before I arrived in Warragurra. Welcome back, Kate.'

'Thanks.' Her eyes softened. A wistful tone entered her voice. 'I hope it's going to be good.'

'Coming back from a long break is always a bit of an adjustment.' He remembered how tough it had been when he'd returned to work after Annie's death. All those sympathetic faces. He pushed the memory away. 'Still, two weeks working with me will be a good way to ease back into the routine and then you'll be set to take over your usual clinic runs.'

She blinked twice and her smooth brow creased in a fine line. 'This is my usual run.'

His gut tightened, his unease strengthening. 'But Emily—'

'Was filling in for me while I was on leave.'

Her quiet words exploded like a bomb in his brain. *No. No.* He didn't want this. 'So you and I, we're now Flight Team Four?'

'We are.' She smiled again.

Her enthusiastic vibes radiated around him, sparking off a trail of heat that coursed through him, completely disconcerting him. His mind creaked to the inevitable, unwanted conclusion. 'And Emily has been reassigned?'

'She has.'

'Right.' The tightness of his throat strangled the word. *Think.* This wasn't really a problem. He'd just ask for another nurse.

The booming voice of the regional director sounded in his head. *Teamwork is the key. Get your hormones under control and deal with it.*

A shadow floated through Kate's caramel-brown eyes before resignation pushed it aside. She laced her hands in her lap. 'I'm sorry this change of roster caught you by surprise but I'm sure it won't take too long for us to get used to each other.' She gave a throaty laugh. 'After all, I don't bite.'

An image of her lush, red lips and her white teeth nibbling his neck slammed into him.

This wasn't happening. He didn't react like this to women. He couldn't. For years he'd seen women as colleagues, employees, sisters, mothers, friends. He packaged women into neat, safe boxes.

And that was exactly what he had to do now. Find a box for

Kate. She would go into the workbox. And it would be a very secure, firm box with a lid that would not open.

He could do that. Of course he could do that.

How hard could it be?

# CHAPTER TWO

KATE twisted open the top of a bottle of ice-cold water and drank half of the contents in one go. After recapping the bottle, she ran it across the back of her neck, savouring the coolness against her hot skin. She glanced out toward the endless burnt brown paddocks and beyond to the horizon which blurred with shimmering heat. Cattle clustered under the few available scrubby trees, seeking shade in the midday heat.

Coming out of a European winter and straight back into a Warragurra summer was like crashing into a brick wall, except the wall was all-encompassing, energy-draining heat. She must be mad. She should have delayed her return and spent two more months in France and Italy. But Warragurra was home. At least it had been, and she planned to make it home again no matter what anyone else thought.

'Hot one for you today, Kate.' Barry Sanderson, the taciturn owner of Camoora Station, lifted his hat and ran his forearm across his sweaty brow.

Kate smiled. She'd missed the ironic understatement of the Australian outback. It was *always* hot in February in western New South Wales. 'It's a stinker. Thanks for giving me the shadiest spot on the veranda for my baby clinic.'

'You know for as long as Mary and I are here, you're *always* welcome at Camoora.' Understanding crossed his weatherworn face before his voice became gruff, as if he'd exposed too much of his feelings. 'Besides, we can't have those babies overheated.'

'Thanks, Barry.' She continued swiftly, not wanting to embarrass him but grateful for his support. 'I'd better get back to work. Can't have the new doc beating me on my first day back.'

Barry put his hat back on his head. 'You make sure you have some tea and scones with Mary sooner rather than later.' He strode down the long veranda of the homestead, stopping to talk to Baden.

Kate watched the interchange—the stocky bushman and the tall, athletic doctor. Baden was as dark as Barry was fair. She'd been stunned this morning when he'd turned around and faced her on the plane. Yesterday's pirate was a doctor.

A disconcerted doctor. He'd looked almost worried when he'd realised the two of them were now Team Four. That had thrown her. She was used to all sorts of expressions from half the town—disdain, hatred and loathing. But work was different. At work she was valued, admired, respected. Or at least she had been.

Teamwork was the basis of the Flying Doctors. The working day meant a lot of time was spent with your team colleague. She'd hoped to resume working with Doug Johnston, but he'd transferred to Muttawindi two months ago covering Bronte Morrison's maternity leave. He wouldn't be back in Warragurra for a year.

*We must have just missed each other. I started in September last year.* Her stomach dropped as she recalled Baden's words. He and his family would have arrived in Warragurra just as the Kennedys had finally realised they had no legal standing to contest Shane's will. Just as the vitriol in the local press had reached its zenith. In many circles in the town her name was mud. Perhaps Baden's wife had heard the rumours and not heard the truth.

Tension tugged at her temples with a vice-like grip. Work was her sanctuary while she found her feet again in the town. She must make this assignment with Baden work. Only her actions could dissolve rumours and innuendo. She had to prove to him she was a professional who could be relied on, a team player. Someone he could depend on as much as he'd obviously depended on Emily.

She watched him walk along the veranda toward her, his moleskins moving against his thighs, outlining hard muscle. 'Ah, the baby clinic.' He rubbed his hands together. 'It's one of my favourites.' His smile raced across his face, lighting his eyes, making them sparkle with anticipation.

His smile sent her blood racing to her feet, making her feel light-headed. 'I know what you mean. A roly-poly baby, healthy on breast milk reaffirms that life is good.'

They quickly established a pattern of weighing and measuring babies, reassuring anxious mothers and immunizing babies against childhood illnesses. Kate dealt with any breast-feeding issues and Baden examined the babies with reflux.

With companionable teamwork and a lot of laughter they tested the hearing of all the eight-month-old babies. Baden entertained each mother and baby with his Peter the Penguin puppet, while Kate shook the rattle behind the baby's ears.

Baden's experience as a father came through as he managed to relax the mums and the babies with the antics of the hand puppet. Kate imagined he would have read great stories to Sasha, complete with a cast of voices for the characters.

In the distance a child's scream rent the air as Kate called her next mother and baby.

'Looks like we might be patching yet another knee and dispensing a lollypop,' Baden commented as he filled in an immunisation record.

Kate nodded. 'I think that will be number six for the day. Gravel paths and toddlers don't really mix.' She turned and called her next patient. 'So, Ginny, how's baby Samantha going?'

Ginny cuddled the baby in close. 'Pretty well, although I think she's been having a growth spurt as she's been feeding a lot.'

Kate checked Samantha's date of birth. 'Well, at six weeks you'd expect—'

'Help me! Will someone help me?' A woman's frantic voice carried across the yard, her distress palpable.

'Sorry, Ginny.' Kate spun around, reaching for the emergency kit, her hand colliding with Baden's.

He grasped the handle. 'I've got it. Follow me.'

He ran down the veranda as Mary Sanderson came into view, carrying her four-year-old daughter. Her eldest daughter, Kelly, ran close behind.

Blood covered the little girl's face as she lay whimpering in her mother's arms. 'What happened?' Baden gently guided the woman into a seat.

'She was feeding the chooks with her big sister, like she does every afternoon. Kelly said she heard Susie scream and she turned around to find the rooster had knocked her flat. I can't believe a rooster could knock a child over.' Incredulity marked her face. 'I've spent all my life on a farm and I've never seen that happen.'

Kelly bit her lip. 'The rooster was on Susie's chest and pecking her and I ran at it but it wouldn't let go. I threw the bucket at it but while I was picking her up it flew at her again.' She gave a quiet sob. 'It was really scary.'

Kate squeezed Kelly's shoulder. 'You did a great job, Kelly. Dr Baden and I will soon have the blood cleaned up and it won't look so scary.' She opened up normal saline and began to clean Susie's face with gauze so they could clearly see the extent of the damage.

Susie's petrified screams pulled at her. The little girl's face seemed to be swelling under Kate's fingers as she wiped the blood away. Her puffy eyes were slits in her face and her cheeks were increasing in size.

Baden's long fingers gently sought a pulse in the wriggling child's neck, which he counted against the second hand of his watch. 'Susie, I'm just going to listen to your chest with my stethoscope.' He bent down so he was at the same level as the little girl and showed her the round end that would lie against her chest.

Susie's crying halted for a moment but then she started to cough—probably induced by the hysterical screaming. The coughing eased and she lay exhausted in her mother's arms.

Apprehension skated through Kate as her trauma radar tuned in. Something wasn't quite right. Superficial lacerations didn't usually cause swelling like this. As she grabbed more gauze she caught Baden's worried expression.

He felt it, too—the aura of disquiet seemed to blanket them both.

She quickly and deftly used the gauze to clean away the large amount of blood on the child's neck. Blood oozed out as fast as she could clear it. 'Baden.' She hoped he could decode the tone of her voice.

He immediately pulled the earpiece out of his ear, his concentration firmly on her. 'Yes?'

'There's a really deep wound on her throat and her neck is swelling fast. I'm worried about her airway.'

'So am I. Her air entry is diminished.'

'What do you mean?' Mary's voice wobbled. 'It's just a few scratches, isn't it?'

Baden carefully examined Susie's throat, his fingers gently palpating around the base of her throat. 'There's air under her skin.'

'Air? That can't be good.' Kate reached for the walkie-talkie.

He rubbed the back of his neck. 'It's subcutaneous emphysema. I think the rooster has perforated her trachea—the tube that takes the air to the lungs—and now air is escaping into the skin.'

Mary's hand flew to her own throat. 'Can she breathe?'

'She's breathing on her own at the moment but the risk is that the bleeding and swelling will block the tube. We're going to have to get her stable and then evacuate her to hospital.'

Kate immediately called Glen on the walkie-talkie. 'We need the stretcher, Glen. Susie Sanderson needs oxygen and evacuation, over.'

'On my way, over.' Glen's voice crackled into the dry, hot air.

Mary, her eyes wide with fear, looked frantically at them both as Baden's words finally sank in. 'She'll go to Warragurra Hospital, won't she?'

'No, I'm sorry but she needs to go to the Women's and Children's Hospital in Adelaide.' He rested his hand on Mary's for a brief moment. 'I'm going to need to examine her fully.'

'Glen's on his way with the stretcher, which will double as a treatment bed.' Kate pulled out the paediatric oxygen mask and unravelled the green tubing, making it all ready to connect the moment the stretcher and oxygen arrived.

'Give us a hand, Kate.'

Glen's voice hailed her from the bottom of the stairs. She quickly ran to meet him and helped to lift the stretcher up onto the veranda.

Baden's strong arms gently transferred Susie onto the stretcher, sitting her up to aid her laboured breathing. 'Kate's going to put a mask on you to help you feel better and Mummy's here to hold your hand.'

His tenderness with Susie touched Kate. Not all doctors were at ease with kids. But he was a father and had probably spent a few nights walking the floor.

'I want a drink,' Susie sobbed between fits of jagged crying.

Kate adjusted the clear mask to Susie's face, making sure it was a snug fit by pulling on the green elastic. 'I'm sorry, sweetie, you can't have a drink but I'm going to give you a drink in your arm.' Kate checked with Baden. 'Normal saline IV?'

He nodded, a flash of approval in his eyes. 'Yes, saline. You all right to insert it?' He paused for a moment in his examination of Susie's back.

For a brief moment she was tempted to say no. She'd been out of the field for six months and Shane's parents' campaign against her had dented her confidence. But she had to show Baden she was a team player and totally reliable. 'Sure, no problem.'

*You've done this hundreds of times. Don't let the Kennedys invade work.*

'Susie, this will sting just a little bit, OK? You squeeze Mummy's hand really tight.' She adjusted the tourniquet and palpated for a vein. Her fingers detected a small rise and she swabbed the little girl's arm, the alcohol stinging her nostrils.

'OK, here we go.' Carefully she slid the intravenous cannula into the vein, controlling the pressure so there was enough to pierce the skin but not too much that she put the needle through the vein.

'Mummy, stop her,' Susie squealed as the needle penetrated the skin.

Kate bit her lip. 'Nearly there, Susie.' Holding her breath, she withdrew the trocar. Blood.

*Yes.* She released her breath and taped the needle in place. 'IV inserted, Baden.'

He gave her a wide smile of acknowledgment—a smile that raced to his vivid blue eyes and caused them to crinkle at the edges.

A smile that melted something inside her and sent spirals of molten warmth through her, reaching all the way down to her toes.

*Stop it.* Thank goodness he was married and off limits. Otherwise that smile could batter all her resolutions about staying single. She found her voice. 'Do you want a bolus of three hundred millilitres?'

'Yes, good idea. I'm worried about bleeding.'

'What about pain relief?' It was a tricky situation.

'Morphine would be good for the pain so she would be more comfortable and start to breathe more easily, but it also depresses the respiratory system. It's catch-22.' He frowned and rubbed the back of his neck, the same action he'd used when he'd told Mary about the perforated trachea. 'We'll titrate it in through the IV and that way we can control it and pull it if we need to.'

'Mary?' Kate got her attention. 'How much does Susie weigh? I need as accurate a weight as possible.'

The distraught mother spoke slowly. 'I… It's been a while since I weighed her but she'd be about twenty kilograms, I think.'

'Baden?' He'd lifted her onto the stretcher.

He nodded. 'That's about right.' He gave Susie's knee a rub. 'You weigh the same as the sacks of flour I buy to make bread.'

Susie gave a wan smile.

Kate calculated the dose. 'So two milligrams of morphine.'

'Correct.' Baden checked the dose with her as mandated by the Dangerous Drug Act.

He called to Glen. 'We need to go.' He rested his hand on Mary's shoulder. 'Are you or Barry coming with us or will you follow on your own?'

'Mary's going with Susie.' Barry's gruff voice cracked on the words. 'I'm going to go and kill that bloody rooster.'

'After you've done that, pack them both a case, Barry, and we'll radio you when we get back to Warragurra.' Kate hugged the usually stoic man and ran down the steps.

Kate gave thanks that the airstrip at Camoora Station was very close to the homestead. Station hands, their dusty faces lined with anxiety, carried the stretcher as if it were porcelain, avoiding jolting the adored Susie, hoping their care would help.

Seven minutes after Baden had issued the order to depart, the PC-12 aircraft was racing down the dusty runway.

Kate did the first set of in-flight observations. Susie's heart was racing and her breathing rapid and shallow. 'She's tachycardic and tachypnoeic,' she informed Baden sotto voce the moment he signed off from the radio conversation with the paediatric registrar in Adelaide.

He placed his stethoscope on Susie's back and listened intently. 'Nothing is getting into the lower lobe of her left lung.' Deep furrows scored his forehead as he leant across her to check the IV.

The fragrance of spicy aftershave mixing with his masculine scent filled Kate's nostrils and she wanted to breathe in deeply. Instead, she deliberately leaned back and concentrated on filling in the fluid balance chart. 'Are you thinking pneumothorax?'

'I'm certain the lower lobe of her lung has collapsed but at the moment her body's compensating. I'm not rushing into a needle thoracentesis without X-ray guidance unless I have to.' He shook his head in disbelief. 'It was such a brutal attack. I can't believe a rooster's beak could cause such damage.'

'It wouldn't have been the beak. It was the spur on the foot. They're viciously sharp.'

He raised his brows. 'You seem to know a bit about poultry.'

She shrugged. 'Born and raised a country girl. What about you?'

'City boy. Grew up on the Adelaide beaches.'

She laughed. 'Linton would say that Adelaide and city was an oxymoron.'

Baden raised his brows. 'From Sydney, is he?' He chuckled. 'I'll have you know that peak hour lasts half an hour.'

His rich laugh relaxed her. 'Peak hour in Warragurra is Saturday night when the station hands drive into town. Even from Adelaide it's a big leap.' She checked Susie's pulse. 'What brought you here?'

'It was something I'd talked about doing for a long time.' He had a far-away look in his eyes as if he was recalling memories.

She jotted down the volume of the new bag of IV fluid that she had just attached to Susie's drip. 'And suddenly the time seemed right?'

His relaxed demeanour instantly vanished. 'Something like that.' His voice developed an edge to it, a tone she'd not heard before.

Before she could wonder too much about what that might mean, Susie started coughing. Kate immediately aspirated her mouth but the child continued to gasp, her lips turning blue.

'She's obstructing!' She snapped opened the laryngoscope, the tiny light bulb glowing white. 'Intubation?'

'What's happening?' Mary's petrified voice sounded from her seat at the front of the plane.

'We have to put a tube in Susie's throat so she can breathe.' Kate wanted to go and hug the distraught mother but all her attention was needed for Susie.

Mary's gasp of horror echoed around the plane.

Baden accepted the laryngoscope, a grim expression on his face. 'I doubt I'll be able to pass the tube through the swelling.' He tried inserting the 'scope but a moment later shook his head. 'No go.'

Kate's stomach dropped and she swung into emergency

action. 'Right, then. Tracheostomy it is.' She opened the paediatric emergency cricothyroidotomy kit, which she'd had ready since they'd boarded the flight.

Susie's small chest struggled to rise and fall, each breath more torturous than the last.

Baden snapped on gloves and grabbed the scalpel.

A sharp incessant beeping from the monitor hammered the air as Susie's oxygen saturation levels started to fall to dangerously low levels. Each beep told them Susie was edging closer to cardiac arrest.

'Save my daughter, please!'

Mary's tortured plea ripped through Kate. She quickly laid the semi-conscious child on her back and extended her neck.

Baden threw her a look, his eyes dark with worry. This procedure on a child was fraught with danger but they had no choice. With a remarkably steady hand he gently palpated Susie's neck, counting down the rings of cartilage until he found the correct position. He made a quick, clean cut.

Kate immediately cleared the area of blood with a gauze pad. She pulled the sterile packaging of the endotracheal tube halfway down, exposing the top of the tube and insertion trocar.

Baden juggled the forceps and then grabbed the tube, sliding it into place.

Kate swiftly attached the oxygen. A moment later the monitor stopped screaming as Susie's oxygen level rose. A sigh shuddered out of Kate's lungs as she injected normal saline into the balloon of the ET tube to hold it in place.

Baden raised his head from his patient and turned toward Mary. 'We've bypassed the blockage and she's breathing more easily now.'

Mary slumped. 'Oh, thank you, Baden. Kate. I was so scared that she might…'

Baden nodded. 'She'll probably have to go to Theatre when we arrive in Adelaide to repair her lung and trachea, and when the swelling has subsided, this tube can come out.'

He turned back to Kate and spoke under his breath. 'So much for a quiet first day back at work for you. Nothing like an emergency to pump the adrenaline around.' He stripped off his gloves. 'Thanks, Kate. That was excellent work.' His lips curved upward in a friendly smile. 'It's good to have you on board.'

'Thanks. It's good to be back.' Delicious, simmering warmth rolled through her, quickly overtaken by sheer relief. She'd managed to drive away his doubts, the ones that had shone so brightly that morning in his amazing eyes.

Her plan had worked. She'd shown him she knew what she was about, that her medicine was sound. She'd managed to stay one stop ahead of him during the emergency and at times their anticipation of each other's needs had been almost spooky.

For the first time all day she relaxed. Team Four would be OK. Work would again be the safe sanctuary it had always been—reliable and familiar. No surprises.

Smiling to herself, she adjusted Susie's oxygen and started to dress her lacerations with non-stick gauze.

'Prepare for landing.' Glen's command sounded in her ears and with one final check of Susie she took her seat, snapping her harness firmly around her.

The paediatric team met them at the airport in Adelaide and within minutes Susie and Mary were on their way to hospital and the ICU unit.

As always happened after a high-powered emergency, Kate's legs began to wobble. Coffee. She needed coffee. The refrigerated air of the airport terminal hit her the moment she stepped inside. She ordered three coffees to go and some giant cookies so heavily laden with chocolate chips you could hardly see the actual cookie base. Juggling the capped coffees and her bag of treats, she headed back toward the plane. Glen usually liked to get back in the air as soon as possible.

As she approached she saw Baden striding back and forth across the tarmac, his mobile phone glued to his ear and his other hand rubbing his neck. Agitation rolled off him in waves—a total contrast to the cool and level-headed doctor she'd just worked with in an emergency.

He snapped the phone shut just as she stopped beside him. She passed him his coffee.

'Oh, thanks.' He accepted the coffee with a distracted air.

'Let's move under the wing—at least there's shade there.' She offered him a cookie as they took the five steps into the shadow of the plane. 'Is there a problem?'

He blew out a breath. 'Sasha is refusing to go to after-school care. She's never done this before, she's always been happy to go. I don't know why she had to pull this stunt today, the one day in weeks I've been delayed.'

Confusion befuddled her brain. 'Why is the school ringing *you*?'

He shot her a look of incredulity that screamed she was an imbecile. 'Because I'm her father!'

His frustration hit her in the chest like a ball on the full, almost making her stagger. Rattled, she chose her words carefully. 'Yes, I understand that, but you're in Adelaide and your wife's in Warragurra. Surely she can get away from work for half an hour to talk to Sasha?'

His hand tightened on the cookie, sending crumbs tumbling toward the ground. 'I don't have a wife. It's just Sasha and me.' His phone rang loudly and he spun away to answer it.

*I don't have a wife.* He'd spoken the words softly but they boomed in Kate's head as if she were standing in front of a

500-watt concert speaker. The five small words tangled in her brain like knotted fishing wire, refusing to straighten out and make sense.

He was a single parent.

Questions surged through her, desperate for answers, but Baden had his back to her, his entire being focussed on the phone call.

She watched him end his call and consult with Glen, his dark curly hair, flecked with grey, moving in the wind. Then he tilted his head back, downing his coffee in two gulps, his Adam's apple moving convulsively against his taut neck. Crushing the empty cup in his strong hand, he swung around, his free arm beckoning her forward.

As she drew up beside him he stood back to allow her entry to the plane's steps. 'Glen's ready to leave, so after you…' His eyes sparkled as he gave her a resigned smile. A Pirate smile. Delicious and dangerous.

Her blood rushed to her feet as realisation hit her. *He's not married.* Together they were Team Four. They had to work side by side every day. The attraction she'd easily shrugged off yesterday and earlier today suddenly surged through her like water through a narrow gorge—powerful and strong.

The safe sanctuary that was work, the sanctuary she so desperately needed, vaporised before her eyes.

Baden stacked the dishwasher, his thoughts not on the china but on trying to come up with the best approach to handle Sasha's rebellion. She'd made herself scarce, knowing he wasn't thrilled with her behaviour. He could see her out the window, jumping on the trampoline, her long brown hair streaming out behind her.

*It's chestnut, like Kate's.* The unexpected thought thudded into him, startling him.

Kate had worked alongside him today as if she'd done it every day for a year. Calm, experienced and knowledgeable, she got the job done. Just like Emily. Except Emily didn't wear a perfume that conjured up hot tropical nights and sinful pleasures.

He slammed the dishwasher closed. What was he doing, thinking of Kate, when his concentration should be firmly on Sasha? Guilt niggled at him. He'd promised Annie that Sasha would always be his top priority. Hell, it was no hardship. He adored his daughter. But he missed sharing the parenting journey.

Sasha had finished on the trampoline and was lying in the hammock, which was permanently slung between two veranda posts. It had been a much-adored Christmas present and had saved him from buying the requested pink mobile phone, which he planned to put off for as long as possible.

He pushed the fly-wire screen door open and walked toward her. 'I thought you might like an ice cream.'

Sasha looked up and swung her legs over the side of the hammock, taking the proffered confectionary. 'Cool. I didn't know we had any of these left.'

'I went shopping.' He sat down next to her, his weight sending the hammock swinging wildly, causing Sasha to fall onto him.

'Da-ad,' she rebuked him, but stayed snuggled up next to him, the back of her head resting on his chest. Ice cream dribbled down her chin.

His heart lurched. In so many ways she was still his little girl, but for how long? The signs of impending puberty were beginning to shout. 'Sash, why did you give Mrs Davidson such a hard time this afternoon?'

She licked her ice cream. 'I didn't want to go to after-school care.'

'That bit I understand. It's why you didn't want to go that's bothering me.'

'It's for babies.' A belligerent tone crept into her voice.

He breathed in and focussed on keeping his words neutral and even. 'It's for all kids from prep to grade six.'

'But I'm twelve and can look after myself after school.'

He gave an internal sigh. 'We've had this discussion before, Sash, and because work is sometimes unpredictable and I occasionally have to transport patients to Broken Hill, Dubbo or Adelaide, I need to know that you're safe.'

'But I'd be safe here.' She turned, her earnest green eyes imploring him to understand. 'Besides, Erin isn't going any more. Her mum stopped working and she's getting to do cool stuff, like going to Guides on Wednesdays and swimming on Fridays.'

He ran his hand through his hair. Erin Baxter and Sasha were inseparable friends. Without Erin's company, after-school care would seem like jail. All the other children who attended were in the junior classes at the school. 'Why didn't you tell me Erin wasn't there?'

She shrugged. 'You would have said I still had to go and I hate it without her. There's no one to hang out with. I wish that…I wish I could just come home after school.'

Her unspoken words hovered around them both, pulling at him, twisting his guilt. Before Annie's death Sasha had always been able to come home straight after school.

'I'm sorry I'm not here after school and I'm sorry Mum's not here.' He hugged her tight. 'What if I talk to Erin's mum and ask if she would mind taking you to swimming, too? I have Wednesday afternoons in the office so if we find out what time Guides is on, perhaps I can take you. That only leaves three days of after-school care. Deal?'

Her eyes danced with joy. 'Deal. Thanks, Dad.'

He swung his legs into the hammock and lay down next to her. 'You're welcome, sweetheart.' Another crisis solved. Work was uncomplicated and straightforward compared to this parenting gig.

Sasha cuddled in closer now her ice cream was finished. 'Did Emily have purple hair today?' She'd always been impressed by Emily's extremely short rainbow-coloured hair.

He stretched out, enjoying the companionable time with his daughter. 'Actually, Emily isn't working with me at the moment. Do you remember that lady we met when we were buying your new green top? Well, it turns out she's my flight nurse now.'

'Awesome. She had the best smile and a gorgeous skirt.' Sasha propped herself up with one elbow resting on his chest. Her serious gaze searched his face. 'What's she like?'

'She's very good at her job.'

'Yeah, but do you *like* her?' Hope crossed her face.

Unlike adults, kids always cut to the chase, but even so Sasha's unexpected wishful look, combined with the question hit him hard in the chest. To a twelve-year-old, *like* was serious stuff.

Did he *like* Kate? The image of luminous brown eyes, as warm as melted chocolate, filled his head. A streak of unexpected longing shot through him.

Disloyalty followed closely, jagged and sharp.

He sat up abruptly, setting the hammock swinging wildly. He wasn't up to discussing this with Sasha when his reaction to Kate confused the hell out of him. He rolled out of the hammock and stretched his arms down for her. 'Time for bed.'

'Da-ad.'

He hauled her out of the hammock. 'Come on, hop it. Clean your teeth and get into bed. Otherwise you'll never get *Anne of Green Gables* finished.'

The promise of reading time had Sasha dashing for the door, her question about Kate forgotten.

A long breath shuddered out of his lungs. If only he could find Kate that easy to forget.

# CHAPTER THREE

'So is everyone clear on the rosters?' Jen's right hand rested firmly on her hip as she looked expectantly at the staff. 'Team Four, your roster has changed a lot so you *must* make sure you have the most up-to-date version.' She narrowed her gaze at Baden. 'The email system is back online and I expect you to check it.' Jen ran a tight ship, holding together a staff of twenty strong personalities.

Everyone nodded and those brave enough even mumbled, 'Yes, Jen.'

'Right, then, thanks for your attention.' Jen tapped a pile of brightly coloured files. 'Please collect a folder on the way out.'

Baden winked at Kate. 'We'd better check our emails.'

'I think that line was directed solely at you. I've still got brownie points up my sleeve.' She couldn't resist teasing him. 'After all, it wasn't me who drove out to Opal Ridge for a clinic on the wrong day.'

A sheepish grin crossed his face. 'Lucky for me old Hughie chose that day to have a hypo so it wasn't a complete waste of time. Now he's completely up to speed with his new glucometer.' He faked a serious expression, the corners of his eyes crinkling with humour. 'Patient education is a very important part of our work, Sister Lawson.'

Laughter rolled through her at his self-deprecating humour, bringing a joy that had faded from her life. 'Is that right, Doctor? I had no idea.'

His laughter joined hers and quickly raced to his eyes, which sparkled like sunshine on water. His work-issue blue shirt intensified the vivid blue of his eyes and enhanced his tanned face. Not to mention the way his chest filled the shirt, making the fabric sit flat against what she imagined was solid muscle.

Her stomach flipped as heat rolled thorough her. *Stop it now.* She crossed her legs, trying to halt the tingling sensations that built up inside her.

It was too depressing to be twenty-nine and reacting like a sixteen-year-old. She was too old for a hormone crush. Too world-weary to have stars in her eyes and too bruised to ever think romance was for her. But her body wasn't listening.

It didn't seem to matter that she'd spoken sternly to herself, that she'd instructed her body *not* to react and that she'd willed herself to be impervious to eyes that sparkled with every shade of blue. It took one smile and her body quivered in anticipation.

She stood up and joined the queue behind Linton and Emily to collect the folder as instructed.

'So, Doc, you thought you'd do a spot of opal fossicking the other day.' Emily immediately teased Baden about his mistake.

'Yeah, and I found one this big.' He held his hands a shoulder width apart. 'But it got away when Hughie hypo'd.'

Kate let the laughter and camaraderie wash over her, savouring it. Wednesday afternoon meant staff meeting. All the teams were back in the office after morning clinics to attend. They took it in turns being the standby emergency team, but it wasn't very often that there was a Wednesday afternoon emergency. It was almost as if the locals knew not to get sick after 1:00 p.m.

If they did get a callout it was usually from tourists who'd got themselves into a spot of bother.

With the exception of the staff meeting, Wednesday was pretty much a Baden-free day. Kate ran an early well-women's clinic in the morning before returning to base for the afternoon.

It had been a relief to work on her own this morning, giving her over-developed radar of Baden a rest. It wasn't that she didn't enjoy working with him. She did. She'd loved her first two days with him. He was on the ball medically, good-humoured most of the time, and he related really well to the patients. But this overwhelming attraction that whizzed through her whenever she was near him was wearing her out.

It was crazy stuff. He was her colleague. She should be noticing how thorough he was with the patients, learning from him as he passed on clinical skills, taking advantage of the way he treated her as an equal, seeking her opinion in tricky cases. And on one level she was doing all those things.

But on another level she was very aware of the way he twirled his pen when he was thinking. How strands of silver hair caressed his temples in stark contrast to the rest of his raven curls, and how his deep, rich laugh was as smooth and velvety as a cellared shiraz.

And she kept wondering how he'd come to be a single father. Where was Sasha's mother?

Was he divorced? Perhaps they'd never married. All the different permutations and combinations ran through her head. Baden hadn't volunteered any more information and the opportunity to ask more direct questions hadn't arisen. She supposed she could ask Emily but it seemed a bit tacky, almost like prying. She'd been on the other end of that. Her life had been pried into, opened up and peeled back like a sardine can. She didn't intend to inflict that invasion of privacy on anyone.

'Are you coming for coffee, Kate?' Linton paused by the door. The 'cappuccino club' met straight after the staff meeting each week. 'We've got Florentines.' His expression of delight made him look like a kid who had just discovered Mum had filled the cookie jar.

She glanced at her watch. Four o'clock—the meeting had run late. Wednesday evening was Guides. She'd been a Guide leader for a couple of years and tonight was her second night back after her break.

She didn't want to be late, especially as one of the Guides had asked if she could bring a friend. That was great as the pack could do with more members. The Kennedy clan had pressured some families to withdraw their daughters and some had capitulated. Others had stayed, although they refused to help out, but she was sticking with it. There were three supportive parents and now she was back she planned to rebuild. Guides would be so much fun that the girls of Warragurra would be begging their parents to attend and to get involved. 'Sorry, I'll have to pass this week. Save me a Florentine.'

Linton nodded and disappeared down the hall with Emily.

She picked up her folder and handed one to Baden. 'Aren't you going for coffee either?'

Baden shook his head. 'I promised Sasha no after-school care on Wednesdays.'

She smiled. 'Negotiated a midweek deal, did you, to sweeten the rest of the week?'

Surprise rippled across his face. 'Something like that. I guess I have to accept she's growing up and perhaps growing out of after-school care, but she's not grown up enough to be on her own.'

Kate nodded slowly, understanding his dilemma. 'It's a tricky age. School holidays must be really tough for you.' *What about Sasha's mother?* She bit off the specific question that gnawed at her. 'Can extended family help you?'

'My parents visit in the holidays.' The words came out curtly, as if they were meant to discourage a response.

He did that occasionally—lurched from extremely friendly to completely closed down whenever the conversation turned to personal things. A few times she'd been on the point of asking if Sasha might like to join Guides, but he always swung the conversation back to work and kept it firmly centred on the job.

*Except when he told you he wasn't married.*

She thought back to Monday when they'd been in Adelaide. He'd closed down then when he'd told her that, just like he'd closed down now. For whatever reason, he didn't want to talk about Sasha's mother. Perhaps his relationship with her had been as disastrous as hers had with Shane. If it had been, she could totally understand why he avoided the topic. But that didn't help her rampant curiosity. She hated the fact she wanted to know about this woman and the more he deflected the topic, the more she wanted to know.

He walked to the door, pushing it open for her. She ducked under his arm, her shoulder brushing against him. Tingling pleasure pulsated through her, the sensations intensifying as they dived deeper and unfurled like ribbons in the breeze. Her body's reaction to an inadvertent touch was way out of proportion and she tried to shrug the sensations away. Finally, the tingling receded, leaving her bewildered and unsettled.

As they walked down the corridor she concentrated on work, trying to ignore the maelstrom of emotions churning inside her. 'Have you heard from the Women's and Children's in Adelaide?'

He nodded. 'Susie's doing well. She's out of ICU and will probably be transferred to Warragurra tomorrow.'

'Thank goodness. Mary and Barry will be so relieved.'

'Yes, it was a good outcome.' He paused outside his office. 'See you tomorrow, then.'

'Yes, see you tomorrow. 'Night.' She moved toward the door. Thank goodness she could leave the office now. She didn't have to face working with Baden until tomorrow morning. And all her attention for the next few hours would be on the Guides, which would completely block any errant thoughts of a tall, curly-haired doctor.

An hour later she'd negotiated the supermarket, bought a giant container of maple syrup, set up three trestle tables and plugged in a couple of electric frypans. She crossed her fingers that the old hall's fusebox would cope with the power drain.

She checked her watch. Sandra, her assistant, was usually here by now.

The Guides started arriving and she gave them setting-up tasks, keeping them busy.

'Hi, Kate, Mum's sent some eggs from the farm.' Phoebe Walton put a dozen eggs on the trestle table. 'She says you have to take any leftover eggs home.'

'Thanks, Phoebe. Can you head into the kitchen and help Hannah and Jessica in their quest for cooking utensils?'

'Sure.' Phoebe headed to the kitchen.

'I remembered the lemons!' Erin Baxter proudly held a bag of lemons aloft.

'Sensational effort, Erin.' Kate looked beyond her. 'Where's your friend?'

Erin dumped the lemons down hard, sending three rolling down the hall. 'She's coming but Mum couldn't bring her because I had a dentist appointment.' She grimaced.

'I think the fluoro pink brackets look fabulous on your braces.' Kate's mobile phone vibrated in her pocket. 'Excuse me.' She pulled out the phone, immediately recognising the number on the display. 'Hi, Sandra.'

'Joel has just vomited everywhere for the second time and I really can't leave him. Sorry, Kate. Perhaps one of the mothers can stay and help you out?' Sandra's hopeful voice sounded down the line.

Kate didn't have the heart to tell her that the mothers who might have stayed and helped had departed, and by the time she was able to get one of them to come back they would have lost too much time for the session to take place. 'I hope Joel feels better soon.' She rang off.

Hilary Smithton walked in with her daughter, Lucy, her nose wrinkling as if the air of the Guide Hall was offensive. Hilary always arrived late, although Kate doubted it was from disorganisation. Hilary had grown up with Shane. Along with the Kennedy clan, she blamed Kate for his death.

Kate took in a deep breath. 'Hello, Hilary. Hi, Lucy. Did you remember the sugar for the pancakes?'

Lucy cast a worried look at her mother and then stared at the floor.

Hilary put her palm against her chest in an exaggerated movement, her red nails vivid against the white designer T-shirt. 'Oh, dear, were we supposed to bring sugar?'

Kate forced a polite smile. She'd bet her bottom dollar Lucy had asked for the sugar. 'Not to worry, Lucy. I brought some in just in case.'

Relief flooded the girl's face as she ran off to join her patrol.

Kate did a head count. She had more girls than she could legally have in her care alone. She didn't want to have to disappoint them and cancel. Swallowing hard, she smiled at Hilary. 'Sandra Dodson has a sick child and isn't able to assist tonight. Are you able to stay and help out?'

Hilary's gaze swept the hall, taking in the smiling, chattering girls all lined up in their patrols with the expectation of a fun time ahead shining on their faces.

Kate could almost hear Hilary's brain ticking over, working out that without help Guides would have to be cancelled. She gave it one last shot, planning to appeal to Hilary's maternal side. 'Lucy's been so looking forward to earning her cooking badge. Tonight's the final task. It would be disappointing if it couldn't happen.'

Hilary exhaled on a hiss, her eyes narrowing to glinting slits. 'Disappointment is part of life. The sooner she learns that, the better. You might have been able to manipulate Shane but you can't manipulate me.'

For a moment her attention seemed to slide away, as if she was looking over Kate's shoulder. Then her gaze snapped back. 'I refuse to help you, just like you refused to help Shane. And if you run the group tonight without another adult present, I'll report you.'

Kate's fingers curled into fists, her nails digging into her palms. She welcomed the pain as she forced herself to stay calm. She knew Hilary disliked her but she hadn't believed she would jeopardise the Guides.

Anger and frustration welled up inside her. Her first attempt at resuming her life back in Warragurra and she'd failed. Hilary had her neatly over a barrel. How hard did it have to be to live in this town?

'I can stay and help.'

The deep resonance of the words washed over her, causing her breath to catch in her throat. She'd recognise that voice anywhere. She spun around so quickly she swayed.

Baden stood in the hall with Sasha, his expression congenial but his eyes unusually dark, with swirling puzzlement in their depths.

Then he smiled. 'Hello.'

Kate's knees wobbled and she locked them for support. Her heart had already been hammering from the adrenaline surge Hilary's words had evoked. Now his smile added a crazy jumping third beat. It left her dizzy and disorientated.

'Hello, Baden.' She focussed hard to sound cool and in control.

'Erin Baxter invited Sasha to Guides.' The informative statement filled in the gaps, as if he sensed her confusion at seeing him out of context. 'She's been talking about Guides for days so it would be a shame if pancake night couldn't happen.' He shot a wide smile at Hilary. 'Besides, I'm a bit of a pancake expert.'

Hilary stiffened. 'Well, I'll leave you to it, then, Doctor. Although a man present at Guides is not exactly what the organisation had in mind.' She gripped her shoulder-bag close to her side and strode out of the hall, her high heels clicking on the bare boards. The door slammed behind her.

Relief flooded through Kate, followed by a certain amount of smugness. Hilary had been outplayed and Guides would take place tonight. The situation had been rescued. She turned toward Baden, her thanks rising to her lips.

His clear blue gaze hooked hers. Suddenly she was acutely conscious of his height, his sharply appraising gaze and the unasked questions on his face. Questions that demanded answers.

Her stomach dropped to the floor. Her private life had just collided with her working life.

She'd wanted to keep the two completely separate. No way was she going to tell him about her battle with the town and relive the horror of the last year. But Warragurra's size was conspiring to throw them together.

The exhilaration of the rescue faded fast, leaving dread in its wake.

\* \* \*

Baden had supervised the beating of batter, tossed a hundred pancakes, wiped up more sugar than an army of ants could have consumed and had fought off sixteen girls attacking him with teatowel flicks.

But now peace reigned. Their parents had collected all the Guides and Sasha had gone with Erin for an ice-cream treat on the way home. Although why Erin's mother thought they needed any more food after the feast they'd just had was beyond him. But apparently ice cream was a must with pancakes, even if the ice cream had to be consumed half an hour after the pancakes.

As he folded up the last trestle table he surreptitiously watched Kate, or Koala, as the Guides called her. She wore a vivid pink and blue apron over her casual uniform and flour stuck to her forehead.

Her silky smooth hair, which normally hung in a perfect curve around her face at work, had been pulled back in a blue hair tie. Tendrils had escaped and now stuck to her cheeks, which were bright pink from the heat in the hall. She looked about eighteen. Except for the fine lines around her eyes.

Lines that life had put there. He recognised them, he had some of his own and many more than he'd had two years ago.

Did they have anything to do with the standoff he'd witnessed when he'd arrived earlier in the evening? The moment he and Sasha had walked into the hall he'd recognised the vitriol on Hilary Smithton's face.

And every protective instinct he possessed had gone into overdrive. The intensity of his response had left him stunned. The only other time he'd experienced such feelings had been when Sasha had been a toddler and a large dog had bared its teeth at her.

But Kate wasn't a toddler so this reaction was foolish. Most of him wanted to run a mile. Kate belonged at work. He had no plans to get involved with anyone again. Love was unreliable and he had to protect Sasha.

He'd kept all their conversations at work firmly centred on work. Hell, he hadn't even realised she was the Guide leader until Sasha had mentioned it two minutes before they'd arrived. Spending an evening with Kate hadn't been part of his plan for tonight, but the twist of Hilary's mouth, and the venom of her words, had made him speak.

Kate had treated the episode with Hilary as if it hadn't happened and now, two hours later, he was none the wiser as to the reason for Hilary's antipathy. The Guide meeting had continued as smoothly as if there had never been a threat to the evening.

'Cup of tea?' Kate held out a steaming mug.

'In this heat?' He bit off the words. 'Are you insane?'

She smiled, 'Ah, but it makes you feel cooler.'

'What, after it's made you twice as hot?' He eyed the hot drink with distrust.

'That's right.' She laughed, a mellow, throaty sound. 'Are you judging my mother's logic?'

He stamped down on the rush of pleasure that streaked through him at the sound of her laugh. 'Yes, I am.'

She sank down into a chair, all grace and innate elegance, which was at odds with her current bedraggled look. 'You're right, it's crazy thinking but there's nothing cool in the fridge and I need a cup of tea.'

The thought of a cold beer materialised in his head. 'After sixteen giggling girls and a run-in with Hilary Smithton, you probably need something stronger than that.'

She flinched as if she'd been struck and her relaxed demeanour vanished. 'No, I just need to sit down and catch my breath.' The words came out precise and clipped as she put her mug down by her chair.

It was obvious she didn't want to talk about it. And, hell, he didn't really want to know because asking meant involving himself in her life. He didn't want to be involved in her life. Getting involved with a woman wasn't part of the plan, couldn't be part of the plan. He and Sasha were doing fine on their own.

But something more than curiosity pushed him to ask. 'Why does Hilary Smithton hate you?'

He heard her sharp intake of breath and the scrape of her chair aginst the floorboards. 'I really appreciate you helping me out tonight, Baden. You saved the girls from disappointment and helped three of them get their cooking badge.' Her mouth curved upwards in a smile so tight it threatened to break in half.

Irritation chafed him. 'You're avoiding my question.'

'I'm not sure it's one you have the right to ask.' Coolness clung to the words like frost.

Indignation spluttered inside him, quickly taking hold. He'd bailed her out. That alone deserved an explanation. Now she was treating him as if he was the person who'd treated her so rudely. Righteous anger spurred him on to speak. 'If this issue with Hilary is going to affect Sasha's safety then I have the right to ask and the right to demand an answer.'

Her shoulders stiffened. 'I would *never* jeopardise the safety of the girls. Ever.'

Frustration collided with guilt. Intrinsically he knew she spoke the truth. She was right. Sasha would be safe at Guides. Irritation prickled at the realisation that he'd been out of line. In this situation he didn't have the right to ask that question.

At work it would be totally different. He'd have the right to demand an explanation, especially if it affected her performance. And should it ever happen, he would invoke that right. But this wasn't work.

*This* time he had to let it go.

The fact that bothered him so much upset him even more.

Kate counted silently backwards from ten as Warragurra airstrip seemed to rise up to meet them. Glen brought the plane down smoothly onto the runway, a tiny bump the only sensation that they weren't still in the air. She loved it when she got to zero in her counting just as the plane landed.

'Kate, can you write up your proposal for a "Pit Stop" Field Day at Coonbunga Station?' Baden unbuckled his harness.

'You think it's worth pursuing?'

'Absolutely.' Enthusiasm moved across his face. 'It combines health education, screening and personalised health information. Plus you've tapped into people's competitiveness and made it fun. I think they'll enjoy themselves and learn a lot as they put their bodies through a safety check and determine their "airworthiness". It's a brilliant idea.'

A thrill tripped though her at his praise. A thrill totally connected to his professional recognition of her idea. It was great to be part of a team with a supportive colleague. 'Thanks. I'm glad you liked it.'

'It's really innovative, Kate. Well done.' He stood up, his smile washing over her, his height seeming to fill the plane.

The lingering warmth from his praise immediately flared, spiralling into waves of heat.

*Exactly how long are you going to kid yourself that feelings like this are from professional recognition?*

She hummed to herself, drowning out the voice of reason. They worked together. Nothing could happen. She wouldn't allow anything to happen. Not that she had to worry. If she was honest with herself, it was only a one-way attraction. All her way. She could kid herself that his bone-melting smiles were especially directed at her but she'd seen him smile at everyone in much the same way. Except for Sasha.

When he was with Sasha his aura of a wide personal space seemed to vanish. Lightness came into his eyes chasing away the gloom that sometimes hovered around him. It seemed crazy but she had this feeling that when he smiled at Sasha she was seeing the image of the man he had once been.

Since the night at the Guide Hall ten days ago, when she'd frostily refused to tell him about Hilary, he'd been slightly more aloof than before. That niggled at her. And it drove her mad that it did. She'd respected his silence and hadn't asked him about Sasha's mother. So why did he feel he could be grumpy with her when she kept her private life private, just like he did?

Yet at three o'clock in the morning she was often lying awake, listening to the hum of the air-conditioner and thinking about why Baden and Sasha were on their own.

Thinking about Baden.

About how it would feel to tangle her fingers in his thick black curls. How it would feel to explore golden skin stretched taut over toned muscle.

Suddenly her skin prickled with heat. She quickly exited the plane into a hot, dry wind. At least the forty-degree Celsius day was good for something! It hid the source of her being hot and bothered.

Baden's long stride quickly caught her up but the wind prevented any conversation. As he opened the door into the offices for her, she breathed in deeply, deliberately catching his fresh and spicy scent.

Regret poured through her the moment she did it. 'I'll start on the proposal tonight. See you tomorrow.' She turned toward her office, thankful to be able to put some physical space between herself and Baden and find some equilibrium for her jangled emotions.

He checked his watch. 'Can I ask a favour? I got a ride here this morning from Jenkin's Mechanics. Can you give me a ride back into town?'

Dismay filled her at the unexpected request. She wanted to say no. Baden in her small car was so much closer than Baden in the plane. But no wasn't an option. She tried to sound casual. 'Sure, no problem.'

'Great, thanks. I'll just grab some stuff from the office.' He strode down the hall, the cotton twill of his trousers outlining the tightness of his buttocks.

Kate closed her eyes, refusing to stare, but the after-image burned brightly in her mind.

Five minutes later Baden folded his body into her sports car, appreciation and intrigue written clearly on his face. 'I've always wanted a car like this.' He ran his finger along the dashboard.

She grimaced. 'It's up for sale if you're interested.'

'Really?' For a moment consideration crossed his face but it faded as quickly as it had come. 'Sasha's tennis team would have to ride on the roof. Pity, though. It must be fun to drive. Why are you selling it?'

*Because getting rid of this car is part of my new life.* 'It's not practical.' She quickly reversed out of the parking space and pulled onto the road.

'But no one buys a car like this out of practicality. Why did you buy it?' He swivelled slightly in his seat, his attention completely focussed on her.

'I didn't buy it.' Shane's blotchy face hovered in her mind. *Katie, baby, don't leave me.* Her fingers tightened on the steering-wheel. 'It was a…' *Bribe.* 'It was a gift.'

He whistled. 'Lucky you.'

'That's your opinion.' The muttered words left her mouth before her brain had the sense to cut them off.

His black brows immediately rose, interest clearly etched on his handsome face.

The Jenkin's Mechanics sign thankfully came into view and she pulled up onto the concrete apron. 'Here we are.'

Baden opened the door. 'Thanks for the ride.'

'You're welcome.' She flicked the switch to open the boot so he could get his bag.

He climbed out of the car and paused, bending down to talk to her. 'By the way, Jen asked me to remind you that the dinner for the new physiotherapist is going to be at the Royal.' He inclined his head in the direction of the building across the road.

The newly furbished Royal Hotel was a popular place catering for the coffee and cake set through to discerning diners in the grand dining room. The sports bar with its many large plasma screens had been cleverly contained within a heritage façade. From the outside people glimpsed the Warragurra of old when silver had lined its streets and money had been no object. The renovation had been Shane's last job with Kennedy Constructions.

Out of the corner of her eye she saw three men walk out of the back door of the hotel. Her chest tightened as she instantly recognised two of the men. The tallest of the three—Josh Martin—had been Shane's closest mate, and the best man at their wedding.

A prickle of unease ran through her. She'd avoided this part of town since coming home. Every nerve ending screamed at her to leave. She turned on the ignition.

The noise of the car made Josh look up. His lip curled when he caught sight of her.

*Leave now. Do not pass go, do not collect two hundred dollars.* She put the car into first gear.

Josh and the other man stepped onto the road, supporting Richie Santini, who stumbled, his gait unsteady. As they reached the middle of the road Richie slumped between them, falling against Josh and making him stagger.

A shiver of disgust ran through her. Richie was drunk again. Some things never changed. She willed them to move quickly across the road so she could get away.

'Richie!' Josh's worried voice carried across the street. 'Mate, come on, you'll get run over.'

Kate expected Richie to stand up as Josh jolted him with his body. He didn't. His colour had gone from florid to white to blue.

Hell, he was unconscious. Kate pushed her door open. 'Baden!' she called to him as his hand touched the doorhandle of the shop door. 'Quick, over here.' She ran toward the grass verge where Josh had laid Richie down.

Baden caught up to her, his medical bag in his hand.

'Roll him on his side, Josh,' Kate called out as she reached them.

Josh turned the moment he heard her voice, pure hatred lining his face. 'Get away from here, Kate. You've done enough damage.'

His words pounded her like hailstones, but he couldn't hurt her any more. No more than he and Shane had already. And another person didn't deserve to die.

'Don't be stupid, Josh. I'm a nurse. I can help.' She dropped to her knees to check Richie's airway, the stench of stale alcohol almost making her retch.

Josh's arm shot out from his side, striking her across the shoulder in an attempt to push her away.

She gasped, desperately trying to maintain her balance as pain and the past swamped her.

'Step back from her. Now!' Baden's voice boomed out like a sergeant major establishing control. 'I'm a doctor and I'm in charge.' He pointed to the unknown man. 'You. Restrain your mate before I flatten him.'

Through the fog of shock Kate realised the experienced triage doctor had just secured the scene.

'Kate.'

He spoke her name with caring firmness, centring her. She swung around to face him as if he were a lifeline in a storm-ravaged sea.

His expression was neutral but his eyes swirled with eddies of fury tinged with disbelief. 'Kate, call an ambulance.' He tossed her his phone and immediately turned his attention to the patient, implementing what Kate had tried to do—assess the airway, check the breathing and the circulation.

She stood up and walked five steps away. With trembling fingers she managed to dial 000.

Josh took a step forward.

Kate stood her ground but her grip on the mobile phone threatened to crush it.

His mate put his hand on Josh's shoulder. 'Give them space to do their job, Josh.'

'I am, Trev.' Josh tried to shrug off his hand.

The dispatcher finally answered. 'Police, fire or ambulance?'

'Ambulance.' She wanted the police but that would only make things worse.

Baden called out to her. 'No pulse. Commencing CPR now.'

She nodded, indicating she'd heard him. The professional nurse kicked back in, corralling her shock and fear into a place to be dealt with later. 'We have a collapsed patient with no pulse. Doctor in attendance and CPR commenced. We need a defibrillator.'

'Hell, Richie.' Josh's voice cracked as Baden's arms pushed against Richie's chest, compressing his heart, attempting to get it pumping again.

Kate ended the call and knelt down next to Baden.

His firm voice counted the compressions. 'Twenty-six, twenty-seven, twenty-eight, twenty-nine, thirty.'

She blew two breaths through the Laerdal pocket mask into Richie's mouth and checked for a pulse. 'No pulse. Keep compressing.' She strained her ears for the ambulance. 'We need that defibrillator now.'

They established a rhythm, with Baden compressing and Kate giving the rescue breaths, but she knew how physical CPR was and how arms tired quickly. 'Swap at thirty?'

Baden nodded, still counting, keeping the beat of thirty compressions to two breaths.

The swap had to be fluid. The recent guideline changes for CPR focussed on more compressions with fewer interruptions.

Kate started counting out loud. 'Twenty-eight, twenty-nine, thirty. Change.' Her crossed hands immediately started compressions where Baden's had been. *Don't die on me, Richie.*

But she knew the reality. She'd seen his swollen ankles—unusual in a man in his mid-thirties. His heart muscle was saggy and overstretched, its capacity to start again severely compromised by a lifetime of binge drinking.

A small crowd had gathered, including Baden's mechanic, Scott. All of them stood watching with a mixture of fascination and horror as a life hung in the balance.

'Change of heart, Katie?' Josh's cruel voice exploded above her. 'Saving Rich won't make up for the fact you killed Shane.'

His words struck her as hard as a physical blow. Blood pooled in her feet, silver lights exploded in her head and she started to shake. *Concentrate on the job.*

She counted loudly, the words and the rhythm driving away her fear, allowing her wavering courage a chance to take hold.

'Scott, get him out of here or I'm calling the police.'

Raging fury poured through Baden's words. 'This isn't daytime TV drama.'

Kate heard the barely audible aside as he lowered his head to give Richie another rescue breath.

Except it was her past life unfolding in all its sordid detail in front of the one man she'd wanted to keep it from.

Five men surrounded Josh and guided him to one side as the ambulance screamed to a halt. The paramedic and an intern from the base hospital ran to them, carrying the portable defibrillator.

A flurry of hands worked on Richie. Kate kept compressing while the paramedics attached the monitor pads.

'He's in asystole.' Michael, the doctor, interpreted the readout.

'Shock him now,' Baden instructed as he reached for the intravenous kit.

'Stand clear.' Michael discharged electrical current into Richie's chest.

The monitor flatlined.

'Resume compressions.' Baden nodded to Kate. 'Prepare for stacked shocks.' He slid the butterfly cannula into Richie's arm and drew up adrenaline. 'I don't have a good feeling about this.'

He wasn't telling her anything she didn't already know. The odds were stacked against getting an exhausted heart muscle to start beating again.

'Stand clear.' Michael pressed the button and the pads delivered another shock to Richie's chest.

All eyes focussed on the readout.

'We've got a wobbly rhythm.' Michael sounded uncertain.

'Thank God.' Kate's softly spoken words came out on a breath. He had a second chance.

'Yeah, but for how long?' Baden's bald words indicated the reality of the situation.

'Let's transfer him immediately. He needs every bit of expertise Coronary Care can provide.' Michael nodded to the paramedic. 'On my count.'

They lifted the heavy man onto the stretcher and transferred him into the rig. Michael clambered in to monitor Richie and his co-worker switched on the siren and drove them away.

Kate's legs immediately started to shake, followed by her arms and then the rest of her body. Bile scalded her throat as she gulped in air, trying to still her heaving stomach.

She saw Josh being hustled away but not before he looked straight at her and used his arm to make an offensive gesture.

Baden's strong arm curled around her, pulling her in close. 'It's over now, Kate.' He spoke softly, his words comforting as his hand stroked her hair.

She needed to go, needed to leave this minute. She shouldn't be standing here. She shouldn't want to be in Baden's arms, seeking shelter. She shouldn't want to lay her head on his chest and close her eyes and forget. Forget everything except the touch of his body against hers, the rise and fall of his chest against her breasts and his heat flooding into rekindling sensations she'd long forgotten.

For one brief moment she gave in to temptation, resting her head on his shoulder, feeling the softness of his cotton shirt against her cheek and the hardness of the muscle underneath. Taking a sample to last her for ever.

She wrenched herself away. She had to go before he asked questions. Asked difficult questions she didn't want to answer. 'I have to go.'

His hand gripped her arm. 'You're not going anywhere without me.'

The firmness of his voice startled her. She looked up into navy eyes filled with a hard edge she didn't recognise. Apprehension rippled through her. 'I'm fine, really. I'll make myself a cup of tea with loads of sugar.' She forced a smile onto her face, hoping to placate him.

The flash in his eyes said he'd seen straight through her ploy. 'It's not just you I'm worried about. When your private life impinges on a patient's well-being then it's no longer private. We're going somewhere quiet and you're going to tell me what the hell is going on with you and this town.'

Panic clawed at her as Shane's legacy reared again, determined to haunt her. She desperately tried to think of a way of avoiding this meeting. She opened her mouth to speak and closed it again.

Determination lined Baden's face. He wouldn't let her go until she agreed to his demand.

At that precise moment she knew she had no choice.

# CHAPTER FOUR

BADEN sat on a wicker seat, sipping lemon, lime and bitters, under a thick green canopy of twining wisteria. He had the surreal feeling he'd stepped back in time.

He could feel a stream of cool air at his back, coming from inside the homestead's thick russet and ochre stone walls. In front of him an unexpectedly green lawn sloped down toward the river and the magnificent red river gums. Hundreds of years old, one of their gnarled trunks looked as if it had regrown around the site where Aborigines had once carved a canoe.

Weeping peppercorn trees and towering jacarandas softened the harsh stone lines of the house and perfume from the extensive rose garden scented the early evening air. Visions wafted through his head—people chatting on the lawn, ladies promenading in white muslin dresses, men in suits, a jazz band playing and flappers doing the Charleston on the dock by the river. Their laughing voices echoed around him, memories of the jubilant celebrations of a successful wool clip in days long gone when the merino sheep had been gold on four legs.

He couldn't believe Kate lived in the Sandon homestead, one of Warragurra's eminent homes. A home with a round National Trust plaque at the front door and neatly beneath it a Kennedy Constructions historic brass renovation plate.

How had he not known she lived here? *You never asked.* He hadn't wanted to ask, scared if he did so he'd become even more intrigued by her. Even so, he wasn't certain Kate would have divulged the information freely.

She'd insisted that the only place she would talk to him was at her home. And what a home it was. He remembered Annie showing him an article and photographs from a lifestyle magazine about the house and the million-dollar renovation. It had been around the time they'd first discussed moving to Warragurra. He'd joked at the time that he'd buy it for her if it ever came on the market.

But Annie had never made it to Warragurra or to Sandon homestead. Her illness-ravaged body had succumbed before the final plans had been in place. A twinge of guilt tugged at him that he was here now and that the woman in front of him intrigued him and filled his dreams.

Kate sat opposite him, wound as tight as a drum, with waves of tension rolling off her.

His anger and disgust at the events of the afternoon had abated but the sensation of holding Kate in his arms, her breasts pressed firmly against his chest, the silky feeling of her hair under his fingers, had stayed strong.

Too strong. Too vivid.

When he'd pulled her into his arms he hadn't thought, he'd just acted. She'd looked like she had been about to faint on the pavement. Holding her had been the most natural thing in the world. But want had quickly drowned empathy as her heat had flowed into him.

He hadn't held a woman for two years. He hadn't wanted to hold a woman in that time. Not until today. The guilt dug in deeper as his hazy memory tried valiantly to recall Annie's feel and touch. It came up blank against the vivid feel of Kate.

He ran his hand across the back of his neck. Now wasn't the time to be changing his game plan—his top priority had to be Sasha. That meant keeping his distance from Kate. This was work and the only reason he was here was to find out what the hell was going on in this town.

But asking her outright would just make her defensive so he approached it gently. 'I bet this place saw some parties. I almost feel we should be sipping gin and tonics in deference to the house.'

She raised her brows. 'This house has a long history of wild parties, right up until a year ago.'

He put his glass down on the red gum table. 'Really? What changed?'

She sighed a long shuddering breath. 'Shane...my husband died.'

A dull ache flared then throbbed inside him. He knew the excruciating pain of loss too well. 'I'm so sorry.'

Stunned disbelief scored her face at his well-meant sentiment.

Remorse immediately tugged at him. He'd just exacerbated her pain. 'Words don't do a damn thing to help, do they?'

She blinked, her large eyes swirling with undecipherable emotions. 'Actually, sorry isn't a word I've heard very much, so thank you.'

Bewilderment lurched through him. 'Your husband died and people didn't say sorry?'

She shifted in her seat, folding and unfolding her arms before standing up. 'Seeing as you're insisting we have this conversation, can we do it while we walk in the garden?'

Conflicting needs clashed. His need to know what was going on collided with Kate's evident pain at having to tell him, and meanwhile the clock ticked on. He had to collect Sasha from the pool at seven. He sighed. 'Look, you don't need to tell me

your life story and I don't want to cause you a lot of grief by
asking you to revisit your tragic loss.

'But whatever's going on between you and the people in this
town, it's now impacting on your job. So that involves me. The
only thing I need to know is why the people in the town dislike
you so much.'

She gave a brittle laugh. 'The *only* thing? I wish it was that
simple.' She swallowed hard. 'They blame me for Shane's death.'

Thoughts tumbled through his mind. Car accident? Medical
emergency? 'Why?'

Kate started striding quickly toward the river, shredding a
eucalyptus leaf with her fingers as she walked, the strong, fresh
aroma of the oil trailing behind her. She caught his gaze, her
expression a mixture of culpability and distress. 'Oh, God,
there's no easy way to tell you this.'

Her vulnerability rocked him. The desire to pull her into his
arms, stroke her hair and ease her pain surged through him, immediate and strong. He clenched his hands to keep his arms by
his sides. He didn't want to cause her any more pain and part
of him wanted to say, Don't tell me, I don't need to know.

But he did. As her boss, he had to know.

*Just listen. Support her by listening.* 'Start at the beginning
if it helps.'

She threw him a grateful look. 'You asked me on my first
day back at work if I was Kate Kennedy. Well, I was for five
years. I married Shane, the eldest son of the Kennedy family.'

The image of her flashing eyes the day he'd questioned her
surname rushed through his mind. 'Would I be right if I guessed
the construction Kennedys?' Suddenly where she lived started
to make sense.

She nodded. 'That's right. Warragurra establishment.
Kennedys have been building Warragurra buildings for a very

long time. Shane used to take pleasure in the fact he was often renovating buildings his great-grandfather had built.

'He was a gifted craftsman and his talent was bringing buildings back to life so they shone. At the same time he gave people the opportunity to value the past, while giving them the modern conveniences. He and I renovated Sandon.'

'Did a love of heritage buildings bring you together?' He asked the question, the drive to know more about her straining at his self-imposed restraint.

Her lips tugged slightly at the corners. 'That and his wicked sense of humour. Shane was a funny guy. He was the bloke you'd ask to be MC at a fundraising dinner or a wedding. He was larger than life, he had an air of excitement about him and he didn't take things too seriously. I was working at the base hospital in those days and I think after a day in ICU where life and death can sit so closely together I found him to be a breath of fresh air.'

Her breath shuddered out of her lungs. 'I completely missed the dark side of him, the opposite side of the larger-than-life, fun-loving guy.'

Baden probed gently. 'Was he depressed?'

She hesitated for a few seconds. 'My husband was a hidden alcoholic.'

He tried to keep his face neutral as the unanticipated words settled around them.

Her voice wavered. 'With the exception of my colleagues, no one in this town accepts that because Shane didn't fit the stereotype. He held down a great job, he was well respected in the community and he managed a complex business with his father. But every night he would drink.'

He spoke quietly. 'That can't have been easy.'

A flutter of hurt surfaced briefly in her eyes until she blinked.

She stared ahead. 'At first it was a few beers, and then it was beer and a bottle of wine. Business lunches got added into the mix until he could consume up to four bottles of wine a day plus beer and spirits. His personality at home became dramatically different from his public persona. The man I married had completely disappeared, submerged in a sea of alcohol.'

Her despair radiated through Baden. 'That would have been really tough. What did you do?'

She threw her hands up. 'What didn't I do? I'd married for better or worse, in sickness and in health. But addiction isn't like other illnesses and there's no quick fix. It slowly pervaded every aspect of our lives and insidiously took us down into bleakness.'

He concentrated on her words, every part of him shuddering as he felt her pain.

'I asked him to cut back, I refused to have alcohol in the house, I asked him to see a doctor, have hypnotherapy, go to Alcoholics Anonymous—I even suggested couples counselling, but I was a lone voice.' She tossed her head as if shaking the past away. 'This is a country town and drinking is embedded in the fabric of the community. His mates all enjoyed a drink at the pub. No one could see anything wrong with how Shane led his life.'

Baden had worked with alcoholics before and he knew what a tough fight she must have faced. 'And he didn't see he had a problem?'

She nodded slowly. 'That's right. He didn't believe he had a drinking problem. He told me I was a killjoy and the problem was all mine. His parents refused to accept he was an alcoholic and made continual excuses for him, but mostly they just blamed me.' She puffed out a breath. 'I was difficult, I didn't understand him, I was spoilt. He worked hard, giving me a good lifestyle, so surely he deserved to relax a bit after work.' Her voice caught. 'His mates thought I was an interfering witch.'

She hugged her arms close to her and shivered, even though the late-afternoon sun seared everything in its path. 'The night he got violent and trashed the kitchen was the night I left.'

Irrational resentment toward a sick man consumed him. A man who obviously hadn't valued the wonderful woman he'd married. 'You did the right thing, Kate. No one has the right to abuse.'

She showed no sign she'd heard him, her eyes glazed with hurtful memories. She continued talking—her need to get the story told so great. 'Shane couldn't believe I'd left him. He showered me with presents, including the car; he begged me to come back and he promised me he'd change. I needed to believe he would try and I gave him a second chance.' Her haunted gaze hooked with his, pleading for him to understand.

'You loved him.' He spoke the words, trying to support her, but they unexpectedly speared him like a jagged knife.

Her fingers curled deeply into the muscles of her upper arms and when she spoke the words came out flat. 'His promise lasted a month.'

The low-life! Anger spurted through Baden like water from a geyser. Immediately the doctor in him struggled to override the strong reaction. 'He was sick, Kate.'

She nodded, swallowing hard. 'The hardest thing was knowing that until he acknowledged to himself he had a problem, nothing would change. I officially moved out. His parents harangued me, our friends stopped talking to me and his closest friends hated me.' She raised her troubled eyes to his. 'You met them today.'

The urge to touch her intensified. He wanted to show her he understood. He shoved his hands in his pockets to stop himself. 'That was a very courageous thing to do.'

'Courageous?' Her eyes widened and bitterness lined her face. 'I left him and five months later he hanged himself.'

Suicide.

Air rushed out of his lungs. He hadn't expected that at all. He'd imagined Shane had run his car off the road drunk or had experienced cardiac problems or liver complications like his friend this afternoon. He ran his hand through his hair. 'Hell, Kate, I'm sorry. Suicide leaves so many raw emotions. But surely you know Shane's death is not your fault?'

She stopped walking and stared out toward the river. 'On my good days I know that. I stayed in town for four months after Shane died but when his parents started calling me a gold-digger and tried to contest his will, life in Warragurra became almost impossible for me.'

Understanding flowed through him. 'So you went to Europe hoping things would settle, and the town thought you'd gone for good.'

She swung back to face him and gave a wry smile. 'That's right. I left needing some time and space. I know in my heart that I didn't kill Shane, but his family's hate campaign eroded my confidence, escalated my guilt.' She nibbled her bottom lip. 'But this is *my* town, too, with my friends, and it was time to come home.'

She swallowed hard, her voice trembling. 'But today was the first time Shane's closest friends have seen me, although Hilary would have told them I'd returned.'

He grappled to comprehend the tangled situation of grief, money and power. The reaction of Shane's parents seemed to be pathological grief. 'Surely his parents wouldn't have any claim to Shane's will?'

She shrugged her shoulders. 'Legally they don't but that didn't stop them from seeking advice from numerous solicitors across the country and starting a campaign against me in letters to the editor in the *Warragurra Times*. They'd lost their son, they needed to blame someone. I was the obvious person. His mother had never been thrilled about our relationship and now I was alive and her son was dead.'

'Grief drives people to do irrational things.' The words sounded bald and useless as resentment bubbled through him at the grief-driven spite of Kate's in-laws. Part of him wished he'd known her then and had been able to do something. Support her in some way.

Again she tossed her head, her silky hair swinging around her face. 'But that's all over now. I refuse to be a scapegoat. I love Warragurra. Since my parents died I've called Warragurra home. My job and my friends are here and I refuse to let a minority group drive me out. This is my new start. I will never let anyone take me down to that dark black pit of despair again.'

Her emotional bravery awed him but at the same time sadness enveloped him on her behalf. A beautiful, generous woman deserved more. A lot more. 'Not every marriage is black. It can be a wonderful thing.'

'Yes, well, I don't plan to find out.' Her eyes flashed with determination. 'I do my job well, Baden. The service supports me and as I work out of town, what you experienced today has never happened before. I doubt it will ever happen again. I'm sorry I didn't tell you when you started but I didn't think it would impact on you. I'm sorry you had to encounter my sordid past.'

Her amazing strength radiated through her words. She'd been to hell and back and yet she was apologising to him. 'I've never doubted your professionalism, Kate. As a newcomer I'm not privy to the nuances of the town. I didn't realise life here was so tough for you. I'm surprised you came back.'

She laced her fingers in front of her, pressing down so hard against the backs of her hands that her knuckles gleamed white. 'I have a right to live in this town. I love my job and my friends. I have a right to a happy, single life.' She swung one arm out wide. 'Sandon is too big for me but I won't be moved on by bigotry. When I sell, it will be my decision.'

She stood before him, firm, willowy and tall like the tree behind her. A beautiful woman facing down demons no one should ever have to deal with.

The slightest tremble vibrated along her plump bottom lip as her shoulders quivered. 'But sometimes it's so damn hard.'

He knew exactly what she meant. Sometimes it *was* too damn hard. Instantly, his resolve to keep his distance fell away. She needed his support. He needed to show her he understood. Stepping in close, he reached for her, winding his arms around her waist and drawing her close.

She stiffened in his arms.

He rested his chin against her hair. 'It's OK. We all have bad days.'

Slowly, her breath shuddered out of her lungs as she relaxed against him, languid and warm. She nestled her head into his shoulder and strands of her hair caressed his cheek. Her sweet scent encircled him as her breath fanned out against his neck.

He stroked her hair just like he stroked Sasha's when she was upset, but unlike with Sasha, an overwhelming sense of tranquillity wove through him as he held her. A sensation he'd forgotten.

As he moved his head to drop a light 'it's all better now' kiss onto her forehead, she tilted her head back. His lips collided with hers. Warm, soft lips that tasted like nectar.

Instantly the kiss changed.

His arm tightened around her waist, closing the infinitesimal space between them. Her body moulded itself to his, pressing hard against his length. All space between them vanished. So did every thought of support.

He wanted to touch her, taste her, plunder her glorious mouth, needing it as badly as a man in the desert needed water.

He slanted his mouth firmly against hers as every emotion he'd submerged since meeting her rose to the surface, demanding to be sated.

A low moan of want sounded in her throat as her lips yielded under his.

White lights exploded in his head.

Heat merged with heat.

Longing collided with need.

He lost himself in her hot, velvet mouth, which welcomed him, drawing him in, giving yet taking at the same time. His blood pounded through him, his need strong and hard, crashing easily through every barricade he'd erected.

She reached up, her breasts moving in a caressing motion, her nipples hardening against his chest. She snaked her arms around his neck, pulling his head closer still. Her fingers tangled in his hair as her mouth covered his, her tongue savouring, exploring and branding all at the same time.

The here and now fell away. Nothing existed except the two of them and their driving need.

He tore his mouth from hers and trailed kisses along her neck, tasting the salty hollow at the base of her throat and stroking the curve of her jaw.

She suddenly stepped backwards, pulling him with her as she rested against the tree. Her desire-fuelled gaze zeroed in on his face, all shadows of the past pushed aside.

Through his fog of need he knew instinctively that she wanted him as much as he wanted her.

He lifted her against the tree as her legs entwined with his, her body rising up.

Her fingers fumbled frantically with the buttons on his shirt, pulling the fabric briskly aside before resting her palms flat on his chest. A sigh of pleasure echoed around him.

His breath came in ragged jerks as sensations drove through him, exploding in bursts of pure, undiluted lust. He'd taken and conquered her mouth but he wanted more. He wanted to know how her slick and silky skin felt against his, wanted to feel the full and heavy weight of her swelling breast in his hand, he wanted her legs high around his waist and to truly feel her. He wanted to take her right now under the magnificent stately red river gum with its heady scent of eucalyptus.

*This is crazy.*

But he was past listening.

He pushed her shirt from her shoulders. Smooth, flawless skin greeted him, her breasts round and full, her nipples hard with longing. Groaning, he lowered his head, fixing his mouth around the enticing softness, his tongue flicking her nipple.

Her hands gripped his head hard as she bucked against him. A delicious moan of longing left her lips.

*She wants this as much as you do.*

He lifted her up, supporting them against the tree, cupping her with his hand, burying his face in her neck.

Nothing mattered except their need. Their need to push the past away and lose themselves in each other.

The shrill sound of a phone ringing split the air.

His phone.

The here and now slammed into him so fast it winded him.

Kate pulled back, her chest heaving. 'You'd better take that.'

He nodded mutely and lowered her to her feet before

pressing the answer button on his mobile phone. 'Hello?' His husky voice could hardly speak.

'Dad, where are you? It's way past seven.' Sasha's indignant voice sounded down the line.

*Sasha.* All his blood drained from his head and he swayed. He'd completely forgotten Sasha.

Guilt slammed into him with a sickening thud. He ran his hand over the back of his neck. What the hell was wrong with him? How could he have forgotten his daughter?

*Promise me you'll always make Sasha your top priority.* Annie's words seared him.

He'd just allowed lust to completely take over. He'd been behaving like a teenager. He was a grown man, a doctor, a father, and yet he'd been seducing his nurse in her garden. *Oh, yeah, that's really classy.*

His guilt solidified. 'I'll be there in ten minutes, sweetheart.' He punched the 'off' button.

He turned back to Kate. She stood a short distance from the tree, her blouse rebuttoned and tucked in, her natural elegance and grace giving her a serene calmness. But her swollen lips clearly told the real story, reminding him of their recent folly.

He forced himself to speak. 'I'm sorry.'

'Yes.' A muscle twitched in her jaw.

God, he felt like a louse. He'd taken advantage of a woman in an emotionally vulnerable state, but at the same time every cell in his body screamed for him to leave. 'I'm sorry, I have to go.'

'Of course you do.' Her smile didn't quite reach her eyes where the shadows marched in formation, reclaiming their rightful place.

# CHAPTER FIVE

'MORNING, Baden.' Kate forced the words out praying they sounded casual as well as bright and breezy.

'Morning, Kate. How are you?'

'Good. Yourself?'

'Fine. How's Sasha?'

'She's well, thank you.' Baden's deep voice vibrated with a new reserve.

Tension circled Kate like a boa constrictor. The clipped conversation dripped with unspoken words. Words neither of them wanted to speak.

Many people dreaded Monday morning but she wasn't usually one of them. She loved a new week, all fresh and shiny, ready to be embraced. But not today. On Friday she'd more than embraced Baden. She'd been a hair's breadth away from total abandonment.

Her cheeks flamed at the thought. She'd spent the weekend dreading this morning, knowing she would have to face him. Work with him all day, all week and well into the year.

She'd spent the weekend unable to settle to anything, constantly replaying the moment a simple and kindly sympathetic embrace had fired into the most sensual kiss she'd ever known.

How could one mouth create so many emotions and destroy every particle of her willpower? With one kiss she'd melted against him, every cell in her body humming with an all-consuming yearning to touch him and feel him in every way possible.

She'd completely yielded to the wondrous sensations his mouth had ignited deep inside her, letting them take over absolutely, leading her as a willing follower. She'd lost track of time and place and propriety. She would have made love to him under the river red gum without a moment's hesitation.

The thought both appealed and appalled. She was a grown woman, not a sixteen-year-old with more sex drive than sense. And yet her body had craved him with such force she'd hardly recognised herself.

But had she misread the situation? Had she been the one driving the kiss? The horrified expression that had streaked across his handsome face when his phone had rung had whipped her so hard she could still feel the sting.

He'd realised with stunning clarity what he had been doing and who he had been doing it with. Guilt had scored his face and he'd run so fast from her there was a possibility he'd broken records. Was it to do with Sasha's mother? Or was it all to do with her? Getting involved with Kate Kennedy would make his life in the town difficult. She bit her lip. Most of her understood. A small part railed against it.

So exactly what did you say to your boss post–thwarted seduction?

'Do you have the test results for Lucinda Masterton?' Baden slid into his seat, fastening his safety harness, his face impassive.

*You talk about work and nothing else.*

As the plane taxied down the runway she opened her brief-case. 'I do and I'll be signing her up for my next diabetes education group.'

Baden nodded. 'Good idea. Have you followed up Caroline Lovett? Emily was concerned about her.'

'I telephoned her last week but if she isn't at this morning's clinic I will personally go and collect her.'

'What, in Cameron's ute?' Azure eyes twinkled with a wicked glint.

It was the first sign he'd shown that morning of the Baden she'd grown used to. 'Betsy is the perfect example that you don't need doors for the engine to work.'

He laughed, the tension on his body sliding away. His face relaxed, his high cheekbones softened, even his curls seemed to unwind, brushing against his forehead.

Liquid heat flowed through her right down to her toes. She adjusted her position in the seat, disconcerted by her strong response. In the confined space of the plane her legs collided with his, her foot tangling behind his left calf.

Immediately Baden's rigid tension returned, coiling through him like a snake ready to strike. His eyes darkened to a stormy blue.

Piercing regret stabbed her. She'd just glimpsed the future. Working with Baden had changed for ever. She cleared her throat and focussed. Opening the next folder, she continued, 'I want to refer Prani Veejit to the endocrine unit at the base hospital because of her thyroxine levels.'

Monday morning's mid-air case conference had begun, the first task in a busy day.

Four hours later, Kate stretched her back after working non-stop in cramped conditions. The places she set up her clinics never ceased to amaze her. Today she was in the footy clubroom's kitchen with her portable steriliser and her folding examination table. It was the only room that offered a door that closed and privacy. Space in the kitchen was at a premium and she swore her spine had connected with the black handles of the ancient pie warmer every time she'd carried out the pap test examinations.

Her well-women's clinic had been full as it had been a long time since the service had been offered in the remote community of Gemton. She'd just seen the last patient on her long list. The health clinic doubled as a social event as many of these women lived on remote cattle stations and didn't see each other very often.

Each time Kate had gone out to the main hall to call in the next client she'd felt like she had been interrupting a party. Everyone had brought food—club sandwiches, mini-quiches, fruit platters—and the giant urn bubbled with boiling water for the numerous cups of tea that were required. Kate wouldn't need dinner tonight after consuming far too much delicious passionfruit sponge.

'Cup of tea, Kate?' Esther Lucas stood with a large stainless-steel teapot hovering over a mug.

'That would be lovely, thank you.'

The older woman smiled and poured the tea. 'You've had a big day today. I wonder if the doctor has seen as many men as you saw of us women.' She passed the tea and a plate of sandwiches.

Kate laughed. 'That's why Baden set up at the pub, so he has a better chance of finding the men. In general, women are better at having check-ups.'

Esther leaned forward, inclining her head. 'Not everyone saw you today who should.' She spoke conspiratorially. 'Can you take your cuppa and go have an encouraging chat to Brenda?'

'Sure, if you think I should.'

'I do, dear. Brenda's struggling. The drought has hit them hard and she's putting everyone and everything ahead of herself. She only popped in to give Tilly her birthday present but seeing as she's here…'

Country caring. It never ceased to amaze Kate how a community could care so much. She'd experienced both ends of the spectrum of small towns. This was the end that kept her going and helped maintain her faith.

As she took her tea and sandwiches toward Brenda she caught sight of Baden, who'd just arrived from his clinic. Many of the women immediately gathered around him, overwhelming him with hospitality and battering him with questions.

'Cup of tea, Doctor?'

'Did you get my Geoff to talk to you?'

'Have some sponge or perhaps a sandwich?'

'How's that gorgeous daughter of yours? I bet she's growing up.'

Kate heard the rumble of his deep voice as he politely replied to their questions. She sighed. With them his voice was friendly and open, in stark contrast to the cool and clipped tones he'd used with her that morning.

She took in a deep breath and rolled her shoulders back. None of that mattered. What mattered was that Esther was worried about Brenda and she needed to find out why.

Brenda sat in a chair, her eyes closed and her shoulders slumped. Her workworn hands lay folded in her lap against a pair of faded jeans. A voluminous peasant-style blouse settled over her, not quite hiding a large stomach.

Kate started at Brenda's appearance. In the eight months since she'd last seen her, the woman, in her mid-forties, had gained a lot of weight. Still, that could happen as women approached menopause. She sat down next to her. 'More tired than usual, Brenda?'

Brenda opened her eyes, her mouth curving into a half-smile. 'Kate, you're back. It's good to see you.'

'Thanks, Brenda. How are things with you?'

The woman shrugged. 'You know.'

Kate spoke gently. 'No, I don't really know. How about you tell me?'

She gave a long sigh. 'We're buying in feed, the price of beef has fallen though the floor and Des is looking worse than me.' Her thumbs rolled around each other in her lap. 'I'm up at five and in bed at eleven. I'm so damn tired that I can hardly put one leg in front of the other, but that's normal, right?'

Kate hedged. 'Maybe. But it's always worth investigating so while you're here and I'm here, how about a check-up? I'll do a physical, take some blood and then we'll know if it's just the stress of the drought.'

A shimmer of fear ran through the woman's eyes. 'Des said the doc was aiming to head out by two.'

Kate rolled her eyes and grinned. 'He's so busy being fed by his fans over there that we won't be able to get away in under half an hour.' She stood up, giving Brenda an expectant look.

'I forgot how pushy you could be. All right, let's get this over, then.' Brenda slowly lumbered to her feet and walked to the kitchen.

Kate closed the door firmly behind her. She started off with non-invasive checks of pulse and blood pressure, hoping the familiarity of such routine tests would put Brenda at ease. 'Still having periods?'

Brenda nodded. 'Although they're a bit hit and miss and for the first time in my life I'm getting pain.'

Kate jotted down the word 'pain' on Brenda's history. 'Just with your period or mid-cycle?'

'Both, I guess.' Brenda looked down at her feet. 'It hurts now and then and during sex. Not that I feel like it very often, I'm so damn tired and nauseated.' She threw her head up, despair flashing in her eyes. 'I think I'm pregnant.' She lifted her shirt to expose a bloated abdomen. 'Kate, I can't be pregnant, not now, not at forty-four.'

'Let's do a pregnancy test, then.' Kate handed her a specimen jar.

Brenda grimaced. 'That won't be a problem. I'm needing to pee all the time.'

A few minutes later both women peered at the negative result.

'Well, we've ruled out one thing.' Kate smiled at Brenda. 'So now I'll do the rest of the check-up.'

'I can't wait for that.' With a resigned expression Brenda got undressed and lay down on the examination couch. 'At least in this heat your hands won't be cold.'

Kate checked Brenda's breasts for lumps, checking carefully above and below the breast as well as in the lymph nodes under the arms. 'That's all fine. Now I'm going to feel your tummy.'

She carefully pressed down on Brenda's swollen abdomen, feeling for the ovaries. A lump met her fingers. A sliver of concern whipped through her. She palpated again. The lump remained.

She needed to do a bi-manual examination but if what she suspected did exist, Baden would have to examine her. It would be better if Brenda only had to have one vaginal examination. 'Brenda, I'd really like Baden to do an internal examination.'

'Why can't you do it? You always do it.' Brenda stiffened, instantly wary.

She fudged the answer. 'I'm a bit rusty after six months off.'

Brenda's eyes narrowed as if she didn't believe her, but she nodded her head slowly. 'OK.'

Kate tucked the modesty sheet around Brenda. 'I'll just go and get him.'

Baden was still surrounded by the women of the district but

he turned toward her as soon as he heard the door open. His dark brows rose in question.

She nodded. It was uncanny how often he anticipated her or knew she wanted to discuss something with him.

'Excuse me, ladies. Thanks so much for the late lunch, it was delicious.' He walked over to her. 'How can I help?'

'I've got Brenda Cincotta presenting with erratic periods, nausea, indigestion, urinary frequency, dyspareunia and lower back pain, and on abdominal palpation I can feel a mass. It might be an ovarian cyst.' Her optimism floundered under his intense gaze.

'What did the pelvic tell you?' A fine tremor rippled through his voice.

'I haven't done it. If I felt the mass then you would have to repeat the procedure and I'm trying to avoid her having two vaginal exams. I said I was a bit rusty.'

He cleared his throat. 'I doubt she bought that.'

She shrugged. 'She didn't, but she agreed.'

'Right, well I'll examine her.' He turned and put his hand on the doorhandle then paused, perfectly still. For the briefest moment an unusual expression twisted his face and then he breathed in deeply and rolled his shoulders back.

With a jerk he opened the door and stepped through, a strained smile on his lips. 'Good to see you, Brenda. I caught up with Des today. Sorry to hear the drought is messing you about but I'm really pleased you're both taking a bit of time to look after yourselves.' He pulled on a pair of gloves. 'Kate tells me that things have been a bit haywire with your cycle just recently.'

Brenda grimaced. 'I thought I was pregnant but perhaps it's just early menopause.'

'Let's find out, shall we?'

'I need to get back, and Des has to hand-feed tonight so just get it over.' Brenda lay back and closed her eyes.

Baden gently proceeded with the examination, starting with palpation of her abdomen and then moving on to the internal.

Kate kept her gaze fixed on his face the entire time, searching for clues. His behaviour at the door had mystified her. Now an unexpected sheen of sweat broke out on his brow as his face paled.

He stripped off his gloves and handed Brenda some tissues. 'We'll give you some time to get dressed.' Without waiting for an answer, he walked out of the room.

'Back in a sec, Brenda.' Kate followed him into the small office next door to the kitchen, away from prying eyes.

'It didn't feel like a cyst, did it?' She knew from his expression.

'I felt a solid mass bigger than five centimetres. There's every chance it's ovarian cancer.' His hands curled into a fist. 'I want to evacuate her today, now, for tests at the base hospital.'

'Today?' Shock rocked through her. 'Wouldn't it be better if she went home tonight, got a bag organised and then she and Des could come together to Warragurra tomorrow?'

'No.' The word exploded from him like a shot from a gun.

She started. 'It doesn't have to be this rushed.'

'It has to be today.' He spoke through clenched teeth.

Thoughts charged through her mind, colliding with each other as Kate struggled to understand his over-the-top reaction. 'But it's not likely that you can get the tests organised this quickly. Letting them come in tomorrow would give them both some time to absorb and adjust to the news.'

He spluttered. 'Adjust to the news? No one *adjusts* to cancer, Kate. She needs a CA 125 blood test, an ultrasound, a chest X-ray and a biopsy. And, damn it, she's having it all today.'

Her head spun as she tried to keep track of the conversation. 'But it might not even be cancer…'

He swore softly under his breath. 'You might want to live in fairyland, Kate, but I don't. She has all the vague symptoms that make ovarian cancer the silent killer it is. On top of that, she has a solid mass.' The veins in his neck throbbed as his voice almost growled. 'She needs surgery and chemotherapy yester-day and I'm damn well going to make sure she gets it, even if I have to take her to Sydney or Adelaide myself.'

His anger bore down on her like the wind from a cyclone— powerful and unforgiving. How did she tell him she thought he was overreacting? That if he went into that small room now, as agitated as he was, he'd terrify Brenda. 'Baden, perhaps I should tell her.'

His jaw stiffened and his eyes sparked like flint against stone. 'I'm the *only* one who can do this. I'm the only one that understands.'

Hot, searing pain slashed her. It was as if he'd struck her across the face. But at the same time warning bells screamed in her head. This wasn't the behaviour of a detached doctor about to give a patient bad news. Gut instinct forced her to move in front of the door but she had no idea if she was protecting Baden or Brenda.

He stood before her, his breath coming quickly, his eyes wide and his handsome face contorted. But with what? Pain? Anxiety? Grief?

She didn't know but every part of her knew something was very, very wrong. 'Baden, what's going on?'

He crossed his arms and rolled his eyes. 'Nothing is going on and that is the problem. Stand aside, Kate, so I can talk to my patient.'

'No. She's my patient, too.' She locked her knees against

their trembling. 'I've never seen you react like this. Not even last week when you had to organise tests for Mrs Hutton for suspected bowel cancer.' She took a deep breath and asked the question that plagued her. 'Why is this case different?'

Tension shuddered through him as he swung away from her, gripping the back of a chair so hard the metal strained. 'Ovarian cancer consumed my life for four years.'

Consumed? 'Did you work in the area in Adelaide before you came up here?'

He turned and faced her—his eyes deliciously blue but alarmingly empty.

A chill ran through her.

His face sagged, haggard with sorrow but lined with love. 'Ovarian cancer stole my wife. Annie died two years ago this month.'

She gave thanks the door was behind her, holding her up as a shaft of pain pierced her, taking her breath with it. He'd lost his soul-mate. The mother of his child.

She ached for him. Ached for Sasha. Suddenly his over-the-top reaction seemed reasonable. Shame filled her—she'd just exacerbated his pain by pushing him to tell her. 'I'm so sorry, Baden. I had no idea. I…'

He shrugged. 'I don't talk about it much.' He ran his hand across the back of his neck. 'Thanks.'

The word completely perplexed her. 'What on earth are you thanking me for? I think I just made things worse for you.'

He gave a wry smile. 'No, you stopped me from letting my personal feelings impact on a patient. You're right—if I had gone in to talk to her a couple of minutes ago I probably would have terrified her.' He pulled out his phone and handed it to her. 'I want you to ring the base and schedule all those appointments for tomorrow, just as you suggested.'

A glimmer of anxiety skated through her. 'Don't you want me to come in with you when you talk to Brenda?'

He shook his head. 'No. It's best we combine forces and not waste time. You get everything set up for tomorrow. I'll talk to Brenda and arrange for her and Des to fly in first thing in the morning.'

'Are you sure? Because—'

He shot her a look as if he could read her mind. 'I'm fine, Kate. February's just a tough month, that's all.'

She wasn't sure if she believed him or not. 'Would you and Sasha like to come to dinner tonight?' The words rushed from her mouth, the result of a half thought-out desire to help him get through a tough month. 'I'm sure Sasha would enjoy a horse ride or going in a canoe.'

His shoulders tensed and his eyes darkened with surprise, followed by an emotion she couldn't read.

'I'm sure she would. Thanks for the offer, but she's got school in the morning.'

Unexpected disappointment streaked through her. 'The weekend, then?' She bit her lip, hearing how needy she was sounding. How had an invitation to help him suddenly become more about her?

His azure gaze pierced her. 'Kate, would you have invited me to dinner half an hour ago?'

The question hit her out of left field, completely unnerving her. 'I… Well… Yes.'

His brows rose. 'I think we both know that isn't true. We're colleagues, not friends. You don't have to start treading on egg-shells around me or start cooking for me. I don't need pity. We've had two years on our own and Sasha and I are just fine. Life goes on.'

He walked from the room, leaving her holding his phone,

the only part of himself he seemed willing to share with her. The ache for him and his loss suddenly turned and became part of her, its dull dragging pain trawling through her.

No wonder he'd pulled away from their kiss in her garden. He had nothing to offer her—his heart belonged to another woman.

She was just his flight nurse. Nothing more, nothing less.

She waited for the relief she should feel to fill her. She didn't want to lust after him, she knew the heartache magnetic attraction could wreak. She'd lived it with Shane.

A week ago being Baden's flight nurse had been all that she'd wanted. It had fitted in with her longing for a simple and uncomplicated life. A single life with good friends.

But he'd just returned her attempt at friendship.

Suddenly just being his colleague didn't seem enough.

Baden sat at the kitchen table surrounded by travel brochures. He'd gone to the travel agency on the way home, trying to squash the unsettled feeling that had been dogging him for the last few days. *Days without Kate in them.*

It had been a hell of a week. He'd broken the news to Brenda and Des and supported them through the tests. Brenda's results had been positive for cancer and she'd gone to Sydney for surgery to have her uterus, ovaries and Fallopian tubes removed. Kate had accompanied her and had rung to say the surgery had gone according to plan and Brenda would have her first round of chemotherapy before leaving Sydney.

The times Emily had accompanied patients south he'd hardly thought about her, but although Kate had been absent she'd actually been with him every moment of the day. Images played constantly through his mind—her chocolate-brown eyes that could go from warm and soothing to smouldering in a heartbeat, her delicious curves that had been burned into his memory and her throaty laugh that made his blood pound faster just thinking about it.

Sasha leaned over his shoulder, her arms curling around his neck. His guilt dug in. He'd been distracted all week, thinking of Kate instead of focussing on his daughter.

'I thought you said we couldn't go on a holiday until we'd been here a year?' She peered at the glossy pictures. 'Oh, Queensland?' She slid forward onto his lap and picked up the theme-park brochure.

He pointed to a tropical scene with bright-coloured umbrellas with gold tassels. 'What about Bali? Mum always wanted to go there.'

Her face took on a far-away look. 'The theme parks would be awesome.' Then she focussed and looked straight at him. 'And Seaworld is totally educational.' A familiar cajoling sound played through her voice.

He smiled at her obvious ploy. 'What about Bali this time and theme parks next?'

'I don't want to go to Bali.' Unexpected petulance crossed her face.

Surprise whizzed through him. 'But it's on the planner. The things we talked about doing with Mum.'

'But Mum isn't here.'

He hugged her close, wishing for the billionth time that Sasha could have her mother in her life in person rather than in memory.

She struggled out of his embrace and crossed her arms. 'Why do we always have to do what Mum wanted?'

Baden stiffened in shock as her words hailed down on him. His immediate response was to be the father in charge. 'We don't always do what your mother wanted.'

Sasha stilled. 'Yes, we do. We came to Warragurra because that was what Mum wanted to do.'

He gave her a squeeze. 'And you've made lots of friends and it's been great.'

She wriggled off his lap. 'Yeah, but staying in Adelaide might have been great, too. You didn't always do what Mum wanted when she was alive.' Tears of frustration pooled in her eyes as her anger bubbled up. 'I don't want to go to Bali. I want to do something that I want to do.' Turning on her heel, Sasha stormed off to her room, her door slamming hard behind her.

Hell. He pushed the brochures away and dropped his head in his hands. Puberty hormones had well and truly kicked in. How had a simple idea about a holiday exploded in his face? A ripple of indignation washed through him. She was being over-dramatic, a pubescent drama queen.

Coming to Warragurra had been set in place well before Annie had died. They'd planned it together, both agreeing that the country was the place to bring up a child. He'd promised Annie he would bring Sasha here and he had no regrets.

*You didn't always do what Mum wanted when she was alive.*

But Sasha's comment stuck like the barb of an arrow. She had a point, he'd give her that. Annie had been larger than life, such a powerful force in the family. It had made for heated debate and lively discussions about all sorts of things, and there *had* been plenty of times they hadn't agreed. Would he have gone to Bali for a holiday? Would that have been his first choice?

If the truth be known, he probably would have sided with Sash for the theme parks. There was something about a roller-coaster that had him hustling for the front seat every time. So why was he pushing for Bali now? It was only a holiday.

Sighing, he stood up and poured himself a glass of orange juice. Should he talk to Sasha's teacher about her moodiness? She'd just tell him it was normal developmental behaviour.

Kate's caring face floated across his mind. She had lots of

experience with the Guides so he could get some advice from her. He smiled at the thought.

*You rejected her friendship, remember?*

How could he have forgotten? From the moment he'd rejected her dinner invitation she'd been nothing but the perfect nurse. Gone were all the signs of fire and passion that he'd experienced when he'd held her in his arms, gone was the laughter and mischievous grin. In their place was a cool professional—competent, knowledgeable and proficient.

Which was everything he'd wanted, right? Safety in professional distance. He needed that distance from her. The night he'd kissed her he'd lost himself in her and forgotten his daughter, which had scared the hell out of him. His focus had to be on Sasha. She needed him. Needed him to be her mother and father. She needed stability. He couldn't let himself be distracted by Kate and that was why he'd rejected her invitation.

Curtly rejected it, and at the same time rejected her friendship.

Remorse nibbled at him as he stared out the window at the first stars of the night, twinkling against a pink and grey sky. As if anything had been going to happen at a family dinner. His knee-jerk reaction had changed their working dynamics. He missed the banter and the laughs. He missed how her eyes danced with devilment and teasing. Just plain missed the Kate he'd got to know.

He ran his hand through his hair. They had months ahead of them, working together, and for their patients' well-being they needed to be a team. He wanted his friendly colleague back, rather than the starched version. And the only way that would happen was if he apologised and offered friendship. He could do friendship. Friendship was safe, simple and straightforward. Friendship wouldn't affect Sasha.

Contentment wove through him. He'd apologise the next time he saw Kate.

But first he had to go and hug his daughter and tell her he loved her. Perhaps he could trade off theme parks with a few days of bushwalking in the hinterland. He'd give it some thought.

# CHAPTER SIX

'GOODNIGHT, Koala.' Erin waved enthusiastically as she ran backwards towards the car.

'Tonight was great. Thanks heaps.' Phoebe's eyes shone with delight as she slung her bag over her shoulder.

'I'm glad you had a good time. See you next week.' Kate stood on her veranda smiling, waving and saying her goodnights to the Guides as car doors slammed, tyres crunched on the long gravel drive and young voices called their final farewells from open car windows.

She'd held a special Guide meeting at Sandon. They'd lit a campfire, made damper, toasted marshmallows and had had the best fun swinging from a rope and cannonballing into the waterhole. Two new girls had visited and she was confident they'd join. Word was spreading through Warragurra Public School that Guides was fun.

She closed the front door and walked back through the house to the kitchen, checking her watch. One Guide remained to be collected. One parent was late.

Sasha sat cross-legged on the floor, cuddling a black kitten that squirmed in her arms, his white feet trying to get purchase so he could make a quick exit.

'He's so cute, Kate. What's his name?'

Sasha's bright eyes and animated gaze reminded Kate of a younger version of herself. 'I've called him Snowy.'

'But he's more black than white.' She wrinkled her nose in thought and then laughed. 'Oh, I get it. That's the sort of dumb joke Dad would make.' She immediately slapped her hand over her mouth. 'Sorry, I didn't mean you were dumb.'

Kate laughed. 'That's OK. It's a silly joke but it made me smile, and the day I got Snowy I needed a smile.'

'Why?' Sasha scratched the kitten behind the ears and he stilled.

'I'd had a bad day at work. A lady got some bad news. Sometimes bad things happen to good people and it makes no sense.'

'Yeah.' Sahsa fell quiet for a bit. 'That happened to my mum. She died of cancer when I was in grade four.' Sasha buried her face in Snowy's fur.

Kate's heart bled a little for the young girl. 'That sucks.'

Sasha raised her head, her eyes wide. 'Yeah, it does.' She hugged the kitten close.

'You must miss her.'

Sadness tinged with guilt streaked across her face.

'I do miss her, but I...' Her voice trailed away, her expression uncertain.

Kate sensed she wanted to talk. 'It's OK. You can say what you feel here. It's just me and Snowy.'

'And the horses, the chickens and the dog.' Sasha waved to Rupert, the golden retriever, who stood by the French doors, looking suitably hangdog at not being allowed in the house while that upstart kitten got all the attention.

'Sure, but they've all signed the secrecy act.' Kate smiled, hoping to relax her.

Sasha hesitated and then words poured out. 'Everyone says

I must miss Mum and I really do, but it's not every day.' She gazed at Kate imploringly. 'Some days I even sometimes forget until I go to bed. Is that a bad thing? I feel really bad saying it.'

Kate put her arm around Sasha's shoulders. 'That's a normal and healthy way to feel. Mum wouldn't want you to be missing her every moment of your life. She would want you to grow up, be happy, have adventures and have fun.' *That's what I'd want for my child.*

'I miss her on my birthday and at weird times like last week when we got into the tennis finals.' Sasha blinked rapidly. 'I wanted to tell her so bad that it hurt here.' She put her hand on her chest and sighed. 'But other times I feel bad when I'm having heaps of fun. Like tonight, it was way cool swinging out over the river and letting go of that rope. Mum probably wouldn't have even let me do that! She was pretty strict sometimes.'

Kate smiled and gave her a quick squeeze. 'I think she might have let you do it now you're twelve and have passed swimming survival.' She tightened her sarong and stood up. 'I'm going to make myself an iced coffee. Would you like one of my special ice-cream milkshakes? They always make me feel better about things.'

'Yes, please.' Sasha scrambled to her feet, letting the kitten escape.

'Chocolate, caramel, strawberry or blue heaven?'

'Wow, you have all those flavours?' Disbelief shone from her face.

'Yes, I do. Pretty wicked, isn't it? But why leave behind the great things about being a kid when you grow up?' Laughing, she walked to the kitchen and pulled the blender out of the cupboard.

Sasha sat in the tall chair at the breakfast bar and tapped the top of each bottle of topping trying to decide which one to have.

An idea started to gel in Kate's mind as she mixed the drinks.

'Sasha, you know how we talked about Guide challenges last week and working toward your Junior BP award?'

Sasha nodded. 'I was thinking about doing hiking and camping for one. Once I walked from home to Ledger's Gorge. I really liked it there—it was a good place to think, you know?'

Kate understood completely. 'We all need a place to think when things are tough.'

'Yeah, and sometimes I just need to think.' Sasha seemed to shake herself and she grinned at Kate. 'But I have to do two things off the list, right?'

'You do. Hiking and camping is a fantastic choice for part one. I was thinking what if you chose service as the second topic and you helped raise some money for research into finding a test that can detect ovarian cancer early. That way you're doing something really important and something your mum would be really proud of. It could be your special thing and I'm sure the other Guides would be keen to help. We could wash cars, sell chocolates, that sort of thing.'

Sasha's eyes might be the same colour as her mother's but they sparkled just like Baden's. 'What about a drive-in-movie night like they had in the olden days? That would be so cool.'

Kate chuckled at the 'olden days.' She could remember going to a drive-in herself as a kid. But the idea was a good one. She never ceased to be amazed at the inventiveness of her Guides. Adults needed to remember the enthusiasm of youth and really listen.

She pulled open the freezer and hauled out a large container of ice cream. 'That's a sensational idea. A huge idea in fact. All the Guides could do it as part of their service badge and we could get more help from other organisations. There are plenty of wide-open spaces in Warragurra for a one-night drive-in and I'm sure we can do a joint venture with the hospital and get some publicity. I think we could get it all up and running and do it in two and a half months' time.'

Sasha beamed. 'Erin and I will write down a list of movies that might be good and—'

Rupert started barking as the doorbell chimed. 'Dad's here.' Sasha rose to her feet and raced to the door with Snowy bounding after her.

Baden. Kate's stomach flipped. *Don't do that. We've talked about this.* But talking sternly to her body made scant difference. It betrayed her every time with shimmers of delicious anticipation.

She hadn't seen him for a week as she'd been in Sydney with Brenda. Her reaction was ridiculous, considering the tension-filled few days after Brenda's diagnosis. He was only coming to collect his daughter. He wouldn't be staying; he'd been quite clear about *not* wanting to come for dinner. Not wanting to be friends.

And, really, it was for the best. She wanted an uncomplicated life after the horror of the last couple of years.

She breathed in deeply, steadying her pounding heart, and walked down the long hall. A cacophony of sound assaulted her as she reached the open front door.

Baden stood on her doorstep, his black curls damp and tight as if he'd just stepped out of the shower. His gleaming tanned skin seemed even more golden against his predominantly white open-necked shirt decorated with purple, green and pink stripes. *Sasha chose that shirt.* The thought bounced through her head as she took in the brown leather belt hugging his narrow waist and the long, pleated grey shorts sitting flat against a toned abdomen. Betraying heat quivered inside her. How did he always manage to look so good?

Rupert raced around Sasha and Baden's legs, barking as Snowy meowed frantically and climbed up Baden's shorts.

Kate tried not to laugh as Baden's arm chased a scared kitten across the back of his leg, almost tap-dancing at the same time.

Sasha, oblivious to her father's ripping skin, danced up and down and talked excitedly. 'Dad, this place is so cool and that's Snowy, he's new, and that's Rupert, and he's not new. Sit, Rupert.' Sasha's stern voice surprised the dog, who obediently sat but kept his eye fixed on the kitten. 'And I learned how to light a fire plus we're going to have a drive-in for money for a test for cancer like Mum's and—'

'Whoa, there, Sash.' Baden raised one hand while the other one finally gripped the kitten around the scruff of its neck. Love and laughter shone from his eyes. 'That all sounds fantastic, but how about one bit of news at a time for your poor old dad?' He glanced over the top of Sasha's head, catching sight of Kate. His dancing eyes faded to serious.

Her stomach dropped at the change in his demeanour.

'Sorry I'm late.'

Kate swallowed hard. 'That's OK. The others only left fifteen minutes ago and Sasha and I were getting to know each other.' She bit her lip. 'Sorry about the kitten using you as a climbing post.'

He gave a wry smile as he clamped the squirming kitten with one large hand and scratched Rupert behind the ear with the other. 'Cats love me. Personally, I'm siding with the dog.'

'Dad, Kate's making me a milkshake so can I stay and have mine? Please?' She slid her hand into Baden's. 'You can have one, too.' She immediately swung back to Kate. 'I mean, if that's OK.'

Kate saw a ripple of tension race across Baden's shoulders, and the residual stiffness that remained. It matched his taken-aback look. Steeling herself for his polite refusal, she opened her mouth to confirm Sasha's invitation but Baden spoke first.

'How does that suit you, Kate?' Electric blue eyes questioned her. 'Would we be imposing if we stayed for milkshakes?'

Astonishment burst through her, making her giddy. 'That would be fine.'

'Dad, she's got blue heaven!'

'Has she, now?' He winked at Sasha and then turned to face Kate, his face relaxing into a devastating smile. 'In that case, we have to stay.'

Suddenly an innocuous invitation took on dangerous undertones. The serious, aloof Baden was so much easier to resist.

Baden watched pure ecstasy race across his daughter's face as she sat outside at Kate's large wooden table, sipping a blue heaven milkshake with whipped cream and a cherry on top.

They'd spent an enjoyable and relaxed half-hour making and drinking milkshakes along with a lot of talking, laughter and teasing. Sasha, who could be quiet with adults, was a veritable chatterbox with Kate. Her animated face glowed and her eyes shone when she talked about the fundraising idea of the drive-in.

Kate treated her as a young woman rather than a little girl, asking her opinion on a range of things and gently steering her enthusiasm into achievable ideas. Baden had a sneaking suspicion that the idea of raising funds for ovarian cancer research was Kate's idea but it was a great idea and would help Sasha feel more connected to her mother's memory.

But most of all he loved the fact his daughter was having so much fun.

'This was such a random idea.' Sasha used her long spoon to get the froth from the bottom of the glass.

Baden laughed. 'That's the ultimate compliment, Kate.'

Her lips curved into a soft, enticing smile. 'If I hear random or awesome, I know I'm on the right track.'

Rupert trotted over, a large stick in his mouth, and gazed up at Sasha.

'Can I go and play with him?' She half rose as she asked the question.

Baden checked the time. 'Just for a bit—we have to leave soon. Oh, and put on some insect repellent. The sun's setting and the mosquitoes are coming out. You don't want to get Ross River fever.'

Sasha rolled her eyes. 'Da-ad.'

Kate casually reached behind her to a trolley and picked up the repellent and some matches. She handed the roll-on to Sasha and the matches to Baden. 'You put on the roll-on and your father can light the citronella flares and then we're all protected.'

'Deal.' Sasha grinned. 'Come on, Dad, on with the job.'

'Cheeky!' He grabbed his daughter, tickling her.

Delighted shrieks rose in the air before she managed to escape his grasp and run off with the roll-on, with Rupert racing after her, his golden coat flying.

Baden lit the citronella candles as instructed, thinking about what had just happened. In the most casual way Kate had just deflected a potential standoff between him and Sasha. In fact it had turned into one of those special moments of fun with Sasha that he treasured so much.

He turned back to see Kate sitting in the fading light. The rays of the setting sun danced across her face, highlighting the honey streaks in her hair, the way her soft skin stretched across her high cheekbones and the plump lushness of her mouth. Her laughing eyes caught his.

A jolt of heat flared deep inside him. He returned the matches to the trolley, wishing he could extinguish his reaction to Kate as easily as blowing out the match.

Kate's gaze followed Sasha and the dog across the lawn. 'You have a lovely daughter, Baden.'

Pride filled him. 'Thanks. I think so. Well, most of the time anyway.' He sat down next to her.

'That's pretty much representative of all of us, isn't it?' She rested back in her wide cane chair, all long-legged gracefulness.

His gaze centred in on the toned expanse of skin that the fall of the sarong exposed. *You came in to apologise, so get on with it.* His brain pulled his attention back to the job in hand.

'You're right.' He cleared his throat against a husky voice. 'Last week I had a moment when I should have behaved better.'

Her sculpted brows rose slightly in question as surprise tickled her cheeks, but she remained silent.

'I was insensitive and rude to you when you invited Sasha and me over to dinner. I want to apologise for that.'

She shrugged. 'February is your tough month. We all have to get through things in our own way and not everyone wants company. I understand that.'

She said it as if it was common knowledge but he knew so many people didn't get it. Well-meaning friends had almost smothered him when Annie had died. He hooked her gaze. 'Yes, but you were trying to be a supportive colleague and instead of responding to that I threw your good intentions and your friendship back in your face. I completely overreacted to a simple invitation for a meal.'

Intelligent brown eyes looked straight at him, seeing clear down to his soul. 'You don't have to worry about me chasing you, you know.'

Her candour hit him in the chest. She'd pegged him so accurately it was as if she was in his head, reading his thoughts. Knowing that he feared she might expect more after that kiss. Knowing he couldn't give it.

She continued, a wry smile tugging at her lips. 'After the last few years I'm not in the market for any sort of relationship and I doubt you are either. But I'd like to think we can be friends.'

He grinned as a sensation of lightness streaked through him. 'Friends would be good.' The delight of shared understanding flowed through him. 'Your insight's pretty spot on. Sasha is my top priority now and I'm flat out just keeping up with being a doctor and a father.'

She nodded slowly, her previous expression evolving into a gentle, warm smile, which raced to her eyes. 'You're doing a great job on both fronts.'

He wanted to take her praise and hold it close but a nagging truth spoke up. 'The doctoring compliment I'll accept.' He sighed. 'The parenting, well, I'm not so sure. Sasha hasn't had the uncomplicated childhood that a parent hopes for. Annie's illness was tough on her.'

'It would have been tough on you both.'

Her quiet words circled him with understanding, calling to him, relaxing him. 'The only thing cancer gives you is a chance to tie up all the loose ends, say all the things you ever wanted to say to the person who is dying. Annie and I had been together since high school. We knew each other so well that sometimes we'd finish each other's thoughts and sentences.'

He frowned, remembering some of their arguments. 'Other times we weren't so in tune with each other, but at the end we were both able to put our disagreements aside, say what needed to be said and plan for what would be best for Sasha.

'But cancer steals away everything else.' He shifted in his seat and sighed. 'It stole Sasha's mother. Sash still has all those "firsts" ahead of her and her mum won't be there to help her celebrate them.'

She reached out and touched his hand with the briefest

caress, her warmth spreading through him, almost intoxicating. A chill immediately followed when her fingers left his skin. 'But her father will be there to celebrate.'

His fears for Sasha rose to the surface, almost choking him. 'But will it be enough?' He ran his hand through his hair. 'I'm trying to help her by keeping things the same as they would have been if her mother was still alive.'

Kate tilted her head, confusion creasing her brow. 'How can you do that when her mother has died and everything has changed?'

He shrugged. 'It's not that hard. I've just continued with the family five-year plan.'

She blinked rapidly, as if trying to absorb his statement. 'And that involved leaving extended family and coming to Warragurra, even though your circumstances had changed so much?'

A niggle of annoyance zipped through him at her lack of understanding. 'That's right. It was important to stick to the plan.'

'Really?' Scepticism sounded in her voice. 'You know, Sasha strikes me as pretty mature for her age. I think she's more resilient than you give her credit for.'

Ire simmered inside him. Kate didn't know Sasha like he did. 'She's settled because we've stuck with the plan.' He heard the defensive note in his voice. 'Coming here was important for Sasha because it was what her mother wanted.'

'I think perhaps coming here was important for you. It gave you a map in uncertain times.'

Her words punched him hard, taking the air from his lungs, making his head spin. *Important for you.* His brain railed at the thought. No, she was wrong! Everything he did, he did with Sasha first and foremost in his mind. She always came first.

Resentment surged through him, breaking out against his

imposed control. 'Coming here was a considered decision. I'm not so grief-stricken that I'm blindly following a path.'

'I didn't say you were.'

Her calm tone infuriated him but at the same time it released unexpected feelings, which swirled inside him in a maelstrom of indignation. 'I could have worked anywhere but kids need stability and that's what I'm giving Sasha. She misses her mother and I'm trying to make things as easy and as uncomplicated as possible for her.'

Wide eyes as lush and rich as melted chocolate stared back at him. Understanding tangoed with disagreement.

She bit her lip. 'We can't protect the people we love from everything, no matter how much we want to. Sometimes sheltering them too much is the worst thing we can do.'

He wanted to say *What do you know?* and ignore her comment, but experience showed in the lines around her eyes. He knew then she was thinking of her husband and his parents.

'I'm *not* sheltering Sasha.' He grabbed a calming breath and dropped his voice. 'I'm doing what's best for her. She's lost her mother so doing things her mother wanted for her is the next best thing.' He waited for Kate's response, to hear her agreement. For some ridiculous reason he needed her to say he was doing the right thing.

But her expression, which up until then had mirrored her thoughts, smoothed into neutral, doing little to reassure him.

'Dad, Kate, grab the frisbee off Rupert before he gets to the hedge,' Sasha's breathless voice called as the dog raced toward them.

Laughing, Kate rose to her feet and started to run, her long legs quickly eating up the distance. She threw herself at the animal, rolling onto the lawn, her arms full of dog, her face full of joy.

Devastating loneliness pounded him, leaving behind an aching longing. He wanted to be part of that joy. Hell, he wanted to be in her arms. But that wasn't part of his plan. She didn't want a relationship and he had a daughter to care for.

*Make Sasha your top priority.* He had a promise to keep and a relationship would take his attention from Sasha. His focus couldn't waver from Sasha. He and Sasha were a team with a plan and he was doing what was best for them both. He was an adult and he knew best, no matter what his daughter said or a childless colleague with eyes that he could sink into and a body that he longed to hold against his own.

His plan was right. It had to be right. He squashed the tiny seed of doubt that had raised its head.

# CHAPTER SEVEN

THE hospital lift opened at the second floor and Kate stepped out, immediately turning left. The antiseptic smell mixing with the aromas of the evening meal met her at the ward door and instantly took her back four years to when she had worked here.

She walked to ward 7E and knocked as she pushed the door half-open. 'Brenda, it's Kate.'

A tired voice answered. 'Come in, Kate.'

It had been two months since Brenda had gone to Sydney for surgery. Kate quietly closed the door behind her and sat down in the chair next to the bed. 'I heard you were in for a visit so I thought I'd pop in and say hi.'

Brenda gave a weary smile. 'That's kind of you, Kate. Visiting sick people after a day of working with them isn't exactly R & R for you.'

Kate gave Brenda's hand a gentle squeeze and caught sight of a bright red turban hanging on one hook of the IV stand. The chemotherapy cocktail of drugs hung on the other. 'How's the chemo going?'

'Fine. This is my third cycle and boy, those three weeks between treatments fly past.' She gave a resigned sigh. 'I'm halfway—three down and three to go. The first was the worst because I had no idea what to expect, but now I know about the nausea. As long as I take the antiemetics at the right time I can keep it under control.'

She ran her hand over her head. 'And I haven't got any hair left to lose so that's one less thing to worry about. You have no idea how much time I save in the mornings now I don't have to dry it.' Her dry humour radiated through the words.

Kate tried to smile as sadness settled in her belly. Brenda's no-nonsense approach to life extended to battling a really tough illness. Stage-two cancer was no walk in the park. 'Are you eating enough? You're looking pretty thin.'

Brenda nestled back onto a bank of pillows. 'I eat when I feel like eating. The hospital food isn't always what I want.'

'Can I get you something or make you something you'd enjoy? I make a terrific rice soup and I could whip up a batch tonight for you.' Cooking was the least she could do to help, and she wished she'd thought of it sooner.

'That's kind but—'

A knock sounded on the door. 'Ta-dah! Your take-away order has arrived.' Baden walked into the room, clutching two plastic food containers.

A flush of warmth spread through Kate at his thoughtful gesture. She finished Brenda's sentence for her. 'But Baden has already cooked for you, I see.'

He grinned as he put the food down. 'I wish. But although my chicken soup is good, there's nothing like Walter Wong's chicken and sweetcorn wonton soup for feeding body and soul.' He produced a wide, flat Chinese spoon. 'Eat it while it's hot, Brenda.'

Anticipated delight played across the sick woman's face. 'It smells so good. Thanks for thinking of me, Baden. Des usually brings it in but he had to go home and feed the stock.'

'My pleasure.' He caught Kate's gaze.

She knew immediately he was thinking that compared to what Brenda was facing, him buying some soup was a minuscule effort. But not everyone would have thought of it and that was what made it so special to Brenda.

*And to you.* The familiar voice chimed in her head. Not every doctor would do something like that. Not every man.

Baden picked up the chart.

Kate chuckled. 'You just can't help yourself, can you?'

He shot her a guilty look. 'Just checking to see that the oncologist is on the money.' His eyes darkened and his expression became serious. 'Brenda, make sure the nurses give you the dexamethasone on time.'

'Yes, Doctor.' Brenda gave him a mock salute with the plastic spoon.

He laughed. 'OK, so while I'm being bossy I'll add one more thing. Sleep. As soon as you've finished that soup then sleep so you can enjoy Des's visit tomorrow. Kate and I will leave you in peace but we'll see you in two weeks at the Gemton clinic between chemo courses.'

Brenda put down her spoon and reached out a hand to touch them both. 'You're both doing too much, but thank you anyway.'

'Glad to help.' Baden's voice sounded unusually gruff.

Kate breathed in deeply, feeling unworthy of her thanks. 'I'll look forward to seeing you in one of your bright coloured turbans when we catch up in Gemton.'

'I'll see you both before Gemton. I'm coming to the drive-in night and I'm bringing the entire family, including the cousins who are flying in from Dubbo. All the women are going to wear teal green turbans—it's the worldwide colour to represent ovarian cancer.'

'That sounds fantastic.' Kate marvelled at Brenda's strength.

'Baden explained to me how the CA 125 test can give false

positives.' She shrugged. 'In my case it wasn't a false result but no woman needs the stress of thinking she has cancer when she really has fibroids or endometriosis.' Brenda started waving her spoon. 'Every woman deserves to have a test that is going to be accurate for this disease and I plan to push this cause for as long as I have breath in me.'

She laughed. 'That's enough on the soapbox. Right, off you both go, my soup will get cold.' Brenda shooed them away with one hand and dipped the spoon into the soup with the other.

Kate felt Baden's arm lightly circle her waist to guide her out of the room. Automatically, every particle of her tried to flatten itself against the contact, absorbing as much of his touch as possible. *You're so weak, Kate.*

Guiltily, she stomped on the voice, knowing it to be true, and once out in the corridor she stepped forward, breaking the contact. She put on a no-nonsense voice to cover her lapse. 'I didn't realise you were calling in.'

He shrugged. 'I wasn't, but Sasha got an unexpected invitation for a pizza and movie night so I thought I'd drop by. What about you?'

'Oh, I didn't have any plans so I called in on my way home.' She didn't want to admit that the house was far too quiet, even with Snowy and Rupert.

He shoved his hands in his pockets, his eyes suddenly twinkling against his dark five o'clock shadow—the incredibly sexy pirate look. 'We're both pretty pathetic, then, aren't we? It's Friday night and we're standing in a hospital with empty houses to go to. How about we grab some dinner together? That gives us three hours before I have to pick Sasha up at ten.'

'Sounds like a plan.' Since their conversation at her place they'd settled into a comfortable friendship. Well, comfortable on his side. He treated her like a mate and they talked about all sorts of things. But she still had this crazy super-awareness of him, which had her spinning in circles. His casual touches when he opened doors or moved past her made her dizzy with longing, and she ached with a growing need she'd never experienced before.

But nothing could come of it and she had to learn to control it. Friendship was all she wanted.

*Liar.*

She refused to listen to the traitorous voice in her head that grew louder daily and played havoc with her dreams at night. 'So where shall we go?'

Baden pressed the 'down' button on the lift. 'The Royal Hotel is the closest and Jen raved about the beef she had there the other night.'

*The Kennedy hotel.* Fear clawed her. Bile burned her throat and her heart pounded so fast she thought it would bound out of her chest. 'I can't go to the Royal.'

He spoke quietly. 'Can't or won't? There's a difference.'

She struggled to think against her rising panic. 'You know why I can't go there.' His betrayal fizzed in her veins. 'I can't believe you would even suggest it.'

The light above the lift lit up and the 'ping' sounded as the doors opened. Wrapping her arms tightly around her, Kate stepped into the empty silver box. Anger started to overtake the panic as she punched the ground-floor button.

Baden followed. 'Kate, you live in this town and you have the right to dine where you choose. It's the best restaurant in Warragurra. It just won three hats for country cuisine and I want to take you there so you can enjoy the food.'

She shook her head in disbelief. 'You don't get it, do you? Shane's family owns part of that hotel.'

He stood tall and implacable. 'You can't hide out for the rest of your life, Kate.'

'But if I go there it's as if I'm thumbing my nose at Shane's family's pain.' The lift opened and she stormed out, walking as fast as she could without running.

'Kate.'

She heard his plea for her to slow down but she kept walking.

His hand caught hers and he gently steered her into an interview room and closed the door. 'Let's talk about this.'

Furious with him, she shook his hand away. Immediately the fury turned back against her as the loss of contact throbbed through her like a dull ache. She hadn't wanted to let go. She'd wanted to grip on to his hand tightly, using it like a life raft in a stormy sea.

Baden raked his hand through his hair. 'Don't you think it's time to stop taking the blame for something that wasn't your fault? You're letting Shane's parents' grief control your life. Hiding out won't solve the problem.'

'I'm not hiding out.' How dare he accuse her of that? 'I'm here, back in town, running Guides and—'

'Avoiding this part of town.' He stepped in closer.

His heat washed over her, diluting her anger. 'I don't want to push this. Shane's parents need time.'

'They've had over a year already. You're a lovely person, Kate. Anyone who truly knows you will realise that it's grief that's making the Kennedys act so irrationally.'

'Yes, but—'

'No buts. You need to be seen in town. We have this big fundraiser for the ovarian cancer predictive test research coming up. You've put in hours getting the hospital on board, the flyers printed, you've liaised with the school and you've brokered a deal with the movie-hire company. I haven't even mentioned the diplomatic juggling act of getting five social service groups to work together with the Guides for the fete and food stall side of the night. It's bigger than big.'

Warmth filled her at his praise.

He continued, his face serious. 'The Kennedys and their rich and influential friends need to know what you're doing. They need to know that most of the people in this town respect you enough to back this project. Having them on board will only help ovarian cancer research.'

'So you just want me to do this for fundraising purposes, irrespective of my feelings?' Anger and dread swirled together in the pit of her stomach, forcing nausea to rise. She couldn't believe he was so blinkered that he would put his own feelings ahead of hers.

He shook his head, his eyes dark with thought. 'No, I want to do this for you. If you walk into the pub with me tonight, we're a united front. We're showing people that time has moved on.'

*I want to do this for you.* His thoughtfulness scared her almost as much as walking into the Royal. No one had done anything like this for her. Sure, she'd had lots of support from people out of town but no one in town had offered such solidarity.

He kept talking, ignoring her silence. 'I've already spoken to the manager and he's happily put up a poster for the drive-in and has flyers on the bar tables. You'd be welcome. You can do this. I know it's a big step but it's a step you have to take.'

A thousand thoughts zipped through her mind, colliding and jumbling as she tried to think past her panic. She hated it that he was right.

Baden's arm touched hers. She looked into the clearest of clear blue eyes. Eyes that held understanding and determination. 'If you won't do it for yourself then do if for Brenda and other women like her.'

*Like Sasha's mother.*

Sasha had lost her mother. Baden had lost his wife to this

silent killer. All she had to do was face down a crowd, and perhaps not even that. She breathed in deeply and bit her lip. 'You'll be there all the time?'

He smiled, his face creasing in familiar lines. 'Right beside you.'

Tendrils of longing winged through her, flattening her fear. With Baden next to her she could do this. 'If Brenda can face down cancer and chemo and still crack jokes then I guess I can face down the Kennedys.'

'Fantastic. Let's go.' He reached for her hand.

She spun out of his reach. 'I'll dine at the Royal on two conditions.'

He raised his dark brows in silent question.

'I'm having the seafood platter and you're paying.'

He laughed, the sound so deep it vibrated in her chest.

'What, no dessert?'

She grinned. 'Oh, good idea. I hear their lemon pie is a must.'

He stepped in close, his hands lightly touching her shoulders and slowly trailing down her arms until his hands held hers.

Her mind blanked at his touch.

For a moment she thought she saw desire sparkling in his eyes like sunlight on water, but when she looked again she could only see humour.

He spoke softly, his voice husky with laughter. 'You drive a hard bargain, Kate Lawson. Have you been taking lessons from Sasha?'

'Us girls have to stick together, you know.' Girly giggles bubbled up on a trail of sheer lightness and joy. It took her a moment to recognise the sensation. Happiness. It had been a long time since she'd felt like this…if she'd ever really felt like this.

'Come on, then, before I change my mind or you add French champagne into the mix.'

'That would be an idea if I drank, but I'll happily have French mineral water.'

He pulled her toward the door and out onto the street, their laughter filling the early evening air.

'Race you.' He dropped her hand and started jogging down the street, quickly turning a corner with a wicked wave.

'Hey!' Surprise stalled her for a moment before she began to run, giving thanks she was still in her flat work shoes. She caught him up at the steps of the Royal.

He was leaning casually against the highly polished brass banister, his face devastatingly handsome. 'What kept you?'

She panted indignantly and slugged him playfully on the arm. 'That was cheating. I'm sure I deserved a handicap start.'

He caught her elbow and steered her up the stairs, his head close to hers. 'You're here now, though.' The soft words caressed her hair, her ear and all the way down to her toes.

Realisation slammed through her. He'd used the race to distract her so she wouldn't start to stress on the short walk. She bit her lip. His brand of friendship was everything anyone could want. *Except you want more.*

She tossed the treacherous thought away.

His arm touched the small of her back as he ushered her through the door. As he joined her at the maître d's lectern, his arm circled her waist, the pressure reassuring.

Her heart pounded as she glanced into the dining room but all she could see was a sea of heads.

'Just walk. I'm right here.' Baden gently pushed her forward as the maître d' led the way to their table.

She stared straight ahead, her sight blurred and her mouth dry. Why had she let him talk her into this? Was she such a fool for sky-blue eyes that she'd agree to anything?

In a flurry of scraping chairs and white napkins, Kate found herself sitting opposite Baden, staring hard at the menu.

'I thought you knew what you were having. You can look up, you know.'

His cheeky tone made her lower the tall menu. 'It's all right for you, you're not about to be lynched.'

A serious look streaked through his eyes. 'Neither are you.'

She glanced around. She recognised a few faces. Some tilted their heads to acknowledge her. She forced a returning smile.

Baden ordered and the waiter returned with mineral water, nutcrackers for the lobster legs and hot bread rolls. Kate used every ounce of willpower not to down the glass of water in one go. Instead, she mangled a bread roll.

'Dr Tremont, Katie.'

She looked up to see Richie Santini standing next to their table, holding a glass of mineral water.

Baden rose to his feet and shook Richie's extended hand.

She swallowed hard and tried to sound relaxed. 'Hello, Richie. You're looking better than when I saw you last.'

'That wouldn't be hard, would it?' The man grimaced. 'I saw you come in and I just wanted to say…'

Kate flinched, waiting for the expected words of hatred to follow.

Richie cleared his throat. 'I just wanted to say thanks. They told me at the hospital that without the two of you doing CPR, I wouldn't be here.'

Incredulity stole her breath.

'We're just glad we were there, aren't we, Kate?' Baden's voice filled the gap as he tilted his head encouragingly, his gaze saying *It's your turn to speak.*

She nodded, desperately trying to find her voice against a tight throat filled with emotion. 'It's good to see you, Richie.'

She clinked her glass of water against his, acknowledging the fact he wasn't drinking alcohol.

'Yeah. I'm off the grog. Josh is trying it, too. He's gone to Adelaide for a bit to a clinic there. The Kennedys are paying him sick leave and the cost of the rehab.' He shifted his weight from one foot to the other. 'Turns out you were right after all, Katie. We've been drinking too much for years.'

A rush of thankfulness filled her. At least two of Shane's friends had a second chance. 'It's not about being right, Richie. I'm just glad both of you are getting some help.'

He nodded, his expression resigned. 'I'll see you at that drive-in night, then. Enjoy your meal.' He walked away to his table.

'I can't believe that just happened. And Josh...' She shook her head, bewildered by the thought that Josh was in rehab and that Shane's parents were funding it.

Baden's lips curved into a self-satisfied smile. 'I told you that coming here wouldn't be a bad experience.' He raised his glass. 'To your future in Warragurra.'

*My future.* She should be thrilled that the town was thawing, and on one level she was. On another level she peered into the future and saw only herself. It looked lonelier than it had a few weeks ago.

As she raised her glass to his, the seafood platter arrived at the table. Laden with crayfish, prawns, oysters and Moreton Bay bugs, the table almost groaned under the weight.

The waiter proceeded to clip a bib around each of them. 'Enjoy it. It's absolutely fresh, flown in from the coast this morning.'

'I feel like I'm at the dentist.' Kate chuckled at the white paper bib.

'I'm hoping dinner will be a more enjoyable experience.' Baden smiled his devilish smile as he cracked open a crayfish leg. 'It's not an elegant meal, that's for sure.'

They laughed their way through sensational food, sticky fingers, dribbles down chins and stray squirts of liquid as they cracked, peeled and shucked seafood. They covered a wide variety of topics and never once talked about work. Kate couldn't remember the last time she'd had so much fun.

As she washed her fingers in the lemon-scented water provided for the purpose, she caught sight of Hilary Smithton, bearing down on their table like a rhinoceros at full charge.

The wonderful food curdled in her stomach. She tried for the upper hand. 'Hello, Hilary.'

The seething woman laid her hands palms down on the table, her eyes glittering with anger. 'You've got a hide, coming in here, Kate. Shane made the biggest mistake of his life choosing you over me.' Her voice cracked. 'If he'd married me, he'd still be here.'

And suddenly the years of vitriol all fell into place. Hilary had loved Shane. She blinked rapidly against the futility of hatred. Instinctively she reached out to touch Hilary's hand, to acknowledge that she, too, had lost something, someone.

Hilary pulled her hand away as if the touch had scalded her. 'You might be duping everyone with your saintly fundraising act but I'm not falling for it.'

Baden leaned back casually in his chair, a pleasant smile on his face, but Kate caught an unusual steely glint in his sparkling eyes.

Hilary barely flicked him a glance, her concentration one hundred per cent on Kate. Her lips thinned. 'I won't be coming to your drive-in night and Lucy won't be part of the night either.'

'That's your choice, Hilary, although sad for Lucy.' Kate kept her voice even.

'Good luck with that.' Baden's smooth, controlled voice chimed in, his tone sceptical. 'I know I wouldn't want to be the parent who had to break the news to their kid that they would be the *only* senior student at Warragurra Public School not involved in making fairy floss, cooking sausages or selling smoothies at the drive-in.'

Disconcerted, Hilary swung around to face him. 'What are you on about? It's just the Guides.'

Baden shook his head. 'No, Hilary, it's the town. The town has taken on this project. The hospital is backing it and the school is making it the social service activity of the term. Sure, the Guides are involved, but it's much, much bigger than the Guides. It's bigger than any single person with a personal beef. Every person in this town who has a mother or sister or daughter wants to see a screening test for ovarian cancer become a reality. They're backing the research with their time, money and support.'

All colour faded from Hilary's face before surging back, her cheeks turning bright red. 'Don't preach to me, Dr Tremont. I have the right to choose my own causes.' She spun away from the table and walked out the door.

Baden's words resonated in Kate's head. Was *this* what it was like to be cared for? He had this knack of making her feel special...cherished. *Your mind is running away from you. The fundraising is special to him, too.* Of course it was.

He grinned at Kate, his eyes dancing with wickedness and his curls bouncing with laughter. 'Well, you can't have the whole town liking you, Kate.'

'No, that wouldn't seem right, would it? Hilary will keep me very grounded.' She ran her fingers around the edge of the linen napkin. 'I feel sorry for her, though. She lost Shane twice. Once to me and once to death.'

'But you lost him twice, too. Once to alcohol and once to death.' His quiet voice seemed to caress her.

'I guess I did. It sounds an awful thing to say but I think her loss is greater than mine. Shane is my past and now I'm only looking forward. I've moved on.'

'Have you?' His serious gaze penetrated deeply, as if exposing all her feelings.

'I have.' She caught a shudder of tension ripple through him. 'And what about you?' The words left her mouth on a jet of need before her brain had the sense to cut them off.

His jaw stiffened and his eyes darkened to unreadable before his gaze slid to his watch.

A chill raced through her. Why had she asked? Had she thought if she asked the question it would give her a different answer from the one she knew dwelt in his heart? His situation was so very different from hers. He'd lost a wife he'd loved, lost a happy marriage, a companion, a mother to his child. Of course he hadn't moved on.

She drew on every ounce of acting ability she had, looked at her own watch and jumped to her feet. 'Thanks for a lovely meal, but look at the time. You'd better not be late for Sasha.'

He immediately stood, his expression a jumble of feelings she found impossible to decode. 'Sorry. I do need to go. But it's been great.'

His bonhomie flew to her heart like a poisoned arrow. Until this moment she'd never realised that friendship could be so painful.

Baden stood on Phoebe Walton's veranda at nine-fifty p.m.

He'd hardly noticed the twenty-minute drive out to the farm— his mind had been full of Kate. He could have sat opposite her for hours, just watching the way her smile danced along her cheekbones, how her hair fell so silkily, framing her heart-shaped face, and how her long, thick eyelashes brushed her skin.

But it was the image of her lush lips that stayed with him.

Vivid memories of their touch and taste hovered so very close to the surface of every hour of every day that it terrified him.

He'd loved before and had lost everything. *Except Sasha.* He still had Sasha and she was where his priorities had to lie.

*But Kate...* He jabbed the doorbell viciously, driving the voice away.

Phoebe's mother, Evelyn, opened the door. 'Hi, Baden. Come in, I'll just get Sasha.'

'Thanks.' Baden stepped into the hall and admired Evelyn's artwork, which was going to be on display in the foyer of the hospital as part of the fundraising drive.

Two minutes later he heard Sasha politely thanking Phoebe's mother for having her, but when she appeared in the hall she stomped toward him, her expression grumpy. 'Dad, you're early. None of the other parents are here yet.'

He waved goodnight to Evelyn, picked up Sasha's backpack and slung his arm around her shoulder as they walked toward the car. 'I'm not that early. Mrs Walton said ten o'clock.'

'But the second movie hasn't finished.' She glanced longingly back at the closed door.

'Sorry, sweetheart, but you've got tennis in the morning.' He unlocked the car doors and they both got in.

Sasha tugged at her seat belt, jamming the latch into place with a loud click. 'It's Friday night, Dad. You should have gone out like other parents. I bet you stayed at home and got bored and that's why you're early.' She fixed him with a glare. 'You need some friends, Dad. I've got friends. You need some, too, so you're not just worrying about me all the time.'

Her words chafed at him, irritating and grating. He didn't worry about her—he just wanted what was best for her. 'As a matter of fact, I did go out.'

'What, on your own?' She slumped into the seat, all petulance and peevishness.

'No.' He had an idiotic desire to puff out his chest and boast,
proving to her he wasn't the boring old fuddy-duddy she obviously thought him. 'With Kate.'

Sasha sat up so fast her seat belt locked against her.
Incredulity shone in her eyes. 'Really?'

'Yes, really.' He grinned foolishly.

'Cool! Kate rocks.' She studied him for a minute. 'What did
you do?' Active interest radiated from her.

'We had dinner at the Royal.' The grin stayed on his face,
refusing to slide away.

'Didn't you have a nice time?'

'What sort of question is that? Of course I did. I had a great
time.' Images of the enjoyable evening rolled out in his mind.

'So why are you here early, then?'

Her penetrating stare sent guilt snaking through him.

*Because I was having too much fun.*

*Because I'm thinking more about Kate than about you and
your mother, and that scares me rigid.*

The love he'd had for Annie, the girl next door whom he'd
married, had never felt like this all-consuming rush he experienced with Kate. His marriage had been comforting, dependable and companionable. He'd grieved for Annie but just
lately when he thought of her he didn't ache with loss. He
should still be aching. He should still be missing her as much
as Sasha missed her.

But he couldn't tell his daughter any of this.

He gently prodded Sasha in the ribs. 'Why was I early?
Because, my darling daughter, you know I'm never late.'

Sasha laughed. 'Dad, your jokes are so lame. You are
*always* late.'

'OK, I confess. Kate reminded me of the time so it's her fault. Next time you see her, you tell her how you missed the end of the movie.'

'As if!' Sasha rolled her eyes and turned on the CD player, finding her favourite track. 'Dad.'

'Hmm.'

'It was fun the night we made milkshakes with Kate. Do you think now you've been to dinner with her she might invite us back to Sandon again?'

He caught her wistful expression. 'I don't know, sweetheart. Perhaps.' But the rush of hope that raced through him at the thought matched Sasha's.

# CHAPTER EIGHT

'KATE, I think the allergies have started early this year. I've never had headaches like it. I've even been wearing my sunglasses inside.' Debbie Grayson's colour matched her surname as she slumped in the chair at her kitchen table.

Kate and Baden had finished their clinic and were waiting for Glen to return to collect them. Baden had wandered off with Cameron, Debbie's husband, to look at the new quad bikes Cameron had bought as part of his foray into tourism on the Darling.

'That's no good. Do you want me to have a look at you?' Kate put down her cup of tea.

Debbie looked relieved. 'Would you mind? I feel like I'm taking advantage of you.'

'Don't be silly. You've hosted the day and if you're not well, it's crazy for me to leave without examining you.' She opened her bag and pulled out the ear thermometer.

'They sure beat shaking down the old mercury thermometers.' Debbie tucked her hair behind her ear in readiness.

A moment later the thermometer beeped. 'You've got a slight fever.' Kate gently palpated Debbie's glands. 'And your glands are up but that just tells us your body is fighting something. You said the headaches were different—how are they different?'

'I can't stand bright light and I feel like I've got ants crawling on my skin, around my eye and up into my scalp.' She grimaced. 'The pain is so intense sometimes I feel like crying.'

'And that's not like you at all.' Kate had known Debbie for almost as long as she'd lived in Warragurra. Debbie had been the medical records clerk in ICU at the base hospital until Cameron Grayson had swept her off her feet and brought her out to Bungarra station. Kate snapped on some gloves. 'I'm just going to look in your hair.'

'I said it felt like ants, but I don't have ants or head lice.' Debbie sounded indignant.

Kate parted Debbie's hair and saw a faint rash running along her scalp in a straight line, with occasional blisters. She peered closely at Debbie's forehead and could see a faint red line, a sign of things to come. 'Have you had any sick tourists here lately? Kids?'

Debbie frowned in thought. 'No, I don't think... Oh, yeah, a few weeks ago one poor family had to leave early because both their children came down with chickenpox. But I had chickenpox as a kid so it can't be that, thank goodness.'

Kate stripped off her gloves. 'No, but you can get shingles.'

A horrified look crossed her face. 'Shingles! But I'm only thirty-one and that's an old person's disease.'

Kate shook her head. 'Sorry. You've been flat out getting this new tourist venture up and running, and anyone who's a bit run down and who comes in contact with the herpes zoster virus can have the virus reactivated. Only this time you don't get chickenpox, you get shingles, and the virus runs along the nerve it's been hibernating in for all those years. In your case, it's running along the fifth cranial nerve.'

'So what happens now?' Debbie stared at her anxiously.

'We get Baden to confirm my diagnosis and then we start

you on antiviral medication. I'll just go and give the boys the hurry-up. They should have talked torque and RPMs and all that engine stuff by now, as well as test driven the bikes.' She walked outside and saw the men, both deep in conversation and striding back toward the house.

'Coo-ee.' She gave the bush call.

Baden immediately looked up, and gave her a wave and a smile.

A smile that sent tendrils of pleasure spiralling through her. A smile she hugged close and revisited too often on long, lonely nights.

The men increased their pace and Baden was the first to reach the bottom of the veranda steps, his long legs taking them two at a time. 'Are we ready to go?'

'No, Glen hasn't called yet. But I think Debbie has shingles.'

'What's that?' Cameron's concerned voice broke into their conversation.

'Come inside, mate, and I'll explain it to both of you at the same time.' Baden opened the wire door and ushered everyone inside.

Baden examined Debbie. 'You're lucky we're here today because the earlier you start to treat shingles, the better the prognosis and the shorter the illness. It can be excruciatingly painful, as Deb's finding out. So bed rest for you, young lady, a dark room, painkillers and sleep.'

Debbie groaned. 'I can't just stop. How's Cam supposed to run the station *and* look after the tourists?'

Kate reached out and squeezed Debbie's shoulder, hating that she had to break the bad news to the hard-working couple. 'Debbie, you're in quarantine. The tourists can't be in the house while you're infectious. Each blister contains the virus and just like chickenpox you have to stay isolated.'

'But we're fully booked.' Debbie dropped her head into her hands.

Cam sat down next to Deb and wrapped her in a hug, his large arms enveloping the petite woman.

Did Debbie know how lucky she was to be loved like that? Kate pushed away the errant and slightly jealous thought.

Cam stroked Deb's hair. 'I'll call in Beth Johnson and she can cook for the guests in the shearing shed—that will keep everyone out of the house.'

Debbie burst into tears.

Cam looked bewildered as his usually in-control wife sobbed on his shoulder. He patted her back. 'The tourists will be fine, love, honest.'

Debbie sniffed. 'But I'm going to miss Brenda's fundraiser on Saturday, and I can't even visit her. If Brenda got something like this now, with her immune system whacked from chemo, she could die.'

Kate exchanged a worried look with Baden. Debbie was clearly exhausted, sick and overwrought.

'Well, she'd get pretty sick and you're right, you wouldn't want to risk it.' Baden produced some tablets and poured a glass of water. 'Take these, Debbie, they'll ease the pain. We'll leave you with the famciclovir, some cream for the rash if it gets really itchy, and some strong painkillers. I want you to phone the base tomorrow to report in.' Baden suddenly became unusually stern, his gaze fixed on Debbie and Cameron. 'If the rash develops near your eye, you're to radio the base immediately.'

'Why?' Debbie raised her head from Cam's shoulder.

'There is a slight chance you might develop shingles running through your eye and if you did it's serious and we would need to fly you to the Base Hospital to see an ophthalmologist.'

Fright raced across Debbie's face. 'How can I stop that from happening?'

Baden sighed. 'You can't, but you *can* take the antiviral medication and get plenty of sleep, which will help your body heal.'

'I'll make sure she takes the tablets and rests, Baden.' Cam pulled his wife to her feet. 'You go to bed, honey.'

'I'll come and get your room set up, close the blinds and make sure you have what you need.' Kate picked up a jug and a glass and followed Debbie down the hall into a large bedroom. French doors opened out onto the veranda to catch the breeze on hot summer nights.

'You put your nightie on and I'll make your bed.' Kate pulled the bottom sheet taut and executed hospital corners. She always got a great sense of satisfaction from making beds and settling patients so they were comfortable. She pulled the curtains closed, blocking out the light to lessen Debbie's photophobia.

'Oh, that bed looks so good.' Debbie sank into it.

Kate tucked her in. 'The analgesics will kick in soon and they might make you feel dizzy so don't go trying to do anything, OK?'

'Yes, Sister.' Debbie snuggled into the pillows and then fixed Kate with a piercing look. 'That Baden's a bit of a dish, isn't he?'

Kate groaned inwardly. Ever since Debbie had married Cam she'd been trying to matchmake everyone else. Initially Kate had been safe from Deb's scheming because she'd been married, but not any more. 'I suppose he is if you like the rakish dark-haired look.'

Debbie raised her brows. 'And you don't?'

*I adore it.* 'I think it's dangerous.' She set up the jug of water and put it on the bedside table along with a little hand bell she'd found on the bookshelf.

Debbie adjusted her top sheet. 'Now, that's where you're

wrong. You're mistaking danger for adventure. Don't you think it's time you tried some adventure, Kate?'

'Shane gave me enough adventure to last a lifetime, Deb. I don't want complications, I want a quiet life.' She tucked the sheet in briskly, hoping to put an end to the conversation.

'Shane gave you grief, sweetie, not adventure. There's a big difference.' Debbie squeezed her hand and yawned. 'Just think about it.' Her eyes fluttered closed.

Kate quietly closed the door behind her and rested against it for a moment. *Don't you think it's time you tried some adventure?* For a few moments the idea played across her mind, weaving daydreams and delicious thoughts.

*It's ludicrous.* She pushed herself off the door. She didn't want to get involved again and even if she did, Baden wasn't offering her anything, let alone adventure. It was just the strong painkillers making Debbie babble on and she shouldn't be taking anything Deb said seriously.

There was no point thinking about adventure with a raven-haired doctor. The *only* thing she should be thinking about was getting home tonight and making some final calls for the drive-in fundraising night. Surely Glen must be arriving soon.

Baden passed Kate her satellite phone, which started ringing the moment she walked back into the kitchen. He watched her take the call. He'd observed her so often over the last few weeks he could now recognise many of her expressions. Rapid blinking meant unexpected news.

She snapped down the antenna of the phone. 'That was Glen. He's worried about the weather so he wants us to meet him at the old strip out by Dog Tired Hut.'

'Dog Tired Hut?' Baden laughed at the name. 'Why would there even be an airstrip at such a place?'

'My great-grandfather built that hut after a particularly difficult droving season.' Cam rinsed out the teacups. 'He used it for rest and shelter on the big drive south. These days when we're mustering, we use the hut as a lunch stop and an Av-gas station. The helicopter lands there to refuel so the strip's in good nick.' Cameron glanced out to the west. 'I don't like the look of those clouds, though. Still, Glen will have seen the radar so he must reckon he can get in before the rain turns the strip to mush.'

Baden followed Cam's stare. 'Those clouds have come across the sky every day for a week, just teasing us with the idea of rain.'

'Yeah, but Dad was complaining of aching knees this morning and as a rain predictor, they rarely fail.'

'That's pretty scientific, Cam.' Baden raised his brows at his host.

Cam looked suitably embarrassed. 'I know, but despite my postgraduate qualifications in agriculture, including a unit on weather patterns, Dad's knees are the most constant predictor.' He fished a set of keys out of his pocket. 'Take Betsy out to the hut and I'll get out there later in the week to collect her.'

He tossed the keys to Kate. 'You'd better drive her but teach the doc the trick with the column shift so he's set for next time.'

Kate caught the keys and grabbed her gear. 'I'll go and sweet-talk her into starting first time. Keep a close eye on Deb, Cam, and ring us any time.' She peered into the sky. 'I hope you get some rain but not until I'm home.'

He nodded slowly in agreement. 'Take care.'

Baden shook Cam's hand. 'Thanks, mate. See you next month.'

He followed Kate out to Betsy. Cameron's door-less ute was legendary but this was the first time he'd had ever had to use it. He put their medical bags in the back tray under an old hessian wheat sack before sliding in next to Kate on the old bench seat.

She grinned and handed him a surgical mask.

He turned it over in his hand. 'What's this for?'

'Dust. Move away from the door to avoid the worst and find somewhere to hang on because there are no seat belts.'

*Somewhere to hang on.* His gaze settled on Kate. He quickly took advantage of a legitimate invitation to sit really close to her. His palm itched to settle on her thigh.

Moving toward her, he slung his arm casually along the back of the seat. Faint vestiges of her floral perfume wafted toward him. How did she manage to smell so good after a day spent in heat and dust? The question lay unanswered as he lost himself in her scent.

Her brow creased in concentration as she pushed the key into the ignition. 'Right, then.' She patted the dashboard. 'Sweetie, you're going to behave for me today, aren't you?'

He pulled his sunglasses down over his eyes, his mouth twitching. 'You're talking to a *car.*'

'Shh, she's really sensitive. She comes through on emergencies, but if she knows it's just a regular drive she can play up.'

He put on his mock serious expression. 'Perhaps I should introduce myself to put her at ease?'

She shot him a derisive look, but humour spun through her eyes. 'That won't be necessary as you're not driving, but it's absolutely essential when you do drive.' Her fine-boned hands closed around the large steering-wheel. 'Now, you pump the accelerator twice before you turn her on.' Kate's foot pumped then she bit her lip and turned the key.

The engine roared into life and Kate gave him a broad smile of delight. He loved they way she got such a thrill out of the little things in life. 'Well done. What's next?'

'Put your mask on.' She pulled her own on and then pushed the column shift toward the wheel and down and Betsy moved forward. 'The problem isn't getting into first gear but into second. Relax the pressure on the gearstick as you pass neutral.'

He watched the concentration crease her forehead as she changed into second. 'You seem to know a lot about cars.'

She laughed. 'I know squat about cars but Emily taught me all about Betsy. She's the one who will whip up the bonnet and fiddle about. I guess it's the legacy of five brothers.' She relaxed as she manoeuvred the shift into third gear, her leg brushing his. 'No, I'm a real girl. If the battery plays up I can hit the terminals with my shoe and that's about it.'

'Does it work?'

She suddenly looked sheepish. 'It usually gets a man to come to my aid who's prepared to get his hands grimy and jump-start the car.'

'Ah! So all this feminist independence is a front.' He loved teasing her.

'No.' Her voice sounded huffy but her eyes sparkled above the mask. 'I am completely independent, except for cars. I just hate getting my hands covered in grease, or anything dirty for that matter.'

'But it just washes off.' He shook his head. 'You sound just like Sasha.'

'Wise girl, your daughter.'

Her high-wattage smile radiating from her eyes hit him soul deep. Her eyes reflected laughter and affection, backlit by something more. Instinctively his hand curled around her shoulder, easing his body into hers, closing the slight gap between them.

As the ute bounced over unmade road and plumes of dust billowed out, conversation became impossible. Kate's body was touching his as she headed Betsy toward the hut. He could feel the rise and fall of her chest, strands of her hair blown by the wind caressed his cheek and her soft skin lay against his own.

All thoughts of his work responsibilities and his worries about Sasha drained out of him. Nothing existed except the two of them alone on this long, straight and dusty track. *Just the two of them.*

It felt…right

He hoped it would take a really long time to get to Dog Tired Hut.

The rain started to fall three kilometres from their destination. Kate sat forward, concentrating on the track that was fast becoming red, sucking mud.

For the last twenty minutes she'd driven with Baden's arm curved around her and his leg pressing against hers, just as if they were two teenagers sneaking off together. She hated it that it felt so good. So right.

'I don't like the look of this rain.' She scanned the horizon, hoping to see the plane. 'I thought Glen would have been waiting for us.' A niggle of anxiety skated through her.

'He can't be too far away.' Baden gave her shoulder a reassuring squeeze.

Occasional drops that splattered them turned into driving rain that came straight into the ute as they approached the hut. Kate pulled to a stop, the wheels skidding in the mud. She whipped off her mask. 'Let's make a run for the hut. We'll be drier in there.'

Her feet hit the ground and she immediately sank into ankle-deep mud. 'Oh, yuck.' She looked sadly at the red mud that had trapped her shoes. Pulling each foot out with an audible slurp, she gingerly made her way to the back of the ute.

Baden picked up her medical bag and passed it to her. She extended her hand to grab the handle but her grip was slick with rain and it slipped. She leaned forward, reaching to catch the bag before it sank into the mud, but she overbalanced. Her feet gave way and she fell head first into the quagmire.

'Are you OK?' Baden extended his hand, his lips compressed, trying to suppress the laughter that shook his body.

She glanced down at herself to see red clay caking her from shoulder to toe. Rain and mud plastered her uniform to her, making her look like a cross between a mud wrestler and a wet T-shirt competitor. Her fingers pulled uselessly at her clinging shirt, which hid little. 'I can't believe I did this. I'm filthy.'

Baden's hand gripped her wrist and he pulled her to her feet, his face alive with amusement and a flash of appreciation. 'At least your hands aren't covered in grease.'

His laughter carried away her dismay and she joined in. 'I think I can add mud to my list of icky substances I don't like being covered in.' Rain ran down her neck, as well as into her shoes. She tossed her head back and spread her arms out wide, willing the plane to arrive, attempting to wash herself at the same time.

'Come on, you're soaked. Let's go inside.' Holding his medical kit with one hand and her hand with the other, he jogged toward the hut and unbolted the door.

The satellite phone rang in her pocket as they stepped over the threshold. Swallowing her horror, she wiped her muddy hands on the one bit of her shorts that was dry and punched the answer button. 'Glen, I'm on speakerphone. We're at the hut but where are you?'

'Sorry, Kate, Baden, I've had to divert due to the weather. It's very local but I can't risk the plane on the strip. I can pick you up from McCurdy's.'

Baden frowned. 'But that's one hundred kilometres from here and the track will be a bog.'

Kate nodded and spoke to Glen. 'Even if we could get there, which we doubt we can, we couldn't make it before nightfall.'

'I can't land at night unless it's an emergency. Sorry, guys, but I think you're stuck for the night.' Glen's apologetic voice came down the line. 'We'll reassess everything in the morning.'

She glanced at Baden and they spoke at the same moment. 'Sasha.'

'Glen, we have limited battery life. Sasha Tremont needs to be collected from after-school care and looked after for the night. Can you organise that?'

'Sure. I'll radio Jen, who'll sort it out. Don't worry, Baden, she'll be fine, and my kids will love having a visitor for the night. Meanwhile, enjoy your outback adventure, guys. Over and out.'

The line went dead.

Baden started to pace and his hand tugged at his hair. 'Hell. How can I be a doctor and a decent father? She hasn't ever slept over at Glen and Jen's and she shouldn't even have to.'

Kate put her hand on his arm as an overwhelming need to reassure him settled in her belly. 'It's OK. These things happen in the outback. If you were a plumber you could have got stranded by this rain and washed-out roads. Sasha knows the Jacobses. Hannah's in her class and they're in the same patrol at Guides. She'll love having an unexpected sleepover.'

He sighed, his expression not quite in agreement. 'I suppose so but I promised her we'd make toffee tonight for the stall. I hate letting her down.'

A flash of irritation sparked in her. Why was he this hard on himself? 'You're not letting her down. You're raising a kid who knows she's loved and who goes with the flow. At Guides, she's the one who copes with unexpected things when the others panic or just get frustrated because something hasn't gone according to plan. She knows you're not in any danger so she won't be stressing. In fact, if I know Sasha, she'll be organising Jen and the kids to make the toffee.'

A wry smile tugged at his lips as his apprehensive expression slowly faded. 'She organises me all the time so you're probably right. She'll be making the most out of this unexpected situation.'

Tension seemed to flow out of his body and an unfamiliar aura of lightness surrounded him. His eyes danced, his brow cleared and a sinful smile clung to his lips.

The change was intoxicating. She'd never seen him look like this. It was as if he'd discarded the burdens that had been clinging to him from the moment she'd met him.

He glanced around at the spartan hut. 'Meanwhile, *we* need to make the most of this situation.'

The double entendre of his words hung in the air. Her heart hammered hard against her chest.

His desire-fuelled gaze came back to rest on her. She could feel his eyes travelling the length of her body. Her skin, cool from the rain and mud, heated up so fast she could swear she could hear the water sizzle.

He stepped in close. 'I think the first thing we need to do is get out of these wet clothes.' His words rolled out, low and husky.

She swallowed hard at his crystal-clear intent. 'Really? We don't have spare clothes.'

He tucked her wet hair behind her ear. 'It would be the responsible thing to do. After all, we don't want to get hypothermia.'

Every nerve ending was firing off rounds of heat and the idea of hypothermia seemed ridiculous, but her body started to shiver. She couldn't tell if it was from cold or anticipation.

He tilted his head toward the old bed, covered with a couple of even older rag quilts. His grin—one of sheer devilment and daring—raced across his face. 'I think that for *tonight* this is our best option.'

She stared up at him, sinking into eyes so blue, completely

caught in their hypnotic effect. *You're weak, Kate. This is just a moment in time. He's only offering one night.*

But he could have asked her almost anything at that point and she would have said yes. She was done with being sensible. Being sensible had only brought her heartache. She didn't want marriage and commitment and neither did he. No promises were being made, just an agreement of a stolen moment in time.

*I need this. I'm taking this one moment in time because it will never come my way again. The memory will keep me warm in the lonely nights ahead.*

'So you think that snuggling up in that bed for this *one night* would be the best idea?'

His expression registered the deal on the table. 'I do. Body heat is powerful stuff, Kate.' His finger drew a feather-soft trail down her cheek.

She swayed toward him, placing her hands on his chest, her fingers feeling the solid muscle beneath his wet shirt. 'But I'm all muddy.'

'I'll wash you.'

Blood roared in her ears at the image his words created. Then his mouth came down onto hers, his tongue caressing her lips with soft and delicate touches, making her feel cherished and adored. Sending waves of longing pounding through her, setting her legs trembling.

Her hands found his hair, his curls all wet and soft under her fingers. She opened her mouth to his, welcoming him, giving herself to him, letting him take away a year of pain and loneliness. Taking a moment in time for herself.

Her hand found the buttons on his shirt and she started to undo each one, her fingers stiff and shaking with a mixture of cold and need.

Still his mouth stayed on hers, creating sensations she'd

never known. Aching pleasure built inside her and her body quivered, longing for him to touch more than just her lips.

As if reading her mind, Baden eased his lips from hers and trailed kisses along her jaw. He murmured against her neck, 'You're beautiful. You're beautiful covered in mud, you'd be beautiful covered in grease, and you've been driving me crazy for the last three and a half months.'

'Have I?' She needed to hear him say it again, to drive away the nightmare of her marriage.

His hands slid under her shirt, dextrously releasing the catch on her bra. 'You have and I can't wait to see all of you, muddy or not.'

A thrill zipped through her, heading straight to her core. She pushed his shirt from his shoulders and pressed her lips to his chest, tasting rain mixed with salt and feeling taut muscle under skin. Hers for tonight.

He pulled her shirt over her head, dropping it onto a chair before pulling her close, his hands splayed against her back, kneading her spine.

Skin against skin. Breast against chest.

Waves of need crashed through her.

She fought to memorise every moment of this brief time with him but as pleasure surged through her, she let herself be swept away on a tide of bliss.

'You're cold.' He pulled her toward the bed and with a scrambling of hands—belts, bra, shorts and pants cascaded into a heap. Laughing, they both fell onto the bed, the old springs creaking under their weight and the mattress sinking in the middle, rolling them together.

Legs entwined. Cold flesh met cold flesh, instantly flaring into heat.

'Let me warm you,' he murmured gently into her hair as his

hand cupped her breast. His thumb brushed her nipple, which instantly rose to his touch.

White lights danced in front of her eyes as rivers of wonder flowed through her. Wonder that he touched her with such tenderness, wonder that he wanted her.

She wanted him. Her body vibrated with need as her hands raced all over him, touching him, feeling him, making sure this was all real but knowing it was really an illusion—a fantasy in a moment of time.

She didn't care.

He caught her hands loosely and held them above her head, his focus entirely on her pleasure. With a low guttural moan he trailed kisses across each breast and then closed his mouth softly over her tingling nipple, his tongue gently lashing the sensitive nub.

A groan of ecstasy escaped her parted lips, the sound completely foreign to her. Nothing she had ever experienced before had been like this.

She gripped his shoulders as she unconsciously rose toward him, never wanting him to stop.

He raised his head, his eyes simmering with wickedness. 'So that works for you, does it? What about this?' He dipped his head, his tongue trailing a curving path past her belly button and beyond.

Her hands frantically gripped his head as he wove his magic. It was too fast, she wanted to savour it moment by moment but her body disagreed. Her mind shut down completely, driving out all thoughts, all arguments, all common sense. Her mind gave over to her body to glory in everything being offered. She took it all greedily, like a thirsty person took water, not knowing when it might be offered again.

Layer upon layer of tingling, glorious sensation built on

itself deep inside her, like a furnace being constantly stoked, intensifying with every stroke of his tongue, taking her higher and higher until she teetered on a precipice, sheer pleasure and pain blurring. She called his name, then shattered into a million shards of light as ribbons of liquid paradise poured through her, mellowing her completely.

She lay back on the lumpy pillow, Baden's smiling face above her, looking very self-satisfied. The wondrous feelings suddenly faded, leaving her muscles twitching, aching and empty. She reached for him. 'That was very nice, thank you, but I think you can do better.'

He brushed her damp hair from her face. 'Is that so?'

'Hmm, yes.' She traced the contours of his face, the pads of her fingers absorbing him like a blind person absorbed Braille.

He lowered his head and whispered deliciously wicked suggestions into her ear.

All thoughts of teasing faded as her body thrummed with aching need for him. She rose up against him, welcoming him into her, needing him to complete her in an age-old way. Glorying in his need of her.

Together they created a rhythm that drove them higher and higher until they cried out together and tumbled over the edge, freefalling—forever entwined.

Baden stoked the fire and spread Kate's rinsed clothes out along the fireguard to dry. Kate stood beside the fire wrapped in a quilt, all rosy pink after her wash in the hipbath, all dark hair and dark eyes. She looked lush and delectable.

Memories of how lush and delectable she was had him pulling her into his arms. He sat down with her cuddled on his lap.

'Your clothes will be dry soon.'

She snuggled against him. 'Thanks for looking after me. The

bath was divine and somehow you even made instant noodles taste palatable.'

He laughed and dropped a kiss into her hair, which smelt of lavender shampoo. 'I think you were just so hungry you weren't as discerning as usual.'

'Perhaps.' She stifled a yawn. 'What time is it?'

He glanced at his watch. 'Nine o'clock. Why?'

She put a finger to his lips before slipping off his lap and pulling him to his feet. 'Come and look at this.' With the quilt trailing behind her like a bride's train, she padded over to the door and stepped outside.

He'd never seen a sky like it. Silver lights danced across the ink-black sky. Twinkling stars in all their sparkling glory rained their light down on them. The Southern Cross constellation hovered on the horizon and the moon was yet to rise. 'It's beautiful.'

Kate picked up his hand and pointed with it. 'Look over there.'

He peered up, his eyes straining to discern something special amongst the mass of stars. Then he saw a streak moving across the sky. He couldn't believe his eyes. 'Is that a comet?'

She turned to him, her face alive with excitement. 'Yes, and not only is tonight the best night to see it, we're out here with no light pollution.'

He pulled her close, loving the way her curves fitted into him. 'It's a special night all round.'

She laid her head on his shoulder. 'One worth remembering.'

Her quiet words unexpectedly speared him. *One night.* It was what they both wanted, what they had both agreed to. Neither of them was able to offer more. He couldn't risk loving again, he had to protect Sasha. Kids loved easily, but as Kate didn't want a relationship he couldn't risk Sasha getting attached. Another loss could devastate her.

But he had tonight. They had less than twelve hours before real life returned. Before he was a doctor again, before he was a father again. Before life returned to what it had been.

So why the hell was he out here, looking at stars?

He swung her into his arms and took her back inside.

# CHAPTER NINE

'MINE!' Sasha dived for the ball, catching it and hugging it to her chest with one arm as she swam with the other toward the water polo goal.

'Not likely.' Baden ducked under the water and came up next to her, tickling her around the waist until she surrendered the ball.

'That's cheating.' Her indignation came out on a wave of laughter as she grabbed her father by the feet.

Baden disappeared under the water in a haze of bubbles, the ball bouncing up to the surface of the water.

Kate grabbed it, shimmied up onto the edge of the pool and sat watching father and daughter do battle, not even aware their target had been poached. She hated to admit it but she could watch them together for hours. Baden was a wonderful father and he and Sasha had a very close relationship, which wasn't surprising, considering what they'd both been through.

It couldn't be easy, raising a daughter on your own, and she was happy to help but Baden kept Sasha to himself. Stupidly, she couldn't shake the irrational thought that after their wonderful night together at Dog Tired Hut, he might just want to spend a bit more time with her. That he might want Sasha to spend some more time with her. She sighed. It seemed that was just a giant flight of her imagination.

The only reason Sasha and Baden were swimming in her pool was because they'd spent the morning making sausage rolls in her kitchen for the drive-in night. And the only reason that Baden had come was because of the purpose of the night. He was committed to the ovarian cancer fundraiser. He didn't want anyone to lose a loved one like he had.

Lose a wife.

Baden might have *made* love to her three nights ago but he was still *in* love with his wife. So much so that he was still trying to live his life as if she were still alive.

She didn't think it was healthy for him or Sasha but, then again, what did she know? Her marriage had been a disaster and his, she suspected, had been wonderful, so it was like comparing apples to oranges. She couldn't imagine what it would be like to lose someone who completed you.

*Baden completes you.*

The random thought thundered through her. Immediately, every part of her tried to eject it from her brain. No, it wasn't possible—she wouldn't allow that kind of thinking.

Sasha and Baden both surfaced from their underwater chase, spluttering and still trying to dunk each other when they saw Kate holding the ball.

They pulled themselves out of the pool and sat next to her, flanking her, catching their breath. Cosy warmth spread through her as Sasha's arm wrapped around her waist and she cuddled in close.

'Lost something?' Kate smirked as she stroked the ball, the thrill of oneupmanship streaking through her. 'You two are hopeless. You're so busy trying to outdo each other that you took your eye off the main game.'

Sasha giggled. 'You sound like a mum, Kate. My mum used to say Dad and I were too competitive.'

Kate surreptitiously glanced at Baden, expecting the usual tension to enter him like it always did whenever Annie was mentioned. But his demeanour didn't change at all.

He gave a deep, rumbling laugh. 'I can still beat you, Sash.'

'Wanna bet?' Sasha flicked water at him with her feet.

Kate spun the ball on her index finger, taunting them both. 'I'm thinking that as neither of you actually *have* the ball then I win.'

Baden and Sasha instantly exchanged knowing looks and suddenly their arms circled Kate. For a moment she was cocooned and a flash of what it might be like to be part of their lives spooled through her mind. Loved by a man who was defined by his caring. Mother to a girl with great spirit and determination. Part of a loving team—part of a family.

Then the arms tightened around her and she felt herself moving. 'Hey!' But her cry was lost as she was pushed into the water by four hands and then tickled mercilessly. She kicked to the surface. 'You two fight dirty.'

'Yeah.' Baden grinned and pulled her close, his arms and legs immobilising her against him. 'Sash, I've got her, you get the ball.'

Sasha ducked under and tickled Kate under the arms.

Kate released the ball in self-protection as her chest muscles ached with laughter. 'Not fair—two against one.'

'Got it, Dad.' Sasha swam toward the goal.

Kate expected Baden to swim after Sasha, but he unexpectedly stayed put.

She looked up into eyes full of fun that suddenly darkened with longing. His arms pinned her against his length, nothing between them but thin Lycra.

Her blood pounded in her ears as it raced his heat through her, waking every part of her. Reminding her of the night they'd spent together and refuelling the need that simmered permanently under the surface into boiling yearning.

Water dripped from his flattened curls onto her face, the droplets making a slow and erotic trail down her cheek. With each breath his chest rose and fell against hers, his heart beating hard, matching her own.

For the shortest moment he looked over her head toward Sasha, who was concentrating hard on shooting a goal, then his gaze returned, searing her with need. He swooped his lips down against hers, hot, hard and urgent. He kissed her, seizing her breath, branding her with his touch and taste and tantalising her with a glimpse of what she knew he could offer.

Then he spun her out of his arms and swam like a man possessed toward Sasha. 'Great goal, sweetie.' He gave her a high five. 'What a team.'

Panting for breath and completely stunned, Kate trod water as the world regained its axis, and all vivid colours faded. Ordinary life returned, looking pale and wan.

His naked need stayed with her. She recognised that need, she was intimate with it as it mirrored her own. She knew in the depth of her soul he wanted her in his arms. That one night had not been enough.

And she so wanted to be back in his arms, feeling cherished and treasured. Back in the arms of this wonderful man who'd quietly supported her as she'd faced the town. He'd pushed her to take a risk, but he'd been with her every step of the way. This brilliant, caring doctor, this considerate and adventurous lover, and this devoted father with a huge capacity to love.

She loved him.

She gripped the side of the pool as the muscles in her legs went weak with realisation and stopped treading water.

Oh, this wasn't good. She rested her head on the curve of the bull-nose pavers. She'd fallen in love with a man locked in the past. A man whose love for his dead wife still coloured his decisions and governed how he raised his daughter. A man who kept himself and his daughter locked away from the love she had to offer.

For weeks she'd tried not to love him. He didn't want to be loved and she knew only too well that love didn't work for her. But despite everything she'd tried, love had sneaked in. She loved him and she loved his daughter.

Sasha.

*Sasha is my top priority now.* Baden's determined voice resonated in her head. Sasha came first, which was how it should be. But what if she could show him that Sasha came first with her as well? Could that possibly open his eyes to the idea that he could love again? That he could love her? The thought embedded in her mind, sinking down deep with penetrating roots.

'You're cutting it really fine.' Gwen Lloyd, the sister in charge of the Opal Ridge Bush Nursing Hospital, filled the burette on Hughie's IV, diluting the penicillin infusion.

Baden checked his watch. 'I'll just make it as I've only got Dimity to assess and I can dictate the referrals at home.'

'Sorry, me sugars have gone haywire, Doc. It's this bloody cough.' The old miner sat forward as his frail frame shuddered with a racking cough.

Today's clinic had been frantic. The current virus had swept the small town and everyone had called into the clinic, hoping he could prescribe a magic cure. For most people all he could prescribe was TLC, bed rest and plenty of fluids. But the elderly had been hit harder and he had two suspected cases of pneumonia.

'Cough that goop up, Hughie.' Gwen put her hand on Hughie's bony back and held a specimen jar under his mouth.

Baden had started Hughie on penicillin but he needed to drop the specimen of sputum off at Warragurra Base Pathology for an accurate culture. He put the small plastic container with its bright yellow lid into a cooler bag. 'I'll ring through the results. We might need to change the antibiotics.'

Gwen nodded. 'I'll call you if he doesn't improve.'

Baden put his hand over Hughie's work-scarred one. 'Don't you worry about me, Hughie. I've got enough time to get back to Warragurra. You only need to concentrate on getting well.'

The old man slumped back onto the pillows, his eyes bright with fever. 'Don't you think it's time you got yourself another wife, lad, instead of all this rushing about? She could be looking after your little girl.'

Baden forced a smile to his face. All his elderly patients who lived alone thought he should have a wife. 'It's a different world, Hughie. Even if I did marry, which I'm not going to do, my wife would probably be working and I'd still have to collect Sasha.'

'Humph.' Hughie wasn't impressed. 'Well, all this gadding about, it's not what a family is all about.' He closed his eyes, ending the conversation.

Baden sighed. 'Gwen will look after you, Hughie, and hopefully we won't have to fly you to Warragurra. Remember to eat all the food so your blood sugar is stable.'

Thirty minutes later, he kept his eye on the speedometer as he sped down the bitumen road toward Warragurra. A speeding ticket was the last thing he needed on top of his frantic day. He wished he could drive and dictate at the same time. All the paperwork would have him up until midnight.

Paperwork Kate usually did for him if she was rostered on with him. But Kate never came with him to Opal Ridge. Today she'd stayed in Warragurra, running an in-service for the nurses. Gwen did a great job but she wasn't Kate.

Kate.

Kate, who four nights ago had made love to him with a passion that had taken his breath away. Together, their lust for each other should have set the old hut on fire. Yet, when he thought about their stolen time, those few hours in the outback, it was the joy of holding her close, the wonder of her comforting heat snuggled against him and the banter and serious discussions late into the night that stayed uppermost in his mind.

But it had been a 'once only' night—they'd both been adamant about that. So why did his arms ache at not being able to hold her?

Today had seemed twice as long without her. He'd missed her friendly smile and her jokes and their conversation. They talked about all sorts of things and today he'd wanted to get her advice on the best way to broach the topic of periods with Sasha. Last night he'd tried, but Sasha had immediately changed the subject. He could just see her saying, 'Ee-uuww,' Dad,' and escaping to her room when he tried again. Kate taught puberty education and probably had some natty pink sample pack he could give Sasha, as well as a few tips.

Sasha talked about her all the time and since Kate had taught her how to French braid her hair, she proudly wore it that way. Kate genuinely seemed to enjoy Sasha's company.

He turned into School Road and slowed to the obligatory forty-kilometre school zone speed limit. Sasha, who was playing outside, gave him a wave and ran back inside to get her bag. Baden followed and signed the in-out book.

'Thanks, Gloria, see you next week.' Baden handed over an envelope with the week's fees enclosed to the after-school care co-ordinator.

Gloria spoke, sotto voce. 'I thought without Erin we were going to have problems, but Sasha's the happiest and most settled she's ever been.'

Baden nodded. 'I think that Guides and swimming has helped.'

'Hmm.' The experienced teacher vacillated. 'I think there's more to it than that.'

Sasha reappeared from the bag cage. 'Thanks, Mrs Davidson.' She pulled on her backpack. 'Are you coming to the drive-in on Saturday night?'

The matronly woman smiled. 'I wouldn't miss it for anything, dear.' She suddenly had a far-away look in her eyes. 'I remember going to the drive-in with my Stan and a big box of chocolates.'

'Oh, we have heaps of great food, Mrs D. Kate, my Guide leader, well, actually she's dad's nurse but really she's my friend, she has had us cooking loads of yummy stuff.'

Baden smiled at how kids needed to mention every connection they had to people. He would have just said 'Kate.'

'That's wonderful, dear.' She shot Baden a meaningful look.

He had no idea what it meant. Sasha was very excited about the fundraiser but so was the whole town. Kate had organised the Guides into a food-creating machine. He put his hand on his daughter's shoulder. 'Honey, we have to go.'

They waved goodbye and headed to the car. As Baden turned back onto the road he remembered the sputum container. 'We just have to go to the hospital to drop something off.'

'OK. Will Kate be there?' Sasha selected a CD from the collection.

'I don't know. I didn't see her today.' He flicked down the sun visor against the glaring late afternoon sun.

She slid in the CD. 'You like Kate, don't you, Dad?'

He slowed down at a give-way sign and checked for oncoming traffic, his mind half on the conversation. 'Of course I do. She's a good friend to both of us.'

'She must get lonely in that big house.'

He waited for the oncoming car to pass and then turned right into Settlement Street. 'She's got Rupert and Snowy.'

'Yeah, but they don't talk.'

He squinted through the sun glare, thinking he really should wash the windscreen from the inside. 'Well, she's thinking of selling Sandon anyway.'

Sasha spun so fast that her seat belt snapped tight. 'No, she can't do that!' Her voice sounded horrified. 'She invited Erin and me for a sleepover after the fundraiser and I've already chosen a room.' Her voice started to rise. 'And she said I could visit whenever I want to and ride Thumper and…'

He sighed at her reaction. If only Mrs Davidson could see Sasha now. 'Calm down, sweetheart. I just said she might sell Sandon. It's her home and her life and her decision. It's nothing to do with us.'

'But it's such a cool house and she should stay. I love it there.'

An irrational irritation zinged through him. He and Sasha lived in a lovely house full of love. 'There are more important things in life than a nice house, a swimming pool and horses. Besides, when we visit Kate we're just guests at Sandon. It's not like we're part of her family.'

Sasha folded her arms across her chest. 'I *know* that, Dad. But I still think that Kate is lonely. She needs someone.'

Am image of Kate in the arms of another man speared him so sharply he flinched but then her words on marriage pounded him. She had no plans for another relationship. 'I think she's happy with her life the way it is, Sasha.'

'I don't know, Dad.' Sasha sounded unconvinced. 'I think she needs someone.' Her green eyes flashed with conviction. 'Just like you need someone.'

His throat dried at the unsubtle matchmaking. Sasha was twelve, with no idea what relationships meant or how they would affect her. How another person in their life would take his focus away from her. 'I don't need anyone, honey. You and I are a team and I'm happy just the way things are.'

But the words sounded unexpectedly hollow to his ears.

Warragurra had been buzzing for days. Finally the drive-in night arrived and kids and adults alike bounced with excitement.

A huge semi-trailer with an enormous screen hanging from one side was parked in the paddock next to the school. The school grounds had been turned into a carnival with white-topped marquees selling everything from sausages in bread to de luxe hamburgers, fizzy drinks to fairy floss and the always popular lolly stall.

Music blared from the loudspeakers and kids charged around the grounds, waving their glow-in-the dark sticks. The pre-movie picnic was in full swing. Nothing this big had happened in Warragurra for a long time. The airport even had a parking problem as so many light planes from outlying stations had flown in for the event. People stood around in groups, enthusiastically chatting, the gathering having a second purpose—breaking the isolation of outback life on the land. Even Shane's parents had come along.

Last week they'd written to Kate, wishing her well for a successful night and enclosing a large cheque as a donation. They might never be close friends but at least the rift seemed to have eased.

The Guides were helping out at a variety of stalls with their parents' assistance. Kate had left it up to Sasha which stall she wanted to work on with Baden, but Sasha had been adamant she was working with Kate. Baden hadn't said a word. He'd arrived with Sasha two hours ago, donned a barbecue apron that made him look like he was wearing a dinner suit and took his place at the hotplate with Phoebe Walton's father, Richard. He looked as mouth-watering as the food he was cooking.

Whenever she turned his way he gave her a grin and a flourish with the tongs. Kate dragged her gaze away from him for the zillionth time. What she really wanted to do was throw her arms around his neck and trail kisses along his jaw, his neck, his chest… She pulled her attention back to assembling souvlaki, Malaysian satay and hamburgers with all the trimmings, including pineapple and beetroot.

Sasha stood next to her, beaming at the customers as she happily took their money. 'Enjoy your dinner and remember to stock up at the lolly stall before the movie.'

Kate gave her a quick hug. 'You're a born salesperson, Sasha.'

The girl seemed to stand a bit taller. 'This is just so totally awesome. I've never had so much fun.'

Kate's heart swelled. 'I've had a lot of fun working with you and getting to know you. It's great that we've made friends and we're helping to raise money for a really worthwhile cause.'

Her elfin face became serious for a moment. 'I know Mum would be really pleased I've done this. She always said that helping others made you feel good about yourself.'

The more Kate learned about Annie Tremont the more she thought she would have liked her had she known her. 'Your mum sounds like a clever woman.'

'She was, but so are you, Kate. I couldn't have done anything like this without your help. You're not really moving, are you?'

The question surprised her. 'I wasn't planning on moving. Why?'

Sasha looked a bit embarrassed. 'Oh, it was just something Dad said.'

The memory of the time she'd told Baden about Shane came

flooding back. 'I once said to your dad that I was thinking I might move but I don't feel that way any more.'

Sasha unexpectedly flung her arms around her waist. 'I'm *so* glad you're not going. I'd really miss you if you left.'

The intensity of the heartfelt words stunned her and she treasured them, holding them close to her heart.

'Kate, Sasha, we're starving here.' Des Cincotta stood at the front of the queue, a teal green turban on his head and a smile a mile wide as he held tightly to Brenda's hand. Behind them stood a long line of people, all wearing the same teal green turbans.

'Oh, those head scarfs are so funky.' Sasha gazed at them with longing.

Brenda pulled two turbans out of her bag. 'I have one for both of you. The big one is for Kate and the smaller one is for you, Sasha. I thought it might be a good symbol for remembering your mum and looking to the future.'

The young girl's eyes widened in delight. 'Thanks heaps, Mrs Cincotta.' She immediately turned to Kate. 'Can you help me put it on?'

'Sure.' Kate took off her gloves and wound the material around her own head and then placed the smaller one on Sasha's chestnut hair. 'You look gorgeous.'

'You're just saying that.' Sasha glanced down at her feet.

'No, Kate's absolutely right. You do look gorgeous.'

Baden had wandered over from the barbecue to see what was happening. Fatherly love glowed in his sky-blue eyes.

The familiar lump in her throat formed when Kate caught sight of that look. Father and daughter, a strong bond.

Then his gaze met hers over the top of Sasha's head. 'In fact you both look gorgeous.' Fatherly love suddenly vanished, replaced by a simmering of something stronger. Something she knew was for herself alone.

Her body tingled from the tip of her head down to her toes and then settled deep inside her.

'Don't listen to him, Kate. He's clueless,' Sasha's no-nonsense voice chimed in. 'I can be covered in paint after art and he tells me I'm gorgeous. And no offence but you have sauce on your nose.'

Kate laughed as she wiped away the sauce. But Sasha's comment suddenly brought back Baden's words in a powerful surge. *You'd be beautiful covered in grease.*

Her head spun. If he told his daughter she was gorgeous no matter what, completely unconditionally—did this mean something more? Did he love her? Her heart tripped over itself in happiness at the thought there might be a chance for the three of them as a family.

'So, how many hamburgers, Mr Cincotta?' Sasha focussed back on the important things.

'I reckon twenty-five should do it.' Des handed over a large green note.

Sasha looked stunned as she held the hundred-dollar bill. She carefully put it in the cashbox. 'Hey, Dad, stop slacking, we've got a huge order of twenty-five hamburgers. Come on, Kate, you need to set out the buns.'

'I think we've just been organised.' Baden winked at Kate, and saluted his daughter. 'Coming right up, Miss Tremont.'

Baden walked toward the drinks area, having been released from his cooking duties by Kate as long as he brought back coffee. Although he wasn't sure that a double mocha frappuccino with extra cream really counted as coffee, but he wasn't going to argue with a woman who'd been working flat out since five a.m.

She needed a break; she'd been like a whirling dervish all day.

'Hey, Baden, how's it going?' A woman grabbed his arm, breaking his reverie.

'Emily.' He hugged his ex–flight nurse, taking in her teal turban and a few strands of purple hair that had escaped. 'Great to see you.'

'I hear that Kate Lawson is a star and you're not missing me at all.' She raised her brows, her double meaning clear.

The comment caught him unawares and he found himself clearing his throat. 'If I had to lose you, Kate is a worthy replacement.'

Emily rocked back and laughed. 'Well, that's one way of looking at it. Although you never looked at me the way you look at her.'

His serious doctor voice took over. 'Kate is a valued colleague, just like you are. You're letting your imagination run away with you.'

Emily's smiling face suddenly turned serious. 'No, I don't think I am. I had a *long* wait for my dinner tonight and I watched you at the barbecue. You spent more time looking at Kate than my charred hamburger.'

Hell, had it been that noticeable? He knew he'd lost the battle not to watch her a long time ago, but had he lost the ability to be surreptitious? He tried to deflect Emily with humour. 'Charred! Richard must have cooked that one.'

She put her hand on his arm, her touch and her voice full of understanding. 'I think it's wonderful. You've been alone long enough.'

He breathed in deeply. 'I'm *not* alone. I've got Sasha.'

Emily put her hands on her hips. 'You're being deliberately obtuse. You know what I mean. Your wife died and you miss her, but you've grieved, you've started a new life and it's normal and healthy to want to love again.'

He waited for the usual anger to fizz inside him when people tried to match him up but for some reason it didn't come. That in itself worried him. He changed the subject to something safer. 'So, how's your eldest brother? Did he manage to get the loan for the new dam?'

But Emily wasn't listening to him. She'd turned her head away, her attention one hundred per cent on Linton, who stood on the stage speaking into a microphone. His voice boomed over the PA system. 'Can everyone make their way over to the drive-in area, please? The film's going to start in fifteen minutes.'

Baden raised his brows knowingly. 'So how's Linton?'

Emily turned back with an overly casual shrug. 'No idea. I haven't seen him since he finished his rotation with the Flying Doctors three months ago.'

He crossed his arms and grinned at her. 'Really? I thought I detected more than a casual interest.'

'I think you're letting your imagination run away with you.' She tilted her jaw in the stubborn way he remembered so well and played him at his own game of changing the subject, which spoke volumes. 'Say hi to Sasha for me and I'll catch up with you later.' With a quick wave she walked over to another group of people and made her way to the drive-in paddock.

He joined the coffee queue behind Evelyn Walton. 'Getting a caffeine shot to keep you alert while you supervise the Guides at the movie?'

Evelyn nodded. 'They'll be fine. Richard's filled the back of the ute with foam blocks and cushions and I have enough lollies to keep the dentist in business for the next year.'

Baden ordered the coffees. 'Sounds like we'll be coping with sugar highs.'

Evelyn laughed. 'Probably, but that's all part of the fun.' She moved to the side to wait for her coffee. 'Baden, can you do me a favour?'

'Sure.'

'Richard and I are on duty, along with Sandra, and Hannah's parents, plus there are bound to be other Guide parents who sit with us. Kate's done a huge job getting tonight off the ground and she deserves to watch the movie in a civilised way, rather than being pelted by Guides with foam blocks during the quiet bits.'

He put his hands in his pockets. 'Good luck convincing her not to sit with the Guides.'

Evelyn wrinkled her nose. 'Actually, that's the favour. I want you to convince her.'

A slight tremor of unease ran through him. 'You know Kate, she'll just do what she planned on doing.'

Evelyn picked up her coffee and fixed him with a steely look. 'You're the doctor—tell her she'll collapse from exhaustion or something. Better yet, buy her ice cream and chocolates and nail her to the picnic rug way off to the side so no one can see her to bother her. I'm sure you'll think of something.'

An image of Kate slammed into him. Kate lying down on a picnic rug beside him, her body snuggled against his, her head nestled into his shoulder, her hair tickling his cheek and her lips warm against his own. His breath rushed out of his lungs.

He'd just lost his 'safety in numbers' buffer, the buffer he'd been depending on all day. It had become an increasing battle to keep her out of his arms.

A germ of an idea slowly turned in his brain and the floundering tatters of his resolve to stay away from Kate vanished. He now had the perfect solution that would suit both Kate and him and protect Sasha's feelings.

'Sure, no problem, Evelyn.' He hoped she hadn't noticed just how husky his voice had become.

# CHAPTER TEN

KATE'S knees knocked together so hard she was sure people at the back could hear them. She could deal with bleeding bodies and hysterical relatives, she could pull together a huge fund-raising night like tonight, but she dreaded public speaking.

Baden leaned in close and whispered in her ear. 'Just imagine them all naked.'

An image of Baden's golden body illuminated by moonlight came into her mind. Her knocking knees melted on the spot. She threw her hands out wide. 'How is *that* supposed to help?' Her voice started to rise. 'I could never understand how that is a useful tip.'

His eyes sparkled at her, and a grin raced across his cheeks. 'Trust me, just try it.' He gave her a gentle push onto the stage.

She took in a deep breath, tossed her head and walked across the stage, which was really the flatbed of the semi-trailer. Her hand curved tightly around the microphone. 'Ladies and gentlemen. I'm Kate Lawson and…' She looked out onto a sea of over three hundred faces, many of them wearing teal green turbans. Her mind instantly blanked. With a hammering heart she turned her head to the left catching Baden's gaze.

He mouthed at her, 'Think naked,' and gave her a thumbs-up.

She stared straight ahead picturing the crowd only wearing

turbans. She felt a giggle start to rise out of her as her constricted throat relaxed. 'I just want to take a few moments of
your time to thank everyone who has been involved in making
tonight happen. It wouldn't have been possible without an ex-
ceptional team effort and I'm really excited to announce that
together you have raised a staggering seven thousand dollars
toward finding an early diagnostic test for ovarian cancer.'

Whoops, wolf whistles and car horns sounded as everyone
clapped. Somewhere in the crowd a 'Go, Kate' chant started.

Kate waved and the crowd quietened. 'Clinical trials for the
test are under way and this money will be used to support these
trials, bringing us ever closer to an accurate and fast way to
detect this silent disease.' She tucked her hair behind her ear
against the early evening breeze. 'But now it's time for the two
movies so sit back and enjoy. Thank you very much.'

She almost skipped off the stage toward Baden, so delighted
was she to have the speech finished. 'Thank heavens that's
over. Now, where are the Guides parked?'

Baden linked his arm through hers and captured her hand.
'The Guides are under the strict supervision of the Waltons and
you are off duty.'

'No?' She stared at him and his black brows rose in confirmation. A puff of longing rose up from deep inside her and
swirled through her, at odds with a strange sensation of disappointment. She had thought that perhaps she would watch the
family-rated movies with Sasha and Baden.

*But you'll have Baden all to yourself.*

Another voice countered, *Only because Sasha's not around.*
Just like the stolen kiss in the pool, Baden would sometimes
unexpectedly touch her or kiss her, but only when Sasha was
otherwise occupied or absent. Without her having realised it,
he'd drawn an invisible line that was only now starting to be

visible to her. And yet often when the three of them were together they felt like a family. Uncertainty ran through her.

*Stop it! You're over-analysing.* She tried to shake off the melancholy that had settled over her by flirting. 'So, do you have a date for this movie?'

'I have a picnic rug, some Irish coffee and Swiss chocolates.' His voice deepened caressingly. 'Would you care to join me?'

*Of course you'll join him.* His words washed over her, stealing away the tiny squeak of rebellion that had stirred. She let him draw her away from the crowds to a dark and quiet area. Next to his car, in the glow of the fading light, lay a rug covered in cushions and the biggest box of chocolates she'd ever seen.

She tilted her head enquiringly, trying to keep her face straight. 'It's not the best view of the screen—in fact, I doubt whether I'll be able to even see the film.'

His arm swung around her waist, pulling her against him, his heat surging into her. He cupped her cheek with his free hand and stroked her face tenderly with his thumb.

His smile streaked through his five o'clock stubble, dark and deliciously dangerous. His voice, low and husky, rumbled around her. 'Now you're catching on.'

Shimmers of delight raced along her veins as she gazed at him with complete freedom as she'd longed to do all day, losing herself in his smile and everything it promised.

He lowered his mouth against hers, his tongue barely skating across her lips in the softest yet most erotic kiss she'd ever known.

This was where she belonged. She tilted her head back, opened her mouth under his and gave herself up to him.

With the same delicate pressure he roved over her mouth, exploring and tasting every part of it in a slow, deliberate manner, as if he was exploring and tasting every part of her.

She gripped his shoulders for support, her fingers pressing

into solid muscle as her legs lost all power to hold her upright. Languid pleasure rolled through her like the ripple of wind on water, making her ache for more, making her stand perfectly still so she didn't miss a moment.

Time stood still. Colours intensified, her perception of space and place altered as she lost herself in the kiss from the man she loved.

Eventually he lifted his head as the last light faded and the moon rose. 'I've wanted to do that all day.'

Her heart sang. 'Really?'

'Really.' He tucked her hair behind her ear. 'Did you know you're incredibly sexy when you're in organising mode?'

Laughing, she sank down onto the picnic rug and opened the chocolates, suddenly famished. 'I doubt Linton sees me that way, especially when I told him he *had* to be MC. I'm pretty sure he'd say I was just plain bossy.'

Baden sat down next to her with a growl, his hand curving around her thigh in a proprietorial way. 'If Linton was to ever think you're sexy, he would have to contend with me.'

A smile opened up deep inside her, expanding into every part of her, filling her with inexplicable happiness. Baden wanted her just for himself. She hugged that knowledge tightly.

She lay down on the cushions and stretched out, blissfully happy. 'A duel at dawn, perhaps?'

He lay down next to her, his fingers trailing across her almost bare shoulders, toying with the spaghetti straps of her dress. 'Hmm, something like that.' He kissed the hollow at the base of her neck and then gave her a light nip. 'Or perhaps I'll just brand you as mine.'

She laughed and rolled into his arms where she belonged.

He hugged her close. 'I'm planning on us having a *lot* of moments like this in the future.'

A thrill of wonder wove through her. He wanted her *and* they had a future together. This time she'd got it right, this time she'd fallen in love with the right man.

A man with a daughter she adored. Suddenly she'd gone from living alone to a woman with a family. An image of the three of them living together at Sandon filled her head. It felt so very right.

'It sounds perfect to me.' She whispered the words against his mouth and gave herself up to his bone-melting kisses.

Lost in the ministrations of his superb mouth, it took a moment for her to realise that a narrow beam of weak torchlight was suddenly splayed over them. Giggles and shrieks sounded from the bushes behind them.

Baden immediately stilled, his lips sliding away from hers.

'Isn't that Sasha's dad kissing Koala?' a young girl's voice asked in a loud whisper.

The beam of light suddenly veered sideways, as if someone had grabbed the torch. 'Shh, they might hear you. Come on, we have to get back before Dad misses us.'

Kate recognised Phoebe Walton's voice and started to chuckle. 'I think we've just been sprung.'

Baden sat up, his body rigid. 'Hell. What if they tell Sasha?'

Kate pushed herself up and sat beside him, taking his hand in hers. 'If they do, it's no big deal.'

'No big deal?' He ran his free hand across the back of his neck. 'I didn't want her to find out this way.'

Kate shrugged. 'I agree it's not ideal but you can tell her in the morning or, better yet, *we* can tell her together after the film.'

'Tell her?' His bewildered expression made her smile. He looked like a little boy who'd just got lost. 'I wasn't planning on telling her anything.'

She frowned, surprised by his comment and suddenly

feeling a bit bewildered herself. 'Do you really think that's wise, not telling her?'

Disbelief showed on his face. 'I don't know about you, but I don't expect my twelve-year-old to understand an affair. And that's what we're having, right? What we both want. No relationship, no ties, but some time together.' He reached for her. 'Just the two of us.'

Her stomach rolled and she gagged as his words pounded her. *I'm planning on us having a lot of moments like this in the future.*

Oh, God, he meant clandestine moments. Stolen times like now and in Dog Tired Hut. Times without Sasha. Times Sasha would not know about.

He had no intention of making her part of his family. He and Sasha were the family. She was only a bit of fluff on the side.

Her world, so perfect a few moments ago, imploded—caving in on her with suffocating reality. She pushed his hands away and found her voice. 'You might have been talking about an affair but I certainly wasn't.'

The lines on his forehead deepened. 'But you said it sounded perfect. What did you think I was talking about?'

She tossed her head high, trying to hold on to her shredded dignity. 'I thought you were talking about a future together. You, me and Sasha.'

A stunned expression crossed his face. 'But you told me you didn't want another relationship.'

She stood up, wringing her hands as her own words came back to bite her. 'I know I told you that and at the time it was the truth, but things change.'

He'd risen to his feet and now leaned against the car. 'We can't be together. I have to do what's best for Sasha. Surely you understand that.' His troubled gaze appealed to her for understanding.

Her brain struggled to make sense of what he was saying. 'No, I'm sorry, I really don't understand how not moving forward with your life is better for Sasha.'

His expression hardened. 'Sasha needs my total attention and I can't allow anything or anyone to get in the way of that. At least, not until she's an adult.'

His words stung like salt on a wound. 'But it's OK to have sex with me once a month while she visits her grandparents in Adelaide?'

He flinched and she knew her words had hit the target with pinpoint accuracy. Obviously that had been his plan. A convenient affair.

He ploughed his hand through his hair. 'You're making it sound sordid and you know it isn't like that at all.'

Anger fizzed in her veins. 'Well, forgive me if I don't see it quite the way you do.' She breathed in deeply, trying to slow her pounding heart. His line of thinking was illogical.

She formed her thoughts carefully. 'Baden, you and Sasha have the most amazing relationship and I would never, ever want to come between you or change what you have.'

Relief flooded his face. 'Which is why my plan will work so well for us.'

Her heart tore, the ripping reverberating through her. He had no idea what she meant. She shook her head. 'Your plan is not going to work. Your plan denies Sasha everything she needs. Your plan locks your daughter into this unhealthy cloister of an existence. You're denying her a chance of a normal family life, to be part of a loving family, to have brothers and sisters and pets.'

She mustered every ounce of courage she had and hauled her gaze to his. 'Over the last few months I've fallen in love with you and your wonderful Sasha. I want to create a family with you, to give Sasha the chance to be a big sister.'

His look of horror was like a knife through her heart.

'Oh, hell.' He started to pace. 'Oh, Kate, I had no idea.'
He spoke quietly, his eyes full of contrition. 'I made a promise
to Annie that Sasha would always come first and I plan to
honour that.'

She swayed as if she'd been hit. How could she compete
against a dead wife who stood between them? She closed her
eyes for a brief moment, hoping to steel her legs into holding
her up for just a bit longer. Sasha's words about her mother
played through her mind. From what she'd gleaned, Annie had
been a loving, sensible and wonderful mother. She didn't sound
like a selfish woman who had feared losing her daughter's love
after death.

'Did she really mean that you couldn't love again?'

His eyes flickered with emotion, but sadness illuminated
them most strongly. Sadness for her.

The truth suddenly rushed in with all the devastating power
of a tsunami.

He didn't love her.

Pain like she'd never known travelled through her, searing
her, scarring her, sapping every particle of joy and happiness
from her soul. Blackness seeped in, staining her with misery.

'Time for bed, Sash.' Baden dropped a light kiss on his
daughter's head.

Freshly showered and dressed in her pink pyjamas, a
yawning and exhausted Sasha snuggled up to him on the couch,
her head against his chest. 'My brain's all spinning around
though, Dad. I don't think I'll be able to get to sleep.'

'Once you're in bed, you'll soon go to sleep.' His words
sounded false to his ears. He knew he'd be lying awake,
thinking about tonight. Thinking about Kate. Hell, what a mess.

Never in a million years had he expected her to fall in love with him. He hated it that he'd hurt her so much but he couldn't give her what she wanted. He had to take the safe path through life for Sasha's sake.

'Tonight was the best night I've ever had.' Sasha looked up, her eyes shining. 'Wasn't Kate awesome? She and I had so much fun selling the food, and the movie was a crack-up.' She paused for a beat and then tickled him. 'That means funny, Dad.'

He raised his brows. 'And here I was thinking the film was, like, totally random.'

'Ha-ha, Dad—not.' She smiled to herself. 'When the first movie finished, we all pummelled Mr Walton with foam and sat on him until he bought us ice creams. It was cool and I can't wait to visit Sandon tomorrow and tell Kate all about it.'

He tried to sound casually matter-of-fact. 'We won't be seeing Kate tomorrow.'

Sasha pushed herself up, her expression one large question mark. 'Why not? We've visited her most days lately.'

*Because I've hurt her deeply. Because she won't want to see me again.* Kate's huge brown eyes filled with anguish haunted him. He breathed in deeply, thinking carefully. Sasha must never know what had gone on between him and Kate; she wouldn't understand.

'The fundraiser's over now, Sash, and we won't be visiting Sandon again.' He kept his voice even. 'Go on, now, off to bed and I'll be there in a minute to tuck you in.'

Sasha stayed put, her mouth taking on a mulish look. 'But she invited me over and I want to go.'

He stroked her hair. 'I know you and Kate did some special things these last few weeks but that's finished now. You'll still see her at Guides on Wednesdays.'

'Why are you being so mean?' Sasha unexpectedly pushed her finger into his chest.

He wrapped his hand around hers, stopping the jabbing, trying to keep calm. 'I am *not* being mean. I'm just pointing out that all good things come to an end and life goes back to normal. Kate's busy with work and Guides and she doesn't need you taking up her time.'

'But she's my special friend. She understands stuff.'

Her expression told him she clearly thought he didn't understand stuff and she mumbled something.

'Pardon?' His tone demanded she repeat it.

A defiant look streaked across her face. 'I said she's like a mum, except different.'

*Like a mum.* The words sank into him, exposing a set of emotions he didn't want to explore. Sasha had *him*, that had to be enough.

'She's your Guide leader, Sasha, and you can see her there.' He heard the thread of impatience in his voice.

Sasha suddenly looked coy. 'Phoebe Walton said she saw you kissing and cuddling Kate so that makes her your special friend, too.' Sasha was like a dog with a bone. He'd never seen her this determined or intense. Her eyes shone with hope and she wheedled, 'That makes her *our* special friend, doesn't it, Dad? And you visit special friends.'

The room suddenly seemed airless as the walls pressed in on him. He went into damage control. 'Phoebe must have seen me giving Kate a quick thank-you kiss. That doesn't make her a special friend. She's my work colleague and my flight nurse and that's all.'

*You keep telling yourself that, mate.*

He blocked the voice out of his head. He was a father and it was time to start acting like one. 'I'm sorry but you can't go and see Kate at Sandon any more, and that's the end of the discussion.' He gave her a gentle nudge. 'Now, go to bed.'

Sasha launched herself off the couch, tears streaming down her flushed and angry face. 'I hate you, Dad, I hate you so much!' She turned and ran, her bare feet pummelling the polished boards in the hall. A moment later her bedroom door slammed, setting all the windows vibrating.

*Hell.* What was it with the women in his life tonight?

*You're the problem.* He stood up and walked over to his CD player, turning on some quiet music to drown out the voice in his head.

As much as Sasha and Kate hated him right now, he knew what was best for him and Sasha. He had to stick to his plan. It was all he had. It was the only safe thing he could depend on. Annie had died. Kate could decide she didn't love Sasha after all and leave. He wasn't going to risk his daughter's happiness when there were no absolute certainties.

But why did being in the right have to be so damn lonely?

The grandfather clock chimed two. Baden looked up from the glow of the computer screen, last year's tax figures blurring in front of his eyes. Kate and then Sasha had sent his brain into overdrive so there'd been no point going to bed. Instead, he'd tackled his overdue tax figures. At least his accountant would be pleased with him.

*He's about the only person who will be.*

Snapping down the top of his laptop, he cleared the cups off the table, dumping them in the sink. Walking down the hall, he paused outside Sasha's room. Usually he tucked her in even if she'd been moody, but with tonight's exhaustion-induced tantrum, he hadn't gone in, thinking it wiser to wait until she was asleep.

In the morning, when she wasn't exhausted any more, he'd suggest she visit Erin and together they could rehash the events of the drive-in night, as girls liked to do. That would satisfy her and Kate would recede to being the Guide leader.

He quietly opened the bedroom door. He never went to bed without peeking in on Sasha. The day may have been a beast but she always looked angelic in sleep and his heart filled with the joy she gave him.

The glow from the moon came through the open window. He was surprised the window was fully open. He crept over and slowly dropped the sash halfway into its usual position and then lowered the Roman blind. Sasha needed a good eleven hours' sleep and the sun rose early.

As usual the room was a jumble of clothes, books, CDs and open dressing-table drawers, with clothes spilling out of them. What was it with not being able to open *and* close a drawer? He bent down to pick up the pink quilt, which had slid to the floor. As he stood up he caught sight of the bed. It was empty.

Without thinking, he reached out and put his hand on the bottom sheet. Cold.

He swung back to the window as fear slithered through him. The window was never wide open like it had been. Surely Sasha hadn't crawled out and run away?

The clothes she'd been wearing at the drive-in were still on a heap on the floor. Perhaps she hadn't gone very far.

He strode out into the hall. 'Sasha? Sweetheart, are you here?' He opened every door in the house, calling her name, each time sounding more frantic than before.

He tugged open the hall cupboard, grabbed the torch and ran out the back door. 'Sasha!' He swung the torch around the garden and scanned the tree house.

She wasn't there.

He sprinted around the side of the house to her bedroom window. A bush with a few broken and flattened branches declared Sasha had left the house.

Panic flooded him and chaotic thoughts ricocheted around his brain. His twelve-year-old daughter was out in the dark, alone. His throat constricted.

*Think!* He started to pace. She was upset so where would she have gone? Erin lived three streets away. He belted inside and grabbed the phone, his fingers thumping the numbers hard and fast. *Pick up, pick up.* He willed the Baxters to hear the ring, and have it wake them from their slumber.

The ringing stopped and a clunking noise sounded before a sleepy voice came down the line. 'Hello. James Baxter.'

He breathed out slowly so that he didn't gabble. 'James, Baden Tremont. Sorry to bother you but Sasha's missing. Is she with you? She might have sneaked into Erin's room.'

There was a short silence, as if James was digesting the request. 'Right, I'll go and check for you, but I think you'd better speak to Trix.'

Erin's mother came on the line. 'Baden, what's wrong?'

He sighed. 'Sasha and I had an argument and she's run away. You're the closest house so I thought she might be with you.' He heard James's voice murmuring in the background.

'James says Erin's asleep and there's no sign of Sasha.' She paused for a moment. 'Think about the argument—that might give you a clue to where she's gone.'

*Kate.*

'Thanks, Trix, you're brilliant. I'll call you back.'

He scribbled a note. 'I love you, Sasha. Ring me on my mobile if you're reading this.' Grabbing his car keys, he left the front and back doors unlocked and reversed the car down the drive.

He drove slowly all the way to Kate's, his lights on high beam, hoping to see a small figure walking along the road. Shadows jumped out at him but they were shadows of his imagination.

She must be at Kate's. She had to be at Kate's.

Of course she would be at Kate's.

He turned into Sandon's long curving drive, the tall cypress trees lining the road casting moonlight shadows on the gravel. Rupert started barking as soon as he stepped out of the car.

'Shh, Rupe, it's just me.'

Veranda lights sensed his movement and illuminated the thick oak front door. Panic made him pound on it. 'Kate, answer the door.'

A moment later her anxious voice came from the other side of the screen door. 'Baden? Is that you?'

Hell, he'd scared her. 'Yes, it's me.'

He heard her sharp intake of breath before she opened the door. Dark rings hovered under her eyes, which stared at him in wariness as she tied a dressing-gown around her.

'Have you been drinking? It's two o'clock in the morning.' Her arctic tone told him he wasn't welcome, that his unexpected arrival had brought scarring memories back.

He hated himself for doing this to her, but he couldn't deal with that right now. Right now only Sasha mattered and his fear for his daughter did away with any preliminaries. He pushed past her, opening doors, looking left and right.

'What are you doing?' She pulled his arm. 'Baden, what's going on?'

Guilt almost choked him. He couldn't hurt Kate any further by telling her that he'd told his daughter she couldn't come and visit her. 'She was overtired after the drive-in, we had an argument and she's run away.' He started to pace. 'She's not at the Baxters', and I doubt she'd be at the Waltons' so I thought she might be here.'

Silently Kate stared at him, her large eyes filled with astonishment and then fear.

A shiver ran across his skin and his chest tightened. At that moment he knew with dazzling clarity that, no matter how much he'd hurt Kate, if Sasha had come to Sandon, she would have telephoned him immediately. She would put Sasha ahead of how she felt about him, no matter how much he'd hurt her.

She opened her mouth. 'What was the arg—' She stopped, breathed in and her expression changed from shock to crisis planning. When she spoke again she was all business. 'How long do you think she might have been gone for?'

'It was eleven when she went to bed.' The words sounded stark in the darkness. 'She could have been gone as long as three hours.'

A look of horror rolled across her face on hearing about the elapsed time. 'Surely if she was with one of her friends, their parents would have rung you.' She started to walk toward the kitchen. 'Oh, but then again the girl she fled to might be hiding her because they're both scared that you or her parents would be angry.'

A glimmer of relief sparked inside him. 'You're right, I never thought of that. I'll start ringing.' He pulled out his mobile.

'Hang on. You need to do this systematically.' She rummaged through her sideboard cupboard and pulled out a manila folder of phone numbers. 'This is the Guides' contact list. Take it and start ringing from your house in case Sasha has returned or is about to return. Mark off each name as you phone so you don't miss anyone.'

Her sensible words started to break through his fog of fear. Thank goodness he'd come here. Kate was the most amazing woman he'd ever met. 'Good idea.'

She picked up her mobile phone, checking the display. 'I've

got a full battery and I'll have this in my pocket all the time I'm driving around town looking for her. Contact me any time. Better yet, ring me after an hour, unless one of us finds her before the hour is up.'

She put her hand on his arm. 'We'll find her.'

Her warmth seeped into him, soothing and reassuring at a time he thought those feelings to be impossible. He covered her hand with his. 'Thanks, Kate. I really appreciate your help.'

She jerkily pulled her hand out from under his. 'I'm doing it for Sasha.'

Her words sliced through him. He knew he didn't deserve her sympathy and understanding, but it hurt more than he'd anticipated.

He nodded and walked to the patio door.

'Baden.'

He turned at the sombre tone of her voice.

'If you draw a blank, you *must* ring Daryl Thornton at the police station. As soon as it's first light, a search can be started.'

She voiced the thoughts that he'd held at bay for the last hour.

Jagged fear ripped through him, sucking his breath from his lungs. Where the hell was his beautiful daughter?

# CHAPTER ELEVEN

KATE pulled on her jeans, thick hiking socks, a long-sleeved T-shirt and a polar fleece. If this turned into a full-on search and rescue then she was going to be prepared. Daryl Thornton, the police sergeant, would shoot her otherwise. Good preparation was vital and he'd drilled it into all the members of the emergency service.

When she'd heard Baden's pounding on the door every nightmare of Shane coming home drunk had rushed through her. Why would he be on her doorstep sober? He'd told her to her face that he didn't love her so there was no reason for him to visit.

But the moment she'd seen him standing on her veranda, his face ashen under the yellow light, his hair standing up on end from being ploughed through by agitated fingers, she'd known something was desperately wrong. His blue eyes had been stark as he'd stared through her as if searching beyond her.

And she understood completely.

Sasha was missing. Sasha, whom she loved like a daughter. What had possessed her to take off in the middle of the night?

She stowed medical gear into her backpack, filled her water bottle, packed some sustenance bars and headed out to the car.

If Sasha hadn't been found by dawn, she was all prepared to join the official search, which Daryl wouldn't start until then.

Meanwhile, she'd start her town search at the school, although she doubted Sasha would have gone there. Her headlights swept the streets, which were eerily empty, as they usually were a few hours before daybreak. She searched the school, the bus depot, the Guide Hall, the pool—all the places in town that were familiar to Sasha.

But she found nothing. No sign of Sasha.

Where would she have gone? She banged her head against the steering-wheel. *Think like a girl.*

Her brain was grey fog. She stared through the windscreen at the green road sign displaying names of places out of town.

Sasha's sweet voice sounded in her head. *Once I walked from home to Ledger's Gorge. I really liked it there, it was a good place to think, you know?*

If you'd had an argument with your father, you'd need to think. Ledger's Gorge was a decent walk in daylight. It would be almost impossible in pitch darkness. The arguments went around in her head. Still, it was the best shot she had. She started the car and headed out of town.

The only sign of habitation at the Ledger's Gorge picnic spot were two wombats grazing in the moonlight. Kate got out of the car, cupped her hands around her mouth and yelled into the darkness. 'Sash-a.'

She held her breath, wishing for a reply. All she got was an echo of her own voice.

She swung her high-beam torch around the area. It illuminated the carved wooden sign that marked the start of the steep walk down to the gorge. Even in daylight it was a tricky walk. Surely Sasha wouldn't have gone down there?

The crazy thought took hold, niggling her until she couldn't ignore it any longer. She strapped on her backpack, put her mobile phone in her pocket, gripped her torch and started to walk along the narrow and rough track. Every ten steps she called out Sasha's name and waited, her ears straining for a reply.

Twigs snapped underfoot, making her jump. *Go back, no kid would do this in the dark.* But Sasha could be determined, almost as determined as her father, and for some reason Kate couldn't rule this crazy venture out of her head.

She reached the top of the steep and narrow steps that were carved out of the red rock. She gingerly took the first step. *One down, ninety-nine to go.* 'Sasha!'

Her voice came back to her. Then she thought she heard a small sound. She held her breath.

Silence.

She lowered herself onto the next overly large step and slid her bottom along it, the darkness making her feel dizzy. This was why they didn't do search and rescue in the dark. *But this is Sasha.* She managed another ten steps that way.

'Sasha!' She swung her torch in an arc, squinting to see any sign of anything that wasn't a tree. One side was blackness, the side that fell to the gorge only black space between her and the bottom.

At step forty-seven she decided she was the one who was crazy, unwise and foolhardy. If Sasha was here, she would have heard her calls by now. *Go back to town.* She stood up and gave one more almighty yell, shining the torch from side to side and down.

The white light cut through the darkness, catching a flash of colour. She moved it back. Pink. She blinked in disbelief. Below her she could see pink. 'Sasha.'

But the pink didn't move.

Her heart hammered wildly in her chest as she sat down and

bottom-shuffled another fifteen steps. She shone her torch. On a ledge just below the stairs, cushioned in thick bush, lay Sasha's inert body clad in pink pyjamas.

*Be alive. Be alive.* She scrambled to the edge, and shone the torch. The drop from the steps wasn't much more than six feet. *You can get down there without a harness.* Somehow she managed to lower herself down, her feet finding footholds, her fingernails digging into the crevices, until she dropped the last bit.

Prickly branches scratched her as she tumbled onto the ledge. She took in a deep breath and wriggled. Everything moved, nothing hurt. She crawled slowly to Sasha and immediately pulled her away from the edge of the ledge.

Gently shaking her shoulder, she tried to rouse her. 'Sasha, sweetheart, it's Kate.'

The girl's eyelashes fluttered open and closed again.

*Thank you, thank you.* She sent up a prayer. She shone the torch on Sasha's face. Blood had clotted at her temple and her face was badly scratched by the bushes. She checked her airway and breathing, then gently opened each eye, and tested her pupils. The black discs contracted. At least she could rule out a brain injury.

'Sasha, I'm going to see if you have done yourself any more damage.'

The girl moaned as Kate systematically ran her hands down Sasha's arms and then her legs, feeling for misalignment, pretty much dependent on her sense of touch rather than sight as she juggled the torch in her mouth.

A sob broke from Sasha's lips as Kate's hands pressed on her lower left leg, which lay at an angle.

'I'm sorry, Sash. You've broken your leg.'

The young girl started to cry, the pain from her leg seeming to have jolted her back to consciousness. 'Oh, Kate, I was so scared. Daddy's going to kill me.'

Kate stroked her temple and kissed her forehead. 'Shh, no, he's not. He's going to be thrilled you're safe.' She pulled out a space blanket and tucked it around Sasha to keep her warm. 'I'm going to ring him now and when the sun comes up he'll be here to take you to hospital.'

She set the torch securely in the fork of a bush and pulled out her phone. Leaning in close to the torch, she auto-dialled Baden's mobile and then put the phone to her ear.

The sound of ringing never started.

She held the phone under the beam of light. The signal detector was blank. Her heart slammed against her chest. *You idiot!* She was so used to using her work satellite phone she'd never even thought that her mobile phone wouldn't work out here.

She was stuck on a ledge, with a child with a concussion and a fractured leg, and no way of getting any help.

Daryl would string her up and ditch her from the search and rescue squad.

Baden would never forgive her.

'So what do you think she was wearing when she left home?'

Daryl opened his spiral-bound notepad as he stood in the middle of Sasha's room.

Baden tried to pull his fried brain together. 'She's got a lot of clothes but I've looked through them and I think the only things missing are her pink pyjamas and her walking boots. The lantern torch is gone but her backpack is still here.'

'It's cold out there tonight. Would she have a jacket?'

Baden opened the drawer where Sasha stored her hoodies and polar fleeces, his hands riffling through the contents, trying to keep his thoughts calm enough to think. 'Perhaps a red hoodie, but I'm not certain.' In thin pink pyjamas, hypothermia was a real concern. Regret slashed him. Sasha was out there somewhere, alone and cold, and it was all his fault.

'And you've rung her friends, you say, and no one's seen her?' The fatherly policeman's bushy eyebrows rose in question.

Baden pulled his mind back to the details. 'That's right and Kate Lawson has been doing a town search while I did the ring around from here in case Sasha came home.'

'Wise idea. Well, she's been gone five hours now so I'll put the call out to our volunteer searchers. We'll meet at the station in an hour.'

'I'll be there.' Relief flooded him that he could finally do something more tangible to look for Sasha.

Daryl flipped his notebook closed. 'Doc, someone has to be here at the house in case she does come home under her own steam.'

'I can't sit around here any longer. I have to do something.' His voice rose in frustration.

Daryl scratched his head. 'The kiddie knows Kate, doesn't she? Ring her and get her back here. She can man the house and that frees you up to search. I'll see you at the briefing.'

'Right, I'll be there.'

*Sasha, be safe, please, be safe. I promised to keep you safe.*

The moment Daryl left the house, Baden dialled Kate's number. 'The number you have telephoned is either turned off or out of range. Please try again later.' The recorded message droned on. In his haste he must have dialled the wrong number. He tried again but this time he used the number already listed in the contacts list to avoid a mistake.

The same message played.

*I've got a full battery and I'll have this in my pocket all the time I'm driving around town, looking for her.*

He glanced at the clock. He'd missed the check-in phone call because he'd been with Daryl. His unease ramped up. Kate wouldn't have turned off her phone. She was experienced in search and rescue and she knew the vital importance of communication. He knew she would have rung him when she hadn't heard from him.

His stomach curdled. Something was wrong. Very wrong. The only reason she wouldn't have rung him was if she wasn't able to. If something serious had happened to her.

An insidious thought edged though him, taking hold. Two females missing. Shocking things, unmentionable things sometimes happened in small towns as well as in big ones.

His blood turned to ice as his fear for Sasha, already at breaking point, compounded with his dread for Kate. He collapsed into a chair, dropping his head into his hands. First he'd lost Sasha, now Kate was missing. What if he lost them both?

Crushing pain bore down on his chest, sending silver spots wavering before his eyes. He couldn't lose either of them. He couldn't lose his daughter and the woman he loved.

*The woman he loved.*

He loved her. He dragged in a ragged breath. Oh, God, he'd been such a fool. He'd got it all wrong. His promise to make Sasha his top priority didn't mean he couldn't love again. It meant he should love a woman who loved Sasha. A woman Sasha loved, too.

Kate was that woman and he'd pushed her and her love away.

Now she was missing and he couldn't tell her he loved her. And that Sasha loved her, too.

*Move!* a voice roared in his head. *Go!*

He had to find the two most important people in his life. He had to find them, hold them and tell them he loved them both.

He rang Daryl as he ran to the car. 'Kate's missing, too. I want the helicopter brought in and I'll be on it.'

\* \* \*

Kate's fingers burned from cold as she checked Sasha's pulse. It was rapid but that could be due to pain. The birds started to twitter, their cacophony of sound heralding the rise of the sun. A large red ball, it rose from behind the gorge, banishing the dark and bringing much-needed warmth.

At any other time the beauty would have awed her but not today. She'd spent the last hour cuddling Sasha close, using her own body heat to warm the frightened child and the space blanket to trap the heat around them.

The unforgiving rock and dirt had dug into her hip while the bushes poked her. She'd never complain about her mattress again. Sasha had slept fitfully in between being woken up for head-injury observations.

Kate sighed. At least she knew that Baden would have contacted Daryl and a search would be getting into full swing. But they would start searching from Baden's house and move out in concentric rings. Did Baden know Sasha loved the peace of the gorge? Had she ever told him she liked to come here to think?

They could be here for hours. Why, why hadn't she rung Baden to tell him she was heading out this way before she'd left town? But hindsight was a wonderful thing. She chewed her lip. At least her car was in the car park if someone from town thought to come out here and made the connection.

'Kate.' Sasha gripped her hand and started to sob. 'It really hurts. When are they coming to get me?'

Her stomach sank but she couldn't lie. 'Honey, I don't know. But you need to use some of that bravery that made you walk out here in the dark alone.'

A small voice replied, 'I don't think it was bravery. I think it was probably stupidity.'

Kate gave a wry smile. 'Perhaps, but sometimes when we're angry or sad we don't think things through very well.'

Sasha nodded. 'I was so angry with Dad. I wanted to come out to see you at Sandon this morning and he said I would only be seeing you at Guides.'

Kate's heart sank. The one person she and Baden wanted to protect most had ended up getting hurt. 'Well, you're seeing me now and when you're all tucked up in a hospital bed we'll talk to your dad about you coming to visit me now and then. I don't think he realised it was quite so important to you.'

*Or to me.*

If Baden hadn't been able to share Sasha before, he certainly wouldn't be able to now. The fear of losing her would only make him hold her closer and push Kate further and further away. Not that there was any room left to push. He'd left her in no doubt—he didn't love her. The bleak thought chilled her as much as the dawn air.

She reached for her medical bag now that the light was bright enough to see by. She gasped as she caught sight of the precipitous drop a mere ten metres away from where they lay. She didn't want to think about what could have happened if the bushes hadn't broken Sasha's fall.

'Sasha, I'm going to examine you again now I can see and put in an IV so I can give you something for the pain.'

'Will it hurt?' Sasha shivered under the silver space blanket.

'Not compared to falling off those steps.' She slipped the tourniquet around Sasha's arm. 'Your job is to look upwards toward the steps and see if you can see anyone. We'll start calling out in an hour when there might be a chance a tourist is visiting.'

'OK.' Sasha flinched as the cannula went into her arm.

Kate attached the five hundred millilitre bag of saline to the cannula and hung it from a tree. Then she pulled her polar fleece over her head. 'I'm going to take off your pink PJ top and you can wear this.'

'Why?'

'Your fluoro pink top is really bright and I'm going to spread it out on top of this bush. Then if we hear or see anything, I'll wave it over my head.'

'And the rescuers will see it because it isn't green like the trees or red like the dirt.'

'Exactly.' She gave Sasha a reassuring stroke of the head. 'I found you because of this pink so they'll find us, too.' *I hope.*

'And Dad said I had too much pink.' Sasha tried to laugh but grimaced in pain.

Kate splinted Sasha's leg, giving thanks it wasn't a compound fracture. She didn't need a bone sticking out through skin in this dirt. The sun rose higher in the sky and every five minutes she called out, "Coo-ee! Help!"

The only response she got was a visit by geckos and skinks, the tiny lizards that hid in the crevices, who came out on the rocks to sun themselves. She took a slug of water from her drink bottle, munched on a sustenance bar and waited.

Sasha moved abruptly.

'What's wrong? Does it hurt somewhere new?' Kate was instantly alert.

'No. Listen.' Sasha stared up. 'Can you hear that noise?'

A faint whirring sounded in the distance. *A plane.*

Kate struggled to her feet and grabbed the pink pyjama top, shoving a long stick through the arm.

The whirring grew louder. 'Will they see us?' Anxiety vibrated from Sasha as she squinted into the sky.

'I hope so, sweetie, and then they'll tell the rescuers where to come.' Kate raised the stick over her head.

A yellow helicopter suddenly appeared above the red cliffs, banked and flew up the gorge.

'Wave it, Kate, wave it,' Sasha yelled above the deafening noise of the rotors of the approaching helicopter.

With feet planted wide apart she waved the pink pyjama flag high over her head in an arc, back and forth, as if she were signalling the end of a Grand Prix race, praying the occupants of the helicopter would see it.

The helicopter flew past, the noise receding as it rose up out of the gorge.

Kate lowered the stick. 'They should fly round again, Sasha.' *Please, please, see us.*

'It's getting louder.' Sasha craned her neck, trying to see.

The muscles in Kate's arms screamed but she raised the flag again and started waving it. The helicopter approached more slowly this time. Her breath caught in her throat. Had they seen her?

The helicopter inched closer, until it hovered close to them, the noise deafening as dirt and dust swirled from the updraught of the rotors.

She caught sight of Baden's face, white with relief and fear.

She gave a thumbs-up, hoping to ease his fright. She yelled to Sasha, 'Your dad's just found us, sweetheart.'

Sasha gave a watery smile.

The helicopter rose and turned, positioning itself over them, the pilot skilfully hovering, not moving the chopper an inch from its position. An electric winch lowered a container onto the ledge. Kate grabbed it and opened it up to find a two-way radio.

'Kate do you read me, over?' Baden's reassuring but strained voice rumbled through the speaker.

Relief rushed through her. 'I read you loud and clear, Baden.

Sasha is safe. She has a suspected fractured tib and fib and a slight concussion but she's conscious and alert. Over.'

'Thank God. I'm coming down, over.' The relief in his voice was palpable.

Above her, Baden, dressed in bright orange emergency services clothing and a hard hat, connected his harness to the steel line, which was lowered toward her. As his hips came within arm's reach, she steadied his descent until his feet touched the ground.

His arms wrapped around her for an infinitesimal moment, their pressure reassuring and wonderful. Then he stepped back and a sense of loss hit her.

'Strap your radio to your body.' His command came through the radio so he could be heard over the noise of the helicopter.

The doctor in charge had arrived. There was a job to be done and he was reminding her of her role in the rescue. Failed co-worker. Her heart, already torn and bruised, broke a little more.

He moved away from her and dropped down next to his daughter, stark relief and love shinning from his eyes as Sasha reached up and wrapped her arms around his neck.

Kate bit her lip. Father and daughter reunited—as it should be. She hated the cold and heavy emptiness that dragged through her at the knowledge that she couldn't be part of this reunion.

He motioned for her to bob down on the other side of Sasha so the patient and the pilot could hear both radios.

Baden checked the air splint on Sasha's leg. 'Has she had any pain relief?'

Kate nodded. 'An hour ago.'

'Great. Thanks.' He lowered his head to Sasha. 'I need you to be really, really brave. I'm going to put you into the harness and hug you against me. Your leg might hurt but it's the best way to get you out of here. Together we'll be winched back to the helicopter and James will pull us on board.'

'I can do it, Daddy.' Sasha turned to Kate, seeking confirmation. 'Can't I, Kate?'

Her battered heart took another pummelling. 'You can do whatever you put your mind to, sweetheart.' Kate squeezed her hand. 'And in a few hours, after your leg is all plastered, you'll be sipping blue heaven milkshakes in hospital and thinking this was all a bad dream.'

'Will you bring Kate up, too, Daddy?'

Baden shook his head, his shuttered gaze catching Kate's. 'No. Kate will go out on foot.'

Of course she would. She wasn't injured and there were other medical personnel present. But none of that knowledge stopped a lump forming in her throat.

She flicked into work mode. Pushing away every personal feeling she had, she supported Sasha while Baden's strong and steady hands fitted the harness. Together they positioned Sasha against Baden and he crossed his legs over Sasha's to hug her against him then gave the signal to James.

The winch started to wind. Kate watched as the two people she loved most in the world moved upwards and away from her.

The tears she'd been holding back for twelve hours spilled over.

Kate's head pounded. Daryl had harangued her from the moment he'd dropped the rope ladder down to her so she could climb off the ledge, he'd berated her as she'd walked up the fifty steps back to the car park and he'd lectured her as he'd driven her to Warragurra Base Hospital. Then he'd hugged her, thanked her and left her sitting in A and E drinking hot tea.

'Warming up now?' Linton stuck his head into the doctors' lounge. He smiled his playboy grin. 'I hear you're being a difficult patient and have refused to sit in a cubicle.'

She rolled her eyes. 'That would be because I'm *not* a

patient. I'm fine. Nothing that a hot shower and some sleep won't cure.' She warmed her hands around the mug as she rested back in the soft couch. 'Besides, I look in better shape than you do. Big night last night, was it?'

He looked sheepish as he spun a chair out from under a table and sat astride it. 'I was merely being a good host as you'd instructed, and after the drive-in I introduced the newly arrived physio students to Warragurra's night life.'

Her tea almost spurted out of her mouth. 'I only asked you to be the MC.' She gave him a long look. 'So now you've dated every nurse at the hospital, you're moving on to students? Don't you think they're a bit young for you?'

For a moment he looked affronted but then his expression smoothed into its usual urbane lines and he teased her. 'Hey, you and I haven't dated. I promise a fun time.'

She laughed. 'And a don't-call-me,-I'll-call-you policy. Thank you, but I think I'll pass.'

He stood up and swung the chair back under the table, his eyes dark with understanding. 'Sasha Tremont is out of Theatre after a straightforward reduction and internal fixation of her left leg and she's ready for visitors.'

'Thanks, Linton.' She ran her finger around the rim of the cup. Baden would be with her. She hadn't seen him since he'd been winched away. 'I'll visit her a bit later. Hope A and E isn't too busy for you today.'

He grinned and disappeared back to the action.

She should go home and have a shower. She should tie up all the loose ends after the drive-in. She should plan next week's Guide activity. She should do a million things.

But inertia claimed her and she just sat there.

The door clicked open and she glanced up from her thoughts. 'Linton said you were here.' Baden's hoarse voice spoke quietly. He looked like hell. His curls lay flat after being jammed under a hard hat and dark stubble covered his jaw while black smudges ringed his eyes—testament to the raw fear he'd lived with through the night.

She smothered her overwhelming desire to wrap her arms around him and tell him it was over now. Guilt immediately surfaced, turning inside her. Four hours of his fear she could have alleviated if she'd planned before going to the gorge.

He sat down next to her. 'Sasha's asleep.'

She nodded, feeling the tension between them. 'That's the best thing for her.'

'Yeah, it was one hell of night.'

His sigh shuddered through him and she felt some of his dread as the memories came back.

Unspoken words spouted from her mouth. 'I'm so sorry I didn't tell you I was going to the gorge. I could only think of Sasha and I'm so used to the satellite phone…'

His blue eyes glittered when her words stalled. No matter what she said, he'd never forgive her.

'Don't you *ever* do anything so stupid ever again.'

His harsh words slapped her hard, their sting sharp and tingling.

She could understand his anger. She tossed her head to try and maintain her composure. She just had to keep it together a little bit longer.

Suddenly his hands rested on her shoulders, his fingers digging into her skin, almost shaking her. 'Do you hear me? I never, ever want to feel like that again.'

A tickle of fear skated along her veins and then he pulled her hard against his chest, his arms vice-like around her. She could feel his heart pounding against her own.

'What a crazy, stupid, wonderful thing you did, haring off into the bush to find Sasha. But you could have plunged off those steps and missed the ledge.' His voice rose with distress. 'You could have died.'

'But I didn't.' She spoke softly, needing to reassure him, needing to reassure herself.

He gently cupped her face with his hands and stared into her eyes, his own filled with emotion. 'When I couldn't contact you, I thought that some crazed person had abducted you and Sasha. I thought I'd lost you for ever and all I could think was that you were gone and you didn't know that I love you.'

*I love you.*

Her breath whooshed from her lungs and her brain seized, trying to make sense of his words. 'You love me?' She couldn't hide the bewilderment in her voice.

He dropped his hands from her face, folding his hands over hers, holding them tight. 'I love you with every part of me.'

She wanted so desperately to believe him, to be in his arms, but she didn't understand what was going on. She pulled her hands free and stood up, wrapping her arms around herself to prevent her shaking. 'Last night you told me you couldn't love me. That you'd made a promise and we couldn't be together.'

'I've been such a fool, Kate.' He stood up and walked toward her, his face full of regret. He tried to reach for her but she spun out of his reach, needing the physical distance from him so she could order her thoughts.

He stood still. 'My world was rocked when Annie died and all I could think of was if I lived my life how we had planned, if I kept things the same, then that would give Sasha the security she needed so she could grow up feeling safe.' He ploughed his hand through his hair.

'But life doesn't stand still, does it?' She knew that only too well.

He shook his head. 'No, it doesn't. Sasha realised that before

I did but I was blind to her many attempts at pointing it out. And blind to yours.' He sighed. 'I thought that the promise I made meant never falling in love again and that would keep Sasha safe from being hurt. But that wasn't what it meant at all and all I've done, as you so succinctly put it, is deny her a full and happy life.' He gripped the back of a chair. 'She loves you, Kate.'

She bit her lip and asked the hardest question of her life. 'Is that why you love me, because Sasha does?'

'No!' The word exploded over her as he strode to her side. He gently cupped her face, forcing her to look at him. 'If I'm honest with myself, I've loved you from the moment I glimpsed your long, shapely legs leaning out of the storage unit in the plane on the first day we worked together.'

He stroked a finger down the side of her face. 'You've filled my dreams, my waking thoughts. You've made me laugh and cry, but most importantly you've woken me up. I don't just exist any more. With you I truly live.'

His gaze dazzled her with love and at that precise moment she knew she wasn't a consolation prize. He loved her and she belonged in his heart.

'Will you marry me and be a mentor and friend to my daughter?'

Her heart exploded with joy. 'I think that is the most wonderful question I've ever been asked.'

His eyes twinkled. 'Yes, but do you have an answer?'

She laughed and placed her lips against his, seeking entry to his mouth, giving her answer to him and part of herself.

He kissed her back, long and hard, pledging love, friendship and security, all tied up with a swirling passionate heat.

She reluctantly pulled away, catching her breath.

He gave his wicked laugh. 'We've got the rest of our lives for kisses like that in less public places.' He grabbed her hand.

'Come on, let's go and celebrate our engagement with our daughter, and she can toast us with a blue heaven milkshake.'

*Our daughter.* Her dream had come true. 'That sounds like a perfect idea.'

His smile rained down on her like sunshine from a cloudless sky. 'Oh, and by the way, good luck talking Sasha out of a pink or purple bridesmaid's dress.'

She raised her brows. 'Pink saved us today so I think it should become our signature colour. Besides, a pink shirt under your tuxedo would look exceedingly good.'

A look of horror streaked across his face. 'There's no way known that I'm—'

She stole his argument with a kiss.

And he didn't object at all.

# The Outback Doctor's Surprise Bride

## AMY ANDREWS

**Amy Andrews** has always loved writing, and still can't quite believe that she gets to do it for a living. Creating wonderful heroines and gorgeous heroes and telling their stories is an amazing way to pass the day. Sometimes they don't always act as she'd like them to, but then neither do her kids, so she's kind of used to it. Amy lives in the very beautiful Samford Valley, with her husband and aforementioned children, along with six brown chooks and two black dogs. She loves to hear from her readers. Drop her a line at www.amyandrews. com.au.

To my sister-in-law Jeanette for reading all my books. Thank you, your support means so much.

# CHAPTER ONE

DR JAMES REMINGTON flipped open his visor as he sped down the arrow-straight highway. He revelled in the power of the vintage Harley engine growling between his legs, the air on his cheeks and the way the softening light of the encroaching dusk blanketed the thick bush in its ghostly splendour.

He raised his face to the sky and let out a long joyous whoop, his gypsy heart singing. This was the life. The open road. The sun on your face. The wind at your back. Freedom. He felt a surge of pleasure rise in his chest as a familiar affinity with the environment enveloped him. He felt a part of the land.

A solitary road sign appeared in the distance, announcing Skye, his destination, was only five kilometres away. It loomed large and then was gone in the blink of an eye. He felt anticipation heighten his senses. On a deeper level an unwanted thought intruded. Maybe this time he'd find what he was looking for. A place to hang up his helmet. A place to call home.

He shook his head to quell the ridiculous childhood longing. The wind was on his face, he had freedom—why did he need roots? The township of Skye was just another outback stop in the many he'd made in the last few years. And after Skye there'd be another and then another until he reached the Cape and then he'd…figure out his next move then.

The road started to twist and turn a little as it wended its way through thick stands of gumtrees and heavy bush. James eased back on his speed as he leant into the curves, enjoying the zigzag of the powerful bike.

He rounded a bend and came face to face with his worst nightmare. His headlights caught the silhouettes of several cows meandering across the highway in the waning light. He had seconds to respond. He braked and swerved and in the split second before his bike slid out from underneath him and he was catapulted across the tar, James knew that, whatever happened next, it wasn't going to be good.

Helen Franklin was annoyed. It was nine p.m. She'd been hanging around for a couple of hours, waiting for the locum doctor to arrive. Had he arrived? No. His bags had arrived by courier earlier but he was still a no-show. The casserole she'd cooked for him sat uneaten in the fridge.

She could be at the Drovers' Arms, joining in the weekly trivia night. Her team was at the top of the table and she hated missing it. She'd tried phoning his mobile number the agency had furnished her with a few times but had had no response. Not that that necessarily meant anything. Mobile phone reception out here was dodgy at best between towns and only marginally better in them.

An uneasy feeling bunched the muscles at her neck and she hoped some catastrophe hadn't befallen him. But as he was only two hours late she doubted she'd manage to convince anyone to send out a search party for him. No, she just had to wait and hope that he showed or at least rang in to explain.

He'd probably just changed his mind about coming to Skye and hadn't bothered to tell anyone. Country towns were notoriously hard to attract medical staff to. She'd had a request in for a locum since Genevieve had announced her pregnancy and she was now thirty-six weeks gone.

Well, damn it all, she wasn't going to hang around all night, waiting, when the new doctor couldn't even be bothered to let her know of his delay. He'd better be here by the start of business tomorrow, though. Genevieve should have given up work a month ago. Her blood pressure was borderline and her ankles were starting to swell. She needed the break. She'd admitted only yesterday that she was completely exhausted by lunchtime most days.

Helen left a terse note on the dining-room table, gathered her stuff and left, pulling the door closed behind her. There was no need for a key. This was Skye. Nobody locked their doors. And when she saw him in the morning, she was going to give Dr James Remington a piece of her mind, and if that set the tone with her flatmate for the next four months then so be it.

James woke to birdsong and the first rays of sunlight stabbing at his closed lids. The pain in his right leg grabbed at him again and he gritted his teeth. He felt like hell. He'd had a fitful night's sleep on the hard ground. He was hungry, his bladder was full and his mouth tasted as if an insect had crawled inside during the night and died there.

His broken leg throbbed unmercilessly despite the splint he'd managed to fashion from the branch of a tree. At least it was daylight now. His hopes of rescue had improved dramatically. He looked at his watch. He was now twelve hours past his ETA—surely someone would be worrying?

All he had to do was get himself to the roadside and hope that the highway to Skye was busier during the day than it had been during the long hours he'd lain in the dark. He'd only heard two vehicles all night. The bitumen was probably only a few metres or so away, but he knew just from the small amount of moving he'd done after the accident that with his broken leg, it was going to feel like a kilometre by the time he'd got there.

He'd decided against moving too far last night. Dusk had turned to darkness quickly and visibility had been a problem. The night was impossibly black out here, the bush incredibly thick. Through a mammoth effort he'd managed to drag himself over to his nearby bike. He hadn't been able to see it and had had to rely on his sense of hearing, heading towards the sound of the still running engine.

Thirty minutes later he'd been sweating with effort and the excruciating pain of every bump jolting through his injured leg. He'd pulled his torch out of his bike's tote bag and located some paltry first-aid supplies to help him with his leg. He'd had his swag and some water and with his mobile phone showing no reception, he'd known he was there till the morning.

As tempting as it had been to push himself, he had known it would be sensible to wait for daylight. Apart from

his leg and some minor scratches, he'd escaped remarkably uninjured so the last thing he'd needed had been
to reach the road and then be run over by an unsuspecting
car. He was in black leathers and a black T-shirt. Even his
hair was black. He had hardly been the most visible thing
in the inky outback night.

James relieved himself with difficulty and with one
final look back at his bike gritted his teeth and began the
slow arduous crawl through the bush to the road.

Helen woke to the ringing phone just before six a.m. and
was dismayed to find the spare bedroom not slept in and
the note she'd left last night untouched on the table. She'd
come home from the pub to an empty house but had hoped
the missing locum had crept in during the night.

She answered the phone tersely, preparing to give
James Remington a good lecture. But it was only Elsie and
she spent ten minutes listening to the latest calamity before
she was able to get off the phone. *Damn it!* James
Remington had better have a good excuse for his tardiness.

A feeling of unease crept over her again and she quickly
punched in the local policeman's number.

His sleepy voice answered. 'Sorry, Reg, it's Helen. I
know it's early. I hope I didn't wake you.'

'It's fine. What's up?'

'The new doctor still hasn't shown. Have there been any
accident reports?'

'Not that I know of. Do you think something's happened?'

'Not sure.'

'I'm sure he's fine, Helen. Like I said last night, he's
probably just been delayed.'

'Probably,' she agreed, thinking dark thoughts about their new locum.

'He'd have to be missing for at least twenty-four hours before we could mount an official investigation.'

'I know.'

'But if you're worried I can start making some enquiries straight away. I can take the patrol car down the highway a bit.'

Helen pursed her lips, unsure. She knew Reg was probably right but she couldn't shake a nagging sense of unease. 'No, it's OK. I'm off to Elsie's now. Some of their stock broke through a fence last night and she's all het up. I'll keep my eyes peeled. I'll ring later if I still haven't heard from him.'

She rang off and looked around the empty house. *You'd better be in a ditch or laid low by a severe illness, James Remington, because this is just plain rude.*

James grunted as he inched himself slowly closer on his bottom. His movements were awkward, like a dyslexic crab. His arms were behind him, his left leg, bent at the knee, was used to push himself backward as his right leg slowly dragged against the ground as it followed.

The morning sun wasn't even high in the sky yet and he was sweating profusely. Although his leathers contributed, it was pain that caused moisture to bead above his lip and on his forehead. Every movement was agony, his leg protesting the slightest advance. He'd have given anything for a painkiller.

At just about halfway there he lay back to rest for a moment, the road now in sight. A silver car flashed by and he raised his hand and yelled out in the vain hope that he was spotted. Of course, it was futile—he was still that little bit too far away to be detected.

But he was slightly cheered by the presence of traffic. All he had to do was get the rest of the way and wait for the next car to come along.

Helen left Elsie's still distracted by their missing locum. The Desmond farm was on the outskirts of Skye and her little silver car knew the way intimately. Helen had lived with Elsie and her family on and off most of her life, permanently from the age of twelve after her mother's death.

Her mother's mental health had always been fragile, necessitating numerous hospital admissions, and her gypsy father, overwhelmed by his wife's problems and gutted by her eventual demise, had been ill equipped to care for his daughter. He'd flitted in and out of Skye as the whim had taken him, leaving Elsie to raise her.

And she had, providing stability and a much-needed loving home despite the fact that she had also been raising Duncan and Rodney, her grandsons, after their father—Elsie's son—and mother had been killed in a car accident. Duncan, who had stayed in Skye to run the farm, was the same age as Helen and they were still close.

At eighty, Elsie was a much-loved part of the family. She still lived at the homestead and now Duncan's children were benefiting from Elsie's love and eternal patience. Unfortunately in the last couple of years Elsie's health had started to fail and things that once would never have bothered her now weighed on her mind.

More often than not, when she was in a state, it was

Helen she phoned. Duncan was busy with the farm and Denise with the kids and Helen never minded. It was the least she could do for a woman who had helped her through some of the darkest times of her life.

She knew that half an hour of chit-chat and a good cup of tea soon put Elsie right. How often had Elsie taken the time to allay Helen's own fears as she'd lain awake at night, scared about the future? Elsie's hugs and calm, crackly voice had soothed her anxieties and had always loosened the knot that had seemed to be permanently present in her stomach. Easing the old woman's own fears now was never a hardship.

Helen put thoughts of Elsie aside as she concentrated on the road. Her eyes scanned either side and checked the rear-view mirror frequently. Just in case.

James mopped at his face with his bandana. He was nearly there. So close. He could hear a car approaching from a good distance away and he tried to move the last few metres quickly. Pain tore through his leg and halted his desperate movements. He swore out loud as he realised by the sound of the rapidly approaching engine he wasn't going to make it in time for this car.

In a final act of desperation he stuck up his arm and frantically waved the red bandana, even though he could tell the car had already passed. He lay back and bellowed in frustration.

Helen's gaze flicked to her rear-view mirror. Her eyes caught a blur of movement. Something red. She took her foot off the accelerator. She didn't know why. It was probably nothing. She searched the mirror again. Nothing. It was gone. But the same feeling of unease she'd had since last night was gnawing at her gut. The car had slowed right down and acting purely on instinct she pulled over and performed a quick U-turn.

She drove back slowly towards where she had seen the flicker of red. Her green eyes searched the side of the road. Nothing but red dirt and brown bush greeted her. She'd almost given up when she saw him. A figure lying just off the edge of the road.

'Hell!' She braked and sprang out of the car, giving the highway only a cursory glance as she crossed it to get to him.

James could see a woman's legs as she strode towards him. She was in long baggy navy shorts that fell to just above her well-defined knees. They were nice legs. Tanned. Smooth. In fact, they were the best damn set of legs he'd ever seen. He'd never been so happy to see a set of legs ever in his life.

If he hadn't been in so much pain he would have laughed. James Remington, gypsy loner, who prided himself on being beholden to no one, was so grateful to this set of legs he'd have traded his bike for them. He shut his eyes and rubbed his St Christopher medallion thankfully.

Helen threw herself down in the dirt beside him. Was this her locum? He looked younger than she'd expected. 'Are you OK?' she demanded, clutching at his jacket.

James opened his eyes and found himself staring into her worried green gaze. Her eyes looked like cool chips of jade. Amber flecks added a touch of heat. It was the only time a demanding woman hadn't scared the hell out of him. In fact, had he not been practically incapacitated with pain, he would have kissed her.

'I am now.' He struggled to sit up.

'No, don't move,' Helen said, pushing him back against the ground. 'Are you James Remington?' she asked as she ran her hands methodically over his body, searching for injuries. Her hands moved dispassionately through his thick wavy hair, feeling for any irregularities or head injuries. Down his neck. Along his collar bones to his shoulders.

He wasn't surprised that she knew who he was. Maybe he should have been but the pain was all-encompassing. As her hands moved lower to feel his chest, push around his rib cage and palpate his abdomen he absently realised he would normally have cracked a joke by now. The pain was obviously altering his persona.

He was pretty suave with the ladies but he'd never had one become so intimately acquainted with his body so quickly. She had a nice face and a distracting prim ponytail that swished from side to side as she assessed his injuries.

'Yes, I am,' he said as her hands gripped his hip bones and she applied pressure down through them, glancing at him with a cocked eyebrow in a silent query. He shook his head.

'We've been worried about you,' she said. 'What happened?' Helen felt methodically down his left leg from groin to toes.

As her fingers brushed his inner thigh James felt his body react despite the pain in his other leg. 'Came off my bike. Cows on the road.' He grimaced.

'Ah. Elsie's,' she said absently as she concentrated on

his other leg, starting again in his right groin. 'You been out here all night?'

'Yup. Look, I'm fine,' James said, batting her hand away. 'It's just my right leg. The tibia's broken.'

Helen sat back on her haunches and surveyed the crude but effective splint. She didn't want to disturb it if she didn't have to. 'Is it closed or open?'

'Closed,' he confirmed. He'd cut open his jeans to investigate the damage by torchlight last night.

'Were you knocked out?'

'No. Conscious the whole time.'

She nodded, grateful to discover that he didn't appear to be too injured at all and trying not to dwell on the fact that their desperately needed locum was now totally useless to them. Helen made a mental note to get onto the agency as soon as she could to organise a replacement.

'Well, we'd better get you to Skye. Do you think between us we can manage to get you into my car? It'll be quicker than calling the ambulance.'

James ran assessing eyes over her. He doubted she'd be much help at all, there wasn't much to her. But he was strong and at the moment he'd go with any option that got him to medical attention as fast as possible. 'Sure.'

Helen nodded and left him to bring her car closer. She performed another U-turn and pulled it up as close to James as possible. She opened the back door.

'You might as well lie along the back seat.'

Helen hoped she'd sounded more confident than she felt. Looking down at him, she wondered how they were going to manage it. There was a lot of him. He was a tall, beefy guy, his build evident despite his recumbent posture.

She remembered the things she had resolutely ignored during her assessment of him. The bulk of his chest, the span of his biceps and the thickness of his quads beneath her hands. He was all man. Still, his musculature had hinted that he took good care of himself. She hoped so. She hoped he was strong enough to lift his bulk because at a petite five two he dwarfed her.

James looked behind him and shuffled his bottom until he was lined up with the open door. 'I can lift myself in if you can support my leg.'

Helen nodded. She knelt to position her hands beneath his splint. She felt him tense and glanced up at him. She noticed the blueness of his eyes for the first time. They were breathtaking. A magnificent turquoise fringed by long sooty lashes. Was it fair for a man to have such beautiful eyes?

She blinked. 'Does it hurt?'

He nodded.

Even through his overnight growth of stubble she noticed the tautness around his mouth and realised what it was costing him to sit stoically.

'It's going to hurt more,' she said softly, knowing there was no way they could accomplish the next manoeuvres without causing more pain.

He nodded again. 'I know.'

'We could wait for Tom. He carries morphine in the ambulance.'

He shook his head and she watched as his thick wavy hair with its occasional grey streaks bounced with the movement and fell across his forehead.

'No. Let's just get it over with.'

She nodded. 'Ready?'

James placed his hands on the car behind him, bent his left leg again and pushed down through his triceps, lifting his bottom off the ground. A pain tore through his fracture site and he grunted and screwed up his face as he placed his rear in the footwell. He shut his eyes and bit his tongue to stop from groaning out loud at the agony seizing his leg.

'You OK?' Helen asked, supporting his leg gently as she noted the sweat beading his brow and his laboured breathing.

James nodded. He felt nausea wash through his system as the pain gnawed away unabated. He had to keep going. If he stopped now he'd never get himself in the car and the pain would kill him. He placed one hand up on the seat and repeated the movement again, lifting his buttocks onto the padded material.

James muttered an expletive and then looked at Helen with apologetic eyes. 'Sorry,' he panted.

Helen grinned. 'Quite all right. I think a swear word is entirely appropriate, given the circumstances.'

'Hardly appropriate in front of a lady.' He grimaced.

Helen looked around her and threw a glance over her shoulder before turning back to face him. 'No ladies here.'

He gave a hearty chuckle and then broke off as pain lanced through his leg and he clutched at the splint. 'Don't make me laugh,' he groaned.

'Whatever the doctor orders.' She grinned.

She held his leg while he shuffled back in the seat and helped him manoeuvre into a position of comfort. Well, of less pain anyway. He dwarfed the back seat. It was impossible for him to recline. Instead, he sat in a semi-supported position, the door propping him up.

'I have some cushions in the boot. Hang tight.'

James closed his eyes wearily feeling grittiness rub like sandpaper against his lids. *Where the hell was he going to go?*

Helen arranged two cushions around his fractured leg to try and support it better. She shut the door and moved around to the driver's side, opening her door and flipping her seat out of the way.

'Here, put this behind your shoulders. Might make the ride a little more comfortable.'

She levered him forwards and stuffed the cushion behind his back, fussing a little to get it just right. James caught a whiff of her perfume and opened his eyes. They were level with her chest and he could see the pink lace of her bra and the curve of her breast as she leaned over him to adjust the cushion.

He shut his eyes again in case she thought he was staring at her breasts, and her ponytail brushed lightly against his face. Her hair was nut brown and smelled like roses. It swished back and forth a few times, caressing his face, and after a night in the cold, dark bush it was strangely comforting. He wanted to wrap it around his fist and pull her closer.

'All set?' she asked.

James slowly opened his eyes. He nodded and smiled. She turned to go and he put a stilling hand on her shoulder. 'Thank you. I don't even know your name.'

'It's Helen. Helen Franklin.'

'Ah. The nurse. That explains your tender touch.'

Helen stilled, suddenly mesmerised by his blue eyes. He was without a doubt the best-looking man she'd ever met. She'd not risked such thinking until now, but it was the inescapable truth.

'Yeah, well, don't count your chickens,' she quipped, pulling away from his touch and resetting her seat. 'We've got a few kilometres of potholed highway to travel first. I'm sure by the end of that you'll have changed your mind.'

Helen buckled up and started the car.

'Be gentle with me, Helen.'

Her eyes flew to the rear-view mirror and found his blue flirty gaze staring back at her. He was teasing her. *Great. Not only sexy but flirty, too.* Fortunately, she knew the type well. Her own father was a classic example. It was typical that not even a broken leg could stymie the natural urge men like James felt to flirt.

But there was a shadow in his eyes that she recognised, too. Something that haunted him. Maybe it was just the pain. But maybe, like her father, it was something deeper, older. Something that he'd carried around for many years. Something that made him wary. Something that made him guarded.

Something that made him…intriguing.

Something that was a big flashing neon sign to her and all women to stay the hell away. Charming and charismatic had their good points but there was always a down side. She'd seen enough to know that men like James Remington, like her father, wouldn't be held back or held still.

She rolled her eyes at him. 'Hang tight.'

She let the tyres spin a few times as she skidded away.

\* \* \*

They made it to the hospital ten minutes later and within half an hour James had been X-rayed and given a shot of morphine.

Helen checked her watch. If she didn't go now she was going to be late for work. They were already one doctor down, necessitating the need for Genevieve to take a patient load when she was supposed to only be working two half-days to show James the ropes before commencing her maternity leave.

Helen worried about Skye's only general practice and what they were going to do without a replacement for Genevieve as she gently drew back the curtain that had been pulled around his cubicle. James lay on the gurney, his eyes shut, his size taking up its entire length, his feet hanging over the end.

He was shirtless and her mouth dried as her gaze skimmed over the planes and angles of his smooth, tanned chest and abdomen. A silver chain hung around his neck, a dainty medallion hanging from it. It looked surprisingly manly and strangely erotic sitting against his broad bare flesh and her fingers itched to touch it.

A light smattering of hair around his flat nipples was tantalising and she followed a trail of hair that arrowed down from his belly button until the sheet cut the rest from her view.

He shifted a little and she looked away from his abdomen, feeling a jolt of guilt at such voyeurism. He smiled to himself and Helen watched as a dimple in his chin transformed his stubbled features from Greek God-like to pure wicked. He looked relaxed for the first time since she'd met him, no tense lines around his mouth or frown marring the gap between his eyebrows.

James was drifting through space, floating. It felt good and he almost sighed as pink lace and roses flitted through the fog in his head. He felt the swish of her hair against his face again, across his lips, and it was as if she'd stroked her hand down his stomach. He could feel himself reaching for her, hear himself murmur her name.

He jolted awake and grabbed the side rails of the gurney as the sensation of falling played tricks with his equilibrium. His foggy mind took a moment to focus and when it did he found himself staring across into green eyes.

'Morphine dreaming?' She smiled.

James had never had anything stronger than paracetamol in his life before so he supposed that was exactly what he'd been doing. 'Strong stuff.' He grimaced.

The floating sensation had been pleasant and the relief from the constant feeling that his leg was in a vice was most welcome, but the sense of not being fully in control of his body was disconcerting and he wasn't entirely sure he liked it. He was always in control. He'd spent too many childhood years feeling helpless to be remotely comfortable with this drug-induced vulnerability.

'I hear you copped a lucky break.'

James grinned at her joke despite the odd feeling of being outside his body. 'Yes, simple fracture of the tibia, not displaced. Long leg cast for six weeks.'

'You got off very easy.'

'Indeed.' James remembered the worst-case scenarios that had careened through his mind as he had been hurled into the bush and knew that he could just as easily be dead or very seriously injured. 'How's my bike?'

She rolled her eyes. Of course, he would be worrying about the machine. 'Alf's recovering it now.'

'You don't approve?'

She shrugged. She was a nurse. Orthopaedic wards were full of motorbike victims. 'Mighty thin doors. No seat belts.'

He regarded her seriously, her no-nonsense ponytail swishing slightly as she spoke. Not a single hair had managed to escape. He grinned. 'You need to live a little. Nothing like the wind on your face, whipping through your hair.'

Helen sucked in a quick breath as his smile made his impossibly handsome face even more so. It made him look every inch the freedom-loving highway gypsy he so obviously was. She understood the pull of the wind in your face—she'd often ridden on the back of her father's bike over the years. But a life of chronic instability had left her with feet firmly planted on the ground.

'I have to get to work. I'll check back in on my lunch-break. Can I bring you anything?'

James shut his eyes as the room started to spin again. 'Food. I'm starving.'

She laughed. 'They do feed you here, you know.'

'Hospital food,' he groaned. 'I want proper stuff.'

'Like?'

James thought hard as the foggy feeling started to take control again. He allowed it to dictate his stomach's needs. He rubbed his hand absently over his hungry belly. 'Pie. Chips with gravy. And a beer.'

Helen laughed again and tried not to be distracted by the slipping of the sheet as his hand absently stroked his stomach. Pies were her favourite bakery item. 'A pie and chips I can do. Don't think morphine and beer are a good mix, though.'

James opened one eye. 'Sister Helen Franklin, you are a spoilsport.'

'Yeah, well, I also sign your cheques so be nice.'

He chuckled and, despite his efforts to fight it, a wave of fog drifted him back into the floating abyss. Being nice to Helen conjured up some very delectable images and with his last skerrick of good sense he hoped it was just the morphine. The feel of her hair in his face and her pink lace was already too interesting fodder for his narcotic-induced fantasies.

If he wasn't careful she might become way more fascinating than was good for him. Helen Franklin looked like she was the kind of woman men stayed with. And James didn't stay. He didn't know how.

# CHAPTER TWO

AT SIX o'clock Helen walked into the hospital to find James entertaining three nurses. It had been a shocker of a day. From Elsie and her cows, to finding James, to the news that another locum would be difficult to find. She wasn't feeling particularly jovial.

'Feeling better, I see,' she said dryly.

Her colleagues greeted her warmly and then fluttered their hands at James, promising to catch him later. She frowned at the very married nurses and felt strangely irritated.

'Thank God you're here. Break me out, will you?'

He was sitting propped up in his bed, a black T-shirt thankfully covering his chest, his leg supported on a pillow. She shook her head. Did he think he could just snap his fingers and she'd jump to attention? 'The med super wants to keep you overnight.'

James snorted. 'Don't be ridiculous. I broke my leg, that's all.'

'Jonathon's just being cautious.'

'I'm going stir crazy in here and this bed is frankly the worst thing I've ever lain on. The ground in the bush last night was softer than this.'

Helen laughed despite her irritation because it was true. The mattresses left a lot to be desired. 'How's the cast?' she asked, moving to the end of the bed. 'Wriggle your toes.'

James sighed and wriggled his toes for the hundredth time since he'd had the damn thing put on that morning.

Helen touched them lightly to assess their colour and warmth. 'Do they—?'

'No,' he interrupted. 'They don't tingle. I don't have pins and needles,' he said testily. 'They have perfectly normal sensation.'

Helen quirked an eyebrow. Good, now he was irritated, too. 'So this is the doctors-make-the-worst-patients demonstration?'

'I'd like a decent night's sleep in a comfortable bed before starting work in the morning if it's all the same to you.'

Helen's hand stilled on his toes. 'Work?'

'Yes, work. You know, the reason why I'm in Skye in the first place?'

Helen became aware of her heart beating. She hardly dared to hope. 'Oh…you still want to…take up the contract, then?'

James frowned. 'Of course? Why? Are you withdrawing the offer?'

'No, no, of course not,' she said, absently stroking his toes peeking out from the end of the cast. 'I just assumed… I mean I thought…you'd want to rest up until your leg was out of the cast.'

He snorted and tried not to be distracted by the light touch of her fingers on his toes and how strangely intimate it was. 'It's just a broken leg. I may not be as mobile as I'd like but I'm still capable of sitting in a chair and seeing patients. You do still require a doctor, don't you?'

Helen couldn't believe her luck. Her dark mood lightened. She smiled. 'We most certainly do.'

'Excellent. I'm your guy. Now,' James said as he swung his leg down off the bed and reached for his crutches, 'if you know where my luggage is, perhaps you could get me some clothes and the appropriate paperwork so I can get the hell out of here. I'd like to check on my bike.'

Helen watched him fit the crutches into his armpits, her hand now lying on the empty pillow.

'It's fine. I went and checked. Alf has it at the garage. He's shut now. You can go visit tomorrow.'

'It'll be safe there?'

She smiled. 'Of course. This is Skye.' Although she did understand his reticence, his classic Harley must be worth a fortune.

He nodded. 'I'll call in on my lunch-hour tomorrow.'

'There's no need to start straight away,' she protested. They could cope for a bit. 'You should take a few days off, James, we'll manage. Your leg should be elevated as much as possible initially.'

'I'll keep it up all night. I promise.'

He turned on the crutches to face her and she tried not to think about the unintended double meaning behind his words. But he was dressed only in his black T-shirt and a pair of black cotton boxer shorts that came to mid-thigh and left nothing to the imagination.

He looked like he could have modelled for them. He would have been perfect in a glossy magazine somewhere with his full pouting mouth and brooding dark looks. She could almost picture him clad only in his undies, his magnificent turquoise eyes making love to the camera. Maybe even straddling a gleaming chrome Harley. James Remington had clearly missed his calling.

She blinked and then swallowed. Hard. For goodness' sake, she was a nurse, not some swooning teenager. She'd seen plenty of completely naked men. It made no sense to be affected by someone who was practically fully clothed. Hell, she'd seen more male skin exposed on a beach.

'Right, then, I'll bring you some clothes. Hang tight.' And she fled from the room.

'Hang tight' seemed to be a favoured expression of hers. Again, as he looked down at his attire, he wondered just where the hell she imagined he would go in his underwear.

James was surprised to find on the way home that he would be living with the very capable Helen Franklin for the duration of his time in Skye. The agency had assured him accommodation was provided so the details hadn't mattered at the time. For someone who'd spent a good part of his life between jobs camped out in a swag on the ground, any roof over his head was welcome.

But as she helped him out of the car and the smell of roses enveloped him again he felt a tug in his groin. The memory of her light touch on his toes earlier returned to him, as did the look she'd given him when he'd stood before her. The amber flecks in her eyes had glowed with warmth, hinting at passion, but she'd also looked a bit like a rabbit caught in headlights.

He could tell she was attracted to him. But he could also tell she didn't want to be. A fact he understood perfectly. He was most definitely attracted to her. Who could resist being plucked out of the bush by pink lace and ponytails? But, like her, he didn't want to be either.

He'd had his share of casual flings on his travels but always with women who'd known the score. Helen Franklin sent up a big red flag in his head. Warning bells were ringing loudly. Some women were best left alone— and she was one of them.

'So this is it,' Helen said, dumping her bag on the hallstand and holding the door open for him. He brushed past her on the crutches and her breath hitched in her throat. 'Your bags are in your room, through there.'

Helen pointed to one of the three bedrooms that ran off the main living area and tried not to blush at the memory of going through his bags to find the clothes he was now wearing. There had been a lot of boxers in his luggage and she felt as if she knew him more intimately than she'd ever known a complete stranger.

'Kitchen through that door and dining room beside it.' Helen could feel his gaze on her. 'I have a casserole from last night I plan on heating up, if you'd like some.'

James nodded, his stomach growling at the suggestion. 'Sounds good. I wouldn't mind a shower first, though. I feel like half the bush is still clinging to me.' He looked down at his leg and grimaced. 'I guess a bath's going to be easier.'

Helen nodded while desperately trying to not think about him in the bath. Naked. 'Probably.' *Oh, God, he wasn't going to need a hand, was he?* 'Will you be OK to…?'

James watched the play of emotions flick across her face and toyed with the idea of exaggerating his injury. 'Why? Are you offering?' he murmured.

Helen felt her cheeks grow hot just thinking about something that was second nature to her. Something that she had helped hundreds of patients with. Running a bath for him…helping him off with his clothes…supporting him as he lowered himself into the bath. She opened her mouth to tell him she wasn't his nursemaid but no words come out.

James chuckled. 'It's OK, Helen. I think you've already gone above and beyond the call of duty.'

She cleared her throat and tried again. 'Damn right,' she said, and stalked into the kitchen, his hearty laughter following her.

An hour later Helen was starting to worry when the door to the bathroom was still closed. She hadn't heard any pleas for help and she hoped he was just taking his time rather than stuck in the bath, unable to get out. She turned the volume on the television up to distract her from her steamy thoughts.

He joined her a few minutes later, hobbling on his crutches. He was wearing a white T-shirt that hugged his well-defined musculature and a pair of black boxer shorts. His dark wavy hair was damp and wet strings of it brushed the back of his neck. He smelled like soap and something else, some spicy fragrance that she knew was going to stick around long after he'd hit the road.

He was clean shaven and her fingers tingled with the urge to touch his smooth jaw.

'Better?' she asked him, hoping she sounded normal and that the husky strain in her voice was just her imagination. She'd known him for less than a day but already he made her acutely aware that she was a woman.

He nodded. 'Heaps.'

James turned to sit on a lounge chair.

'No, wait, hang on,' she said, springing up from the couch she'd been sitting on. 'You have the three-seater—that way you can put your leg up. I'll sit there.'

James stopped and stared down at her. She was fussing around with cushions. She seemed nervous. Her ponytail swished with her movements and from his vantage point he could see the nip of her waist and the nape of her neck.

'OK.' He sat and put his leg up gratefully. It had started to throb again and he'd just taken two painkillers.

'Hang tight. I'll just nuke your casserole.'

Helen fled to the kitchen and leant heavily against the sink for a moment. *What the hell was happening to her?* She was acting as if she'd never seen a man before. OK, they didn't really get men of his calibre in Skye. For God's sake, there were only three unattached men under forty and not one of them looked like James. Locums who deigned to come to the bush usually only came in one flavour—fiftyish, balding and, more often than not, condescending.

But she was going to need to get a serious grip because she had to live with this man for four months and acting like a tongue-tied teenager every time she saw him less than fully dressed was going to get really embarrassing really quickly. So he redefined tall, dark and handsome. One thing was for sure. He'd get back on that bike in four months' time and ride off into the sunset. And she was damned if he was going to ride off with her heart.

James looked up as she came back into the room carrying a steaming bowl of something that smelled divine, and his stomach growled. He took the tray from her and was pleased to see she'd served him a hearty portion and also added a hunk of fresh grainy bread.

'This smells amazing,' he said as he ripped off a chunk of bread and dipped it into the thick, dark gravy.

Helen nodded. 'It tastes pretty good, too.'

James mouth was salivating even before he could put the soaked bread into it. He shut his eyes and sighed as the meaty flavour hit his taste buds. He chewed and savoured it for a few moments before swallowing. 'Oh, yes. Yes, it does.'

Helen resolutely turned her attention to the television and tried not to be turned on by the sounds of pleasure coming from his direction. Elsie had always said there was nothing more satisfying than filling a grown man's belly. Helen had secretly thought that was kind of old-fashioned but being privy to James's appreciation was strangely gratifying.

As James ate he watched his new housemate surreptitiously through his heavy fringe. She seemed engrossed in the television, sitting with her shapely legs crossed and her hands folded primly in her lap. She was quite petite and the big squishy leather chair seemed to envelop her.

She was still in her clothes from that morning, navy shorts which had ridden up to mid-thigh and a plain white cotton blouse. He assumed it was her uniform. Apart from the tantalising glimpse of her leg, it was kind of shapeless. If he hadn't known about the pink lace beneath he would have even said it was boring.

'So, what's the story with this place?' James asked as he mopped up the dregs of his bowl with the last piece of bread. 'It looks quite old.'

Helen steeled herself to look at him and was grateful he was looking at the fancy ceiling cornices. 'It's a turn-of-the-century worker's cottage that's been added onto over the years. It's been used as a residence for the Skye Medical Practice for about forty years since Dr Jones bought the property and built the original surgery at the front of the land.'

'Did he live in it?'

Helen nodded. 'Until it got too small for his growing family. He had seven children. And it's been used ever since by successive doctors. Frank lived in it when he first came to Skye until they bought something bigger, so did Genevieve until she moved in with Don.'

'Frank's the boss?'

Helen nodded.

'Has it ever been empty?'

'Off and on.'

'How long have you lived here?'

Since Duncan and Denise's growing brood had made her realise it had been time to move on. They hadn't asked her to go, had been horrified when she had suggested it, but she'd known it was the right thing to do. As welcome as they'd always made her, as much a part of the family as she'd always been, the facts were the facts. They'd needed an extra room and she was an adult.

It had been an odd time. She'd realised that she'd never had a place she could truly call her own. A place she'd felt like she'd belonged. That deep down, despite Elsie's love and assurances, she'd always felt on the outside. Her mother was gone and her father was more comfortable with the open road than his own daughter.

She looked around, feeling suddenly depressed. Even this place wasn't hers. 'A couple of years.'

James heard a sadness shadowing her answer. He saw it reflected in her eyes. He recognised the look. Had seen it in his own eyes often enough. Beneath the surface Helen Franklin was as solitary as him. Looking for something to make her feel whole. Just like him.

He felt a strange connection to her and had a sudden urge to pull her close, and perhaps if he hadn't been encumbered with a cast that seemed to weigh a ton he might have. She seemed so fragile suddenly, so different from the woman who had dragged him from the bush. 'Is that how long you've lived in Skye?'

Helen laughed. 'Goodness, no. I was born here.'

*Of course.* Everything about her screamed homey. From her casserole to her prim ponytail. She looked utterly at home in this cosy worker's cottage in outback Queensland.

He felt a growl hum through his bloodstream as the affinity he'd felt dissolved with a rush of hormones. She wasn't his type. In fact, she was the type he avoided like the plague.

'Have you lived here all your life?'

Helen didn't miss the slight emphasis on the word 'all'. Obviously staying in one place was a fate worse than death for him. She looked at his beautiful face, into his turquoise gaze, and saw the restlessness there. The same restlessness she'd grown up seeing in her father's eyes. He was a drifter. A gypsy.

'Except for when I went to uni.'

James nodded his head absently. *Definitely not his type.* He preferred women who had lived life a bit. Travelled. In his experience they were much more open-minded. They knew the score and didn't expect an engagement ring the second a man paid them a bit of attention.

'You don't approve.'

He shrugged. 'Not at all. It's just not for me. I'd feel too hemmed in.'

*Heed his words, Helen, heed his words.* But a part of her rebelled. The arrogance of the man to assume that because she was still living in the place she'd been born that she'd not done anything with her life. 'There's nothing wrong with being grounded. Doesn't running away get tiresome?'

He chuckled at her candour. She didn't look fragile any more. She looked angry. 'I prefer to think of it as moving on.'

God, he sounded like her father. 'I bet you do.' He chuckled again and goose-bumps feathered her arm as if he'd stroked his finger down it. 'So where are you *moving on* to from here?'

He shrugged. 'Central Queensland somewhere. Wherever they need a locum. I haven't seen much of the state and I want to make my way up to the Cape. It's supposed to be spectacular.'

Helen had been up to Cape York with her father during a very memorable school holiday. It *was* spectacular. But stubbornness prevented her from sharing that thought. She wasn't going to elaborate and spoil his image of her as a small-town, gone-nowhere girl.

'Where are you from originally?'

'Melbourne. But I haven't lived there since I finished my studies.'

'Let me guess. You've been travelling?'

James laughed. 'Very good.'

'Do you still have family in Melbourne?'

'My mother.'

Helen noticed the way his smile slipped a little. It didn't appear that they were close. 'Your father?'

James sobered as he fingered the chain around his neck. 'He died in my final year of uni.'

'I'm sorry,' Helen said quietly. She met his turquoise gaze and she could see regret and sorrow mingle.

He shrugged. 'We weren't really close.'

There were a few moments when neither of them spoke. The television murmuring in the background was the only noise. So James's relationship with his parents had been as fraught as hers had been with her parents? She felt a moment of solidarity with him.

James stirred before the sympathy he saw in her gaze blindsided him to the facts. Helen Franklin was a woman who liked to be grounded. He'd avoided her type for years.

They were incompatible. He was just a little weakened from the pain that was starting to gnaw at his leg again and her terrific home cooking.

'Still, I inherited his bike. I guess I have that to thank him for.'

That explained why he'd been so concerned about the

machine. It wasn't just because it was highly valuable, it obviously had sentimental value to him.

'She's a beautiful Harley,' Helen commented. 'Is it a '60 or '61?'

James regarded her for a moment. 'You know something about bikes?'

Helen stifled the smile that sprang to her lips at his amazement. 'I know a little.'

'It's a 1960.'

'It seemed to survive the crash OK.'

He smiled. 'An oldy but a goody.'

She grinned back at him. It was something her father would have said, his own classic Harley being his most prized possession. Looking at James, she could see why her mother had fallen for her father. The whole free-spirit thing was hard to resist. James's handsome face was just as charming, just as charismatic as the man who had fathered her.

She blinked. 'So…what…you just roam around the country, going from one locum job to the next?'

He nodded. 'Pretty much.'

'Sounds…interesting.' Actually, she thought it sounded terrible. No continuity. No getting to know your patients or your colleagues or your neighbours. It sounded lonely.

'Oh, it is. I love it. The bush is drastically underserviced. There are so many practices crying out for locums. Too many GPs working themselves into the ground because they can't take any time off. Much more than city practices. I really feel like I fill a need out here. And bush people are always so friendly and happy to see you.'

'But don't you ever long to stay in one place for a while? Really get to know people?'

He shrugged. 'I prefer to spread myself around. Locums are in such high demand out here—'

'Tell me about it,' Helen interrupted.

He smiled. 'I'd like to think I can help as many stressed out country GPs as I can rather than just a few for longer. And, anyway, it suits my itchy feet.'

She suspected James Remington could have done anything he'd put his mind to. He looked like a hot-shot surgeon at home breaking hearts all over a big city hospital yet he chose to lose himself in the outback. 'Not a lot of money in it,' she commented.

'I do all right,' he said dismissively. 'General practice has its own rewards.'

As an only child growing up in a very unhappy household, James had never felt particularly wanted by either of his parents. Oh, he hadn't been neglected or abused but he'd been left with the overwhelming feeling of being in the way. Being in the way of their happiness. They'd stayed together for him and had been miserable.

Being a GP, especially in the country, looking after every aspect of a patient's health, had made him feel more wanted and needed than his parents ever had. Not just by his patients but by his colleagues and the different communities he'd serviced. And James knew through painful experience you couldn't put a dollar value on that. Some rewards were greater than any riches.

Helen nodded. 'I agree.'

They watched television for a while. Helen found her gaze drifting his way too frequently for her own liking. She yawned. 'Think I'm going to turn in for the night.' She stood and leaned over to take his tray, his spicy scent luring her closer.

'Yes, I'm kind of done in myself.'

She straightened, pulling herself away. 'See you in the morning.'

'Night,' he called after her retreating back.

James woke at two a.m. his leg throbbing relentlessly. He shifted around trying to get comfortable for fifteen minutes and gave up when no amount of position change eased the constant gnaw. He reached for his crutches and levered himself out of bed. He'd left his painkillers in the bathroom.

Quietly he navigated his way through the unfamiliar house to the bathroom. He didn't want to switch on any lights in case he woke Helen. He didn't know whether she was a light sleeper or not and the last thing he wanted to do was annoy her on their first night under the same roof.

He located the pills and swallowed two, washing them down with some tap water. The thought of trying to get back to sleep before the painkillers had worked their magic didn't appeal so James decided to sit in the lounge, put the television on low and try and distract himself.

He picked his way gingerly through the lounge room, trying not to make too much noise or bang into any furniture. He felt for the couch as he balanced himself on his crutches and was grateful when he finally found the edge. But as he manoeuvred down into its squishy folds his crutches wobbled and one of them fell.

James made a grab for it but the sudden movement

jarred through his fracture site. He cursed to himself as he clutched his leg, helpless to prevent the crutch from crashing down loudly on the coffee-table.

Helen sprang from her bed as the noise pulled her out of her sleep. James? Had he fallen? She dashed outside pushing her sleep-mussed hair out of her face.

She snapped on the light, flooding the lounge room in a fluorescent glow, putting her hand to her eyes at the sudden pain stabbing into her eyeballs. 'What? What's wrong?'

James squinted, too, the pain in his leg still gripping unbearably.

'Are you OK?' Helen asked, slowly removing her hand as her eyes adjusted.

He nodded. 'Sorry, I didn't mean to wake you.'

James's eyes came open slowly and he wondered if the pain and the medication were making him delirious. Before him stood a very different Helen Franklin. Gone was the prim ponytail. Her hair was down, a deep rich brown tumbling in sleep-mussed disorder to her shoulders. It made him want to put his face into it, glide his fingers through it.

Gone was the shapeless uniform. She was wearing some kind of silky sleep shirt the colour of a fine merlot, which barely skimmed the tops of her thighs and clung in interesting places. It left him in no doubt that her pert breasts were no longer encased in pink lace. In any lace at all. He could see the jut of her hip and the curve of her waist and a whole lot of leg.

A sudden image of her riding on the back of his Harley

dressed as she was right now, her breasts pushed against his back, stormed his mind and he was rendered temporarily mute. That medication he'd been given was powerful stuff!

'Oh, no!'

James roused himself at her plaintive cry and tracked her progress with eyes that seemed to be seeing in slow motion only. Her body moved interestingly beneath her silk shirt.

She was kneeling beside the coffee-table, gathering some broken glass from a photo frame, before he registered what had happened.

'Oh, hell. Sorry. I didn't realise I'd broken anything. I'll replace it.'

Helen looked down at the broken glass that had framed a picture of her at fifteen and her father on his Harley. 'It's OK,' she said dismissively, tracing his devil-may-care smile. 'It's just glass. I can replace it. I should remove my pictures anyway. I've been here by myself for so long I kind of took over.'

'No, please, don't.' He placed a hand on hers. 'I'm only here temporarily, it would be silly to put them away.'

Helen looked down at his big hand covering hers. *Only temporary.* Just like the guy in the photo.

James removed his hand and watched the way she touched the picture with a strange kind of loving reverence. 'Your dad?'

Helen nodded, still staring down at the photo.

'Is he…?'

She glanced up at him as he trailed off. His hair was sleep-tousled, his wavy fringe flopping across his forehead, and she was pleased that the coffee-table was between them. 'No. He's very much alive and roaming some highway somewhere.'

He saw the love in her eyes as she gazed at the picture but heard the bitter note in her voice. Obviously her father aroused intense emotions. It also explained how she knew about Harleys. And maybe it even explained her desire to stay grounded.

'Anyway,' she said, becoming aware of his intense gaze and the building silence and belatedly the fact that she was in her pajamas, 'are you going to be OK?'

He nodded. 'I'm just going to watch some telly until the painkillers start to take effect.'

Helen rose and backed away, still clutching the frame. She was suddenly acutely aware of her state of undress. How bare her thighs were. How braless she was. How her shirt barely covered her rear. How…interested he seemed.

'See you in the morning.' She took a deep breath and turned at the last moment, praying that he wasn't watching her.

But he was. James caught a brief glimpse of firm cheek as the shirt flared when she whipped around. And leg. A lot of leg. Suddenly his time in Skye had become very interesting indeed.

He was living with someone who was as sexy as hell underneath her ponytailed primness and knew about Harleys.

Suddenly she seemed more and more his type.

# CHAPTER THREE

HELEN didn't dare come out into the main part of the house until she was dressed the next morning. She'd lain awake for an hour, thinking about James's heated gaze and how liquid heat had pooled low in her belly. She knew that even after a day in his company she was treading on dangerous ground.

She was attracted to him. Not such a bad thing to admit to, she supposed, except for the fact that he was way out of her league. The regular attentions of Skye's bachelors paled into comparison with one hot look from James. She'd do well to remember he was only there for four months and she'd never had a casual relationship in her life.

When she was dressed she made her way out to the lounge room to find James fast asleep where she'd left him. She stopped in mid-stride and almost tripped. The man was utterly gorgeous. A dark shadow adorned his jaw and his broad chest rose and fell in hypnotic splendour. His jet-black hair lay thick and luscious across his forehead.

His leg was raised on some cushions. His other leg

positively exuded testosterone, its well-defined quadri-
ceps and calf muscles complemented by a perfect covering
of dark hair. His large bare foot seemed oddly out of place
with his sexy he-man image, made him seem vulnerable
somehow, and the nurturer in her wanted to go get a
blanket and cover him up.

She gave herself a mental shake and ordered herself to
stop gawking like a teenager. She turned away and headed
for the kitchen. Damn him for lying around her house,
looking sexy and vulnerable all at once. She got two slices
of bread and jammed them into the toaster. She pushed the
lever down harder than required and hoped he had almighty
backache this morning. If she had to trip over his barely
covered body every morning, it was going to be a long four
months!

James awoke slowly. He could hear music and noises
coming from the kitchen and the mouth-watering aroma
of toast teased his nostrils. He grimaced as he sat up and
rubbed the crick in his neck. There was a slight ache in his
leg but it was feeling much better than it had last night
when his midnight wanderings had disturbed Helen.

A vision of her in her sleep shirt played in his mind again
and he smiled to himself. Maybe it had been the medication,
maybe it had been seeing a scantily clad Helen in the middle
of the night, but something had fuelled some fairly erotic
dreams and he felt his loins heat as he recalled the images.

He rose awkwardly, using his crutches for support. He
needed a shower. A cold one. But given how logistically
impossible that would be, he'd settle for coffee instead. He
hoped Helen owned some decent stuff, not some horrible
instant brand.

Even on the road he made sure he carried a supply of freshly ground coffee. Life was too short to drink the instant stuff. In fact, that was pretty much his motto for life. Life was short, grab it by the horns and ride it for all it was worth. He'd grown up seeing his parents waste their lives stuck in a situation they hadn't wanted to be in, and he was damned if he would.

He drank good coffee. He went where he wanted. He followed his own rules. He worked wherever the road took him and kept his relationships short and sweet. And even if his heart did occasionally yearn for something more, he hadn't been in a place yet or met a woman yet who could ground him. In fact, he seriously doubted either existed.

He swung into the kitchen and stopped in the doorway. Helen was standing at the sink, her back to him, eating toast as she bopped along to a country song playing on the radio. Her head was moving to the beat, her hips were swaying and her feet tapping.

He leant heavily on his crutches for support. She was back in her uniform again, her hair tied back in its prim ponytail, not a hair out of place. But it didn't stop the leap of interest in his groin or a pang of something he couldn't quite name hitting him in the chest. He knew she probably had some lacy concoction on under that prim white blouse, knew the contours of her hips from the cling of fabric last night, knew that her bottom cheeks were cute and perky as hell.

*She could be the one.* James clutched the handles of the crutches harder as the insidious voice invaded his head. Preposterous! Yes, he fancied her. He was a man, for crying out loud, and she was a very attractive woman. But that was it.

For God's sake, he'd only known her for a day. OK, it had been a tumultuous day. She had, after all, rescued him and his broken leg from the bush, but there was no need to let his imagination get carried away.

The funny feeling he'd got in his chest when he'd looked at her just now was easily explained. It was lust. The tantalising stirrings of sexual attraction. The allure of possibility. And that was all. He was a thirty-five-year-old man. *He* was in charge of his life—not his hormones.

He cleared his throat. 'I don't suppose you have any decent coffee in this neck of the woods?'

Helen jumped. She hadn't heard him approach. She turned. 'You nearly gave me a heart attack,' she said accusingly, talking around her last mouthful of toast.

He grinned. 'Sorry. I was enjoying the show, though.'

Helen swallowed the remnants of her breakfast. How long had he been standing there? She straightened and gave him a don't-mess-with-me look. 'Show's over.'

He shrugged. 'I prefer rock music anyway. Does the local radio station play any of that?'

'Sure. Country rock.'

James chuckled. 'About that coffee?'

Helen pointed to the percolator sitting on the bench and the expensive coffee-jar sitting beside it.

James eyes lit up at the unexpected sight of his favourite Italian blend. Helen Franklin may live in outback Queensland but she obviously had style. 'Ah, a woman who appreciates fine coffee.'

Helen shrugged. 'Life's too short to drink bad coffee.'

James gaze caught and held hers as she echoed his sentiment. Living with a gorgeous woman who shared one of life's most basic truths with him was going to be a bigger challenge to his powers of resistance than he'd first thought. 'Couldn't have put it better myself,' he said softly.

Helen swallowed at the silky quality to his words. His magnetic presence made the small kitchen seem even tinier. 'Why don't you go and get dressed?' *For God's sake, put something on...* 'And I'll get a pot started.'

James nodded noticing how she clutched her hands together. 'Deal.' He grinned and executed a perfect about-turn on his crutches.

They walked the short distance to work in a silence broken only by the crunching of their feet on the pebbles that lined the drive. The day was already hot and James turned his face towards the sun.

'Here we are,' Helen said, opening the back door for him and indicating for him to precede her.

James swung in on his crutches into what appeared to be a staffroom and was greeted by a very pregnant freckled redhead.

'Ah, you must be James. Thank God you're here,' Genevieve said, and gave him an enthusiastic hug.

James laughed. It wasn't often that he was greeted like Santa had dropped him under a tree. 'You must be Genevieve.'

'Yes, sorry,' she said, blushing a pretty shade of pink. 'Probably not the most appropriate way of saying hello but you are a sight for sore eyes...or feet, as the case may be.'

Helen envied the easy way Genevieve handled herself around James. She felt all tongue-tied just looking at him—there was no way she could have just casually hugged him. Although Genevieve did have a compelling motive so greeting James like he was a long lost-brother seemed entirely appropriate.

'Well, I aim to please.' James smiled.

Helen heard the flirty tone to his voice and wanted to roll her eyes. Did the man never switch his charm off? Genevieve was happily married and hugely pregnant.

'Genevieve's right,' said a gruff voice from the doorway. 'You are a sight for sore eyes.'

James looked up and saw a big bear of a man with a thick bushy beard standing in the doorway. 'You're not going to hug me are you?' he joked.

The man roared laughing. 'Hardly.' He walked forward, extending his hand. 'Frank. Frank Greer. Nice to have you in Skye, James. Are you sure your leg's up to it?'

'It aches a little still but work will help to keep my mind off it.'

'I hope Helen's been looking after you.'

The image of a silky sleep shirt flared against his retina. He looked at a glowering Helen. 'Yes, she has. She's been great.'

Helen glared at Frank. If her boss thought she was going to play doctors and nurses with James Remington, he could think again. 'In case it has escaped your notice, it is not part of my job to nursemaid every locum that decides to crash his bike and break his leg. Nursemaiding you two is more than enough!' She glared at James for good measure. *Don't get any fancy ideas.*

Frank roared with laughter. 'You're right. What would we do without you? She's marvelous, James, just marvellous.'

Genevieve nodded. 'She runs this practice like clock-work.'

'Damn right I do. Best you both remember that at lunch when I intend to ask for a pay rise.'

They laughed and James could feel the easy affection between the three of them as a palpable force.

'Well I'd love to stand around and chat but I've got work to do. Guess I'll start with the coffee as no one else has done it.'

Helen flicked a reproving glance at her two colleagues. She did love them but would it kill either of them to put the coffee on for once? This was what she got for being indispensable and babying them all these years. She stowed her bag in a cupboard and approached the sink.

'Come on, James, I'll show you the ropes,' Genevieve said, rubbing her belly.

He looked at the mother-to-be and saw the dark circles under her eyes, noted the way she shifted from foot to foot and pushed at her ribs as if she just couldn't get comfortable. She looked exhausted and it wasn't even eight in the morning.

'There's no need,' he said. 'All I need to know is the way to my office. I'll figure the rest out as I go along. I've been a locum for the last five years, I'm used to feeling my way.' True, each practice was slightly different, but the fundamentals never changed.

'But—'

'Really,' James insisted, moving towards her and pulling out a chair from the table behind her. 'Sit, you look done in. It's my fault you had to work a full day yester-day. I think you should just go home and put your feet up. Look after that little one and yourself.'

'I…' Genevieve said as she sank into the chair and looked at Frank.

'It's more than OK by me.' Frank nodded.

James saw the flare of hope and longing in her eyes battle with the weight of her responsibilities. 'Really, I'll be fine. And Helen will be able to tell me what I need to know. Right, Helen?'

Helen turned to face them. Her conscience battled with her libido. She didn't want to spend the morning in such close quarters with him and, damn it, she was busy enough without his professional needs to see to. But one look at Genevieve's weariness and she knew she couldn't deny him. He'd been sensitive enough to Genevieve's obvious exhaustion and it'd be churlish of her to ignore it.

She plastered a smile on her face. 'Sure, absolutely. James is right. Go home. We'll manage just fine.'

'It would be nice to…take a load off,' Genevieve admitted.

'Well, that's sorted, then,' James said, placing a brotherly hand on her arm and easing her up out of the chair. 'Off with you now. We don't want to see you around here until you come to show the little guy off.'

'How do you know it's going to be a boy?' she asked.

Helen handed Genevieve her bag. 'He's a male. They're kind of egocentric like that,' she said dryly.

James's swift laughter took her breath away. It was deep and sexy and one hundred per cent male. The man was impossible to insult! She watched him and Frank usher Genevieve out of the room and contemplated her day. A traitorous thrill ran through her body. If this was day one, how the hell was she ever going to get through the next four months?

* * *

He was right, Helen decided half an hour later. He was a quick study. She'd shown him his office, Frank's office, the reception area, the treatment rooms, the phone system, the chart system and the storeroom. He'd asked a few intelligent questions and clarified several points, but otherwise had listened and not interrupted.

'Here's your appointment book,' she said as she sat in her chair behind the front desk.

James scanned the bookings. 'Doesn't look too intense.'

'You're fairly light today because Genevieve's been taking a reduced patient load. That'll change by week's end.'

'Oh?'

'Once the town finds out you're here, we'll have an influx of patients with all sorts of fictitious conditions, coming to check out the new doctor.'

James laughed. He'd witnessed that phenomenon before. 'I'll try not to disappoint them.'

Helen doubted he'd disappoint at all. The man was going to set off a swooning epidemic all over town.

'So we break at one for lunch?' he asked, studying the book.

Helen nodded. 'One till two.'

'That'll give me time to go to Alf's and check on the bike.'

*The bike.* 'You're not going to be able to ride it for a while,' she pointed out as she tapped a pencil against his cast.

He grimaced. 'I know. Not quite sure how I'll take that. I'll probably go stir crazy.'

'Trapped in a small town with no way of escape your worst nightmare?'

He shook his head. 'Not at all. I just rarely go a day without riding it. I like the sense of freedom it gives me.'

James's words echoed her father's in her head. Her very lovable, very charismatic, very absent father. Freedom? It seemed to her he was as shackled as the next person. Always out there looking for something he could never quite find. 'Are you free or just lost?'

James looked down into her earnest face, her steady green gaze. How did you explain the call of the road to a homebody? But gazing at her, the frission between them pulsing steadily, he wanted her to understand.

'It's hard to explain.'

They gazed at each other for a few moments, his turquoise stare meeting unwavering green. 'Try me.'

The door opened and the first customer of the day stepped inside. Their eye contact held briefly until the patient spoke and then Helen looked away and smiled at one of Frank's regulars. She felt James's intense gaze for a few more moments and almost sagged against the desk when he hobbled to his office and shut the door.

James sat at his desk and mulled over the strange conversation. How could he explain something that was so innate? And why was it so damn important that she understand? He was out of Skye in four months and whether Helen Franklin got it or not was neither here nor there. She was just another pretty face in just another small town. And out of bounds at that.

His intercom buzzed and her husky voice announcing his first patient pushed past his resolve and made a mockery of his don't-give-a-damn attitude.

'Send them in.'

It was lunchtime before he knew it. He'd seen fifteen patients all with varying conditions who had welcomed him warmly to Skye. His leg ached slightly and he had garnered a lot of sympathy over the course of the morning. He'd even managed to find most things without having to hassle Helen too much.

Yes, he thought as he made his way across the main street to Alf's Garage, he had slipped into the routine of Skye's only general practice easily. It was going to be a very pleasant time here indeed. The Helen factor was something he hadn't counted on but it was nothing he couldn't handle.

It was hot outside. The summer sun high in the sky beat down on him relentlessly and shimmered off the bitumen in a haze as he waited for a couple of cars to pass. He looked up and down the main street with interest.

It was like a hundred other small towns he'd seen throughout rural Australia. Wide and a little potholed, there was a central strip for parking along which jacaranda trees had been planted to provide shade and a dazzling carpet of purple in October.

There were the required four pubs, one on every corner, their beautiful wrought-iron latticework decorating the wide verandahs and tin roofs of the solid two-storey structures. Locals strolled down the streets, taking respite from the heat under the shady shop awnings. A bakery. A butcher. A newsagent. A milk bar. The usual array of bread-and-butter services lining main streets everywhere in outback towns.

James spent ten minutes chatting with Alf and looking over his banged-up bike. Assessing the damage, he was

amazed he hadn't been more injured. He gave Alf the
number of a classic Harley specialist in Melbourne and left
reluctantly.

The bike was more than just something that had been
bequeathed to him in his father's will. More than just a
connection to a man who'd always considered his son as
some sort of cross to bear. The Harley was the bike his
father had finally left on after years of a miserable
marriage and as such symbolised freedom to James.

Freedom to be happy. Freedom to plot your own course.
Freedom from blame. He'd never seen his father happier
than the day he'd ridden away, the Harley between his legs.

His stomach grumbled and James decided to cross back
over and buy a pie from the bakery. The one Helen had
bought him yesterday had been amazing and he'd been
craving another ever since. He spotted Helen walking by
as he queued and he bought two on impulse.

He exited the shop and looked down the street in the
direction Helen had been heading. He saw her in the
distance and hurried to catch her up, his crutches a hin-
drance to speed. She stopped, turned right, opened a gate
and disappeared from sight. When he finally drew level he
saw it was an old hall. It stood on stumps, a rickety-looking
staircase leading to an open door. The sign above the door
read SKYE COUNTRY WOMEN'S ASSOCIATION. Helen was in
the CWA? Wasn't that for oldies?

He shrugged, opened the gate, swung down the short
path and manoeuvred himself up the stairs, following her
in. The hall was spacious inside, its bare floorboards and
pitched roof causing the low murmur of voices to echo

hollowly around the room. A raised stage at the far end was overlooked by a framed picture of the Queen.

About twenty elderly women sat on chairs arranged in a circle. Behind them a trestle table groaned with food. The voices cut off as he entered. The click-clack of dozens of knitting needles ground to a halt.

They looked at him. Helen looked up from her knitting as the silence stretched. Her heart slammed in her chest. *What the hell was he doing here?* Wasn't it bad enough they had to live and work together?

'I bought you a pie,' he said, holding up the brown bakery packet, acutely aware of his very attentive audience.

Helen met his turquoise gaze, refusing to pay her hammering heart any heed. 'Are you following me?'

He smiled. 'Just repaying the favour.'

Elsie looked at Helen and saw the slight flush to her cheeks. She looked back at the stranger. He must be the missing locum Helen had been telling her about yesterday. Fine specimen of a man. 'Do you know how to knit, son?' Elsie asked.

'No, ma'am.' He shook his head. 'My grandmother tried to teach me once.' James smiled at the memory. His mother's mother had always made him feel wanted. 'She said I had two left thumbs.'

The women chuckled. 'Well, never mind, bring that pie over here then and pull up a pew. Helen needs some meat on her bones.'

James gave Helen a doubtful look. He loved the sense of community in small towns and had been in enough to know that the CWA ladies were the queen bees. But he hadn't been in town long enough to get a good sense of everything yet and he didn't want to blow it in front of Skye's matriarchs. 'I don't want to intrude.'

'Nonsense,' Elsie said. 'We never knock back the company of a handsome young man, do we, ladies?'

There was a general murmur of agreement and James smiled. He acquiesced, making his way towards the circle, and the knitting needles started up again.

Helen pulled up a chair for him next to Elsie. 'You're really getting around on those things,' she said testily.

He grinned and passed her the pie. 'I'm getting better.'

She took the packet from him as he settled himself down. 'Lucky for you I have a pie fetish.'

*Too much information.* The less he knew about her fetishes, the easier the next four months would be.

'So, you're the locum our cows upended in the bush,' Elsie said with a twinkle in her eye.

James chuckled. 'Apparently.'

Helen went around the circle and introduced all the ladies. She watched as each of them, none under seventy, primped and preened at James's effortless flirting. The man was lethal.

She ate the pie, luxuriating in its rich meaty flavour, trying her best to ignore the conversation and the deep rumble of James's voice as he spoke.

'So, what are we working on, ladies? Is this a general knitting circle or is this a specific project?'

'It's for the Royal Children's Hospital in Brisbane,' Elsie said. 'We knit trauma teddies and bootees and bonnets for the little kiddies.'

'That's very admirable,' he commented.

'Keeps us occupied.' Elsie shrugged. 'Tell us a bit about yourself.'

James was used to the questions and gave the ladies a potted history of his time as an outback locum. He regaled them with his travel anecdotes and skilfully sidestepped any questions that got too personal.

'He reminds me of Owen, don't you think, Helen?' Elsie asked.

Helen ignored the general murmur of agreement. 'Not really,' she said briskly.

'Owen?' James asked.

'Helen's father,' Elsie said.

James saw the shuttered look on Helen's face and gave a noncommittal 'Ah.' He knew how closely he guarded his own history. The last thing he wanted was to encourage these chatty women, even though he was curious.

Elsie also got the message loud and clear and changed tack. She was getting old. And Helen was like the grand-daughter she'd never had. Helen had had such a tough life, Elsie would love to see her settled soon. And there was something about this man, about the way Helen was around him, that brought out the matchmaker in her.

'I hope you're looking after my girl, James. I do so worry about her living by herself.'

Helen almost inhaled the tea she'd been drinking. 'Elsie,' she warned, after she'd recovered from a coughing fit. 'I don't need anyone to take care of me.'

'Nonsense,' Elsie said. 'Everyone needs someone. Isn't that right, ladies?' The circle backed Elsie's statement vigorously. 'You should both come over for tea one night. I make a mean lamb roast, isn't that right, Helen?'

Helen shot an apologetic look at James as the other women agreed. She stabbed her knitting needles through the ball of wool. 'We'd better get back,' she said, standing abruptly.

James bit the inside of his cheek. He felt sorry for Helen. He'd been put on the spot so many times by so many elderly ladies at such gatherings he'd come to expect it. But Helen looked totally mortified, comically so.

They were out in the sunshine in under a minute.

'I'm very sorry about Elsie.'

He laughed. 'It's OK. I think it's some unwritten law that once you get past seventy you have to embarrass as many of the younger generation as possible.'

Helen laughed, relieved that he didn't seemed worried by Elsie's attempts to matchmake. 'I think you're right.'

'You and Elsie seem very close.'

She nodded. 'She practically raised me.'

He looked down at her. 'Your parents?'

'My mother was…ill…a lot and my father…well, let's just say my father didn't cope well. I lived out at Elsie's farm on and off for a long time and when my mother died I just…stayed.'

Helen's childhood sounded as bleak as his. 'That's pretty amazing of her.'

'Yes,' she agreed. 'She's a pretty amazing woman.'

They continued on in silence for a little longer, James reflecting on his own barren childhood. 'Do I really look like him? Your father?'

Helen stopped abruptly. 'Elsie had no right to say that,' she said sharply.

'Do I?' he insisted. 'Everyone else seemed to agree.'

Helen sighed and eyed him critically, knowing from the stubborn set of his jaw that he wasn't going to let it drop.

'Yes and no. He has a dimple in his chin like yours. And you're…' She searched for a word that wouldn't betray how utterly sexy she thought he was. 'Handsome…I guess, like he is…'

James laughed, which emphasised his dimple. 'Why, thank you.'

'It's probably more your persona. I think maybe she recognised the swagger, your confidence, the whole easy-rider look.'

'Are you close?'

*Good question.* Helen started walking again. 'I love him, sure. He's this larger-than-life kind of guy who sweeps into town on his Harley every once in a while and we talk and we laugh and it's just like old times, and then he starts to get that look in his eyes and I know he'll be leaving and…sometimes that's hard.'

'Hard because you don't know when you'll see him again?'

They were nearly back at the practice and Helen stopped and looked up at him. 'Hard because he chooses the road over me. Every time.'

She walked inside and left him standing on the pavement. The pain in her words grabbed at his gut. No wonder she had her feet planted firmly on the ground. He sensed her abandonment and it cut him like a knife.

Helen Franklin was definitely not a woman you could love and leave. She'd been through enough.

# CHAPTER FOUR

His first week went well. The cumbersome cast was annoying and basic things such as walking, bathing and dressing were frustrating experiences, but his leg rarely ached any more. There had been the suspected influx into the practice and Thursday and Friday he was fully booked.

Living with Helen was an interesting experience. There'd been no more early morning incidents for which his sanity was grateful. In fact, outside work, he saw very little of her. A bit around the house as she flitted from one social engagement to the other but otherwise she was largely absent. He began to wonder if she was avoiding him.

She was polite, even invited him along to places, but he got the impression she was doing it only to be civil and the last thing he wanted to do was cramp her style. And the broken leg made everything just that little bit more difficult so he was content to stay at home. He loved to read and his enforced confinement gave him the perfect opportunity.

But even the most engrossing read couldn't block out the distracting presence of her in the house. Even absent, she was everywhere. Her rose perfume permeated everything. The lounge chair smelled like her, the cushions. The bathroom smelled like her and the cabinet was cluttered with her things. The house was cluttered with her things. Photos and mementos and ducks. Lots and lots of ducks. Wooden ducks, ceramic ducks, bronze ducks.

'Ducks?' he had said.

She had shrugged dismissively. 'I collect them. Have for years.'

*A duck collector—definitely a homebody.*

But it wasn't just her stuff. It was more. The way she hung the teatowels on the oven handle reminded him of her. The vase full of flowers on the dining-room table that she picked fresh from the garden every few days reminded him of her. Her chirpy message on the answering-machine made it hard to forget he was living in her house.

At night he'd let the phone ring until the machine picked it up. He told himself it'd be for her anyway but he suspected it was more to do with enjoying the sound of her voice even if it was on a tape.

By the week's end he was starting to go a little stir crazy, trapped in the house with her smell and her machine message and her bloody ducks. He wasn't used to this level of inactivity. Not having his bike and not being able to physically go for a ride whenever the whim took him was frustrating. He didn't like the feeling of being grounded. His itchy feet were almost as bad as the itch beneath his cast, which sometimes drove him quite mad.

Helen took pity on him on Sunday night. 'Come on,' she said. 'Get dressed. You've got ten minutes.'

He looked up from his book. She was wearing jeans that clung to her legs and a lacy button-up shirt with a V-neck in almost the exact shade of her nightdress. He could just see a glimpse of pink lace at her cleavage and he wondered if it was the same pink bra she'd been wearing the day she'd dragged him off the side of the road.

Her hair was down and had been brushed until it looked like burnished wood—sleek and lustrous. Her lips shone with a clear gloss and her green eyes were emphasised further by lashes accentuated with a coat of sooty mascara.

'Where are we going?'

'Trivia night at the pub.'

James stared at her. He seriously doubted he could go anywhere with her looking like that and not want to touch her. Maybe staying home was a better tactic.

Helen stared down at him, waiting for an answer. 'You need to get out and the team's down a player.'

When he still didn't do anything, she said, 'You don't like trivia?'

'Um, no, it sounds fun.'

She waited for him to move. When he didn't she gave an exasperated jiggle. 'You suck at trivia?'

He laughed. 'I can hold my own.'

'Good, 'cos we're winning. You now have…' she checked her watch '…eight minutes.'

James felt the last semblance of his good sense slip. He really did need to get out of the house. And should the desire to touch the much-grounded Helen Franklin overwhelm him, there'd be plenty of people around to discourage what was most definitely a very bad idea.

He hauled himself upright, using his crutches. 'Time me.'

Six and a half minutes later he swung into the lounge room. 'Will this do?'

Helen's breath caught in her throat. She always under-estimated his impact. His height and width were striking. His body dwarfed the crutches, making them look like spindly matchsticks.

He was wearing baggy denim shorts and a blue polo shirt almost the exact shade of his turquoise eyes. He'd brushed his unruly locks into a semblance of order but still his fringe did that endearing flop. His aftershave wafted towards her and she was overcome with the urge to bury her face in his neck.

*Do?* He was going to treble the pulse rate of every woman in the pub. 'Fine.' She nodded and briskly looked away. 'Let's go.' She grabbed her bag off the coffee-table. 'Normally I'd walk but we'll drive so you don't have to hobble too far.'

Helen was relieved when they arrived at the Drovers' Arms. James's presence in the house was unsettling enough—in the close confines of the car it was completely unnerving. Last time he'd been in her vehicle he'd been a safe distance away in the back. Having him sitting beside her, his large hand resting on his leg in her peripheral vision, his spicy fragrance drifting her way was a real test. She clutched the knob of the gear lever tightly and kept her eyes glued to the road.

There was a fair crowd inside the pub and a country rock song blared from the jukebox. Helen was grateful for the noise and distraction. Her team mates cheered when they spied her and waved her over.

'Do you want a drink?' James asked as they passed the bar.

'Diet cola,' she said, and left him to it. She didn't know how he was going to manage two drinks and his crutches and she didn't care. She needed space.

Of course, she needn't have worried. Glynis on the bar insisted on bringing the drinks to the table and fussed over him while he sat down. She batted her eyelids and patted James's shoulder sympathetically, her crimson-tipped nails like an exotic bird flying high against the plain blue of his shirt.

Helen rolled her eyes. Glynis was the only other single woman in town. She'd been in to see James on Thursday with some vague symptoms and had left grinning like a Cheshire cat. Still, half the town had been in to see him with vague symptoms so she could hardly single out Glynis for her displeasure.

James had taken the seat beside her and she was very conscious of his heat, his smell as he sipped at his beer. She introduced him to the rest of the team and then Alf took the small stage used for visiting bands and other acts and the evening commenced.

Helen was impressed. James was good. As good as she was. In fact, better than her tonight. His solid presence beside her was very distracting. Why couldn't he have been as dumb as a rock? He would have been much easier to dismiss.

Sure, she knew he was intelligent. He was a doctor. But she had often found that intelligence and general knowledge didn't always go hand in hand. She'd met a surprising number of doctors and other supposedly intelligent people whose general knowledge was rubbish. His, however, was brilliant.

James was enjoying himself. It felt good to be socialising and everyone at the table had greeted him warmly. It was interesting to sit back and watch Helen interact with her friends. She was obviously well liked and, as leader of the team, no slouch at trivia either.

He motioned Glynis to bring him another drink. Beer was definitely required, sitting this close to her. When she laughed it went straight in his ear and her breasts bounced enticingly. Her arm rubbed against his occasionally and it took all his willpower not to slide his arm around her shoulders, glide his fingers through her hair.

There was a good mix at the table. Frank and his wife were there. He was sitting in for Genevieve. There was Bev, who worked as a receptionist at the nursing home, and then, interestingly, Skye's three bachelor boys. The vet, Graham. The paramedic, Tom. The pharmacist, Brendan. And they all seemed more than a little interested in Helen. Tom in particular. Every time James glanced down the end of the table, he was watching Helen. And if he wasn't watching her, Tom was keeping a close eye on him.

The evening drew to a close with the team—Helen's Heroes—staying at the top of the leader board.

'I can walk you home if you like, Helen,' Tom said as the group headed for the door.

'Thanks, Tom, but I've got the car so Hopalong…' she slapped James's cast as he swung past '…didn't have to walk too far.'

'Hey,' James protested, pulling up. 'Watch it. I'm not going to be Hopalong for ever.'

He grinned down at her and she grinned back. She'd touched up her gloss and her mouth looked very, very inviting.

Tom glared at him and James met his hostility without flinching and then turned and headed for the car. He felt sorry for the younger man. He looked about Helen's age and was living in a place where eligible women were as rare as hen's teeth. No wonder he was acting like a dog protecting an exceedingly juicy bone.

He waited in the car while she chatted with Tom. He heard her laughter and fought the urge to wind down the window and eavesdrop. It was none of his business who she talked to or what they said. Helen Franklin was none of his business, full stop.

Helen climbed into the car a few moments later. 'Well, you were a hit,' she said. 'I hope you had fun.'

*Not much of a hit with Tom.* 'I had a great evening.' He smiled.

She started the car and pulled away from the kerb. 'That question about the termite mounds—we wouldn't have got that without you. It was pretty obscure—how did you know about it?'

'I travelled all around the territory on my bike last year. The termite mounds up there are pretty amazing. I went through a stage where I read everything I could on them.'

'Well, thank you. Hope that head of yours is full of more useless trivia.'

He laughed. 'Now, there's a backhanded compliment if ever I heard one.'

She ignored him. 'Because we intend to win the cup for the third year in a row.'

He whistled. 'A hat trick.'

'That's the one.'

He looked at her and smiled. She smiled back. The amber flecks in her eyes glowed with zeal and her lip gloss glistened as passing streetlights accentuated the lustre. He looked away before he did something stupid. Like reach across and kiss her.

He had to fight this attraction at all costs. She couldn't give him what he needed—a casual affair. And he couldn't give her what she needed—a lasting relationship.

They pulled into the drive and Helen's hand shook slightly as she removed the keys from the ignition. She'd had such an enjoyable time and driving home with him seemed so very intimate. She had felt his gaze on her as she'd driven and she desperately needed air.

'So, you and Tom, huh?' James asked as he manoeuvred his leg and the rest of him out of the car.

Helen took a few gulps of cool, fresh air. 'What? Don't be ridiculous.'

James raised his eyebrows at her vehement reaction. 'Me thinks the lady doth protest too much.'

Helen felt her heart hammering. She didn't want to be talking about her love life with him. Again, it was too intimate. Something that people who knew each other really well did. She sighed. 'We're just friends. We went to school together. He's like a brother.'

James looked at her dubiously as he followed her into the house. 'You can't be that blind surely? I'm pretty sure he doesn't look at you as a sister. He fancies you like mad. In fact, all three of them seemed pretty interested.'

Helen was glad the darkness hid her blush. She'd been aware of the subtle competition between the men for her favour for quite a while. 'Well, I'm not,' she said briskly, heading to the door.

'Oh, yeah? Never even been on a date with one of them?' He hobbled along behind her.

'No.' She opened the door, flicked on the light and threw her bag down on a lounge chair.

James watched her from the doorway. He could see a faint tinge of pink in her cheeks. 'Have they asked?'

Helen kicked off her shoes and gave him an exasperated look. 'And this is your business, how?'

He grinned. 'Want a coffee?'

'If you're making.'

He swung past her on his crutches. 'Make the cripple do the work,' he teased.

Cripple? Even slightly incapacitated, he looked more virile, more capable than any man she'd ever met. 'I'll supervise.'

She followed him into the kitchen, his powerful triceps bunching and relaxing as he exerted his weight down through the crutch, his denim-clad butt taut as he supported his muscular frame on one leg.

James put his crutches to one side as he prepared the percolator, hopping occasionally and using the cupboards for support. Helen hiked herself up on the bench and watched him, idly swinging her legs. The coffee was dripping into the pot within minutes and the whole kitchen smelled divine.

'Mmm, I love that smell,' Helen said, inhaling deeply.

James turned and caught the very interesting expansion of her chest. 'Mmm,' he agreed. *Almost as good as you.*

He held her gaze for a long moment. She was beautiful. Her hair loose, her shapely legs swinging lazily.

'What?' she asked.

He shrugged, breaking eye contact as he took two mugs off the mug tree. 'I was just wondering how come one of those three eager guys hadn't managed to snare you.'

Because they didn't do anything for her. Because they didn't make her feel the way she felt when she was around him. All light-headed and giddy and like she was going to suffocate. Sure, she liked them but she wasn't ready to settle for lukewarm. Not yet.

She watched him pour steaming coffee into their mugs and add milk and sugar. 'It's difficult in a place like Skye. There's me and Glynis from the pub. And there are only three eligible men under forty. Few of the kids that grow up here ever stay. They head for the city. The bright lights. So when your choices are limited you start to see possibilities that you wouldn't have done if you'd had a wider choice.'

James slid her mug over to her. 'I don't think you're giving yourself much credit.'

She stared into the murky depths of her coffee, feeling suddenly depressed. She inhaled the aroma again, hoping for an instant pick-me-up. 'It's just the way it is.'

James slid his coffee along the bench too so he could stand closer to Helen. He stopped about a foot from her thigh and leaned a hip against the counter. 'So you're not interested in any of them?'

Helen blew on the scalding liquid and sipped. She may have been sitting on the bench but she still had to look up into his face. 'No. And they know that.'

Her voice was pensive and emphatic all at once. Her jade eyes were illuminated by the flecks of amber. James had his first real insight into dating in a small town. It obviously wasn't easy.

They sipped at their coffees for a while. James was acutely aware of her thigh a mere arm's length from him.

'I get the feeling,' he said after a few minutes, 'they're all just circling, though. Waiting for you to change your mind.'

Helen nodded. So did she. She gently swirled the contents of her mug. 'I probably will. Sooner or later.'

James almost choked on his mouthful. 'What? Why?' he demanded.

Helen was instantly annoyed at his tone. All right for Mr Wind-in-Your-Face, Easy-Rider. Mr Sex-on-Wheels, Girl-in-Every-Town. 'It's just practical,' she said defensively.

She had to be insane. Right? 'Practical? How?'

'I do want to marry, you know. Have children. If the right guy doesn't come along then I guess I'll have to take what I can get.'

James couldn't believe what he was hearing. 'Don't you want more? A grand love? I thought that's what every woman wanted.'

Helen snorted. 'I'd settle for someone who preferred me over the highway.'

'What about passion?' he pushed.

'Passion is overrated.' Her parents' union had apparently been highly passionately but it hadn't equipped them to cope with the day-to-day realities of life. With the sickness part of their wedding vows.

He gaped at her. 'Are you kidding? Passion is vital. Only someone who's never experienced true passion would say something so naive.'

'Hey,' she said, putting down her mug, 'just because I live in the sticks, it doesn't mean I haven't experienced passion. I did go to university, you know.'

James snorted and put down his mug. 'If it was anything like my uni years, it was more clumsy fumblings and sloppy kisses.'

'Yeah, well, don't judge me by your ineptitude.' Helen could feel her breath getting shallower, her voice getting huskier. She could see his chest rising and falling more quickly, hear the rough edge to his breathing. Suddenly the small kitchen felt positively claustrophobic.

How dared he imply she didn't know about passion? She'd had a six-month relationship with an ancient history student in her second year that had blown her socks off. They'd been nineteen and insatiable.

'Just because you're a lousy kisser.' She knew she was goading him but who the hell had died and made him master of all things passionate?

James had been called a lot of things in his life but a lousy kisser wasn't one of them. He noted the agitated rise and fall of her chest, the catch in her breath as she spoke. This conversation was totally ridiculous and he'd never been more turned on in his life. *Lousy kisser indeed. We'll just see about that.*

He put his hand on her thigh. 'Care to put that to the test?'

His touch was burning a hole in her jeans and Helen realised she had moved them into dangerous territory. His turquoise eyes were blazing with something she'd never seen before. But on some base level she knew what it was. Lust. Pure and simple. At nineteen there had been desire. This was more. This was grown-up. This was virile male animal ready to pounce.

She swallowed. Her heart tripped. 'James, I...'

He applied pressure through his hand and slid her petite body across the bench, easily obliterating the small space separating them. He put his hands on the bench on either side of her thighs, capturing her in one easy movement.

Their faces were close. He could feel her breath on his cheek, smell the coffee. 'You think I'm a lousy kisser?' he asked softly, staring at her mouth.

Helen swallowed again, her throat suddenly as dry as day-old toast. His mouth was so close, well and truly invading her personal space. She flicked her tongue out to moisten her lips and saw his pupils flare. 'I—'

His mouth descended on hers swiftly, cutting off her words. Her lips were soft and pliant and he plundered them in a brief, hard kiss.

'You were saying?' he asked, breaking away with the little willpower he had left.

Helen was breathing heavily, dazed and reeling from the onslaught. His lips were moist and she wanted them back on hers again. She wanted them everywhere.

'I—'

He cut her off again, claimed her mouth again and her moan went straight to his groin, stoking the heat raging there another degree or two. Her arms wound around his neck and he moved his hands from the bench to cup her backside. In one swift, bold movement he pulled her forward and gave a deep satisfied groan when her legs parted to cradle his hips.

His tongue demanded entry and she opened to him as she had opened her legs. He probed her mouth and her tongue danced with his, revelling in the taste of him. He pulled her against him harder and she could feel the ridge of his erection pressed against her.

Without conscious thought she wound her legs around him. His groan empowered her, the squeeze of his hands at the juncture of her buttocks and thighs emboldened her. Her hand snaked up into his hair as she rubbed herself against his hardness. His swift indrawn breath was dizzying.

Their breathing was the only sound in the room. But it was loud enough. Harsh gasps, desperate pants and flaring of nostrils sucking in much-needed oxygen. Just listening to the lack of control in his breath, the way his hand trembled as it pushed through her hair was making her hot.

In fact, she was hot all over. Hot and needy. She didn't want this kiss to end. She wanted to lie back on the bench, stretch out and let him kiss her all over. Afterwards she could plead temporary insanity but right now she wanted more.

The harsh jangle of the phone split the air. Helen pulled back from the kiss as abruptly as if someone had poured cold water on them.

'Leave it,' he said, breathing hard, dropping a chain of kisses down her neck.

She closed her eyes and felt the pull of his lips against

her skin. Oh, dear God, how had they ended up here? The phone rang despite her turmoil. 'No,' she said in a shaky voice, pushing against his chest. 'Let me down.'

James drew in a ragged breath, curled his hands into his pockets and stood back to give her her freedom. His heart pounded in his chest, his head spun and his groin ached as she walked away.

Helen strode into the lounge room. It was nearly eleven o'clock. The caller ID alerted her it was Elsie calling. *Good timing, Elsie.* She picked up the phone with shaking fingers.

'Elsie?'

There was silence at the other end but Helen was still a little distracted from the kiss.

'Elsie?'

Helen thought she heard some noise. A bit like heavy breathing. A prickle of alarm shot up her back, dissipating the sexual energy.

'Is that you, Elsie? Is everything all right?'

Still nothing. She hung up the phone and picked up her bag.

'What's up?' James asked, swinging into the room.

She glanced up at him and then wished she hadn't. His hair looked all tousled from where she had run her fingers through it and his gaze still smouldered with turquoise heat.

'Not sure,' she said briskly, searching around the bottom of her handbag for her keys. 'That was Elsie's number but when I answered there was silence.'

He frowned. 'Could it be a prank call?'

'Hardly. She's in her eighties.' She located her keys and slipped her shoes back on.

'Where are you going?'

'To Elsie's,' she said, heading to the door.

'It's eleven o'clock.'

'Exactly. Something's up.'

'There can't be too much up if she was able to dial your number.'

'I'm on speed dial, she'd only need to hit one button.'

'Call an ambulance, then,' he said, following her.

Helen stopped, her hand on the doorknob. 'I'm not going to get Tom out of bed until I know if he's required. If an ambulance pulled up only to find that Elsie's accidentally knocked the phone off the hook she'd be mortified to have wasted poor Tom's time and precious resources. I'll check on her first.'

'All right,' he said, following her outside.

'Where are you going?' she asked as she realised he was right behind her.

'With you.'

'There's no need,' she said.

'I'm not letting you go out in your car on the highway by yourself in the dead of night.'

Helen laughed. 'Well, thanks for being all proprietorial, but this is Skye.'

He shrugged. 'If something's happened, you'll need a doctor anyway, right?'

Helen weighed the pros and cons quickly. Having him in close confines after what they'd just shared was going to be awkward, but what if Elsie needed a doctor? She couldn't take the risk to save herself ten minutes of strained conversation with a man who had just kissed her senseless.

'Right.'

She climbed into the car and started the engine, pulling away as soon as James had shut his door. The silence built between them and Helen searched for an inane topic. But her head was too full of a hundred dire possibilities over Elsie and a blow-by-blow rerun of the kiss.

James cleared his throat. 'About before…'

Right. Yes. Good idea. Clear the air. Get in before he gave her the it-was-great-but-it-didn't-mean-anything spiel. 'It was a mistake. I know.'

It was. It definitely was. He'd made enough in his life to know. OK, usually they didn't make him feel this good but there was a first time for everything. 'Yes,' he said absently, trying to grapple with his buzzing body.

'You're here for four months. I'm a lifer. It doesn't matter how good it was—'

James turned to her. 'It was good, wasn't it?'

*Oh, man, it had been incredible!* She rolled her eyes. 'That's not the point.'

'Isn't it?'

'No,' she said, shooting him an exasperated look.

James had forgotten the point. 'What was the point?'

'I believe it was to prove that you weren't a lousy kisser.'

He chuckled. 'That's right. So?'

As her face flamed she refused to look at him. 'Look, I don't make out on kitchen benches. This isn't me.'

'Yeah, well, maybe you should.' He grinned. 'You're really good at it.'

Her toes curled traitorously in her shoes at his hearty compliment.

'That's not the—'

'Point,' he interrupted.

'You're leaving. That is the point. And I'm not going there.'

He sighed. She was right. He didn't do serious relationships. The only serious relationship he'd ever been exposed to had been his parents' and that had been enough to put him off for life. It was imperative he didn't let a mind-blowing kiss and a woman he barely knew negate hundreds of painful reminders.

'You're right, of course. And I will drop it. But only if you admit I'm a terrific kisser.'

She rolled her eyes at him. 'How old are you?'

He laughed. 'It's fair enough. A man has his pride. You called me inept. Lousy, even. You dented my ego.'

'Your ego needs a dent or two.'

He laughed again. 'Come on, Helen. Say it. I promise there'll be no more repeats for the rest of my stay. Just friends.'

'Friends? You promise?'

He nodded. 'Unless you beg me to take you, of course.'

He was grinning at her again and she smiled because his dimple made him look like a cheeky little boy. 'You're incorrigible.'

'I know.'

She stared at the road, her headlights illuminating the darkness. She took a deep breath. 'You're not a lousy kisser. There…I said it.'

'Can you give me a rating?'

She laughed. Typical male. He'd probably been rating women since he could count to ten. 'No, I can't.'

'Well, for what it's worth, I give you an eleven. That's the best damn kiss I've ever had.'

Helen blushed and concentrated really hard on not running the car off the road.

'I bet you say that to all the small-town girls,' she quipped.

His chuckle washed over her and she squirmed in her seat to quell the ache deep inside her. Four months stretched ahead as endlessly as the road in front of her.

# CHAPTER FIVE

THE farm dogs were barking furiously by the time Helen pulled the keys out of the ignition at Elsie's. They ran towards the car in a pack, Shep, the blue cattle dog, leading. His threatening bark melted into whines of recognition as Helen called to him quietly.

'Hey, Shep, you're a good watchdog, aren't you, boy? Where's Elsie, boy? Is Elsie OK?' She bent down and gave the dog a scratch behind the ears.

Helen didn't wait for James, although she was aware of his crutches crunching on the loose gravel and his deep voice crooning a welcome to Shep. The sensor lights had come on and it was bright enough for him to see the way.

Now she was here, she was keen to check on Elsie. The door opened and a bleary-eyed Duncan gave her a confused look. 'Helen?'

'Evening, Duncan. Sorry to disturb you in the middle of the night. Is Elsie OK?'

Duncan frowned. 'Yes. She was fine when she went to bed.'

'I've just received a phone call from your number. She's

probably just knocked the phone off the hook but I thought I'd better check it out.'

Duncan's frown turned to worry and he stood aside to let his visitors in. Helen made a quick introduction and Duncan led the way through the house at a brisk pace. He didn't even knock on his grandmother's door but burst straight in.

'Gran!'

Helen heard his strangled exclamation before she'd even entered the room, and prepared herself for the worst. Elsie was lying on the floor on her back beside her bed, the telephone that usually sat on her bedside table sitting on her chest, one hand clutching the receiver.

'Gran, Gran.'

Duncan was down on the floor beside Elsie, shaking her shoulders, his distress evident.

Helen knelt beside him, pushing aside her own fear. She felt for and quickly found a weak carotid pulse. Elsie's eyes were wide open and Helen felt gutted at the frightened look there. You'll be all right, Elsie, everything will be fine, she wanted to say, but her heart sank at the very obvious droop to the right side of Elsie's face. She was drooling and her breathing was noisy.

*No, no, no. Please, let her be OK.*

'Call Tom,' she said to Duncan.

Duncan turned and looked at her as if she were an alien life form. She saw fear in his gaze and she could tell the last thing he wanted to do was leave. She understood. She may not share the same blood as Elsie, but she was as dear to Helen as she was to Duncan. Helen looked at the man she regarded as a brother, stricken by the grief she saw there. She wanted to hug him and weep into his shoulder.

'Duncan,' James said quietly but firmly, having quickly assessed the situation. 'Let Helen and I take care of her now. We need Tom here. I need you to ring him. Tell him Elsie's collapsed. Tell him I think it may be a CVA.'

Helen was grateful James had jumped in. Grateful too that he had chosen the correct medical terminology— cerebral vascular accident—rather than the colloquial term 'stroke'. She didn't want to panic Duncan or Elsie. Not yet. Knowing it herself was awful enough.

It was too hard to judge right now how extensive it was. The next few days would see swelling around the site in the brain where the stroke had occurred and it wasn't until it started to subside that they'd have a clearer picture of Elsie's recovery.

Duncan looked at Helen for confirmation. She nodded, pleased beyond words that James had insisted on accompanying her. She was too close to Elsie and her family, too worried about the old woman herself to be the person Duncan needed her to be. Strong and positive.

Duncan stirred himself. 'CVA…right,' he said.

'Use the phone outside,' James said, prising the receiver out of Elsie's hand and replacing it in its cradle. Elsie's bedroom wasn't exactly small but it wasn't palatial either and with he and Helen in here it was already crowded enough. 'It'll give us room to work.'

'Outside…right. Collapsed. CVA. Right.' Duncan left, still on autopilot, shock blunting his reactions. Helen hoped he remembered the information.

James lowered himself to the floor, gingerly using one crutch, his powerful arm muscles supporting his weight. He sat, his legs spread and outstretched on either side of Elsie's head. Helen shuffled over to make room for him.

'Hi, Elsie,' he said gently, smiling down at her. 'I was hoping we'd next meet over a lamb roast.'

Helen felt tears spring to her eyes at James's tenderness. She needed to pull herself together. She was of no use to Elsie if she was a blubbering mess.

James didn't like the older woman's colour. She was very pale and her lips had lost their pinkness. The stroke had obviously compromised her airway and he wanted her in a more manageable position. 'Elsie we're just going to roll you onto your side while we wait for Tom.'

He glanced at Helen and noticed the shimmer of tears in her eyes. He squeezed her hand and she seemed to visibly straighten then she nodded her readiness. Elsie was quite skinny and he knew they'd be able to manage her easily.

Elsie opened and shut her mouth a few times but no words came out, just gurgly vocal sounds. Her eyes bulged in fear.

'It's OK, Elsie, we're here now,' Helen reassured her, her heart breaking, unable to bear the anxiety she saw in Elsie's gaze. 'We'll take good care of you. Tom will be here soon.'

James supported Elsie's neck, protecting her C-spine in case she'd done any damage when she'd fallen. He counted to three and Helen rolled Elsie onto her left side. James wedged his broken leg against her back and spread his good leg further.

Helen felt more in control now and arranged Elsie's limbs into the recovery position, pulling the pillows off her bed to make it a little more comfortable.

'Put one under her head,' James said. He maintained neck support as he lifted Elsie's head so Helen could slip a pillow underneath it.

He was happy with the improvement in her lip colour and a reduction in her noisy breathing. He could still hear a faint rasp, however. And he was worried that if she vomited, a common occurrence post-CVA, the stroke might have knocked out her gag reflex, which existed primarily to protect the airway from aspiration. He'd have given anything for some oxygen and suction.

'Elsie, my love, I'm just going to hold onto your chin so your airway stays clear.'

He placed two fingers under Elsie's chin and gently lifted her jaw. The rasp disappeared and he was able to simultaneously monitor her carotid pulse with the same hand.

'Tom's coming,' Duncan announced from the doorway. Denise, his wife, was standing beside him.

After Tom's display in the pub earlier James would have been happy to never see him again, but now he was grateful. Elsie's pulse was rapid and weak—Tom couldn't get there fast enough.

'Is she going to be OK?' Duncan asked.

Helen looked at him and felt conflicted about what to tell him. She also wanted to be careful when she wasn't sure what Elsie could hear or understand. She wasn't sure she could open her mouth without crumpling into a heap.

James could see Helen's uncertainty. 'She's in good hands now,' James reassured him. 'We'll know more when we can do some tests.'

Duncan looked at James as if he was seeing him for the

first time. His shoulders sagged. 'Thanks, Doc. I don't know what we'd do without her.'

Helen was pleased that James's quick noncommittal reply had alleviated Duncan's worry. Pleased that it had let her off the hook. She'd been next to useless and she didn't know what she would have done without *him*.

They stayed by Elsie's side while they waited for Tom. Helen monitored her pulse and talked to her reassuringly. James maintained her airway. Denise packed a bag. Duncan paced outside the room, making frequent trips to the window, searching for the red and blue lights.

Tom arrived ten minutes later with an oxygen kit and a portable monitor. He greeted Helen warmly and gave James a curt nod. He assembled an oxygen mask and handed it to James to apply and passed the ECG electrodes to Helen to place on Elsie's chest.

They watched the screen as a heart rhythm appeared. She was tachycardic but the rhythm was essentially normal. Tom wrapped a blood-pressure cuff around Elsie's thin arm and pushed a button. The cuff pumped up automatically and they watched and waited for the number to appear on the screen. Two hundred and ten over one hundred and fifty.

'Does she have a history of hypertension?' James asked Helen.

She nodded. 'She's on a beta-blocker. It's always been well controlled.'

'Let's get an IV in before we move her,' James said.

Tom nodded and within a minute or two had efficiently placed one in the back of Elsie's left hand. Between the three of them they got Elsie onto a stretcher and bundled her into the back of the waiting ambulance.

'You go in the back with Elsie,' Helen told James.

'She'd probably prefer you,' Tom said stiffly.

Helen looked at Tom. She could tell he wasn't keen to have James in his vehicle. *Great!* Just what Elsie needed now was Tom in caveman role.

'He's a doctor, Tom,' she said, not bothering to keep the reproach out of her voice. 'And he has a broken leg. He can't drive the car back to Skye.'

Tom stared for a moment then nodded stiffly. 'Fine.'

James raised an eyebrow at her as Tom stalked back into the house. He grinned. 'Better not tell him about the kiss.'

'This is not funny,' she said sternly. She obviously needed to have another talk to Tom.

'No, of course not.' He grinned again.

She rolled her eyes. 'Get in.'

He chuckled and saluted. 'Yes, ma'am.'

Given the limited space, getting into the back of an ambulance wasn't easy at the best of times, but trying to do it on one leg was especially challenging.

'I'll take your crutches with me and follow you in,' Helen said once he'd lowered himself into the seat next to Elsie's stretcher.

James saluted again. 'Yes, ma'am.'

She shut the back doors on his grinning face and the heat in his turquoise eyes. *Damn the man to hell.* He said that so sexily. She wanted to climb in with him and pick up where they had left off.

When Tom emerged from the house a few minutes later she was still standing with her fingers on the handle, staring at the ambulance doors. 'You OK?' Tom asked, touching her arm lightly.

After tonight she seriously doubted whether she'd ever be right again. Between that kiss and Elsie, things had changed for ever.

She looked down at where Tom's hand rested. Nothing. She felt nothing. James just had to look at her with heat in his eyes and she could barely think straight. She roused herself. 'No, Tom. I'm not. I'll see you there.'

It was around one in the morning before they finally made it back home. They'd stayed until after Elsie's CT scan and bloodwork had come back. The diagnosis of stroke was confirmed, with a clot evident on the left side of her brain. It wasn't as extensive as they had feared and she was being administered a special clot-dissolving medication as they left.

The smell of coffee hit her as soon as she opened the door and Helen remembered she hadn't even turned the percolator off before they'd left. She headed for the kitchen. Their half-full coffee-mugs sat on the bench. She stared into the cold murky depths of her mug and remembered why they'd been discarded. Her cheeks grew hot just thinking about it.

'Want another coffee?' James asked from the doorway.

Helen shook her head, collected the mugs and placed them in the sink, emptying their contents and filling them with water. 'I'm going to hit the sack.'

She didn't look at him. She'd barely spoken in the car. James could tell she was taking Elsie's stroke hard. 'Are you OK?' he asked softly as he moved closer.

She nodded. 'Fine.'

'You don't seem fine.'

She shrugged. 'I'm just sad about Elsie. She's such a proud woman, she's going to hate being incapacitated in any way.'

James nodded. 'Will they be able to care for her at home?'

'I'm not sure.' Helen's brow furrowed. 'They both work long hours on the farm. It will depend on how much care she needs, I guess.'

It was hard to tell from the CT scan and James knew they wouldn't have a clearer picture for a few more days. 'Is there a waiting list at the nursing home?'

'Not usually.' Helen dried her hands, pushed away from the sink and flipped the switch on the percolator. 'Do you want one?' she asked.

'I'll get it,' he said, swinging closer to her.

Helen let go of the percolator. He was very near now and she could feel his heat encompass her. His shoulders were broad in her peripheral vision and she had a sudden desire to lay her head against his chest.

Elsie's plight was turning over and over in her mind and she wanted to cry for the proud old matriarch who had been part of the land and the town for over eighty years. She'd run the farm single-handedly after her husband had died and her three boys had still been toddlers. Not being able to communicate or feed, wash or go to the toilet herself would be the ultimate indignity for such an independent lady.

Her heart was so heavy Helen didn't think she could bear it. She desperately wanted to feel James's arms around her. Seek a little solace. A little comfort. But how would a man who had no roots anywhere understand her despair?

James lifted a hand and gently removed a lock of hair that had fallen across her downcast face. 'I'm sorry,' he whispered.

She looked up into his face and his breath caught. The amber flecks in her eyes were glowing with unshed tears. She was beautiful and so very sad and he wanted to pull her into his arms. But her gaze was also wary and her fingers were gripping the bench so hard her knuckles were white. She'd made herself very clear earlier and she'd been right.

Helen blinked rapidly. She nodded. 'Thanks.' And with every ounce of willpower she possessed she unfurled her fingers, skirted around his bulk and left the kitchen.

James poured himself a coffee, leant against the bench and pondered the two faces of Helen Franklin he'd seen tonight. Hot and moaning into his mouth. Heavy-hearted and serious. Curiously, both of them made him want more.

Much to everyone's delight, Elsie improved dramatically over the next fortnight. She'd been left with slight weakness to her right hand and leg and her speech, which had initially been very difficult to understand, improved every day until there was only a slight slur.

She was having daily sessions with the physio and speech therapist, and the occupational therapist had already made a house call at the farm to see what modifications could be made in preparation for her return home.

Two days after Elsie was admitted to hospital the heavens opened. Torrential rain fell relentlessly on the thirsty landscape, turning browns to greens and dry creek beds to lively waterways. Everyone agreed it was nature's way of encouraging Elsie back to the farm. As with all farmers, rain, or the lack of it, was a constant concern in their daily battle against the elements. The township of Skye felt sure that the rain would put a real spring in Elsie's step.

Often when Helen went to visit, she'd find James already there. He always left as soon as she arrived but the stroke hadn't knocked out Elsie's matchmaking centre— in fact, it seemed to have intensified it.

Elsie had an even greater sense of urgency, having faced her mortality once, and the hints she dropped were becoming more and more obvious. Not even the continuing rain that drummed loudly on the corrugated-iron roof of the hospital or her impending day release for her eighty-first birthday party could keep Elsie's mind off getting Helen and James together.

Despite Elsie's urgings, they hadn't had another incident like on the night Elsie had had her stroke. Thankfully James had kept his promise to just be friends and Helen was grateful for that. She really was. She'd had enough on her mind, worrying about Elsie, without any strange sexual vibe at home. In fact, it had been great, just kicking back and relaxing with him in the evenings. They took turns at cooking and they honed their trivia skills by watching television game shows.

It was just like the last time she'd had a house guest. Craig had been a learner GP on country rotation and had spent two weeks at the practice and boarding at the residence. The company had been good and it had been nice to have someone to talk to. Of course, he'd been fifty, married, balding and overweight, with a dreadful habit of picking his toenails, but apart from that it was practically the same.

Helen was sure that when James hit the big five zero his thick dark wavy locks would be starting to thin, too. His powerful leg muscles would, no doubt, have started to atrophy. His washboard abs turned a little soft—more jelly than jut. And his turquoise gaze would have lost its smouldering intensity, the chin dimple its boyish charm. No man could look that good for ever.

Two weeks after she'd left the farm in an ambulance, Elsie arrived back—even if it was just for the day. Helen, Denise and Duncan had gone all out, the homestead was decked out in balloons and streamers and all the old gumtrees sported yellow ribbons. Elsie was going to get a party to remember!

As they drove Elsie out to the farm James marvelled with her how much the landscape had been transformed by the rain. Water lay everywhere. Every depression was now a puddle or a small pond. The river that the highway out of Skye passed over, which had been no more than a muddy pond when he'd arrived, now ran so vigorously beneath the bridge that James felt sure he could lean over the railing and touch it.

The entire population of Skye clapped as Helen pulled up in the car and Alf hurried forward to help Elsie from the vehicle. The township had laid on quite a spread and Elsie beamed with joy at everyone as she sat in her wheel-chair like a queen receiving foreign dignitaries.

A marquee had been set up in the back yard and people mingled in small groups all happy to still have Elsie around for another birthday. Children darted in and out of the groups and Elsie clapped excitedly at their squeals of delight.

The rain had stopped momentarily and a few meek rays of sunlight pushed through the leaden sky. A brilliant rainbow shone over the farm and raindrops dripped from leaves and flowers and clung to spider webs.

James watched the scene as only a newcomer could. The dynamics of the town were fascinating and no more evident than at a celebration. He kept an eye on Helen as he mingled. She was wearing a black and white dress that clung in all the right places and he'd thought nothing but indecent thoughts ever since she'd put it on. Her hair was caught back in its usual ponytail and he itched to pull it out and let it tumble to her shoulders.

He'd been standing for an hour, leaning on his crutches, and his leg was starting to ache a little. Three weeks down the track the pain was non-existent for the most part. But if he stood for long periods of time it niggled away, letting him know he should sit down and put it up.

He felt a familiar well of frustration rise inside him. The leg had well and truly grounded him in Skye. Not that it had been a particular hardship but he'd never gone a month without riding his bike before and he could feel the gypsy in him urging him on.

He was impatient to get out and see some of the surrounding countryside. There were supposed to be some great thermal springs nearby and he yearned for a night under the stars with the crackle of a campfire keeping him company.

Helen had offered to take him sightseeing but he had

declined. He wanted to be on his bike, the wind in his face. It gave him such a different perspective to being cooped up in a car. He really wanted to witness firsthand the transformation of the scenery with the recent rain.

As soon as the cast came off he was heading out. He hadn't used his camera in over a month and he knew he'd get some spectacular shots of the land metamorphosing from brown to green. From slow death to vibrant life.

James wandered away from the groups of chatting locals. His crutches sank into the soaked grass, making his progress a little slower. The noise slowly receded as he made his way around the side of the low-set house and disappeared altogether as he reached the front.

He spotted a couple of chairs adorning the front patio and he gratefully lowered himself into one and propped his cast up on the other. He shut his eyes and sighed as the niggle eased immediately.

He opened his eyes and they came back into slow focus on the pond that dominated the circular driveway. He had commented to Helen on the way past today that he hadn't remembered seeing it the night of Elsie's stroke.

'You didn't,' she'd said.

She'd explained that years ago, back in its heyday, even before Elsie's time, the farm had had a large fountain adorning the entrance. After a series of hard-hitting droughts it had been deemed to be a waste of water and dug out. The intention had been to fill the hole in but generations of farm kids had used it to play in and it had been everything from a sandpit to a racetrack for toy cars.

Duncan's boys had a very elaborate system of jumps set up within it. Its depth and width and sloping sides made it perfect for them to practise their skateboard skills. But with the recent rain it had filled to overflowing and the only things benefiting from it at the moment were the ducks.

James's gaze settled on an object in the middle. It was white and quite bulky. It took a few seconds for his brain to work out what it was. A sick feeling washed through him and he stood abruptly as he realised. It was clothing. It was a person. Floating face down.

His heart thundered as his powerful arms propelled the crutches back and forth, back and forth. The wet ground grabbed at the rubber stoppers. How long had the person been immersed? As he drew closer he could see it was a child. How long? How long? Was it too late?

He reached the edge and threw his crutches to the ground, balancing on one leg. He looked down at the cast and knew it was about to become soaked and useless. He heard a noise behind him and he looked back. It was Duncan's twelve-year-old son.

'There's a kid fallen in the pond!' he yelled. 'Get Helen! Get Tom!'

James didn't stop to see if Cameron had obeyed him. He turned straight back to the water and hobbled in. On his stomach his hands could just reach the murky bottom and he propelled himself along, reaching the floating child in seconds.

He turned the little boy over and dragged him back to the edge. He could feel dampness permeating his cast and his leg weighed a ton. He felt frustrated he couldn't easily lift the child from the water and stagger out. He couldn't properly bear weight on his leg so he had to place the child on the ground and half crawl, half drag himself out.

The boy looked about five. His lips were blue, he was cold. James knew everything depended on quick and vigorous resuscitation and how long the child had been not breathing and without a pulse.

James ignored the pounding of his heart and the possibility that he was too late and found the calmness inside that honed his thought processes and sharpened his skills. Lying on his stomach, he grasped the boy's chin, pinched his nose and administered a gentle puff into his mouth.

'James!'

He heard Helen calling him, was conscious of shouts and people coming closer.

'Oh, God, its Josh, Alf's grandson. What happened?' Helen asked, throwing herself on the ground next to him. Josh was always in some scrape or other. He had a fairly thick chart back at the surgery to prove it. But this was extreme even for Josh.

'Don't know. I found him floating in the pond,' he said between puffs. 'Do compressions.'

Helen's hand shook as she ripped opened Josh's sodden shirt and performed quick compressions.

'Where's Tom? We need his kit.'

'He's gone for it,' Helen said.

James could hear a woman sobbing hysterically and guessed it was Josh's mother. She was desperately trying to get to him and people were holding her back so they could work. He tuned her out.

Helen could feel how cold Josh's skin was and knew they stood a better chance of resuscitating him if he was warmer. 'Denise, we need towels and blankets,' she said, not looking up from her task.

'How long's he been missing—does anyone know?' James asked Helen.

'Val thinks only a few minutes at the most.'

James nodded and puffed in more air. He hoped so. The shorter the time in the water, the better his chances. *Come on, Josh, breathe damn it.*

Just as Tom arrived and threw his kit on the ground beside them Josh started to dry-retch and then to cough. A stream of dirty water fountained from his mouth and seeped out of his nose. Helen and James rolled him quickly on his side. Josh took a couple of deep breaths and then opened his mouth and cried a long lusty cry.

The collective sigh of relief from the crowd was audible. Val was released and she threw herself down on the ground and scooped a bawling Josh up into her arms. Denise arrived back and threw a blanket around the bewildered child and the sobbing mother.

James felt his shoulders sag as the tension ebbed. He was still lying on his stomach and he dropped his head momentarily, feeling relief wash through his system.

Helen felt a surge of relief swamp her, too, and looked down to where James was lying. The dark wavy hair on his downcast head tempted her and she didn't bother to stop the urge that overcame her. He'd just saved a child's life. She ran her fingers through his glorious waves. 'Are you OK?' she asked.

James felt his scalp tingle as her fingernails grated erotically. He took a deep breath and raised his head, displacing her hand. 'I am now.'

She nodded and they smiled huge relieved smiles at each other. 'Come on.' She stood and picked up his discarded crutches from the ground, her dress wet and muddy. 'You're muddy, soaked and your cast is useless. You're going to need another one.'

He rolled on his back and sat up. Several of the men from the assembled crowd came forward and pulled him to a standing position.

There was much congratulating, backslapping and tearful cheek-kissing. Helen slipped him his crutches and then stood aside and watched a bemused James accept the thanks of the people of Skye.

'A hero. A bloody hero,' a choked-up Alf said as he vigorously shook James's hand.

Helen returned her attention to a mollified Josh. Tom had some oxygen running and was advising Val to take Josh to the hospital for a once-over. Helen supported Tom and Val agreed reluctantly. Helen could tell she wasn't going to let Josh out of her arms or sight for a very long time.

She glanced back at James. He was wet and muddy, his hair hanging in scraggily strips. But he was laughing at something Alf said and his dimple winked at her. His broad shoulders, flat stomach and slim hips clearly visible through his sodden clothes made her stomach muscles clench. And he had saved a little boy's life. And, damn it all, if it didn't look like he belonged here. He looked for all the world like he was one of them.

'All right, everybody, break it up, enough of the hero-worship. He won't be able to get his head through the door.'

There was general laughter and the crowd broke up. 'You've blown it now. They're never going to let you leave,' she said, watching the retreating backs of the towns-folk.

He chuckled. Somehow the thought didn't bother him so much. Maybe it was the elation of a good outcome or maybe it was her standing before him, mud on her dress, hair escaping her prim ponytail. But he had a real sense of home, of belonging for the first time in his life. 'There are worse things.'

She could see the heat in his turquoise gaze and suddenly she was back on the kitchen bench, her legs wrapped around his waist.

'Remind me of that when there's no more room in the fridge come tomorrow.'

He raised an eyebrow at her.

'Skye likes to feed its heroes.'

He grinned. 'Just as well I have a good appetite.'

She curled her fingers into her palms as reminders of his appetite scorched her insides. She forced her legs to move. 'Come on, then, hero. There's a plaster saw some-where with your name on it.'

He turned and watched her walk away, the two muddy patches covering her rear swaying hypnotically. He felt more than a little turned on at the thought of her packing a power tool.

He so liked a woman who was into DIY.

# CHAPTER SIX

HELEN and James didn't bother shopping or cooking for the next two weeks. As she had expected, the good people of Skye had provided. A steady stream of gourmet dishes arrived morning and night. James flattered each offering and its bearer outrageously as they arrived and earned himself an even more elevated status in the community.

'You are shameless,' Helen said, shaking her head after she'd watched him flirt with Lola from the post office one morning.

James held the apple pie up to his face and inhaled the just-out-of-the-oven aroma. 'The least I can do is show my appreciation for such generosity,' he said with faux injured innocence.

'Appreciation? Lola practically melted into a puddle at your feet.'

He grinned. 'Is there something wrong with making a woman feel good about herself?'

His dimple taunted her and she rolled her eyes.

'What?' He chuckled. 'Can I help it if I have a way with women?'

'Oh, yeah,' she teased. 'You've got the grandmothers eating out of your hand.'

James remembered the heat of her mouth against his. *Not just the grandmothers.* He smiled. 'I seem to recall a certain registered nurse who had a little trouble keeping her hands off me.'

Helen's breath stopped in her throat at his cheeky reminder. Her thoughts froze. It took a second for her higher functions to return. 'A temporary aberration, I can assure you. Your charm may have every woman with a pulse in Skye all aflutter but you can save it with me, James Remington. I don't charm that easily.'

James laughed. 'I've noticed.'

His newfound hero status soon became a little overwhelming. People, strangers, thanked him in the street. His drinks were bought for him at the pub. The *Skye Herald* ran a story on him. The local schoolchildren from Josh's class sent him a poster with his picture from the paper stuck in the centre and 'Our Hero' in bold print at the top.

The community embraced him enthusiastically, like a long-lost son. He'd never felt so adored in his life. It was a total revelation for him. He'd locumed in small towns before but Skye had welcomed him with open arms.

He supposed, aside from Josh, his leg had a lot to do with it. It was harder to stay aloof from the dynamics of the town when he couldn't easily escape it. Not that he'd deliberately kept himself aloof in other places but he had been able to roam away on weekends to explore the local area—and he had. Here he was grounded and when he walked down the street, everyone knew him.

It felt surprisingly good. They were fine people with hearts of gold and their pleasure at seeing him was always genuine. Everywhere he went and everything he did, a strong sense of community prevailed. From the chook raffles at the pub on Sunday night to the friendly Friday night footy competition to the monthly barn dance, Skye thrived on its kinship.

James had never really felt like he'd belonged anywhere. But as Skye embraced him he began to feel a connection. Sure, he was dying to get on his bike and go for a ride. Longing to feel the wind in his face again. But he wasn't as stir crazy as he'd expected to be and his affection for Skye was growing each day.

Alf had made fixing James's bike his highest priority, ringing the Melbourne firm daily to check on the progress of the parts he required and not working on any other job for two days when they finally arrived. And if anyone in Skye grumbled about being bumped, his sharp 'It's for the doc' silenced any criticism.

As far as Alf was concerned, nothing was too much or too good for the man who had pulled his grandson's limp body out of the water and resuscitated him. James spent an hour or so after work each day at the garage, checking on progress and talking engines, and Alf was more than happy to chat with the man who had saved Josh.

Yes, his time in Skye was very pleasant indeed. Except for Helen. His attraction for her didn't seem to lessen with time, no matter how much he told himself it wasn't going to happen. If anything, it seemed to get stronger.

He smelt roses wherever he went. A faint trace of them clung to his clothes, reminding him of her even when she wasn't around. Her ponytail swished enticingly and although she was very careful, he caught the occasional glimpse of her in her sleep shirt.

Once he'd even come home after being at Alf's and caught her coming out of the kitchen munching on an apple, swathed in a purple bath towel, a white one tied turban-style around her hair. Her shoulders had been bare except for the occasional water droplet.

They had both frozen on the spot and stared for what had seemed like for ever. It had taken all his willpower not to move towards her. He had apologised and she had fled the room. They hadn't spoken about it since, but he had dreamt about it often. Too often for his own sanity.

The day finally arrived for James to have his cast removed and he was awake early, raring to go. It was a beautiful Saturday morning and as he swung his legs out of bed he rapped on the cast with his knuckles.

'Not going to miss you, buddy.'

He had taken possession of his newly fixed bike a few days before and had already planned a day trip for tomorrow. He'd noticed a helmet in the garage when he'd been stowing the bike. He recognised it as Helen's from the photos of her and her father and he planned on asking her to accompany him.

He got up and put a pot of coffee on and waited impatiently for Helen to get up. The hospital was on the northern outskirts of town, a little too far to hobble, and she had told him she'd drop him there. He read for a while, got up and poured himself another cup, flicked on the television, turned it off and picked up his book again.

When she emerged at eight o'clock he almost leapt up and kissed her. Even her prim ponytail didn't register.

'You're ready, I see.' She smiled.

The curve of her mouth was as cute as hell. 'For two hours.'

'Can I get a coffee first?'

James suppressed the urge to scream. 'Of course. Half an hour's not going to be here or there.'

Helen downed a cup and they were at the hospital twenty minutes later. She accompanied him inside as she wanted to talk to Jonathon about Elsie, who was being discharged in the next few days.

She left James at X-ray and went in search of the med super. It was bedlam inside and when she finally tracked a nurse down twenty minutes later she was chatting to James.

'We won't be able to get to you for another half an hour or so, James,' she said, looking very harried. 'Sorry, we're down two nurses and Jonathon and the registrar are in Theatre, operating on a ruptured appendix.'

James bit down on a disappointed curse. 'That's OK,' he said. 'I don't want to be a bother. My X-ray's fine. Just give me the saw and I'll remove it myself.'

The nurse exchanged a look with Helen.

'James,' Helen said, 'don't be ridiculous. Removing it yourself will be too tricky.'

He nodded calmly. 'Tricky, but not impossible.'

She took pity on him. 'I'll do it,' she sighed. 'Get up on the table.' She left to get the plaster saw.

He grinned at her when she arrived back. She switched it on and the air filled with a loud mechanical whine. It looked like a bar mix with a round disc attachment. Helen watched the serrated edges agitate back and forth.

He pulled his shorts leg up close to his groin. 'Be gentle with me.'

He had said the same thing to her the first day they'd met and she shot him a withering look as she donned clear plastic glasses. She started at his toe and made her way up his leg. The sharp, tiny teeth made slow progress, kicking up fine plaster dust as they went, and it was too noisy for conversation. Which was just as well. Helen resolutely tried to ignore the fact that she was getting closer and closer to a region of him she'd tried not to think about for the last six weeks.

She didn't let her gaze wander up his leg further than it needed to, concentrating instead only on one patch of white at a time. As she got closer to her goal she realised what James without a cast meant. He would be mobile. Freer. No doubt she'd hardly see him at all now after his enforced respite.

Which was good. Really, it was a good thing. The less time he spent swanning around the house, looking all male and gorgeous, was a bonus. It was bad enough that every corner of the house held reminders of him. A pile of his books lying on the table beside his chair. A pot of percolating coffee every morning. The smell of his spicy aftershave ingrained into the curtains and the carpet and the fabric of the lounge cushions.

James off on his bike would be a good respite for her, too. He was kind of hard to ignore around the house and she was getting far too used to having him around. She found herself looking forward to the evenings as she sat at her desk each day. They ate and laughed and tried to outdo each other on the game shows or just sat in their lounge chairs and read. It was too companionable. Too cosy. It made her want things she couldn't have. She was pleased that it was coming to an end. Six weeks of enforced intimacy was more than enough.

Helen took off her protective glasses. 'Nearly there,' she said. 'Hang tight.'

James chuckled. Again, where could he go with a half-removed cast?

Helen picked up the spreaders, which looked like a giant pair of scissors with flat noses and long industrial-looking handles. She inserted the blunt blades into the furrow made by the saw and pulled down on the handles. The furrow widened, the plaster cracking a little as it split apart.

She repeated the process all the way back up his leg until the cast had been split wide open. She held onto the sides of the shell as he gingerly removed his leg.

'Oh, that feels so-o-o good,' James groaned, rubbing his hands up and down his freed leg. The leg looked ridiculously white compared to his other one, and he couldn't wait to get some sun on it. He grabbed Helen by the shoulders, pulled her close and laid a kiss on her lips. 'Thank you.'

He set her away from him again immediately and returned his attention to the leg. Helen hung onto the table as the brief contact with his mouth sent a shock wave through her body. She knew it was gratitude, pure and simple, that there had been no sexual intent, but it had rocked her nonetheless.

She faded out for a second and when she refocused he was scratching his leg.

'Hell, it feels good to be able to scratch it,' he muttered. 'It was always so damn itchy.'

Helen nodded absently. It was a common complaint. Before she could give it any serious thought her hand was on his lower leg, helping him scratch. It wasn't anything different to what she'd have done for any patient. She could feel the bulky contours of his calf twitch beneath her ministrations. 'Your muscles don't seem too wasted,' she commented.

James almost groaned out loud as her nails scraped against his skin. To be able to finally scratch the area felt wonderful but beneath her nails it was intensely pleasurable. He suddenly knew how a dog felt when the sweet spot behind its ears was hit and it would collapse to the ground in total ecstasy. He just wanted to roll his eyes and pant.

He swallowed. 'They could do with a little work.'

She frowned and knocked his hand out of the way to scrutinise his quad. She ran her hand over the thigh muscle, feeling its well-defined shape. Most men she knew didn't have even half the bulk. She could feel it tense as her fingers stroked over its outline.

'Still not bad for six weeks of no weight-bearing.' She looked at James and was startled to find his eyes shut and his head thrown back. Her hand stilled on his thigh, its bulk suddenly hot beneath her palm.

His eyes flickered open and she was lanced by the heat and desire in his smouldering turquoise eyes. Her mouth went dry as their gazes locked. She suddenly became very conscious of where her hand was and what she'd been doing. And how very un-nurse-like it was. How very unprofessional.

'I…I'm sorry,' she said, her voice husky. 'I…shouldn't have… I was just trying to…'

The rasp in her voice went straight to his already aching groin. 'I liked it,' he said, his voice soft and a little raspy also. *I was hoping you'd go higher.*

'It was…inappropriate,' she faltered. She removed her hand from his thigh and took a step back.

'We're attracted to each other, Helen. This is what happens when you deny it.' There, he'd said it. They'd both been pretending for too long.

*No.* She shook her head. 'It won't happen again.'

He nodded. He knew she was right. Crossing that line was not an option. 'I know,' he whispered.

Helen wanted to turn and run from the look of hunger in his eyes, but it was strangely compelling. She seemed fixed to the spot.

'Looking good, James,' a nurse called as she bustled by.

He smiled and waved and watched as Helen emerged from her trance-like state. The unsuspecting nurse had effectively thrown a bucket of cold water over the flames between them.

Helen took another step back. 'I'll go and see if Jonathon's out of Theatre yet,' she said, and fled.

Helen slept till late on Sunday morning. She'd been awake half the night thinking about the cast incident and wondering where James was. She hadn't seen him since practically molesting him and had noticed his bike had been missing from the garage on her return home a few hours later. He certainly hadn't wasted any time.

And why would he have? She'd probably come across as a gauche small-town girl who hadn't seen a well-built man in her life. So, he was attracted to her but he was also a gypsy at heart and she cringed at how she had pawed his leg and how desperate it must have seemed. She'd probably made him feel trapped. Suffocated.

She'd heard him get in around one a.m. Where had he been? Who had he been with? The questions had roared around in her brain despite knowing that the answers weren't any of her business. It had been another two hours until she had finally nodded off.

It was tempting to just stay in bed and hope he would go out again but hiding from the problem wasn't going to make it go away and they still had ten more weeks of being together. She dragged herself out of bed, dressed and steeled herself to clear the air.

A few moments later she found James preparing food in the kitchen. She watched him from the doorway for a while. It seemed strange to see him walking on both legs and stranger still to see him in jeans. They outlined his legs to perfection and she was reminded again how well defined his muscles were.

He seemed to be favouring his broken leg a little. 'Is it giving you trouble?' she asked.

James turned around. He hadn't seen her since yesterday morning and wasn't prepared for the impact of her ponytail and green-eyed gaze. 'Morning, sleepyhead.' He smiled. 'Thought you country girls were early risers.'

'Sleeping in isn't purely the domain of city chicks,' she

said dryly, pushing herself away from the doorframe and heading for the coffee-pot.

She poured herself a cup, conscious of his stare. 'So is it?' she asked turning to face him. 'Giving you trouble?'

He grimaced. 'No. Not really. I guess after having it so well supported for six weeks I'm still a little wary of putting my whole weight on it.'

Helen nodded. 'That's common enough. You'll conquer that the more you use it to bear weight.'

James nodded. They sipped at their coffees for a little while. Helen felt her heart pick up its tempo as she contemplated her next words until it thumped loudly in her chest. Surely he could hear it?

She stared into her coffee and cleared her throat. 'About yesterday.'

'Helen.'

She kept her gaze firmly fixed on the contents of her mug. 'It was very unprofessional—'

'Helen, you weren't removing my cast in your capacity as a nurse. You were doing me a favour.'

'Still…I shouldn't have touched you the way I did.'

'Not even if I wanted you to?'

Helen swallowed and ignored his question and what it did to her breathing. Thinking about him wanting her to touch him was not what she needed right now. 'What you said yesterday was right. I am attracted to you. But you should know that I'm not going to act on it.'

As James felt his body react to her statement he realised there was a major disadvantage to wearing jeans. Suddenly he yearned to be back in the baggy shorts the cast had forced him to wear. 'Because?'

'Because you'll be gone before too much longer and I'm over being left-behind girl.'

He regarded her seriously. 'I don't know how to be staying-put guy.'

Helen nodded. 'Exactly. That's why we can't do this.'

He knew she was right but…he wanted her. 'And you think it's possible to deny your body such a strong attraction?'

She shot him a scornful look. 'I'm an adult, James. Not some hormone-ridden teenager.'

James raised his eyebrows. 'I don't think it works like that.'

'Of course it does,' she scoffed. 'We have ultimate control over what we do.'

Something told James that Helen hadn't had a lot to do with intense physical attraction. He was one of the most controlled people he knew but one look at that damn ponytail and he wanted to rip her clothes off. *She had no idea.*

'So,' he said as he pushed away from the bench and slowly stalked towards her, 'when we get close like this…' he stopped in front of her '…and all we want to do is fall on each other, you want us to just ignore it?'

She felt suffocated as the breadth of his chest filled her vision and his words ignited a flame that licked her insides. Heat suffused her body. But she looked him square in the face. 'Yes.'

He stepped closer until their bodies were almost touching. 'And when our hands accidentally brush and all we can smell is each other and I know if I kiss your neck that your hair is going to brush against my face and you're going to sigh like you did that night right here on the bench behind me, you want us to ignore that, too?'

Helen could feel his heat as she remembered that night. Remembered how she'd wanted him closer. Wanted him inside her. Her internal muscles clenched as if he had entered her. She gripped the bench hard to stop from melting into a puddle at his feet.

This was a test and he had to know she meant what she said. 'Of course. All it takes is a little self-control.' Her voice didn't sound like her voice but she returned his gaze unwaveringly.

'Self-control. So working together, living under the same roof, sharing meals and a living area, sleeping with just a wall between us, that's all OK? Feeling our blood stir, our hearts…' he pressed two fingers lightly against the pulse fluttering frantically in her neck '…race when we're in the same room, you can just ignore it?'

His fingers slid down to the hollow at her throat and she swallowed. With a supreme effort she pulled his fingers away. 'Yes.'

He smiled. He could see the struggle lighting the amber flecks in her eyes. 'Prove it.'

Helen rolled her eyes and moved away from him, placing her mug in the sink. Released from the magnetism of his closeness, she heaved in some deep breaths. 'If you think I'm going to play truth or dare or some other juvenile game then think again.'

He chuckled as he thought about the things he could dare her with. 'No, nothing like that. All I ask is that you spend the day with me. I'm going out on the bike to the thermal pools. Come with me. Convince me you can get through a whole day without feeling the need to ravish me then I'll bow to your higher power and we'll play it your way.'

Helen wanted to spend the day with him like she wanted a hole in the head. Spending a couple of hours snuggled into his back would be temptation enough without further hours in his company. The more time she spent with him the stronger the attraction grew. She needed to limit their time together. Particularly their time alone together.

'I don't feel I have anything to prove,' she said haughtily.

'Really? You keep telling me it's not going to happen and yet twice now your body has told me different. Are you sure you can resist the temptation so easily? How do you know until you've been properly tested?'

Helen knew he was yanking her chain but to hell with him. She was feeling sufficiently goaded. 'You could give me the apple itself and I'd still be able to resist. I am in control of me.'

An image of Helen in fig leaves rose in his mind and his jeans became even more uncomfortable. He raised an eyebrow.

Helen knew this wasn't going to be over until she could prove it to him. 'What time do we leave?' she asked, returning his doubtful stare steadily.

'Just getting the picnic ready. Thirty minutes sound OK?'

She nodded. 'I'll get into my leathers and dig out my helmet.'

*Leathers?* She had leathers? Suddenly the fig leaves were replaced with the image of a leather-clad Helen removing her helmet and shaking her hair loose. Why did fully clothed biker-chick Helen seem more erotic than a scantily clad fig-leaf one?

It had been a while since Helen had been on a bike. Her father had last shot through town two years ago and she'd gone out with him both days. She distinctly remembered the feel of her arms around his waist, hugging into his back and yet feeling that strange blend of disconnectedness she'd always felt in his company. Her love for him as a father figure warring with years of childhood disappointments.

The exhilaration, the freedom both James and her father thrived on hit her almost immediately and she understood their addiction. To a point. It was thrilling. Stimulating. Invigorating. But not to the exclusion of all else. Not to the exclusion of life's little realities. Or inconveniences. Like a wife and child.

She spent the first ten minutes holding onto James while keeping as much space as possible between them. Her fingers clutched a handful of his leather jacket on either side while she held herself stiffly, trying to maintain some distance. But there wasn't much room on the back of a bike and it didn't take long for her body to protest the rather unnatural position she'd adopted.

James wondered how long Helen could keep the stiff posture up for. Aside from everything else she was messing up the aerodynamics. She was supposed to mould herself to his back, fit into his contours, not sit as if he'd suddenly grown spines like the echidna they'd just seen by the roadside.

'Relax,' he yelled over the engine noise and the wind rushing like a cyclone around them. 'Put your arms around me.'

Helen acquiesced, reluctantly at first, settling herself stiffly against him. But as the growling vintage engine ate up the miles she slowly relaxed, her body easing gradually until her front was in full contact with his back. Her arms crept forward until they were fully encircling his waist. It was easy then to just let all the tension go and melt against him.

James felt the moment she finally succumbed. Her weight pressed against him, her arms tightened around his waist and although he knew it wasn't possible, he thought he felt her sigh. There was something elemental about being on a bike, the sun beating down and the open road in front of you. And a woman draped around you. He smiled a contented smile.

The last twenty-five kilometres of their journey took them into a mountain range and national park. The bike slowed to negotiate the winding road and bends and the shade of towering trees allowed only dappled sunlight through the canopy. There was a bit of traffic about, too, slowing their way, people no doubt keen to visit the springs also. When they finally pulled up in the car park they'd been travelling for nearly two hours.

'That was great,' Helen enthused as she alighted and took her helmet off. She shook her head to unruffle her helmet hair.

James took his time taking his own off. She'd fulfilled all his wildest fantasies with that head shake and he didn't want his eyes betraying the fact that Eve was already tempting him with the apple.

'Yep,' he said, making a show of hanging his helmet over the handlebars. 'Nothing quite like it.'

Helen looked around. 'So, do you have a plan in mind for the day?'

James looked down as he removed his gloves, quelling the suggestion her innocent question had raised. He shrugged. 'You're the local. Is there one spot better than another?'

Helen shrugged the backpack off her shoulders and handed it to him. 'There are two major pools but there are literally hundreds of little springs around here so anywhere's good.'

James took the pack. 'Lead the way.'

Helen grinned. She was pleased he had goaded her up here. It had been a while since she'd been and she'd forgotten what a truly beautiful spot it was. With the towering eucalypts, plentiful tree ferns and numerous thermal pools it was like a little piece of heaven.

Still, she wasn't stupid enough to take him to any of the more secluded pools. She hadn't forgotten the reason why she was up here and she certainly wasn't going to give him an unfair advantage.

She followed the short track to the main pool and was satisfied to see several family groups and couples had set up camp around the edges. It wasn't crowded enough to ruin the enjoyment but it wasn't deserted either.

'This looks perfect,' she said, finding a spot not too close to anyone but near enough to be in full view.

James raised an amused eyebrow. 'You think prying eyes are going to help you keep your hands off me?'

'I don't need any help,' she replied steadily. 'They're to keep you honest.'

He chuckled. 'You think I care about an audience?'

Helen swallowed. No, he probably didn't. She ignored his comment and unzipped her jacket. 'I'm going for a swim.'

She was conscious of his gaze on her as she quickly stripped down to the black one-piece she had on beneath her leathers. She daren't even look at him when she was done, afraid of the desire she'd seen in his eyes. She just turned and plunged straight into the pool.

James stared helplessly after her. She'd pulled off her clothes and was gone in what seemed like the blink of an eye but the bit in the middle would be burned on his retinas for ever. A swimsuit that covered everything but left nothing to the imagination. The bulge of her breasts, the curve of her waist, the slimness of her shoulders and waist and the jut of her hip.

He felt a droplet of water hit his cheek and he looked down to find her splashing him. 'Come on in. It's gorgeous.'

The warmth of the water enveloped her instantly and she lay on her back as she waited for him to join her. The heat was drugging and she pondered the supposed detoxifying qualities of the springs as she stared at the little squares of blue sky just visible through the lush canopy. Local legend had it that spirits lived in the springs.

She felt water land on her face and she popped her head up in time to see him swiping his arm in a wide arc across the surface and thrusting in her direction. She couldn't see what he was wearing. All she could see was his magnificent naked chest decorated with its dainty medallion and she prayed to the spirits, if they existed, for restraint.

They wallowed in the water for an hour, chatting occasionally. Helen gave him the tourist blurb on the local area and he listened attentively. A beach ball landed between them and for twenty minutes they got caught up in an impromptu volleyball game.

'I'm starving,' Helen said as the game came to a close.

'Lets eat, then.'

Helen watched as his powerful arm muscles boosted him out of the pool. Water sluiced off his hair and down his back in a fluid sheet, his muscles flexing as he twisted. He stood and she was treading water in the pool, staring up at him.

It was a very bad vantage point. His usually tall frame looked potently dominant. His legs looked longer, his quads bulkier. His chest broader. Black Lycra briefs, similar to cyclist pants and just covering his upper thighs, moulded his hips, buttocks and the contours of his manhood.

'Here,' he said, and held out his hand to her.

Helen was too dumbfounded to refuse. She took his hand and he pulled her out of the water as if she weighed no more than a feather. She stumbled against him briefly as she found her footing but quickly stepped back and dropped her hand from his.

She found her towel and quickly dried herself off, paying particular attention to her hair. The warmth of the day would dry her skin and costume quickly. It was her thick hair that would take for ever.

James also dried off quickly and then threw the towel down on the ground and sat on it as he pulled things out of the backpack. By the time Helen had sat too he had it all prepared. Mini-quiches, ham and salad rolls stuffed with filling and a fruit platter. He'd even thrown in two long-necked beers.

'Wow, this looks amazing,' Helen said, pulling on her T-shirt. She knew she'd never have the nerve to sit in her costume as he was and not cover up.

She accepted the beer and clinked the neck against his. 'Cheers.'

They ate in silence for the most part, content to absorb their surroundings and let other people's conversation drift around them. James's medallion moved with every movement of his jaw and Helen's eyes were drawn irresistibly to it.

She reached forward and picked the delicate piece of jewellery off the broad expanse of chest. 'Is that a St Christopher?' she asked.

He nodded. 'Patron saint of travellers.'

She dropped it back against his neck. 'Did someone give it to you?'

He gave her a steady stare. 'It belonged to my father. It came with the bike.'

She was surprised. It was so fine, almost feminine she'd assumed that a woman had given it to him. Of course, it looked curiously at home around the corded muscles of his neck. On any other man it may have even looked effeminate but he was so masculine it just looked…right.

Helen took a long swallow of her beer, her eyes focused on the St Christopher, not daring to look lower. 'Tell me about your dad.'

James drained the contents of his bottle. 'Not much to tell.' He shrugged. 'He married my mother because she was pregnant with me. He stayed until the day I left for uni and then he took off.'

He was tense. She could see the muscles of his shoulders and neck were corded tight, the veins protruded, a pulse hammered in the hollow of his throat. 'They weren't happy.'

He gave a harsh laugh. 'Now, there's an understatement! I don't remember a time when they were ever happy.'

Helen could hear the bitterness in his voice. 'They argued a lot?'

James shook his head. 'No. They didn't. No more than any other couple, I guess. They just co-existed. They got married through some twisted sense of obligation to me and then felt trapped by it for the rest of their lives. They were very different people, who didn't really get on. The only thing they shared in common was me. They were polite but distant. Not very demonstrative or emotional.'

Helen drew her knees up and rested her chin on them. Her heart bled for him. His childhood sounded so desolate. At least she'd had Elsie's love and care. At least she'd felt wanted by someone. His turquoise gaze stared past her. He hadn't looked her in the eye since the conversation had begun. 'It sounds lonely.'

'It was,' he said abruptly. He really didn't want to spoil this time with her by dredging up his past.

'I'm sorry, I'm prying. You don't want to talk about this.'

James looked at her then. He saw the compassion warming the amber flecks in her cool jade eyes. He sighed. 'No, it's OK. It doesn't matter. It's...a long time ago now.'

But living in Skye, being embraced by the community, seeing Helen with Elsie, had bought his childhood back into sharp focus. He'd thought about those days a lot recently. Skye's easy acceptance of him had made him acutely aware of what he'd missed out on.

'Families are…complicated,' she agreed.

James nodded. He started to peel the label off his beer bottle. 'I always got the sense that I was in the way of the lives they wanted to lead. Like I was a nuisance. Don't get me wrong. They didn't beat me or anything.'

'They just neglected you emotionally.' The thought of a little boy wandering around a house, aching for someone to pay him a little attention, was awful.

James heard the sharpness of her tone as he pulled at the label. 'No. Not on purpose. They just were too caught up in their own sadness to notice I was there most of the time.'

James dropped the denuded bottle down on the ground beside him and started peeling the label off hers. The St Christopher swung gently with his movements.

'I'm sorry,' she said.

'Hey, its OK. I turned out all right.' He grinned.

She looked at his self-deprecating smile and he looked completely unaffected. Except that shadow in his eyes that she'd seen lurking that first day was suddenly explained. Sure, he seemed fine, but he travelled from place to place, looking for something that not even he could figure out. She knew how devastating parental behaviour could be. How a sense of family, or lack of it, isolated kids in a way that touched every aspect of their lives. For ever. No matter how grown-up they'd become.

'No thanks to your folks,' she said.

James dropped the second stripped bottle to the ground and it clanked against the first. 'They did the best they could with what they had.'

She nodded. She guessed everyone had different standards. But sharing his childhood with him had brought back her own painful memories. She could see the lost, lonely little boy and could totally relate to him. How often had she felt abandoned? How desperately had she craved being part of a real family? Was it right that children had to suffer because they were powerless and some adults made bad decisions?

Helen didn't realise how engrossed they were in their conversation until a shrill desperate plea broke the air of quiet relaxation around the pool.

'Help! Help! Is there a doctor or midwife anywhere?'

James and Helen looked up instantly at the cry for help. The panicked voice was coming from one of the many walking tracks that led from the main pool.

'Don?' Helen gasped, staring as a man and a woman came into view. She was on her feet in two seconds, followed closely by James, their wretched childhoods forgotten.

'Genevieve!' Helen exclaimed, closing the distance as she pushed through the curious crowd that had leapt to their feet at the first sign of crisis.

'Helen! James! Thank God!' Genevieve said, sagging against Helen instantly.

Helen looked into Genevieve's flushed face, her heavily pregnant abdomen looking cumbersome. 'What's wrong?' she demanded.

'I'm in labour,' Genevieve panted, clutching Helen's arm like she'd just been offered the last seat in the last lifeboat to leave the *Titanic*.

'You're ten days overdue, Genevieve, what the hell are you doing all the way out here?' Helen demanded as she glared at Don, a well-known local bushwalker.

The contraction passed and Genevieve looked at her with apprehension in her eyes. 'I was going stir crazy in the house. I had to do something to give the baby a prod. I thought a vigorous walk would stir things along. Oh…' she wailed and clutched at Don's sleeve as another pain swept through her. 'I need to push…' She doubled over.

Helen and James looked at each other. Such a definite statement from a first-time mother was alarming.

'I told her I didn't think it was wise to come so far away,' Don said, visibly paling at his wife's distress. He looked as petrified as some of the wood in the nearby forest. As a botanist, he didn't cope well with human conditions.

'When did the contractions start?' James asked, as a by-stander offered them their picnic blanket and Helen helped her friend to the ground.

'Call the ambulance,' Helen said, looking blindly around and hoping someone in the crowd responded. She had a bad feeling this baby wasn't going to wait. She had a worse feeling that help would be at least an hour away. If the baby did come and there were complications, Genevieve's baby didn't stand a chance.

'We were only half an hour into our walk,' Don said, answering for his wife who was bellowing through another contraction.

'Oh, God! It's coming!' Genevieve yelled. 'I have to push.'

James looked at Helen. This was bad.

'Have a look,' James said to her out the corner of his mouth.

He threw a towel over Genevieve's drawn-up knees. 'Do you think we can have some privacy, folks?' James asked the gathering crowd, and was relieved when they broke away, even though every eye at the rock pool was still trained on them.

Helen helped Genevieve off with her shorts and undies and took a quick peek beneath the towel. The baby's head was right there.

'She's crowned,' Helen told James in a low voice.

'How may babies have you delivered?'

Helen shrugged. 'Hundreds.'

OK. There was no time to transport Genevieve to the hospital and he was with a professional who easily out-delivered him. 'Looks like this baby has its daddy's genes and wants to be born among vegetation,' James said to a panting Genevieve. 'The head's ready to deliver. Do you trust us?'

Genevieve looked from one to the other. 'Yes.'

'OK, then.' James smiled. 'Push with the next contrac-tion. Helen's going to catch.'

'What? No. I can't believe this is happening,' Don said, looking at Helen and James in disbelief. 'We have to get her to hospital.'

Helen took up position at the business end. 'No time, Don. You're about to meet your baby.'

And in three pushes William Redmond Jacobs, all ten

pounds of him, was born, bawling and furious at the world. His lusty cries split the suddenly eerily quiet air around the rock pool. There was a collective sigh and then a burst of applause.

Helen caught him expertly and, satisfied with his condition, handed him immediately into the waiting arms of his impatient mother and father. Someone from the crowd handed Helen a clean dry towel and they covered the squawking newborn.

James squeezed her hand and they smiled at each other as they watched Genevieve and Don stare in utter amazement at the perfectness of their son. The new parents were utterly entranced.

James and Helen knew this was one child who was never going to feel unwanted.

## CHAPTER SEVEN

GENEVIEVE'S baby took over the rest of the afternoon and, needless to say, they got through the day without ravishing each other. Helen accompanied the new mum as Don drove them back to Skye and James rode back alone, resigned to the fact it wasn't going to happen between him and Helen. Helen was gaga over the baby and he knew she deserved someone better at the whole family thing than him.

He remembered her saying she wanted children and he knew he couldn't do that. Maybe someone like Tom could. Maybe someone else. But he knew one thing for sure, he didn't know a damn thing about raising a happy child and he sure as hell had no plans to try.

Weeks passed and they returned to their roles as flatmates with reasonable ease. The attraction he felt for her didn't go away and he was damn sure it hadn't evaporated for her either. Sometimes he caught her looking at him and there was such raw hunger in her jade eyes it took his breath away.

But she, as promised, never once acted on it. Never even

looked like she was wavering. 'I'm an adult.' That's what she'd said and she had well and truly proved it. It was actually a good exercise for him in self-control. He'd never been in a situation before where he'd had to keep his libido in check. Pretty much any attraction he'd ever felt had been returned and well and truly acted on. Helen's don't-even-go-there aura was good practice for him should he ever be insane enough to hanker after someone else who could withstand his considerable charm.

Consequently he did a lot of exploring over the next six weeks. He went away on his bike each weekend, discovering a different part of the local area. He usually took his swag and camped out under the stars, returning on Sunday evening in time for the regular trivia night.

That just left the weekdays and nights to deal with. Thankfully work was always busy so although he saw a lot of her, it was impersonal with no time for exchanging longing looks. Nights were the most challenging. But curiously also the most rewarding. Even though it was torturous being near her and not being able to touch her, he loved her company.

She was smart and funny and they'd read a lot of the same books and had the same taste in television. She was a veritable fount of information on the local area and helped him plan his jaunts. They both loved to cook and there was something very fulfilling about hanging out in the kitchen with her, drinking wine and cooking a meal.

Before he knew it he'd been in Skye for three months. The agency he was with had been scouting out locum jobs further north and had secured him another four-month position in central Queensland. His leg was fully recovered and as hard as it was going to be to leave, he doubted he could stay any longer and not make a play for Helen. Only one month to go and it couldn't come soon enough.

'Your next patient is here, James.'

Helen's voice on the intercom stroked over his skin as vividly as the day she had touched his leg newly released from its fibreglass prison. He groaned inwardly. Every day of the next month was going to be hell.

'Send him in.'

He greeted Val and Joshua as they walked through his door a few seconds later and shut the door after them.

James looked at the little blond-haired, blue-eyed boy that he'd saved from drowning. He looked none the worse for it. He had a really mischievous glint in his eyes and James had heard all about what a handful the lad was.

He grinned at the boy. 'Joshua, my man, what have you been up to this time?'

'I have a 'sistent sniffle.'

James noted the stream of clear mucus running from the boys left nostril and laughed. 'That sounds bad.'

'Persistent,' Val said apologetically, pulling out a tissue and wiping her uncooperative son's nose.

Val looked stressed and tired. Exasperated. 'How long has he had it?' James asked, opening Josh's substantial chart.

Val's brow furrowed. 'About a week. But it's really strange. It's just one side. He hasn't had a fever or a cough or even felt unwell. He's been haring around at a million miles an hour into everything as usual.'

James watched Josh as he ran a grubby-looking toy car along the edge of the desk, making brm noises.

'His left eye is really watery all the time, too,' Val continued. 'I thought it was a cold and would go away, but now I'm not so sure. Maybe it's an allergy.'

'Is he allergic to anything?' James asked, flipping though the notes. Josh had produced another car and was crashing the two together, making smashing noises now.

'No.'

'Any itching or welts or rashes?'

'No.'

He nodded. 'Come on, then, Josh, climb up on my bench over there and I'll have a look at your sniffle.'

Josh picked up his cars and followed James over. He placed the cars on the examination couch as he stepped on the footstool and climbed onto the bed.

James took a moment to look at his young patient. He noted the exudate collecting in the corner of Josh's left eye and listened carefully to the boy's breathing. He put his finger against Josh's right nostril. 'Big breath in, Josh.'

Josh puffed up his chest and James noted that the inhalation seemed a little obstructed. 'Again,' he said.

Josh repeated the action and James was even more convinced there was some kind of blockage in his nose. He pulled a penlight out of his pocket, tilted Josh's head back and directed the beam of light into the left nostril. He thought he could see an odd fleck of blue right at the back.

'Josh, I'm going to keep my finger on this nostril and I want you to blow really hard through the other one, OK? Just like you're blowing your nose.'

The boy nodded and blew. Nothing. 'Again,' James said. 'Really hard.' Still nothing. He shone the light up again but whatever the blue fleck was, it hadn't budged.

'Well, Val,' James said. 'I think there may be a foreign body up there. Something irritating the mucous membrane and obstructing the left side of his nose.'

'Oh, no.' Val leapt to her feet. 'Josh, did you put something up your nose?' she asked.

Josh looked at his mother and James could see the sudden look of wariness on his face. He knew he was in trouble. He shook his head but it was plain that Josh wasn't telling the truth.

'What are we going to do?'

James could see the worry and gathering tears on the mother's face. 'It's OK, Val. I'll have a go at pulling it out. If I can grasp it easily, it should be OK. But if it's hard to remove we don't want to push it further into his airway so he'll need an X-ray and maybe he'll need to have it removed under general anaesthetic.'

'Oh, God,' said Val.

'It's OK.' James took a moment to reassure her. 'That's the worst-case scenario.'

Val nodded and James hit the intercom. 'Helen, could I see you for a moment, please?'

Four weeks, Helen thought. Only four more weeks of her stomach doing that silly loopy thing every time his voice purred into her ear.

'You called?' she said as she opened the door.

'Josh appears to have a foreign body up his nose. Do we keep some long-nosed forceps for this kind of extraction?'

'Joshua Lutton,' Helen said, shaking her head at the guilty-looking child. 'Boys, huh?' she said to Val.

'Hey!' James protested.

Val laughed. 'Katrina never did anything like this.'

Helen laughed, too. 'Hang tight. I'll be back in a jiffy.'

Helen returned a couple of minutes later with sterile packaged forceps. 'Do you need a hand?'

'Maybe just to hold him.'

Helen nodded. 'OK, then, come on, Josh. Lie back on the pillow. This won't take a moment.' The child looked at her apprehensively and seemed as if he was about to cry. 'Mummy's going to be here, holding your hand, aren't you, Mummy?'

Val dabbed at her eyes. 'Yes,' she said, smiling at her son as she took his hand.

James undid the packaging and positioned himself near Josh's head. 'You ready?' he said to Helen.

She nodded. 'OK, Josh, we need you to be very still and very brave now.'

'That shouldn't be hard,' James said to Helen. 'I heard Josh Lutton is the bravest kid in Skye.'

'That's right.' Helen smiled at James. 'Isn't that right, Josh?'

Josh's wobbling chin smoothed out and he nodded bravely. 'That's what Grandpa Alf says,' he agreed in a little voice as the three adults loomed over him.

'He's a very wise man is your grandpa,' James agreed. 'All righty, then, Helen's going to tilt your head up and I'm going to pull whatever's up there out. On three. Ready? One.'

James advanced the small metal forceps to sit just outside the nose entrance. Helen held the penlight in one hand and the patient's head in the other. She shone it up Josh's nostril as she held him securely.

'Two.' James inserted the forceps gently. Josh flinched a little and Helen increased the pressure on the boy's forehead, but he stayed still.

'Three.' He opened the forceps and made a grab for the fleck of blue he could see. The forceps scraped against something hard and he manoeuvred them gently to grasp it, hoping he wouldn't push the object further into the airway and possibly block it altogether.

'Got it,' he said, breathing out as he slowly withdrew the forceps. He had no idea how big the object was or if it had any sharp edges that could cause damage on the way out, so he took his time to remove it gently.

James bought the object out into the open and held it up to the light. It was a small, white, hard, plastic figure in a sitting position with blue feet.

Val gasped. 'It's from one of his toy cars,' she said.

Helen released her hold on Josh and he sat up. Val grabbed him and hugged him. 'Never, ever put anything up your nose, Joshy. Never. Do you hear me?' She gave her son a gentle shake.

'It seems like we are constantly in debt to you, Dr Remington,' Val said, turning to him as she rocked a bewildered Josh in her arms.

James shrugged. 'Nonsense. It's my job and boys are natural explorers. Let me just have another look up to make sure he didn't decide to put another one up there in case that one got lonely.'

James shone his torch up again and was satisfied he couldn't see anything more. He asked Josh to breathe again through one nostril and was pleased to hear that it no longer sounded obstructed.

'Thanks again, Dr Remington. He's a gem, that one, Helen,' Val said to her as she gathered Josh to go.

'Yes,' Helen said, conscious of James's amused gaze.

'Are you sure you can't stay? Skye's going to miss you. I don't think Josh will want to see anyone else ever again.'

Helen turned and raised an eyebrow at him. 'James isn't a stayer,' she said dryly.

He ignored her. 'I'm sorry, Val. I've already said yes to another locum job up north. I start in five weeks.'

Helen wasn't prepared for that piece of news. She pulled the white sheet off the examination table to hide the squall of emotions that lashed her insides. He really was leaving. He hadn't even checked to see if they wanted him for longer in case Genevieve changed her mind about coming back so early after the baby's birth. He'd obviously stayed as long as he was going to in Skye.

'Our loss,' Val said. 'Say goodbye to Dr Remington, Josh.'

'Knowing Josh, we should maybe just say see you later.' James smiled.

Val laughed. 'Believe me sincerely when I say this, Dr Remington. I like you. A lot. But I hope Josh never has to see you in a medical context ever again.'

'Fair enough.' James grinned and waved at Josh as they walked out the door.

They watched the empty doorway for a few seconds. 'Where up north?' she asked.

He turned to face her. 'The gemfields.'

She nodded. 'It's nice around there.' She looked down at the sheet bundled up in her arms. 'I'll send your next patient in.'

James watched her go. *It was pretty nice around here, too.*

* * *

A week later the telephone rang at two a.m. Helen, who had only fallen asleep twenty minutes before and was consequently deep in the land of nod, didn't even hear it. It wasn't until James knocked on her door that she pulled herself out of the sticky bonds of slumber.

'What?' she called, completely disorientated for a few seconds.

'The phone's for you. It's Duncan.'

It took a few more seconds for her to wake up properly. She flew out of bed and nearly ran straight into James as she pulled the door open and raced to the phone.

'Hello?'

James stood nearby as Helen took the call. A phone call in the middle of the night could not be good. He watched her face. Her loose hair fell forward and obscured it as she said 'Uhuh' and 'Yep' and shook her head a lot.

Helen replaced the receiver. 'Elsie's been rushed to hospital. They found her unconscious half an hour ago. She was in cardiac arrest. They think she's had a massive heart attack.'

'Oh, Helen,' he said, moving towards her, 'I'm so sorry.'

She looked at him. 'Duncan said Jonathon doesn't think she'll recover.'

He moved closer and held out his arms. He was wearing boxers and a tight T-shirt and his chest looked so cosy, so right, but she daren't succumb to its lure.

'No,' she said, slipping past him. 'I'm OK. I just have to get there.'

When Helen came out of the bedroom James was dressed in jeans and a T-shirt, waiting for her. She stopped short. 'Go to bed, James,' she said. 'You don't have to come with me.'

James shook his head. 'I know. But what kind of human being would I be if I let you go alone? Come on, I'll drive you.'

Helen opened her mouth to argue. She didn't need his help. She was used to doing things alone. She'd been dealing with things alone for all her life. It would be dangerous to get used to having him around. To depend on him.

If only the ache in her arms, in her heart would go away. The need to be held for once, to lean on someone at this moment, was almost unbearable. She'd known this day would come eventually but now it was here her courage was deserting her.

'Helen?'

His voice was soft, his turquoise gaze compassionate, and for a moment her composure teetered. But she snatched it back at the last second, acquiescing with a brisk nod, not trusting her voice.

They drove in silence and were at their destination in under ten minutes. He followed her in and Helen didn't protest. She realised two things. One, she was scared. Scared of what she was about to see. And, two, she didn't want to be alone.

'Hi, Helen,' the night nurse greeted her, and filled her in on Elsie's condition. 'She's in the HDU.' The high dependency unit. Things were serious.

Helen nodded and made her way there. Duncan embraced her, his worried face speaking volumes. She stood at the end of Elsie's bed, the only thing visible from her vantage point was sparse white hair. She was too frightened to get closer.

James could sense Helen was only just holding it all together. She was standing so rigidly not even her ponytail moved. Her hand gripped the bed end with white-knuckled intensity. She looked so isolated, so remote it was painful to watch. He desperately wanted to touch her, pull her into his arms, but he'd never seen her look more untouchable. He doubted she would welcome it.

Instead, he pulled up a chair for her. 'Sit,' he said to her gently, touching her arm to bring her out of her almost trance-like state. She looked at him blankly and he pointed to the chair he'd placed next to Duncan's, on the side Elsie was facing.

'Th-thanks,' Helen said, her legs responding automatically to his command.

Helen sank into the chair slowly. She could see Elsie fully now and her appearance was deeply shocking. She looked like a shadow of herself, a shadow of the woman she'd seen only yesterday. She looked almost unrecognisable.

Helen pulled the lever on the bedframe near her knees and collapsed the side rail that was barricading Elsie from them. She touched her hand tentatively, the sensation evoking a hundred memories.

Suddenly she wanted to be closer. She wanted to crawl into bed beside her, like she had as a little girl. She wanted to hear Elsie's smooth voice singing to her, cuddling her, telling her everything was going to be fine.

She felt hot tears well in her eyes and spill down her cheeks. The one person who'd given her the one thing her childish heart had craved more than anything—a sense of family—was fading away. She dashed them away.

She wouldn't cry. Elsie didn't approve of tears. Elsie believed that when your time was up it was up, and particularly since the stroke she'd known she'd been living on borrowed time. And one look at an utterly devastated Duncan told her she had to be strong for this last part. She grabbed her surrogate brother's hand and gave it a squeeze.

Absurdly, she wished her father was there. Just for once she wished he was there for her. She glanced at James. He was here. Ironic that the one man that was here for her was as much of a gypsy as her father. A man cut from the same cloth. He was here now and she was grateful but in a few weeks he'd get on his Harley and disappear. She'd never felt lonely before. Not ever. Until tonight.

'Hello, Elsie. It's Helen. Duncan and I are here. We're right here. We're not going anywhere.'

Nothing. Elsie's breath misted the inside of the oxygen mask that covered her face. What had she expected? For Elsie to open her eyes and smile at her? Make a last-ditch crack at getting her and James together? She stroked the aged hand, the papery skin, the prominent bones. An IV taped securely into the crook of Elsie's elbow dripped a steady supply of sugary saline into her system to keep her hydrated. A monitor blipped in the background and Helen was alarmed at the frequency of ectopic beats.

She looked at James over her mother's head. He was sitting on the opposite side of the bed, yawning, feigning interest in a two-year-old woman's magazine. 'You should go. You don't need to hang around.'

He shrugged. 'I don't mind.'

'It's not necessary.' Their gazes locked. 'Duncan's here.'

Duncan looked incapable of any higher functions. He looked absolutely gutted. 'I'll stay another hour or so.'

Helen didn't have the inclination to argue with him. It somehow didn't seem peculiar that someone who had been a complete stranger to her three months ago was sitting with her while the woman who had been more of a mother to her than her own mother slowly let go of life. Oddly enough, it seemed kind of right.

Helen shuffled her chair closer to the bed and laid her head on the mattress close to her Elsie's face. It was wrinkled and gaunt, her eyes sunken, her mouth minus her dentures sucked in, her lips thin and dry. This wasn't Elsie. Helen cradled a bony hand against her face and shut her eyes, letting memories of her childhood wash over her.

An hour later the small magazine print started to blur and James's eyes lost the battle to stay open. As he slipped into slumber his neck slowly lost its ability to hold his head up. It nodded forward and he woke with a start, snapping his head back up.

His eyes slowly came back into focus and he rubbed at the crick in his neck. Duncan had nodded off in his chair. Helen appeared to have fallen asleep also, her head resting on the mattress. He stood and stretched, the hard plastic chair not the most comfortable piece of furniture he'd ever sat on.

The air-conditioning was quite cool and he wandered out to the nurses' station and asked for a blanket. They furnished him with one and he placed it gently over Helen's shoulders. She murmured something unintelligible and snuggled into the folds.

Elsie's breath still misted the mask and, along with the monitor noise, James knew she was still with them. For now anyway. James had read Elsie's chart and she appeared to have had an extended down time. At her age, and with her history, her care was purely palliative. He took his seat again.

A nurse came by every half an hour and checked on their patient. One of them bought him a steaming-hot coffee at one stage and he sipped it gratefully. It had been a long time since he had maintained a bedside vigil and he'd forgotten how much caffeine helped. Even bad-tasting caffeine.

The day dawned, soft light blanketing the landscape. The sun rose, pushing the velvety glow aside, streaming in through the windows, its brightness an early warning of another hot day.

Two nurses came in to shift Elsie's position. They shook Helen gently and she stirred, her eyes opening to see the reassuring misting of the face mask.

She sat up slowly and rubbed at her neck. Her bleary-eyed gaze fell on a yawning James. He'd been there all night? 'You stayed,' she murmured, as she moved out of the way.

'Yes.'

The slow smile he gave her banished the tired lines around his eyes and she felt stupidly happy. 'You shouldn't have. You've got to work today.'

He shrugged. 'I'm a doctor. I'm no stranger to all-nighters.'

Helen yawned. 'What's the time?'

'Six. Let's get a coffee while they do this,' he suggested.

Helen saw Duncan off—he needed to duck home for a few hours—and then joined James in the lounge area. She stared out the window while he made her a drink.

'Here. I'm sorry, it's just that horrible instant stuff.'

He nudged her shoulder and she turned away from the view of Main Street, accepting the cup. They sipped in silence for a while.

'I have to make some phone calls,' Helen said. 'I need to arrange for Donna to take over at the surgery.'

James nodded. Donna was a local mother who worked as a part-time receptionist when Helen manned the extra clinics the surgery ran.

'Will she be able to at such short notice?'

'I hope so,' Helen said. 'Given the circumstances, I'm sure she won't mind. It won't be for long.' Helen stood as the import of her words hit her. Elsie was dying. This really was the end.

James watched as she paced to the window and felt completely helpless. She was standing rigidly again, looking so very, very alone.

'I have to ring my father, too. He'll want to know.'

'Where is he at the moment? Will it take him long to get here?' James felt certain that Elsie's death was reasonably imminent. Helen may not look like she needed anyone but surely her father should be there.

'I have no idea where he is. Or if he'll make it in time. I just have a number of a service to ring. He checks it every now and then.'

James nodded. Her voice was curiously lacking in emotion. She'd obviously learnt a long time ago to never get her hopes up where her father was concerned. It seemed so sad in the current circumstances to not be able to lean on the one other person who had given you life.

'How often do you see him?'

Helen shrugged and turned back to face him. 'The last time was two years ago.'

She sounded matter-of-fact. 'You sound very tolerant of him.'

'I guess Elsie had a big influence on me there. She always encouraged me to have a relationship with him. To accept him for what he was. Accept his transience and that the time we had together was finite. She understood he didn't know how to cope with Mum, or with me, and I guess in lots of ways she made excuses for him because I was a child struggling to understand my mother's illness and I didn't need to deal with my father's shortcomings as well. And I guess I bought it.'

'You were a child. He was your father. Of course you wanted to look up to him.' He understood that better than anyone.

'And I did. But as much as I love him, there are times when I've felt really neglected by him.' *Like right now.*

'I'm sorry,' he said. It seemed like they'd both been abandoned by the people who should have been looking out for them.

They stared at each other for a few moments, united in the solidarity of a similar background. The nurse who had been tending to Elsie's pressure-area care bustled into the lounge, breaking their connection. 'We're finished,' she announced. 'You can go back in if you like.'

Helen gulped down the rest of the contents of her mug.

'Go now,' she said to him. 'You need to get ready for work. I'll just make these phone calls then I'll head back in.'

James hesitated. 'Are you sure? I don't like leaving you alone.'

She smiled. 'I know every person in this hospital, James. Heavens, I know everyone in Skye. I'm not alone.'

Still he hesitated. 'I'll pop by at lunchtime. Ring me if…if you need me before that.'

Helen watched him leave. She called to him as he reached the open doorway of the lounge and he turned back. 'Thank you,' she murmured.

He nodded and left.


Elsie died the following day at lunchtime. She'd started Cheyne-Stokes breathing that morning and Helen had known it was close. Every laboured breath Elsie had taken had teetered on the edge of her last, the pause between each respiration stretching interminably. James had been by her side when the next breath hadn't come.

Helen didn't cry, just held Elsie's hand tight and stroked her hair as she comforted a sobbing Denise and a dazed Duncan. James left to give the family some privacy, returning a few hours later after a concerned phone call from one of the nurses.

Helen sat there, her face blank, her hand stroking Elsie's. James touched her shoulder lightly and she shrugged it off. 'I'm fine,' she said, her breath frozen inside her, along with a huge block of emotions. 'I'm fine.'

James sat with her until Helen was ready to let go. He took her elbow and guided her up out of the chair, concerned by her lack of emotion.

She pulled away. 'I'm fine,' she insisted. 'Go back to work. I've got a funeral to organise.'

She left and he watched her go, looking untouchable in her grief.

In control.

*Fine.*

Except he wasn't buying it. Not for a moment.

# CHAPTER EIGHT

HELEN continued to be 'fine' for the next week. They delayed the funeral as long as possible in the hope that her father would be able to make it in time. Elsie had understood Owen better than anyone, had never been judgmental about him, and Helen knew her father would want to be there.

She hadn't heard from him but then she hadn't expected to either. Her father had a habit of just turning up. But the funeral couldn't be delayed inevitably and a week after she died Elsie was scheduled to be buried.

Owen Franklin knocked on Helen's door the morning of the funeral. James opened it and knew who it was instantly. The tall man in leathers didn't seem to have aged any from the photo that stood on the coffee-table. His hair was greyer but there was a vitality about him that belied his years. He smiled, revealing perfect white teeth, and shook James's hand, exuding charisma.

'I'm pleased you got here in time. Helen will be most relieved.'

'Yes, I have cut it a bit fine, haven't I?' Owen remarked as he wandered around the lounge room, inspecting things. 'I was in Broome—only found out a few days ago.'

*What? No telephones in Broome?* James wasn't impressed by Owen's cavalier attitude and felt a curious urge to give him a piece of his mind. He'd been going out of his mind, worrying about Helen's emotional state. Her insistence on being fine, her stoic refusal to grieve.

Hell, she'd been back at work the next day and no amount of persuasion or bullying by him or Frank had swayed her. Would it have killed her father to ring, to reach out to his daughter? Just once?

'What time is the funeral?'

'Eleven.'

Owen nodded. 'Is my girl around?'

'She's in the shower. I'll let her know you're here.'

Owen put a hand on James's shoulder as he passed. 'Are you and Helen…involved?'

What? The man was going to get all proprietorial now? All fatherly? James felt his hackles rise and he stared pointedly at Owen's hand until the older man dropped it. *No, I'm just the one who's been here for her.*

'No. I'm just the locum. Helen's been putting up with me for a few months.'

Helen heard her father's query and James's denial as she walked down the hallway. She remembered the heat of his mouth and, despite knowing it was for the best, his quick dismissal hit her like an arrow to the solar plexus. Had she truly expected anything different?

When she entered the lounge the two men were sizing each other up. 'Hi, Dad.'

Owen opened his arms and Helen went straight to him. 'You made it,' she said, her words muffled as she pressed her face into his chest. She inhaled his familiar aftershave and leaned into him. God, she'd missed him.

'I'm sorry I couldn't get here any sooner.'

Helen pulled back, heard the gruffness in his voice, and knew in his own way that this was affecting him. 'It's OK. You're here now.'

'That's the girl, chin up. Elsie was a tough old bird who lived a great life. She wouldn't have wanted any of us to shed tears over her passing.'

James watched Helen nod, dry-eyed, and despaired. *Chin up?* He had hoped her father's arrival would be the key to unlocking Helen's fettered emotions. That she would see him and all the emotions she'd stored up would be released and she'd burst into tears. But if he was going to give her the chin-up routine...

'Here, I got you this.' Owen pulled a small white packet out of his pocket.

Helen took the offering from him, noticing the dimple in his chin, so like James's. She opened it and peered inside. 'Oh, Dad, it's beautiful,' she said. A small white mother-of-pearl duck lay nestled in some tissue paper.

Owen grinned. 'I thought you'd like it. Got it in Broome.'

Helen ran her fingers over the smooth, milky contours. 'Thanks,' she said, pecking her father on the cheek. She placed it on the shelf with the others and admired it. Her father had brought her most of them from his travels.

'Come on, I bet you've been driving all night and haven't even eaten yet.' She smiled at her father, pleased beyond words that he was there. The only other person in the world who truly understood how much Elsie had meant to her. 'I'll cook you some breakfast.'

'Ah, you know me so well.' Owen chuckled.

James watched them leave the room, hands linked. He marvelled at how close they seemed, given how little Owen had been around. OK, Helen hadn't dissolved into tears as he had hoped, but her body looked more relaxed, her face less taut, her shoulders less tense, the amber flecks glowing warmly in her eyes again instead of the vacant jade chill that had been there for the last ten days.

Her genuine smile had spoken a thousand words. Relief and gratitude and love. She seemed sincerely touched by her father's gift and accepted his presence with no form of censure. He could hear their chatter floating out from the kitchen and it sounded familiar, intimate. As he slipped out of the house James hoped that, whatever their interaction, Helen got what she really needed from her father to help her get through her loss. Not just a lousy duck.

James passed Owen's bike in the drive as he walked the short distance to the surgery. Had he not been so annoyed with the man, James would have stopped and admired the gleaming chrome of the powerful Harley. But for the life of him he couldn't understand what would possess a father to abandon his ill wife and child, and the chrome instantly lost all its shine. His cold, lonely childhood suddenly looked rosy by comparison.

The surgery stayed open until ten-thirty. All the patients that morning commented on Owen Franklin rolling back into town and all had an opinion on his lifestyle. Most were disparaging about it, puzzled by it even, although all agreed he was a difficult man to dislike. And their loyalty to Helen demanded at least a grudging acceptance of him.

James tried not to get involved, his own quickly formed opinion a lot less charitable. He was relieved when they shut their doors and he could have respite from the pros and cons of Owen Franklin. He felt nervous about the approaching funeral, worried about Helen's continuing emotional void and unsure of his place. He wanted to be by Helen's side as he had been since Elsie's death but she didn't need him now her father had returned.

He snorted to himself as he grabbed the jacket he'd brought to work with him that morning. Who was he kidding? She hadn't needed him anyway, with or without Owen. Every person in Skye had been around, comforting her, feeding her, worrying about her. Had she wanted it, any one of them would have lent her their shoulders to cry on, their arms to hold her. No, sirree, she didn't need him at all.

Still, James hesitated as he stepped out of the surgery. Should he call in at the cottage and see if she wanted him to escort her? He wanted to—badly. He'd become quite protective of her these days and the urge to seek her out, check how she was doing was very strong. But she needed this time with her father. To reconnect. To reminisce. She didn't need a third wheel.

It was eerie, walking through Skye. All the businesses were either shut or in the process of shutting down as he passed. Everyone in the town would be at the funeral and most appeared to be there already as he approached the church. The churchyard was almost full. Clusters of people, chatting in low voices, waited for the hearse to arrive.

He nodded to each group as he passed, amazed at the fact that he seemed to know everyone after a few short months. He made his way over to Don and Genevieve, who were standing with Frank.

'How's she doing this morning?' Genevieve asked, bouncing an almost two-month-old William on her hip.

James held out his finger and the baby gave him a dribbly smile as he reached out and clasped it. 'The same.'

Genevieve tut-tutted. 'So she's still fine?'

He nodded. 'Her father arrived just before eight, so I'm hoping she'll have vented with him.'

'Doesn't look like it,' Frank said, indicating with a nod of his head.

James turned and saw Helen and her father walking into the churchyard with the rest of Elsie's family who'd travelled to Skye for the funeral. Helen had her arm around a sobbing Denise. She was dressed in a simple black dress, her hair pulled back in its usual ponytail. She looked a little more relaxed but Frank was right, she didn't look like she'd spent the last few hours sobbing her heart out. She smiled at everyone as she made her way into the church and even stopped to comfort a couple of obviously upset people.

The hearse pulled up, the flower-draped coffin visible through the glass.

'I gotta go,' Frank said. 'Duty calls.' He was one of the pallbearers.

The milling crowd slowly trooped inside. James sat with Genevieve and Don three seats from the front. He could see Helen's erect frame easily, her ponytail brushing the nape of her neck, her father's arm firmly around her shoulders. There was nothing about her stature that indicated she would break down and cry. And it seemed an awful thing to be hoping for but if anyone needed a good howl it was Helen.

Helen went through the motions at the funeral. Sang when the organ played, bowed her head when the minister prayed, even said 'Amen' in the right places. There were some lovely tributes and it was impossible to stop the hot tears that stung at her eyes, demanding release.

But every time a well of emotion rose in her chest she took some deep calming breaths and blinked hard. Her father was right. Elsie wouldn't want any of them to mourn her passing. She would not cry.

The service came to an end and Helen rose, her legs shaking as she watched the coffin being carried out of the church. She put her arm around Duncan as he led the procession outside to the graveyard. She caught James's eye as she passed his pew and saw the concern in his eyes.

He'd been a wonderful support this last week. He'd been largely silent but always there. Making sure she ate, checking on her frequently and screening the number of visitors. She knew he was worried about her lack of emotion, had tried to speak to her about it on a couple of occasions, but he hadn't pushed and had backed off when she had asked him to.

The truth was she couldn't let herself go in front of him. That would take their strange mustn't-cross-the-line relationship to a new level and that was too painful to contemplate with someone who was going to be gone in a few short weeks. She had lain in bed every night feeling so desolate, so alone, craving his embrace but knowing that it wouldn't help. Knowing that she'd just want more.

The ceremony continued at the graveside and her father took her hand. She drew strength from his solidness. Physically and emotionally. She felt the love and support of the entire town surrounding her, and as the coffin was lowered her father squeezed her hand and she squeezed back.

The wake was held in the CWA hall. James didn't stick around for long. The surgery was scheduled to open again at one and he had volunteered to man it, including the reception desk, so everyone else could attend the wake. Helen was surrounded by a constantly changing crowd of locals, all hugging her and passing on their condolences.

James was relieved to see Owen sticking close, his arm around his daughter's waist, being attentive and supportive. Good. If ever there was a time she needed her old man it was now. He hoped she'd lean on him hard for these next few days and find a way to grieve for what she had lost. Owen Franklin certainly owed his daughter that.

It was a slow afternoon with only a trickle of patients. Most people had progressed from the wake to the pub. Very few businesses had reopened. The agency had faxed him a copy of the contract for the next locum job and he read it thoroughly between patients, deciding to sign it later. It was going to be strange, leaving Skye. For the first time in his life he felt like he belonged to a family. The connections he'd made here were strong and walking away would be harder than he'd ever imagined possible.

James didn't go back to the house when he shut up shop for the day. He wasn't sure where Helen and her father had ended up but he wanted to give them some privacy. So he headed for the pub. It was very crowded tonight, many of the funeral attendees still hanging around.

He sat with Alf and a couple of other old-timers as they reminisced about Elsie. They drank cold beer and ate thick steaks. A footy game was showing on the big-screen television.

'Wonderful woman,' Alf murmured, and raised his glass, and they all clanked theirs against his. 'She did a marvellous job with raising those grandkids after the accident. And taking Helen on…'

'Here! Here!' said Doug Phillips. James had been seeing him about the diabetic ulcer on his toe.

'Someone had to,' Billy Dingle threw in. Another patient of James—prostate problems. 'Owen wasn't any help.'

'She'll be missed,' said Alf.

There was general agreement around the table.

James stayed on and watched the next game and it was ten o'clock before he got home. He noticed Owen's bike wasn't there. Maybe he'd garaged it?

He expected to see Helen and her father chatting in the lounge room or the kitchen, but the house was quiet, as if it was empty, when he went inside. There were some photo albums scattered on the coffee-table but no other evidence that they'd even been back to the house. Maybe they'd gone to bed. It had, after all, been an emotionally intense day.

As he was passing Helen's room he heard a strange noise. A plaintive whimper like a wounded animal. He raised his hand to knock and then hesitated. What if her father was in there, comforting her? But he couldn't hear any voices. And then the sound came again and it was so mournful he knocked without giving it any further thought.

'Helen?' he said quietly. No response. 'Helen,' he called again, louder this time.

'I'm fine.'

Her muffled answer didn't sound fine. In fact, he was heartily sick of hearing the word. He opened the door. The room was in darkness but the light spilling in from the hallway behind him illuminated her. She was in a black lacy slip, her hair still up, and she was lying in a foetal position, her arms wrapped around her knees. And she was moving slightly.

'I'm fine.'

It was said tonelessly, like a recorded message. Like a pull-the-string doll repeating the same phrase over and over. She didn't look at him, she just stared. She looked frighteningly expressionless.

He advanced slowly into the room. *Where the hell was Owen?* How could he go to bed while his daughter fell apart in the room next door? 'Helen…'

'I'm fine,' she muttered again.

He reached the edge of the bed and then slowly sank to the floor. 'Where's your dad?'

'Gone.'

*Gone?* 'Gone to bed?'

She gave a harsh laugh, the noise so unexpected that she startled both of them. 'Gone, gone,' she said. 'Left an hour ago. Couldn't stop. Had to go. Too depressing. Too many memories of Mum.'

James stared at her incredulously as she rattled off the words. Owen had left town? His fingers dug into the carpet, fisting in anger. He could feel a flush of heat creep up his neck as a dose of fury flooded into his bloodstream. How could he desert his own flesh and blood like that?

He wanted to leave. Right now. Get on his bike and drag the useless son of a bitch back to town. Demand that he be a father for once. Shake him. Hurt him. Make him suffer as Helen was. Make him see how selfish he was being. Maybe even rearrange that perfect straight smile.

Helen made another low whimpering noise, snapping him out of his vengefulness. He took a deep breath, shocked at the savagery of his response. None of that mattered now. Helen needed him. Helen needed to let go of the grief she'd been burying inside.

'Helen,' he said gently, and placed his hand on her calf. 'It's OK to cry. You need to cry.'

Helen shook her head convulsively. 'No. Elsie wouldn't have wanted me to cry for her.'

James could feel a fine tremor running through the skin beneath his hand. Maybe Elsie wouldn't have—one thing he'd learned out here over the years was that outback women were tough, not prone to emotional tendencies— but he was pretty damn sure Elsie wouldn't want to see Helen like this either. 'Doesn't stop it from hurting, though, does it?'

James felt momentarily lost, he had to get through to her.

'Helen.' He shook her leg. Nothing. 'Look at me, Helen!' He raised his voice and gave her a firm shake. She gasped and looked straight into his eyes.

'You loved Elsie. It's OK to cry and rant and scream and yell. That's what you're supposed to do. You're supposed to beat your chest and shake your fist at the sky. You're allowed to be angry and you're allowed to be sad and you're allowed to want to have your father by your side.'

Helen's eyes filled with hot tears. 'No. I have to keep my chin up.'

James swore. 'No. She raised you, Helen. She's dead. You don't have to keep your chin up. You don't have to do anything you don't want to do.'

He saw a tear spill down her cheek. Felt the trembling beneath his hand intensify, could see her trembling all over as she fought their release.

Another tear fell from the other eye. 'It…it hurts.' Her voice was low, guttural, the admission sounding as if it was wrenched from deep within her.

'Of course it does. When my father died I felt as if my heart had been ripped out of my chest.' And they hadn't even been close. 'It hurts for a long time.'

A sob escaped. 'I don't want to feel this bad any more.'

'It feels worse because you're bottling it up. The pressure's too much. Let it out, Helen. Elsie died. Grieve for her.'

Helen felt overwhelmed by the tide of emotions rising inside her. Her chest hurt, her head hurt, her eyes hurt. She wanted it to stop. She wanted it to be gone. She opened her mouth and released a tiny anguished peep. Like a kitten's meow. And another, more of a moan this time. The moan become a cry, the cry a sob and before she knew it she was blinded by tears and deafened by the noise of the sobs that racked her body.

She didn't feel James moving onto the bed until he was behind her. Pulling her back into him, spooning her, cradling her against his broad chest. She didn't resist, she wasn't capable. It hurt too much inside still and getting rid of it was all that mattered.

The tears came and came, the grief and anguish seemingly inexhaustible. A lifetime of sorrow and heartache falling out at once. She cried not just for Elsie but for years of bottled-up emotion. For her ill mother and for her absent father and an uncertain childhood.

The tears were relentless. Like a tap had been turned on and then broken so it couldn't be turned off. And all the time his chest felt good against her back. Solid. Reassuring. His arm around her waist felt heavy and comforting.

It was a long time before her grief started to wane, her tears started to lessen, her sobs became muted. She slowly became aware of him murmuring soothing words, of his gentle kisses in her hair. She turned in his arms. 'I'm sorry,' she said brokenly, a sob catching her voice.

James rolled on his back and pulled her in close, her body pressed into his side, her head resting against his chest. 'I'm not.'

He stroked her hand which was curled into a fist against his chest. She slowly flattened it and he felt a hard object being pressed into his skin. He lifted her hand and discovered the duck Owen had given her that morning. And he felt another spurt of anger rise in him.

Did her father seriously think it was OK to breeze into town the day she buried probably the most significant person in her life, bearing a mother-of-pearl duck, and then leave again hours later? He removed the object, offended by its symbolism, and placed it on her bedside table. She didn't protest as he'd thought she might and he gently kissed her forehead as he castigated himself for being at the pub when he could have been here with her.

Minutes passed. He lost track of time. He just held her and stroked her arm until her breathing evened out and she slept. Then he slept, too.

Helen awoke in a state of confusion hours later. Her eyes fluttered open and she lay very still, trying to orientate herself. The luminous figures of her alarm clock told her it was twenty past three. Her mouth felt dry and despite her slumber she felt an exhaustion that went deep into her bones. A weariness that came from an emotional rather than a physical source.

Even before the memories came back she knew the solid chest muscles beneath her ear belonged to James. Her nose was pushed against his shirt and she could smell his spicy fragrance. The scent that had been driving her crazy for months. And he was here, on her bed, every magnificent inch of him.

She remembered how he had held her, how he had crooned sweet nothings and kissed her hair. How he had insisted that she let it all go, let it all out. How he had been there for her. How her father had let her down and James had been there to help her through it.

When her father had told her he was going, Helen had been completely shattered. She'd thought he'd stay around for a while, a few days at least. But he had that look in his eye. The one he always got, and she knew any protests would have fallen on deaf ears. She'd needed him to stay but couldn't have borne his rejection. In her fragile state it would have been too much.

The light still spilled in from the hallway and she watched James's face. Relaxed in sleep, it was even sexier. His face was turned away from her slightly and she could just see the shadow at his square jaw and the outline of his full mouth. It pouted deliciously, looking soft and inviting, and then she remembered how hot and hard it could be and she felt heat stir low in her belly.

His chest rose and fell evenly beneath her cheek. Her hand was resting on his stomach and she could feel the tautness of his abs even slackened in slumber. They were warm and solid and she liked the feel of them, liked how, despite his sleep, they reacted slightly as she moved her hand.

Her leg was casually thrown over the top of his thighs. Her own thigh very, very close to his masculinity. All she'd need do was bend her knee a little and she could rub against him. She admired herself against him, her pose possessive. The heat flared in her belly.

*Don't do this. You've just buried Elsie, waved goodbye to your father and slobbered all over James like a deranged baby. You're a wreck. You probably look like hell. He's not going to touch you with a bargepole. And, more importantly, you've already told him it wasn't going to happen.*

But she wanted to. Suddenly it seemed like a perfectly sensible way to end a really terrible day. She wasn't fooling herself or trying to pretend that he wouldn't be gone in a few weeks. This wasn't about the future. She was a woman, with a woman's needs. This was about tonight. This moment.

Earlier tonight she'd needed to be held and he'd done

that. He'd comforted her as if she'd been a child. But now she needed more. Now she needed to feel like a woman. Not Helen the super-organised practice nurse, or Helen of Helen's Heroes or Helen the recently bereaved. Right now she wanted to be Helen the woman.

Was it going to help her forget a little? Yes. Was it going to help ease the sadness a little? Yes. Was that entirely responsible? No. But did she care? Life was short, the day had been long and harrowing and this was an opportunity she'd already passed up. She was damned if she'd do it again.

Helen lifted her hand from his stomach and advanced it slowly through the air, nervous that he might reject her. Could she stand to be rejected again tonight? Her hand hovered for a second above his jaw before she decided.

His stubble scratched against her finger, sending an erotic shiver down her arm. She traced his jaw, up over the contours of his chin, resting briefly in the indent of his dimple. She reached his lips and stroked her finger along their plump softness.

James woke to the sensation of his lips being caressed. It was light, like a feather, like a whisper. He opened his eyes, shifting slightly to try and assimilate what was happening.

Helen's hand stilled but she didn't remove her finger. She held her breath. Was he awake? His hand slid up and captured hers. He kissed her fingertips lightly and she practically mewed. Then he pulled them away, bringing both their hands down to rest on his chest. He patted her hand soothingly. As if she were a child.

*Well, to hell with that.*

'You're awake,' she whispered, rising up on her elbow

to look down into his face. His dark hair fell in unruly
waves and she wanted to touch it. She moved her hand out
from under his and brushed at his fringe.

'Yes.' He smiled, bringing her hand down again.

Helen frowned. In the half-light he looked dark and
dangerous, his gypsy soul shining through. She wanted
him.

'How are you feeling?' he asked, keeping his voice
carefully neutral. Even in the subdued light he could see
the flare of the amber flecks in her eyes and he knew he
was in trouble. She had lust in her eyes and, as much as
he wanted to go there, he didn't think the aftermath of a
huge emotional meltdown was an appropriate time.

He was babying her again. She almost said *Horny,* just
to get a reaction, but she knew he was just concerned.
'Better,' she admitted.

'Good.'

He looked up into her face and saw the honesty there.
But he also saw the passion. He needed to get out. Her leg
was very close to the ache in his groin and he knew if he
stayed for much longer he might not be responsible for his
actions. They'd been right to keep their relationship
platonic. Helen was someone who would demand more
than he knew how to give. He wouldn't let their resolve
falter now.

He swallowed. 'I'd better go.'

*Not so fast.*

As he made to get up she exerted gentle pressure
through her leg and the arm that was slung across his
chest. 'No, wait.' She toyed with a button. 'I told you a
while back that I wasn't going to act on my attraction to

you. And I meant it then. But tonight…tonight I'd like to exercise my female prerogative to change my mind.'

James licked his lips, suddenly very aware of the satiny feel of her slip as it rubbed against him. 'Ah, Helen…I'm not sure that's such a great idea.'

Helen smiled at the struggle she saw going on in his turquoise eyes. 'You don't want to any more?'

He sat up quickly as the line between appropriate and lust blurred, displacing her. He swung his legs over the edge of the bed, keeping his back to her. He couldn't concentrate with her looming over him, her softness pressed into him.

'You've been through an acute emotional upheaval. You're not thinking very clearly.'

'So you do want to?'

'Helen.' He turned slightly to face her, exasperated. 'This isn't about what we want. This is about what's appropriate for the situation.'

She felt like a naughty kid who'd been caught attempting to steal biscuits from the biscuit barrel. *Which may have been OK had she actually got to have a nibble first.* It was time he stopped seeing her as the needy girl of a few hours ago and saw the black-satin-clad woman in front of him. 'I'm not a child, James.'

God, he knew that. She was lying there in black lingerie, looking at him with sin in her eyes. He turned away from her again and ran a harried hand through his hair.

Helen could feel him slipping away from her. Another time she may have admired his self-control but tonight wasn't about control. It wasn't about thinking. Tonight was tactile, not tactical.

She crept up behind him and wound her arms around his neck, pushing her body against him, pressing a kiss to his neck. 'You're not going to make me beg?'

'Helen.'

She loved the warning edge in his voice, the slight crack that told her he was just hanging on. She unwound herself from his neck, slipped off the bed and moved around until she was standing in front of him. Then she knelt between his legs, their heads level.

She moved her face close to his. 'I feel like I've been stripped bare tonight. Emotionally bare. You've seen me at my most vulnerable, my most private. Now I want you to strip me bare physically. I want you to see all of me. You held me before and rocked me and soothed me like you would a child. And I needed that. But I need to feel like a woman now.'

She pressed her lips against his, asking a silent question. There was resistance for a couple of seconds and then he groaned and his mouth softened. And then it opened and his tongue stroked against her lips and she sighed and pressed herself into his body, snaking her arms around his neck and opening her mouth, surrendering it to his.

The long-suppressed passion flared inside her like New Year's Eve fireworks. She moaned and pushed her hands into his hair, wanting, needing to touch him, all of him. Her hands fell to his buttons and her fingers pulled at them impatiently, desperate to feel his naked skin, feeling his heat and needing to get closer.

James could sense her loss of control and pulled away from her mouth, kissing her neck, trying to slow the proceedings down. If she kept going like this, there was no telling how they might end up or how quickly it would all be over.

He'd wanted this for a long time and now they'd thrown caution to the wind, he had no intention of making it less than perfect. And whether she cared to admit it or not, she was still in an emotionally vulnerable state. He wanted this to be slow and easy. Soothing to the ache inside. He wanted it to be thorough, he wanted it to be amazing.

As her hands yanked his shirt out of his trousers and roamed freely over his naked chest and his loins leapt, he knew he had to slow it down. He had to protect her emotional vulnerability. He pulled away from her hot, frenzied mouth.

'Hey, hey, hey,' he crooned, grabbing her hands and bringing them to his mouth, pressing a kiss in each palm. 'Slow down.' He chuckled.

Helen drew in deep ragged breaths, her lips already lamenting the loss of his. 'No,' she croaked.

He laughed again. 'I want this to be perfect. I want to make this right for you. I want it slow and long and gentle. I want to…' he grinned at her '…savour you.'

Helen couldn't believe what she was hearing. Any other time she may have wanted all those things but right now she wanted to feel him inside her more than her next breath.

'Next time,' she whispered, and took his mouth again, revelling in the surge of passion as he met her almost brutal kiss stroke for stroke.

James dragged himself back from the brink of surrender, his erection unbearably tight, straining against its fabric confines. 'Helen,' he moaned into her neck.

Helen drew in some much-needed breaths. He was still treating her with kid gloves. The whole town had been treating her like a fragile piece of china and she was heartily sick of it. 'I'm fine, James. I'm not going to break. I'm not a child.'

'We all need a little tenderness from time to time, Helen.'

She was going to go mad if he didn't take her soon. She needed to prove that she was OK. That she wasn't the grieving girl of hours ago. She was a woman with a woman's appetites.

She pulled out of his arms and stood before him. She whipped her satin slip off over her head and in a second was standing before him in just black lacy knickers. She ran her hand over her naked breasts and watched his pupils dilate.

'Do I look like a child?'

She whipped her undies off, too. 'Do I?'

She pulled her ponytail out and shook her hair free. 'Or do I look like a woman who needs a man?'

James's mouth dried. She was magnificent. Her breasts high and firm, her waist small, her legs slender. Her hair swinging loosely about her shoulders, brushing her delicate collar-bones. The bulge in his pants throbbed with need.

'Because right now I want it rough and hard and fast. Can you give me that?'

He didn't talk, just grabbed her wrist and twirled her around so she landed on the bed on her back under him. He plundered her mouth, all thought of slow and easy totally obliterated. He moved his mouth to a rosy-tipped nipple, savaging it as her hand undid his fly. She pulled his throbbing manhood out of his underpants and squeezed hard. 'Now,' she panted.

She didn't have to ask again. He shed his trousers and was sheathing himself in her hot core seconds later. Her guttural cry spurred him on and he thrust into her again and again, his face at her neck, his hand on her breast.

'Yes. James. Oh, yes.'

He could feel her starting to tighten around him, heard her cries become more desperate, and he rammed into her harder. Faster.

He felt Helen break first, her nails raking down his back. He followed shortly after, joining her in an alternative universe where only their cries and their breath and their rhythm mattered. Not Elsie or Owen. Not their lousy childhoods. Not even his own imminent departure. Just a fantastic, addictive ecstasy which, when they bumped back to earth, left them craving more.

# CHAPTER NINE

HELEN woke at seven-thirty the next morning to an empty bed. She still felt exhausted but in a good way. Not weary any more just deeply, deeply sated. James had made love to her again after their first frenzied session. It had been slow and thorough, he had savoured her as he had promised, and she had cried all over again from the sheer beauty of it. And then he had kissed away her tears and they'd fallen asleep together.

She could smell his scent on her sheets, on her pillow, and she knew she wouldn't wash them until it was completely gone. She could also smell coffee. Divine and rich, its earthy fragrance wafting in through her bedroom door. She stretched and felt the protest of internal muscles and blushed, thinking about her aggression.

She lay there for a while, her stomach growling as the aroma of coffee continued to tease her taste buds, her thoughts drifting to James. Was he out there, freaking out? She imagined him pacing, feeling trapped, rehearsing his you-know-I'm-a-gypsy and we-should-just-be-friends speech. She smiled, giving herself a few more minutes before she put him out of his misery.

He was sitting in a lounge chair in his trousers from last night, no shirt, flicking through her albums. He was sipping coffee and for a few seconds she just drank in the sight of him. He looked magnificent. Her toes curled, thinking about the things he had done to her body, the things she'd done to his.

'Hey,' she said.

James looked up. She was standing in the entrance to the room dressed in his shirt. She'd only done up a couple of buttons and he caught a glimpse of creamy breasts, cute belly button and black lacy knickers. Her hair tumbled in disorder, framing her gorgeous face.

His still unsigned contract sat on the coffee-table on top of the pile of albums, taunting him. Seeing her like this, all tousled from bed and his love-making, to sign it seemed like a really stupid idea. He wanted nothing more than to take her hand and spend all day in bed. But he didn't stay. He didn't know how to stay.

'Hey.'

They gazed at each other for a few moments. No words, just hungry looks that throbbed with yearning, desire and lust.

'Coffee smells good,' she said, her voice husky.

'I'll get you a cup.'

He pushed up out of the chair, grateful for something to do other than stare like a horny teenager. His shirt had never looked so damn good.

When he turned around to bring her cup back out to the lounge room she was leaning against the kitchen doorframe. She advanced towards him, her hand extended, and he passed her the mug. She put it down on the bench and pushed herself up and back until she was sitting on the bench beside it.

He remembered how they had shared their first kiss with her sitting on the bench. His gaze zoned in on the generous display of left breast he could now see, including the rosy tip. Dragging his gaze away, it fell to her thighs where the shirt had ridden up to reveal every silky inch. God, she was too underdressed to be sitting like that.

'So,' she said, admiring the muscular definition of his chest. The dainty St Christopher sat in the hollow at the base of his neck.

'So.' He leant against the sink and nodded.

'Are you freaking out about last night?'

*That was putting it mildly.* 'A little. Are you?'

Helen smiled. 'No.'

James admired her aura of calm. 'O-K.'

'I know what you're thinking. You're thinking, Oh, my God, I took advantage of her in an emotional state, it's not a very honourable thing to do and in the cold light of morning she's going to be upset about it.' She raised an eyebrow at him.

The curve of her breast taunted him, even though he was trying really hard to be a gentleman and not look.

'Something like that.'

'Do I look upset?'

She looked as sexy as hell. She looked like she'd been made love to all night. She looked up for more. 'Not really.'

Helen smiled. 'Right. So get over it. I asked you to do it. In fact, if I remember correctly, I was pretty damn adamant.' She grinned at his grudging smile. 'And it was great. It was just what I needed. So let's just leave it at that. A one-off night that was a great way to end a terrible day.'

He had three weeks left and she really thought that after last night they could live in the same house and not want to repeat the experience? He already wanted her again.

'Really, you shouldn't tell me this is a one-off when you're barely wearing my shirt. In fact, I think we're both a little underdressed for this conversation.'

She grinned at him impishly. 'Do you want it back?'

She was having way too much fun with this. He needed to take back some control here. 'No,' he said, crossing to her, stepping between her thighs, forcing them to part, and reaching for the buttons. He did them all up. Even the top one. 'That's better.' He picked up his mug and headed out of the kitchen.

Helen laughed. 'Speak for yourself.'

She kicked off the bench and followed him, carrying her mug. He was looking through her albums again. She sat opposite him. He was right. If she was trying to convince him this was a one-off then she needed to behave. But she couldn't remember ever feeling this...light. Her weeping last night had purged years' of heartache and it felt good to have it gone.

'You never told me you'd travelled so much.'

She shrugged 'You never asked. In fact, I think you just assumed because I'd lived in Skye all my life that I'd never been anywhere else.'

James nodded. It was true. He had judged her. 'Guilty as charged. I'm sorry.'

'You're forgiven.' After last night she'd have forgiven

him almost anything. 'I guess I inherited a healthy dose of my father's genes.'

He gazed at a photo of a younger Helen, the Eiffel Tower in the background. 'What's your favourite place?'

'Venice.'

He laughed. 'You don't need to think about it?'

She shook her head. 'Nope. There's something special about Venice.'

'Yes,' he agreed, 'there is.'

James flicked through the albums a bit more, the silence between them companionable. Last night had certainly muddied the waters for him. Leaving Skye had become more of a conundrum then it should have been. His wild gypsy soul was calling him on but he knew, like Venice, Helen was special. That there was something special between them. That he wanted to explore what it was. He definitely didn't want to walk away from her.

'Helen…'

She looked up from the fascinating contents of her mug into his serious face. 'James.'

'About last night.'

'Yes.'

'I'm not sure I can live under the same roof and ignore the fact that we had a really incredible night together. Every time I see you I'm going to want to do it again.'

*Amen to that.* But Helen knew the only way she could wave him goodbye at the end of three weeks and not hang onto his leg as he left like a petulant child was to go cold turkey with the sex.

She shrugged. 'Think of it as a one-night stand. You have had those, haven't you?'

James smiled. 'I've had a couple.'

'There you go. We had a one-night stand. There's no follow-through required.'

James stared at her. *Was she for real?* His erection was almost painful. 'I don't usually see the one-night standee every day, though.'

Helen shrugged again, hoping she looked more nonchalant then she felt. 'We'll manage.'

He raised his eyebrows at her. 'I want you again. Right now.'

Helen felt heat slam into her and it took a few moments to regain the power of speech. 'Look. You're leaving in three weeks. And that's fine. Believe me, if anyone knows about the gypsy soul, it's me. I will stand at this door and wave you goodbye and wish you a good life. But if we spend the next three weeks doing what we did last night, I can't promise I'll be able to do that. If my father leaving last night taught me anything, it's not to settle for less. I will cling. I may cry. I will definitely ask you to stay.'

*And I don't want to ask you. I want you to want to.*

'Trust me, it will be messy. I'm trying to be mature about this, James. Work with me.'

'What if you came with me?'

Helen froze, her coffee-mug halfway to her mouth. She placed it slowly back on the coffee-table. 'Why?'

'There's something between us, Helen. I don't want to have to say goodbye. I want to be with you. Don't you feel it, too?'

She nodded. 'And yet I haven't asked you to stay. Haven't asked you to do something I know you wouldn't want to do.'

He thrust the photo album on his lap at her. 'I'm not asking you to do something you don't like. You're a traveller, too, Helen. There's gypsy in you. And with Elsie gone, there's nothing holding you in Skye.'

Helen couldn't believe she'd heard him say that. She felt disappointed and angry. Hadn't he been around her long enough to know her? To sense her connection to Skye was about more than a sense of obligation to Elsie? No, he was looking at her blankly, obviously not getting what she was about at all.

But, then, gypsies never did understand the concept of home and what it meant. Her father certainly never had. Her roots were here. Her memories were here. Her soul was here. Yes, she'd travelled. But she liked being grounded and there was no place like home.

'There's never been anything holding me in Skye, James. I choose to stay here.'

He could tell he'd hit a nerve. She was sitting very straight, the sin that had heated the amber flecks in her eyes moments ago frozen out by the rapidly cooling jade. 'So you're just going to live here…for ever?'

She heard the note of incredulity in his voice. That was why it was good he only had three weeks left. Why she'd never ask him to stay. She couldn't live with a man who didn't understand her and always had one eye on the highway out of town. 'Yes. Is that so hard to comprehend?'

For someone who had spent the last five years of his life on his bike or on a plane, or on some kind of transport heading somewhere, yes. 'I guess I just don't understand the urge to be grounded.'

Which wasn't exactly true. Since coming to Skye he'd

felt the most grounded he'd ever been, like he'd found the elusive something he'd been looking for all his life. And as tempting as it was to blame it on the enforced captivity of his broken leg, he knew that was a cop-out. He knew there was something about Helen that grounded him. But he also knew he couldn't give her the things that she deserved.

'You know, life doesn't have to be one or the other, James. You can have the best of both worlds.'

He blinked at the flint in her voice. 'No, Helen, I can't. I chose the gypsy life because I don't have to be beholden to anyone or any place. I grew up trapped in an unhappy house. Powerless to get out. I'm never going to be trapped again.'

Helen stood. She looked down at him, feeling dismay. 'Look, you want to roam around the country for ever, then good luck to you. You want to become Owen then more power to you. There are worse people out there—'

'I'm not sure about that, Helen,' James interrupted. 'What he did last night was unforgivable. I want to hunt him down and kill him and I barely know him. But you're wrong, I don't want to be him. I'll not repeat his mistakes or my parents'. Which is why it's better to keep moving.'

Helen felt tears prick at her eyes. She felt foolishly moved by James's obvious distaste for Owen's disappearing act but she was angry at him, too. He was selling them short.

Fighting with him now, trying to make him see, she knew that she loved him. That she wanted him to stay. It was a really bad time for such a momentous realisation, but her whole body hummed with it.

And it just made this argument even more necessary.

Deep down she knew that they could have a good life together. Things could work and work well because they both had experience to draw on and a determination not to repeat the mistakes of their childhood. Elsie was gone and her father was always going to be a transient figure her in life. But James could be her family. And she could be his. She could make him see that not all relationships were unhappy.

'So you're just going to roam the rest of your life?'

James shrugged. 'Sure.'

'Because you're too scared to stay in one place and give it a try? That's insane, James.'

'I haven't been equipped to nurture a successful relationship. My upbringing didn't teach me how to give emotionally.'

'You did all right with me last night.'

'That's not the same thing, Helen, and you know it.'

'All I know for sure is that you'll never find whatever the hell it is you're looking for until you stop running, James. Do you even know what it is any more?'

*Good question.* He'd thought he knew but looking at her in his shirt, questioning him, calling him on his beliefs, she was right. What did he want? He'd got away from the sadness of his earlier life but was he any happier? Didn't he want to be happy? To be loved and feel needed? All the things he hadn't had in his younger years.

But what if he stuffed up? What if it didn't work out and he was stuck in Skye in a relationship that was just plain awful? His feelings for Helen were too complicated and, frankly, they scared him. He'd never met a woman who scared him this much.

Helen was someone who would demand everything

from him and he'd been too used to keeping a part of himself back, wary from years of emotional neglect, of not having his feelings returned. It was easier to move on than risk his heart again.

'It's a good life,' he said defensively, as his head roared with conflicting emotions.

'Have you ever thought maybe there's a flipside to your gypsy life that's just as good?'

He'd more than thought it. He'd been living the flipside here in this cottage in Skye with her, and he'd liked it more than he cared to admit.

'I'd hate to stuff up, Helen. I'd hate to hurt you. My past is never far away.'

'Neither is mine, James, but we can't go on like this, forever frightened to live and love and be happy because of what happened decades ago. You know there have been times when I've resented Owen so much. Wished for a proper father, one who was around all the time. I've been disappointed in him and his gypsy lifestyle and his inability to just stay put for a while. But I can't let it—let him—stop me from taking a chance. And you shouldn't let your past mess up a shot at a future either.'

'You don't know how it was,' he said quietly.

'No. Not exactly. But I know it made you sad and that children shouldn't be sad. You had a lousy family.' She shrugged. 'Guess what? So did I. So let's start again. Let's make our own family. Let me be your family.'

James was tempted. Staying here, wrapped up in Helen's arms for ever? Could it be that simple? 'I don't know, Helen.'

She stared at him for a few minutes as her heart broke. If

he didn't know, she was damned if she was going to keep pushing. He had to want this, too. She wasn't going to put her soul on the line, confess her love when he obviously didn't reciprocate. When he still didn't know what he wanted out of life. Because she did know—now. She wanted him.

Helen picked up a pen that was on the coffee-table. 'Then sign the contract,' she said, passing him the pen. 'There's nothing keeping you here.'

And she turned on her heel and stalked into her bedroom before she crumbled in front of him. Her watery eyes scanned the rumpled bed and she just wanted to throw herself on it and cry. *No!* She'd cried enough last night for the rest of her life. No more tears.

James stared after her, pen in hand. How quickly their night of passion and their morning of flirting had vanished when faced with the realities of their very different life-styles. His gaze fell on the contract. She'd painted an attractive picture but he just couldn't visualise how it would work. She deserved to be with someone who could love her with an open heart. Who could see the picture. Who knew how to make it work.

He picked up a pen and signed on the dotted line. She'd thank him for this in the long run.

Courteous was the best way to describe the remaining three weeks of James's locum period. They were polite but distant. A bit like they'd been when their attraction had first flared and she had made it clear that it wasn't going to happen. But it was bleaker than that. He got the impression Helen was marking the days on a calendar.

One with his picture on it.

And a target drawn in felt pen on his head.

He'd tried to approach her the first few days after their argument, tried to explain, but she'd just looked straight through him and said, 'I think we've been over this.'

His body, of course, betrayed him at every turn so her aloofness was a good reminder that they were too different to make things work. The more his body ached for her, the more he craved the open road.

The residents of Skye threw him a farewell party at the CWA hall on his last day of work. Everyone was there. Even Helen. She was tense, her smile forced, but she was there. Alf gave a speech and Josh had made him a poster that said 'Best Doctor in Skye.'

'Are you sure we can't tempt you to stay?' Genevieve asked, rocking a sleeping William as the party flowed around them. 'I don't mind staying on maternity leave. It's going to break my heart to leave him.'

James looked at her guiltily. Looked at the baby he had helped into the world. Looked all around him at the people who had wormed their way into his life with their big hearts and welcoming arms. Each one of them anchored him here.

Maybe he should have checked with Genevieve first. He could have offered to do another four-month stint. But the way things were now with Helen he was relieved to be going. And the road was beckoning him. 'Sorry. I have to be at my next job in a week.'

'That's a shame,' Genevieve mused. 'I kinda thought you and Helen might have…'

James's gaze settled on Helen. She was laughing at something someone was saying. She looked warm and relaxed, so not how she'd been with him, and he found himself yearning for that Helen. 'Ah, no.'

Genevieve nodded. 'Yeah, I guess you're a little too like Owen for her taste.'

James wanted to protest. He wasn't like her father at all. But he supposed, to all intents and purposes, in a lot of ways, he was.

Tom came up and wished him luck, looking more friendly than he ever had. 'Good luck, James,' he said. 'You're going for good, then?'

James clenched his jaw at the smug quality to the paramedic's voice. 'Yes.' The thought of Helen with Tom was more than he could stand. A surge of jealousy ripped through him.

'Well, take care, then. Have a safe trip.'

He moved on and James watched him all the way to the other side of the hall. He turned around and found Helen at his elbow, cuddling William while Genevieve replenished their drinks.

'Promise me you won't settle,' he said to her out the corner of his mouth, smiling at a group of CWA ladies, his gaze still tailing Tom.

'Go to hell, James,' she said sweetly, also smiling at the ladies, and promptly moved away.

Helen lay in bed the next morning, the mouthwatering aroma of brewing coffee wafting into her bedroom. The man she loved was leaving. She wanted to pull the pillow over her head and lock the door.

When it had happened she wasn't sure. Maybe she'd known from their first meeting. Maybe before when an eerie sixth sense had made her uneasy about his delayed arrival. Maybe in some strange, mystical way her soul had sensed the coming of her life partner and her intuition had kicked into overdrive when he hadn't thundered into town on time.

It didn't really matter anyway. The fact was, she did love him. And he was leaving. Which should have been a relief. Loving him and living in the limbo they'd been in the last few weeks was shredding the very fabric of her being. But she wouldn't falter. She'd made it this far without asking him to stay, she sure as hell could make it through a farewell.

It was just such a waste. She'd never been in love before. What on earth had possessed her to fall for an Owen clone she'd never know. A gypsy. She'd get over it, she supposed, eventually, but the loss of what could have been weighed heavily on her as she rose and threw on some clothes. They would have made such beautiful babies.

She padded into the kitchen and he was standing at the sink, his back to her. She headed for the percolator and poured herself a mug. He was dressed in his leather pants and a snug-fitting black T-shirt that hugged the contours of his back and triceps. He didn't turn around.

'When are you off?'

He turned then. 'As soon as I've finished this.'

Her gaze devoured him. The shirt looked just as snug across his chest and his wavy hair brushed his forehead. Her hand shook and her insides performed a series of somersaults. She nodded and looked away, afraid she'd give in despite her resolve. Afraid her body would betray her.

Her legs were shaking as she entered the lounge room and sank into a chair.

He passed behind her a few minutes later, heading to his bedroom. She stared resolutely into her coffee, ignoring him. *I will not ask him to stay. I will not break. I will be fine.*

James re-entered the lounge room. 'I'm off.'

Helen took a mouthful of hot coffee and swallowed it, the heat something to concentrate on other than her breaking heart. She stood. 'OK.'

He walked to the door and she followed, refusing to acknowledge how hot he looked in his leathers. He opened the door and turned to face her. She'd been quite close behind him so consequently they were now very close indeed.

'Guess this is goodbye,' he said softly.

Helen nodded as she watched his mouth form the words. His lips were soft and perfect.

He watched as her ponytail swished from side to side. He was going to miss that ponytail. A silence stretched between them. 'Thank you…for everything. I'm sorry for—'

Helen cut him off, placing two fingers against his lips. Mainly because she couldn't bear to hear it. But also because his lips were so damn irresistible and it'd be the last time she touched them. 'Shh. No,' she whispered. 'Let's not rehash things. Let's just say goodbye and leave it at that.'

His lips tingled where she'd touched them. He wanted her so much. 'Helen…'

His voice was rough, halfway between a whisper and a groan. His lips grazed erotically against the pads of her fingers. She felt a pull down low and was helpless to resist the power of his mouth.

She met his lips with a passion that he equalled and then

intensified. He stabbed his fingers into her hair as he plundered the softness of her mouth and yanked the band from the ponytail. He stroked his fingers against her scalp and her freed hair fell loosely around her shoulders. His lips stoked the furnace that had been smouldering for weeks and her heart hammered even as it broke.

Helen pulled away, breathing hard, knowing this was madness. Her head fell against his chest, his lips against her hair.

James held her tight. 'Ask me to stay.'

Tears pricked her eyes as his voice rumbled through his chest and vibrated into her ear. *Stay.* She looked up at him. 'No, you have to want to.'

James felt torn. He wanted to. He did. But the chains of his past were too heavy to shake. 'Helen.'

She heard the plea in his voice but saw the indecision in his turquoise gaze. She shook her head and stepped away from him. 'Just go, James.'

James opened his mouth to say more. But she was standing there with her arms wrapped around her waist, aloof again. He nodded, picked up his backpack and walked out the door.

Helen stared after him for a moment then slowly shut the door. She leaned her forehead against the wood as the sound of his vintage Harley broke the air.

'Stay,' she whispered.

It wasn't until James pulled into a roadside hotel that evening that he realised he'd been looking back all day. He never looked back. His jumbled thoughts and his heavy heart were yearning for Skye. For Helen.

*Hell.* He loved her. Even as his heart lifted, the thought depressed the hell out of him. This had not been in his plans. He stared at the telephone beside the bed. His fingers itched to ring her. Hear her voice.

What a stubborn fool he'd been. His heart beat loudly at the thought of a future with her. It scared the hell out of him. But a future without her scared him more. She'd asked him to be her family and he'd turned her down. What an A-grade fool!

It was four a.m. when James made it back to Skye. Suppressing the urge to barge into the house, knowing the door would be unlocked, he knocked.

Helen woke with a start.

'Open up, Helen. It's James.'

She stumbled through the house, her hammering heart matching the rapping on the door, beat for beat.

James stared impatiently at the stubbornly shut door. 'Damn it, Helen!'

She reached for the latch and yanked it open. 'Are you trying to wake up the whole neighbourhood?' she hissed.

He opened his mouth to say something else and she grabbed his arm and dragged him inside the house. 'It's four in the morning James.'

She was wearing *that* sleep shirt and her hair was loose and he wanted her so badly he had to shove his hands into the pockets of his leather jacket to stop from reaching for her.

'I love you,' he said. 'I don't know how I'll go or if it will work but you asked me earlier what I was looking for and it took leaving you to realise that I've been looking for you. Someone to help heal the sadness of my past, someone to make a better future with. Together. I've felt more wanted and needed and at home here in Skye than I've ever felt anywhere. And that's because of you, Helen. I knew you were different from the day you pulled me out of the bush. I've just been too busy running scared to see what was right in front of my nose.'

Helen felt a jumble of emotions tumble around inside her as James stood before her, laying his soul bare. Was she dreaming? Love, hope and triumph clashed inside her. Still she didn't dare hope.

'But what about the gypsy rider? What about the freedom of the open road?' She needed to be sure.

'You were right, Helen. I've been running away. I didn't take up the travelling life because it's in my blood, although I've loved it…but because I was afraid of commitment. Afraid of loving someone and not being loved back again. Is it too late to take you up on the offer of being a family? Please, tell me you love me. Please, tell me I haven't blown it before it even had a chance to begin.'

He looked so forlorn standing in her lounge room in his bikie leathers. And he loved her. But still she held out.

'What about kids?'

James expelled a heavy breath. *Children?* The thought was almost as terrifying as loving her and being together for ever. 'You want kids?'

Helen nodded. 'Of course. What about you?' She held her breath—neither of them had had great childhoods. Bringing children into the world was big for both of them.

The amber in her eyes glittered like fiery embers. She was magnificent and he suddenly realised he wanted the whole catastrophe. Even kids, yes. With her…yes. He did. It was daunting but he knew that with them as parents their kids were going to be doted on and loved and the most wanted children on the planet.

He smiled. 'Yes.'

He hadn't been prepared for this. For her. For how grounding love could be. How you wanted to stay when you found that one special person. How you wanted everything. The whole box and dice. But he was damn glad he had.

Helen trembled with the urge to put her arms around him but she needed him to be sure. 'So you think a guy with commitment issues and a girl with abandonment issues can make a go of it? It doesn't sound like a very auspicious start.'

He shrugged and smiled. 'We'll reinvent the wheel.' He looked at the smile that spread across her face and felt encouraged. 'Well? Come on, Helen, you're killing me here. Do you love me too?'

Helen nodded, feeling overwhelmed suddenly by events.

James reached for her and pulled her hard against him. 'Oh, thank you. Thank you, thank you,' he whispered, pressing kisses all over her face. 'I'm never letting you go.'

Helen laughed. She hadn't felt this light, this giddy in weeks. 'I love you James.'

He smiled down into her happy face. 'I'm so sorry—'

'No,' Helen said, placing her fingers on his lips. 'No looking back. We're reinventing the wheel, remember.'

The curve of her bottom felt good snuggled into his palms and he nodded.

'Stay,' she whispered.

James grinned. 'I thought you'd never ask.'

And he dipped his head, sealing their love with a kiss.

## EPILOGUE

IT WAS a beautiful day in Skye when James and Helen wedded three months later. The CWA hall was decorated with yellow wattle flowers, white ribbons and pink balloons. A local band played rock and roll tunes on the stage as the entire population partied with the newlyweds.

Helen sat next to her father and watched her new husband pound the wooden floorboards with an energetic Josh. A bright blue cast covered the five-year-old's newly broken arm. But it hadn't stopped him from wearing the cute little white tuxedo or from relinquishing the white satin ring cushion he'd carried proudly down the aisle.

'He's a good man, darling.'

She smiled at her father. 'I know.' She squeezed his hand.

Owen looked down into his daughter's flushed face. He'd never seen her looking prettier. 'I'm so sorry, Helen. I haven't been a very good father.' He raised his hand and grazed his knuckles lightly down her cheek. 'You're so like your mother. She would have been so proud. Elsie would have been, too.'

Helen covered her father's hand with her own and gave him a gentle smile. For all his failings, she'd always known he'd done his best. 'Thanks, Dad.'

'Come on, dance with your old man.' He stood and held out his hand.

Helen gathered her voluminous skirt and took her father's hand. The band played a jive tune and her father spun her round the floor.

'Excuse me.' James tapped Owen on the shoulder. 'I'd like to dance with my wife.'

Helen melted into her husband's arms as the music slowed to a waltz.

'Are you happy, my darling?' James asked.

'More than I ever imagined possible,' Helen sighed looking into his amazing turquoise eyes. 'What about you? Are you glad you came back?'

James kissed her nose. 'More than you'll ever know.' And he pulled her close and waltzed the night away with the woman of his heart.